THORNS
OF DECISION

BREEANA PUTTROFF

FIRST EDITION
ISBN 13: 9781940481197

~~~~~~~~~~~

Cover Design: Mallory Rock

Formatting & Layout: Mallory Rock

~~~~~~~~~~

Thirteen Pages Press
P.O. BOX 350944
DENVER, CO 80035

Thorns of Decision: The Dusk Gate Chronicles Book 3 is a work of fiction. Names, characters, places and incidents are products of the author's imagination, or the author has used them fictitiously.

ANGRY

THE LOUD KNOCKING ON her bedroom door set Quinn Robbins' fierce anger roaring again. "What?" she yelled; knowing, but not caring, that her voice was too harsh.

Her mother opened the door and came in, barely seeming to notice the way Quinn sat, rolled up in a ball near her pillows, still in her pajamas, even though it was almost noon.

"I've decided you're not grounded from your phone," her mom said, setting the small black object on the nightstand. The little notification light blinked furiously. "You need to use it to call Zander yourself, get things figured out with him."

Quinn raised her eyebrows. "What did you tell him?"

Megan Robbins' gaze was just as steely as it had been since last night, and she looked Quinn in the eyes when she spoke. "I told him that Dr. Rose had a family emergency and that since you were becoming good friends with William, you went along for support."

Quinn's jaw dropped. "That doesn't even make any sense!" Of course, it was eerily close to the truth… but that was the problem. The truth didn't make any sense.

"Well, if you have a better explanation, you're welcome to share it with him. I'm headed down to Denver to pick up Owen and Annie from Richard and Denise's." She turned and left the room, closing the door behind her with an audible *clunk*.

Quinn only barely resisted the urge to hurl the phone at the door. Instead, after a tense moment, she flipped it open and began scanning through the messages…all forty-six of them. Almost every message was from her best friend, Abigail, or from Zander, although there were three from her mother, left on Thursday evening, just after Quinn had disappeared.

She opened the first one.

Where are you, sweetie? Zander just called and said he saw you leaving work.

Oh. So Zander had seen her running away from the library with William? She closed her eyes, trying to remember that evening, which seemed so long ago. Of course, nearly three weeks actually had passed for Quinn, even if it had only been just over two days for her mom.

Still, even if Zander had seen her, it didn't explain how her mom had known where to find her. It didn't explain why her mom had been sitting there at the bridge last night when Quinn returned from Eirentheos.

She had disappeared for two whole days without a word, and she'd come back to find her mother just sitting there…not panicking as Quinn had expected, no police officers searching the river or even dropping by her house for a chat. No, instead, her mother had been sitting, perfectly calm, on a boulder near the gate, just *waiting*, as if she knew exactly where her daughter had been.

Okay, so calm wasn't the right word. Her mother had been furious, livid, as she still was today. But she hadn't been *worried*, even in the slightest. And this was the source of Quinn's wrath now.

Not that she'd *wanted* to worry her mother…actually she'd spent long hours during her time in Eirentheos fretting over what she thought she was putting her mother through. She hadn't *meant* to disappear for so long without saying a word; it had just happened. When William had told her that Thomas was missing, she had gone, making a split-second decision without thinking about the consequences.

But when she'd stepped through the gate and seen her mom there, she had been rocked to the core. What was going on here? *How?* How did her mom know about the gate? What did she know?

Last night in the car, Megan had refused to answer any of Quinn's questions and, even more disturbingly, she hadn't asked any. She'd sat there in the driver's seat, stone-faced for the whole drive. When they pulled into the garage, Megan had turned to Quinn.

"I explained things to Zander and to Mrs. Williams for you, so you still have a job. I picked up your stuff from the library. The perfect attendance at school you were so worried about is blown on that unexcused absence, though. You're grounded from your phone, from everything."

"What do you mean? *What* did you explain?"

But Megan had just climbed out of the car, slamming the door behind her and disappearing into the house. When Quinn followed her inside, she discovered that her mother was locked in her bedroom.

At first, she'd tried knocking at the door and then yelling through it. She wanted answers. But when that didn't work, Quinn had given up and retreated into her own room, slamming her own door so hard she was surprised she hadn't broken it.

The phone in her hand buzzed loudly and then began to play a tune that sent an electric jolt through her. It was Zander again. She stared at the screen, at the picture that had popped up of the two of them. In the picture, Zander's arms were around her shoulders, his cheek close to hers, both of them grinning. She almost answered it, but before she managed to make her finger move over to the answer button, it stopped ringing.

Although she waited for several minutes, there was no notification of a voicemail message.

Sighing, she picked up the phone again. She meant to call Zander back, she *needed* to talk to him, to make things right, but she just couldn't. Instead, she found herself scrolling to the newest entry in her contact list…to the number of the one person she knew she could handle talking to right now.

"Hello?" The voice that answered was immediately comforting and familiar. Her trembling fingers steadied a little.

"William?"

"Quinn? Is that you?"

"Yeah."

"Hey, what's going on with you? Are you okay?"

"I… I think so."

"What was all that at the bridge last night? Why was your mother there?"

"I don't know. She just drove me home and never told me anything. I've never seen her that angry before, but I don't think she could possibly be as mad as I am. Now, she's gone. I guess she took my little brother and sister down to Denver sometime this weekend to stay with their grandparents, and she went to go get them."

William was silent on the other end of the line; she could almost see the look he would have on his face…confused, thoughtful.

"Did Nathaniel say anything to you? My mom didn't seem too surprised when he came out of the gate, either."

"No. I asked him if he knew what that was about, but he said it was between you and your mother."

"What is *that* supposed to mean? Is he there?"

"No. He went into work really early this morning, and he was going to try to spend the day getting things set up for Thomas to go somewhere for the surgery. He was gone before I even woke up."

"Well, crap."

He chuckled for a second, but then his voice grew serious again. "Are you sure you're okay?" The sound in his voice told her he knew the answer, no matter what lie she made up.

"No. I'm not sure about anything right now. Everything is such a mess."

"Do you want to come over and we could talk here? I'm not so good at this phone thing. This is probably the longest conversation I've ever had on one, actually."

That made her smile. "Sure. Give me half an hour?"

"I'll be here. I'm doing homework…you might want to consider bringing yours along, too."

If she rolled her eyes hard enough, would he be able to hear it through the phone? "You would be thinking about homework at a time like this."

He laughed. "I'll see you in a little while."

As soon as she snapped her phone shut, she made a mad dash for the shower. After the days of traveling in the rural areas of William's world, she'd become adept at getting ready quickly. Within ten minutes of hanging up with William, she was in the small mudroom that connected the garage and kitchen, looking for her keys.

She wasn't sure if she was supposed to leave the house, or if being grounded from "everything" besides, apparently, her phone, meant she was allowed to use Jeff's car today, but after a few seconds of consideration, she decided she didn't care.

Somehow, her mother knew about the gate that led to William's world. Even more astonishing was the fact that she had known that's where Quinn would be. *How? What did her mother know that Quinn didn't?* And worse, why was she keeping it a secret?

As she reached for the small ring that hung underneath a bulletin board in the room, one of the papers tacked to the board caught her attention.

A cold chill drizzled down her spine as she recognized it. Her mother had gone through her backpack? It was her most recent

World History exam, the first paper she'd ever gotten a grade lower than a B…and usually she was disappointed with those. The big, red 'D' on the top glared at her mockingly. Even worse, there was a heavy black circle drawn around the letter, and words, written in her mother's perfect penmanship:

'What is THIS?'

The fury welled in her chest again, rising into her throat and nearly choking her. The shaft of the thumbtack ripped a straight line up the center of the page as she yanked it from the display and shoved it into her backpack. Throwing the bag over her shoulder, she grabbed her keys and left.

William was waiting for her in the driveway of the small bungalow he shared with his uncle; she wondered how long he had been standing there in the cold. He directed her to pull all the way up beside the house and then opened the door for her.

A look of shock crossed his face as he took in her appearance. She'd seen, in the rearview mirror, how flushed her cheeks were with her anger. Her hands were still shaking.

"Yeah, you're definitely not okay, are you?"

She shook her head, and he helped her out of the car, steadying her on the slippery concrete. For a second, she wondered if someone came and removed the snow for them when they disappeared, or if William had come out to shovel this morning.

He reached around her to remove the backpack from the passenger seat, zipping it up before slinging it over his shoulder. "Come on," he said.

It was only the third time she had ever been inside Nathaniel and William's house, but somehow right now it felt more like home than the bedroom she'd just come from. A warm fire crackled in the fireplace, and William's books were spread out over the entire dining room table. She felt safer here, almost relaxed, and her anger started to fade.

William set her backpack down on the couch and helped her out of her coat. "Do you want to talk about it?" he asked.

She shrugged, slumping down onto the comfortable leather. "I don't even know where to start."

He sat in a low chair across from her. "Why don't you start at the beginning? What happened last night?"

"That's the problem. *Nothing* happened last night. My mom told me to get into the car and then the only thing she said the whole time was that I'm grounded from everything."

"You're grounded from everything?"

"Well, apparently not from this," she said, pulling her cell phone from her pocket and tossing it on the coffee table. "This morning she told me that I needed to call Zander, and then she left and went to Denver. I don't even know when she's going to be back."

"Are you going to be in trouble for coming here?"

She stared at him…he actually looked concerned about that. "It's not exactly my biggest worry right now, William."

One eyebrow arched into a tiny *v*, but he let the subject drop. "Okay… did you call Zander?"

"No."

"So, you don't know where he thinks you've been for the past two days?"

"My mom told him that you and Nathaniel had a family emergency and that I'd gone along to support you."

William's eyes opened so wide that she was surprised when his eyeballs didn't fall out. "Why would she tell him that?"

"I don't know. Maybe she's psychic, and she never told me that, either."

To his credit, or perhaps as an indication that he was as confused and concerned as she was, he didn't laugh.

"Which leaves us with basically nothing to go on," he said. "You just spent I don't know how long terrified about how your mother was going to deal with your being mysteriously missing for two days, and it turns out you're not the mysterious one at all."

She raised her eyebrows. "Yeah. Pretty much."

"And then there's Nathaniel…"

"Yeah… *What* is between him and my mother? What does he know about this?"

"I have no idea, but with everything that has gone on lately, I'm starting to see that he's awfully good at keeping secrets."

"Okay, but there was at least a *point* to some of the secrets he was keeping in Philotheum. He was trying to protect people. He's not hiding me from Tolliver's troops *here*. So what does he know about my mom that I don't? Why wasn't he surprised to see her there last night?"

William sighed, a deep furrow appearing in the middle of his forehead. "I don't know."

They sat there for several moments, both lost in thought.

"I don't think I've ever been this mad at my mom before in my life," she finally said.

"I don't blame you. I'm not exactly thrilled with Nathaniel right now, and his involvement in whatever this is doesn't affect me nearly as much as what your mom is doing does to you."

"What do I do, William? She's so mad at me that she's not even talking to me."

He studied her carefully for several moments without answering and swallowed hard before he began speaking. "Look, Quinn, you and I have been through a lot together recently, and before I say what I'm going to say, I want you to know that I don't feel the same way about it that I used to. So don't just take this as an 'I told you so,' but the fact remains that coming to my world the way you did, involving yourself the way you have…it was always going to have consequences on your life here."

She was silent for a minute, processing that. "Exactly how is that not an 'I told you so'?"

He chuckled. "I only said that it wasn't *just* an 'I told you so,' I am starting to understand, though, that none of this is as simple as I was trying to make it out to be. And now *this* with your mom… I guess that all I'm really trying to say is that this is just one of those consequences, and it's a crazy one, but we're just going to have to deal with it. I know how angry you are at your mom, but just like in my world, there are other things that need to be taken care of, alongside of freaking out and trying to figure this out."

She sat there, stunned beyond responding right away…not only because he was right, and she needed to wrap her head around all of this and still function, but also because of one little word that hadn't escaped her attention when he'd said it. *We.*

She knew what he was talking about with the "I told you so" speech. Just before the last time she had come home from Eirentheos, she had confronted William about the way he was distancing himself from her, acting like he didn't want her around. Although he had told her that it wasn't personal, he'd said that he believed she was making a mistake trying to divide herself between two worlds and that the lies she was telling to her friends and family were going to catch up with her and result in unpleasant consequences.

And he had been right…exactly right. He had told her so. It wasn't that she hadn't believed him at the time; it was just that she had never anticipated that the consequences would be something like this…that she would discover that she wasn't the only one keeping secrets and lying. She had never guessed exactly *how* entrenched in William's world she would become…never expected the deep connection that she felt to the people and the places there.

And she had really never guessed how much her relationship with William would change. It wasn't only what he had just said, allying himself with her in this situation, placing himself squarely in it with her…there was something else that hung in the air between them.

They had never discussed it, though it was always there, almost visible, tangible, and it was apparent that it influenced them both. *The kiss*. That crazy afternoon in Philotheum when they'd learned another monumental secret as they hid from Tolliver in the basement of his own sister. No, neither one of them had said even one word about it since then, but she knew it had changed everything. And not in the way she would have expected, either.

Somewhere in the back of her mind, she even knew that it hadn't been an accident…it wasn't just something that happened because they'd been so close and so frightened together in that dark place. No… it had been much more than that.

William leaned forward, reaching toward the coffee table, and the movement broke her from her reverie. When he sat back, he was holding her cell phone in his hand.

"You need to call Zander," he said.

That statement yanked her instantly back to reality. *"What? Now? Why?"*

He didn't flinch at her response. He sat, holding her phone in his hand, a patient look on his face.

"Quinn, he's your boyfriend. He saw you running away from the library with me on Thursday evening, and then neither of us was at school on Friday. We are both going to be back there with him tomorrow. He needs to have some kind of explanation, or this could get really bad. You've made the decision to be a part of this huge secret, and now it's time to take responsibility for it."

"But… right now? What do I even say to him?"

"I don't have any idea what you say to him. He's not *my* boyfriend. But yes, right now. Waiting isn't going to make it any easier, trust me."

She nodded, took a deep breath, and reached for the phone.

"You can go into another room, if you'd like privacy," he offered.

She thought about it, but then shook her head. She knew he was right, that she needed to do this, needed to communicate with Zander, now. But it didn't mean she actually had to *call* him. She flipped open the phone and scrolled to the text message menu.

William rolled his eyes.

"What?"

"Nothing," he said, shaking his head. "It's just… as long as I live I don't think I'll ever get my head around the way people in this world do everything they can to avoid actually interacting with one another."

She glowered at him, but it didn't change her mind. Swallowing hard, she began typing.

Hey, Zander,
Sorry I haven't called or texted you back, it's been a crazy weekend.

She glanced up at William. He'd picked up a notebook and was writing in it. "Are we still going with the story that Thomas is your cousin?" she asked.

He sighed. "I don't know. That is what we told him when he saw Thomas at school, but now that this has gotten so much more complicated, I think we should maybe lie as little as possible. It's going to be hard enough to keep the story straight."

Quinn nodded. "I don't like lying to him at all."

He pulled off his wire-rimmed glasses, rubbing the bridge of his nose between his fingers before he looked back up at her, his gray eyes meeting hers with an intensity that made her heart pound. "I know you don't. Just… tell him whatever you need to tell him."

William looked at his notes for organic chemistry, trying to write while Quinn sat across from him on the couch tapping keys on that ridiculous little device. He wasn't sure why it was irritating him so much, to watch her struggle as she tried to figure out how she was going to explain this whole convoluted mess to her boyfriend. He'd known this was coming.

There was a strange, tight feeling in his chest as he surreptitiously glanced up at her. He wondered, briefly, if it was jealousy. Not that he had any right to be jealous. Zander had been pursuing Quinn since before she had ever gone to Eirentheos. He'd known she already had a boyfriend even when they'd kissed.

Besides, however he felt about Quinn…and he wasn't at all sure just what his feelings toward her were…*this* was her world, not Eirentheos. And Zander was part of this world. It was better for her if she did fix things with him and then go on about the business of being happy here, living her life.

The feeling wouldn't go away, though.

"What did you tell him?" he asked when she had closed the phone.

She sighed and pulled her knees up to her chest, the way she did when she was starting to get stressed out. The irritation he'd been feeling at her for not just *dealing* with Zander suddenly vanished, and he had to fight an urge to cross the room to sit next to her and put his arm around her shoulder. They were in her world now, though, and she was texting her *boyfriend.* He wasn't sure she'd respond well if he did that.

"I tried writing several different things, but in the end, I just typed, 'I'm sorry' and sent it."

He opened his mouth to respond, but then thought better of it and nodded, waiting. She'd say more when she was ready.

After a long moment, she looked up at him, her gray eyes filled with a swirl of emotion. "I am sorry, Will. I've made a mess of things with everyone. How can I do this? Lie to Zander? He doesn't deserve that."

"No, he doesn't."

"But I can't tell him the truth."

"Not all of it, anyway."

She blinked. "What do you mean?"

"Okay, so obviously you can't tell him everything. But maybe we should think of what parts you could tell him that are true."

At that instant, the small black phone sitting next to her buzzed. The tiny sound seemed strangely ominous. Quinn jumped away from it as though it might bite her.

"Like what?" she asked when she was breathing again.

"Well, your mom already told him that you and I were becoming friends…that part is true. And she told him that Nathaniel had a family emergency this weekend…also true. We can say that Thomas is actually my brother, and he got hurt, and I was upset. Then, I don't know. Maybe just tell him I needed a friend and since you're the only friend I have here, you were nice enough to be there for me."

Had he really just said that out loud? He watched carefully for her reaction. She glanced up at him, meeting his eyes for a fraction of a second…did her breath catch in her throat? And then she apparently decided not to address it.

"And I didn't call him because?"

He wasn't sure if he was relieved or disappointed. "Because you left your cell phone at work when you freaked out and took off. Again, the truth."

She nodded and picked up the phone. William glanced down at his notes, but the words all seemed to run together and nothing made any sense. He closed the notebook, tossed it on the coffee table, and waited.

She closed the phone again almost immediately.

"Did you change your mind about texting him?"

"I just told him that I wanted to talk to him later in person but that I'm not home right now."

He nodded. "That's probably better."

"Yeah, I don't know exactly what I'm going to say later, either, but I've been pretty awful to him lately. I think he deserves more than just a text message…that's not an invitation for an 'I-told-you-so, though."

He drew an imaginary zipper across his lips, which made her smile. "Do you want to go home, so you can invite him over to have that conversation?"

Her eyes widened, and she shook her head. "No, I'm not quite ready yet. Besides, I really do need to get some homework done today." Her cheeks turned red on the last sentence, which made no sense to him until she pulled a worn piece of paper from her backpack.

He let out a low whistle at the sight of the big red letter on the top of what looked to be some kind of essay. "Quinn! What happened?" He wasn't certain what kind of grades she normally got, but from everything he knew about her, he hadn't imagined 'D's.

"I don't know. I've never gotten a grade like this before. I think I've just been distracted lately. I'm not used to switching back into school mode after being in your world… And now I'll have a whole day of unexcused absences from my classes."

"Okay then, you're right. First you spend the afternoon here getting caught up on all of your homework, and then you go home and you deal with Zander and your mom. I doubt you'll be able to concentrate on schoolwork once you've talked to them."

William finished the last paragraph of an essay for his English class and glanced across the dining room table at Quinn. The way she was so absorbed in her World History textbook, her finger absently twirling a strand of hair as she read, made him smile.

It was nice, he realized, having her here, both enjoying the company as they worked, even if they were silent most of the time. Though he hadn't meant for it to slip out, the little comment he'd made to her earlier, that she was his only friend here, was true.

For a moment, as he watched her, the sunshine falling on her auburn hair, giving it a warm, fiery glow, he almost wished he was just a normal boy from her world…one who might have talked to her before, maybe even done homework together at the library where they both spent so much time.

A boy who might have stood a real chance against Zander Cunningham.

QUESTIONS

ZANDER'S BLACK TRUCK WAS already parked by the curb when Quinn pulled into the driveway, even though she'd only texted him after getting into her car outside William's house.

Part of her was relieved when she pressed the button to open the door of the two-car garage and it was still empty…her mother wasn't home yet. The other part of her was *not* ready for the conversation she needed to have with Zander. By the time she pulled the key out of the ignition, he was already there…standing by her door, ready to help her out and into the house.

Nervous as she was, it wasn't quite as hard as she'd expected when she took William's advice and told Zander the things they'd come up with together, sticking to as much of the truth as she could reasonably tell. It was obvious that Zander didn't quite believe her, but he accepted her story remarkably easily…she got the distinct feeling that he just wanted to believe her and to move on.

They sat together on the couch in Quinn's living room now…a sort of uneasy truce between them as he helped her rework some of her trigonometry problems. She and William had worked on homework together for most of the afternoon, but he didn't help her the way Zander liked to. They'd mostly studied side-by-side, engrossed in their own assignments. Trigonometry was Quinn's most challenging subject, and she had relied a lot on Zander's help over the last couple of months.

"Thanks," she said, as she finished the last problem and closed the book. "I really don't know what I would do without you."

"I don't want to find out," he answered. His tone was joking, but his smile didn't reach all the way to his eyes.

She stared up at him, taking a deep breath. "Zander, I really am sorry. I never meant to hurt you."

He nodded. "I just don't like feeling like you're hiding things from me, Quinn."

"I know. I'm sorry." Did he hear the words she didn't say...*couldn't* say? Because as much as she hated hiding things from him, she would still do it. She couldn't tell him everything. Right then, looking at Zander's hurt expression...*Zander* who had been her 'best fwiend' even before she could walk...she almost wished that she had listened to William when he had first told her that she was going to hurt people...get hurt herself...if she continued to involve herself in his world.

Now it was too late. Even if she never went to Eirentheos again, things could never go back to the way they were before. Now she had already lied to Zander, she'd already seen her mom at the base of the bridge, clearly knowing something she couldn't possibly know.

And, aside from lying to Zander about where she'd disappeared to this weekend, she was still hiding something big from him. Something she *could* tell him, probably she even should, but she just couldn't bring herself to do it.

How could she tell Zander that she'd kissed William?

She looked back up at him, saw the pain in his eyes...yes, he had heard at least some of what she hadn't said. Several emotions warred in his features. When he finally spoke, she knew that he wasn't voicing his first reaction. "I know," he said. "Just talk to me okay?"

She nodded, feeling like a traitor.

Another emotion passed over his already conflicted face; she couldn't get a read on it. "I love you, Quinn," he said suddenly.

She almost fell off the couch. He'd never said that before. It was true they'd been getting more serious, but she hadn't thought they'd gotten to *that* point yet. Terror gripped her insides. *Now* what was she supposed to do? Lie to him in one breath and tell him that she loved him in the next?

She never got the chance to decide. At that moment, the door between the garage and the kitchen opened, and the high-pitched squeals of her little sister, Annie, filled the house.

"Quinn! Guess what Gramma gave me?" she yelled, barreling into the living room, full force, right into Quinn's lap. "Zander! You're here! Guess what my Gramma gave me?"

Annie never stopped for a response. She was happy for any kind of an audience who would look at her new sparkly necklace and ring, prizes from a vending machine in a restaurant in Denver. Richard and Denise had apparently taken them out to lunch earlier.

"Quinn, you left the garage door open," her mother called from the kitchen. Her voice carried an edge that set the anger coursing through Quinn's veins again. Zander looked over at her in alarm.

"Sorry," she yelled back, even though she wasn't. She had to work to keep her voice from shaking.

It was like her mom didn't even hear her. Without acknowledging Quinn at all, she told Owen and Annie to hurry and put their overnight bags up in their rooms and then to get back in the car. When she walked into the living room, her eyes never met Quinn's.

"Your mom is serving dinner in twenty minutes," she said to Zander.

Zander looked over at Quinn. "Do you want to ride in my car?"

"Quinn has too much homework to catch up on after missing school on Friday."

She gaped at her mother in astonishment. "I know you have a lot of World History you need to study for," Megan said pointedly, before she turned and walked back into the kitchen, yelling for Annie and Owen to hurry up.

By the time she could bring herself to look back up at Zander, his expression was stunned, his eyebrows raised so high it was almost comical. Almost. "What is that about?" he whispered.

She shrugged.

"Is it about this weekend? I thought she knew where you were the whole time."

She shrugged again.

"Do you want me to stay here with you? We can talk?"

Though he'd spoken far too quietly for her to have heard, Megan's voice came from the kitchen with uncanny timing. "Zander, I just got off the phone with your mom a few minutes ago. She wants you home for dinner. Now."

He looked back at Quinn with a helpless expression.

"Go," she said, burying her head in her hands.

"Are you sure?"

Megan came back into the living room and stood at the bottom of the stairs, calling for Annie to hurry up, but her eyes were on Quinn and Zander the entire time. After several seconds of frantic glances between her mother's angry expression and Zander's concerned, questioning one, she stood and almost ran for the stairs, brushing shoulders with her mother as she passed.

Quinn was surprised when the shrill ringing of her alarm woke her the next morning. She had anticipated a quick return to the wild dreams and debilitating insomnia that had plagued her for so long now, but she woke feeling like she could have gone right back to sleep. The fact that she was dreading what the day might hold didn't help.

Only the thought of getting to school and talking to William helped her drag herself out of bed. She wanted to know how Thomas was doing, after ten more days in Eirentheos and his trip through the gate yesterday evening.

She'd wanted to go with them, to be there when Thomas came through and maybe spend some time with him last night, but William had convinced her that staying out for longer wasn't going to help the situation with her mom and, in any case, she wasn't sure she was prepared to deal with Nathaniel yet.

It didn't surprise her, as she made her way to the kitchen to grab something quick for breakfast, to discover that she was alone in the house. The sickening anger still tightened her shoulders and stomach though.

Exactly how long was her mother planning on avoiding her completely and not answering any of Quinn's questions? She'd always been close to her mom…always been able to talk to her about anything. In her entire life, they'd never been angry with one another for more than a couple of hours.

Tonight, after her mother returned from work, she was going to confront her and not back down until she had some answers.

The sound of the doorbell ringing startled her enough that it took her a second to figure out what it was. After the second insistent chime, she ran to answer it. Zander stood on the porch with the same strained expression he'd been wearing the evening before.

"Hey," she said. "I didn't expect to see you here this morning."

"I figured you'd need a ride," he said.

She frowned. "Well, I do appreciate it."

Zander looked confused. "How were you *planning* on getting to school?"

"Um, I was going to drive?"

"Your mom didn't *tell* you she took the keys to the Pilot with her to work?"

This was more than anger that filled her now…this was rage, red and raw. "No! The last time she said a word to me was last night while you were still here."

He gaped at her. "Oh my gosh, Quinn. What is going on between the two of you? Your mom was all upset at dinner last night at my house, and she was there half the morning, too. You never told me that you didn't have your mom's permission to go running off with William Rose this weekend. What else are you not telling me?"

"I'm telling you everything I know to tell you, Zander. I'm sorry I didn't tell you to begin with."

"Tell me what, Quinn? Seriously, what is going on?"

But she couldn't answer. Her hands were shaking and her jaw was tight. Tears formed in the corners of her eyes.

After staring at her for a moment Zander shook his head. "Come on, let's go before we're late."

The ride to school was tense, with Zander still wanting answers to his questions and Quinn too enraged at her mother to think clearly. It was bad enough that her mom was avoiding her…did she have to keep saying things around Zander that complicated the situation more?

Once they arrived, her hopes of talking to William were dashed. Zander walked with her everywhere, delivering her to the door of World History, where Abigail was waiting for her expectantly.

She swallowed hard at the sight of her best friend…she never had actually called or texted her back yesterday. Sometime over the weekend, Abigail had dyed several strands of her hair a violent shade of red. Quinn supposed it was futile to hope that wasn't an indicator of her friend's mood.

"What in the heck, Quinn?" Abigail hissed as she and Zander approached. "You can't even be bothered to *text me back?*"

She knew she deserved every bit of her friend's anger, that Abigail had done nothing to deserve this. At the moment, though, she was so wrapped up in her own rage and confusion that she had no idea how to respond. In fact, it was taking every ounce of strength she could muster to stand there at all. All she really wanted to do was run, to get as far away from everyone as possible so she could have a few minutes just to think.

At that moment, the one-minute warning bell sounded overhead, relieving her of the need to explain anything right then. For the hundredth time that morning, she took a deep breath, trying to collect her thoughts and emotions.

"I will talk later, Abbie, I promise. Just... not at school, okay?"

Abigail's eyes narrowed; it was clear that she wasn't going to let Quinn keep getting away with this.

She turned around to look at Zander, a heavy feeling forming in the pit of her stomach. "I'll talk to you more later, too. Can you just be patient with me for a little while?"

He nodded and bent to kiss her on the top of her head, though even as his lips touched her, the gap between them grew.

Although she knew that she absolutely needed to pay attention today in World History...more than in any of her other classes...she struggled to do it. Her thoughts were a tangled mess as she worried about her relationships with Zander and Abigail and stewed in her anger at her mother. For a few minutes, she felt sorry for herself, wishing she'd left well enough alone and never followed William through that gate.

As soon as her thoughts drifted to the gate, though, she remembered that Thomas had come through last night, and she shifted to worrying about whether or not Nathaniel had managed to get the surgery scheduled today. Then all she wanted to do was get to William, to talk to him and, if he was worried, she wanted to be there to comfort him.

Somehow, as she thought about Thomas's surgery, about Nathaniel and William working to get him through the gate and taken care of, her mind cleared a little, and she realized what she needed to do…at least as far as school and her friends were concerned.

In a way, a big way, really, dealing with the details of her life here was no different than what she'd just had to do in William's world as they searched for Thomas, waiting to be able to rescue him.

There were smaller things that had to be taken care of while she waited to solve the bigger ones. They were important, and she just had to do them. Freaking out wasn't going to help anything.

By the time the bell rang again, she was calm. Her rage towards her mother was carefully tucked away, waiting for later. Her friends didn't deserve the way she had been treating them lately, and she wasn't going to take her confusion out on them anymore.

She shoved her notebook into her backpack and hurried to get to Abigail so she could speak first. "I'm really sorry, Abbie. There's no excuse for my not calling you or texting you back. I could say it's because I didn't have my phone with me this weekend, but that doesn't explain why I didn't call you yesterday. There's a lot of stuff going on, and I'm really upset about it. A lot of it, I just don't really *want* to talk about, but I will, later when I'm ready, okay?"

Abigail looked a little stunned at the sudden change in her demeanor, but she nodded.

"I'll see you at lunch?" Quinn asked, already turning toward the door, without waiting for a response, knowing that Zander would appear soon. She was ready for him when he arrived…relaxed and smiling, carefully forming her expression so he would know she was happy to see him.

And she found that her happiness was genuine. Regardless of whatever else was going on, she cared about Zander. Even though she was no longer sure where her feelings stood on the relationship front, she did love him, and she always had. The last thing she wanted to do was hurt him.

He seemed to notice the change, and he visibly relaxed as they walked through the hallway together, carrying her books and slipping his hand inside hers.

The day passed more quickly than she had imagined it would, given the way it had started. She didn't even have the same trouble she usually had re-acclimating to her classes after a trip to Eirentheos. She wondered if she would ever make the trip enough times that the transition would become second nature, the way it seemed to be for William.

The one downside was that she never got the chance to talk to William. Although she had caught a few glimpses of him in the hallways between her morning classes as she walked with Zander, he wasn't in the cafeteria at lunchtime. And after lunch, she never saw him again.

In keeping with her new attitude, she figured it was better not to worry about it. Whatever else was going on, they were friends now, and she could call him tonight and ask.

The biggest threat to her calm came at the end of the day, when her phone buzzed to alert her to a new text message as Zander was walking her to her locker after her last class.

"What's wrong?" he asked, after she viciously snapped the device shut.

"Apparently, my mom talked to Mrs. Williams and arranged for me to go into work this evening to make up for the shift I missed on Thursday night. She said she wanted to let me know in plenty of time, in case I needed to walk."

Zander stopped short. "I still don't understand what you could have done to upset your mom *this* much, Quinn. She's not normally like this."

"I told you what I did. I ran off with Doctor Rose and William this weekend without her permission."

"And what? Got arrested? Boiled a live puppy? It's not like your mom to act like this."

Quinn shrugged. "I honestly don't know. I guess there's some history between Na…Doctor Rose and my mom that I never knew about."

"Between your *mom* and Doctor Rose? What kind of history?"

"If I knew that, Zander, I would not be as confused and angry as I am right now. I don't understand any of it, and she won't tell me anything. I haven't even talked to her since yesterday morning when she came into my room and practically threw my phone at me, saying she'd changed her mind about grounding me from it. Then she left and went to Denver. The only other contact I've had with her is what you saw yesterday, and then this morning when she apparently intended for me to figure out the keys were missing when I went to get into the car to come to school."

"Wow. No wonder you're so upset." He gently squeezed her shoulder.

"I know I deserve for her to be mad at me, but I think at the moment, I'm angrier than she is."

MRS. WILLIAMS

ZANDER OFFERED TO TAKE her over to his house for the hour before her shift at the library, but she was nervous about seeing her boss, and she figured it was best to get it over with. Besides, she knew Zander had to work that evening, too, and she didn't want to take up any of his time to do homework or get ready.

The strangling friction between them was back by the time he pulled into a parking space at the library so long before her shift would actually begin.

For a moment, she thought he was going to start asking her about the weekend again, but then he just sighed. "I'll be here to pick you up later, okay?"

She nodded.

He leaned across the seat and kissed her on the forehead. There was an urgency to the gesture that was palpable in the air between them. She lifted her face, looking into his eyes, and he moved down, kissing her on the lips this time instead. The kiss quickly turned intense; her whole body shifted closer to him, and he grabbed her arm, moving her even closer, as his other hand reached into her hair...

And then it ended abruptly.

Zander pulled back, a look of alarm in his eyes, his hand dropping instantly from her arm. "I'm so sorry! Did I hurt you?"

She was confused for several seconds as she tried to figure out what he meant. Then she remembered. The last time she and Zander had been this close to each other…days ago for him, weeks ago for her…her right arm had still been covered in cuts and bruises, and she'd still had stitches William had put in after an accident in his world.

"Oh," she said, brushing off her sleeve. "Doctor Rose took the stitches out this weekend, and it's not as sore when you touch it now." All still technically true…in Eirentheos William was also known as Doctor Rose. And the stitches *were* gone. "I'm okay."

"Are you sure?" He still looked concerned.

"Yeah. Thanks for the ride. I'll see you in a few hours?"

"I'll be here."

When she first stepped inside the library, she couldn't see her boss anywhere. It wasn't busy at all; there were maybe two or three patrons wandering deep in the stacks and one sat at a table near the gardening books, taking extensive notes from a thick volume.

Behind the circulation desk, there were way too many carts full of books that needed re-shelving…her missing Thursday night meant the job had piled up from most of last week and the weekend, too. It might take her tonight's shift and tomorrow's to get to all of it.

It wasn't time to clock in yet, though, so she made her way to the back room in search of the librarian.

Sylvia Williams was standing on a stepstool by a tall work counter, carefully repairing a plastic dust jacket that had come loose from a book.

"Hi Mrs. Williams," Quinn said, stepping into the room. She tucked her hands in the pockets of her jeans to keep them from shaking.

"Oh, hi, sweetheart. I'm so glad to see you. Is everything all right?"

"Yeah, I just… I'm really sorry for leaving work on Thursday night. I never meant to do something like that. I think I got carried away or something."

Mrs. Williams nodded, her blue eyes shining kindly. The little glass gems on the chain that held her glasses around her neck tinkled slightly with the movement. "It seemed like something pretty serious was going on with William," she said. "I figured the two of you would never have run off like that if it wasn't important."

Quinn's mouth fell open. "So, you're not mad?"

Mrs. Williams smiled. "I've known you since you were a baby, Quinn. I've never seen you make a decision that didn't have some kind of a reason behind it. Don't start making a habit of it or anything, but no, I'm not mad."

"I really am sorry."

"I know you are. It sounds like you got in enough trouble with your mom already, though. You've got a whole lifetime ahead of you to be sorry, sweetheart. You'll make much bigger mistakes than leaving in the middle of a shift at an after-school job as a teenager."

"My mom doesn't seem to think so."

The older woman shrugged, her tiny shoulders moving up and down in an exaggerated fashion. "She's doing what moms do. Besides, your mother has always been the more serious type, like you usually are. I was beginning to wonder if I'd ever see your dad's spunk in you."

Her heart skipped a beat. "Did you know my dad well, then?"

Mrs. Williams' smile lit up her face. "Sure I did. Back before Nathaniel went away to medical school, he was always in here studying, the way William does now, and your father was always here, distracting him."

"Nathaniel *Rose?*"

"Oh, yes. Nathaniel and Samuel were such close friends, always together, those two."

She shivered, taking her hands from her pockets to smooth the sudden goose bumps on her arms. Her father and Nathaniel had been friends? "I didn't even know they really knew each other."

Mrs. Williams nodded, a somber expression on her face. "Your mother was devastated when Samuel died, Quinn. For a couple of years there, I don't think she wanted to be around anyone or anything that reminded her of him. There was even a rumor for a while that she planned to move away, to go to Denver or somewhere else, just to get away from all of the things here that made her think of him. I think Nathaniel was one of those things. Although she didn't end up leaving, she never did have the same kind of friendship with him afterward." She sighed.

"I was really happy for her when she met Jeff and things seemed to start looking so much better for her. You liked Jeff, too. Then you all moved into the new house, and Jeff adopted you and then Owen was born. Megan was really happy again."

"But she still wasn't really friends with Nathaniel." Quinn turned this over in her mind, trying to fit the pieces together. It still didn't explain anything about why her mom had known to be sitting at the bridge.

"No. She and Nathaniel were never good friends again after that. I always thought it was such a shame for you and Nathaniel, too. He was so fond of you when you were little, doting over you and buying you presents every time you were out with him. The shopkeepers on Main Street were always happy to see Samuel and Nathaniel walking up the boardwalk with you. Often, the two of them would take you out on Saturday afternoons, saying they were giving your mom a break…but they loved it just as much…and you never went home empty-handed."

"Wow, I had no idea." Quinn felt moisture in the corners of her eyes. It had been a long time since she'd allowed herself to think this much about her real dad, who had died when she was three. She didn't really remember him, and it was strange to realize that there were other people who remembered her with him. It was even stranger to think that Nathaniel might be one of those people.

"I was pleased when William came to live with Nathaniel, and he had another child to love on. It's been good for him. It's been really wonderful lately to see you and William getting to know one another. I've been hoping it would mean you and Nathaniel reconnecting as well."

"I don't think my mom wants that."

"Your mother loved your father very much, Quinn. In a way, I don't think she's ever completely gotten over losing him, and maybe she never will. And she loves you, too. The two of you will get through your current battle, and you'll come out stronger on the other side."

Quinn nodded, hoping that was true.

"And in the meantime, if there's a reason you need to miss work, or you have something going on…just let me know, okay?"

When Zander pulled up in front of Quinn's house to drop her off, all of the front windows were dark, except for the one tiny light in the window above the front door. Even the window to her mom's room was black.

"Your mom has to be home by now, doesn't she?"

She shrugged. "I'm sure she is. I doubt if they even went anywhere tonight."

"So she's just going to bed this early to avoid you again."

She didn't answer.

He stretched across the seat, reaching for her hand. She accepted it, debating telling him what she'd found out about her dad and Nathaniel Rose. She *wanted* to tell him, but she wasn't sure if bringing up Nathaniel right now would be helpful with the strain already between them.

"What are you going to do for a car when Jeff comes home, anyway?"

The question startled her, and there was a strained quality to Zander's voice that made her suspect this wasn't just a random question. She frowned. "I don't know. My mom and Jeff sometimes talked about buying me one, but I never really wanted to talk about it. I was still sort of freaked out about the whole idea of getting my license when Jeff's team was offered that contract in Afghanistan. By the time I decided I was actually going to do it now, he already knew he was going to be gone. Why? Do you think my mom's going to ground me from his car permanently or something?"

He shook his head. "No. I just… You haven't talked to your mom *at all*, Quinn?"

"I told you what's been going on."

Zander sighed, his brown eyes darker than usual. "Have you, Quinn?"

She swallowed, red coloring her cheeks, though at the moment she was driven more by needing to know what was behind his careful tone than she was by her guilt. "How about you tell me what you're hinting around about, and then I'll tell you something interesting I learned at work tonight?"

He looked taken aback, but he answered. "What I'm hinting around about is whether or not your mom has told you that Jeff might be coming home soon?"

Ice water poured through her veins. "Before June?"

"Yeah. She told my mom the other night that when she talked to him this weekend, he told her that they've been ahead on their project for a long time now. He's had an idea that they might be coming back early for a while, but he didn't want to say anything until he was sure."

"So when you said might…"

"Unless something changes, he'll be back in a month."

Under any other circumstances, this would have been fantastic news. She loved her adopted father, and Owen and Annie missed him like crazy. Having him gone had been really difficult for her mom, too. After already losing Quinn's dad, it really upset her to have Jeff so far away, especially when she worried he might be in danger, even though he assured her all the time that he was only a civilian contractor and he was safe.

At this exact moment, though, the idea of him returning felt like adding another big log onto an already blazing fire. What was *he* going to think about all of this stuff with her? Surely it wouldn't be quite as easy for her to slip off and visit Eirentheos when he and her mom were *both* around on the weekends. *That* thought startled her again…was she really intending on actually going back again, after the way it had already completely complicated her life? But then thinking of *never* going back…*no*, she couldn't say she wasn't going to.

She wondered what Jeff knew about her connection to Nathaniel…if he knew that her father and Nathaniel had been friends. She wondered if her mom had told Jeff what Quinn had done this last weekend.

"What were you going to tell me?" Zander asked, interrupting her reverie.

"Um…" she took a deep breath, trying to regain her train of thought, and then started telling him what she'd learned at work that night.

"Whoa," he said when she'd finished. "And neither your mom or Dr. Rose told you he was friends with your dad?"

"No."

"That's weird. It doesn't make sense that she would just cut him out like that. Your mom has lots of friends."

She nodded. "I don't understand it."

He was silent for several minutes, staring out through the windshield. "You don't suppose something went on sometime between your mom and Dr. Rose, do you?"

Her eyes widened at the implication in his voice. "What do you mean? Like something romantic?"

"Yeah. That would explain some of it, wouldn't it? Why they don't talk to each other now? If they were together before, and then they broke up?"

"He was my dad's best friend!"

"I don't mean while your dad was still alive, Quinn. At least, I don't think your mom would do something like that. But what if, after he was already gone..."

Her heart pounded at the suggestion. "Do you think she would do that?"

"I don't know. Dr. Rose is a nice guy. If he was your dad's best friend, she would have already known him. Why wouldn't she go out with a guy who already liked her kid?"

"And then they broke up." The theory made sense, except... "Why would she keep him as a doctor for us for all of these years then?"

"That'd be obvious and mean, wouldn't it? Everyone in Bristlecone who doesn't go to Doctor Rose has to drive half an hour away, and he's better than that clinic in Pinespar, anyway. They've all had to go there when Dr. Rose's office is closed."

"Yeah... it's just hard to imagine my mom and Nathaniel..."

"You're on a first-name basis with him now?"

Uh-oh. She suddenly had complete sympathy for why William had never gotten to know anyone in Bristlecone well enough to have a real conversation with them. It was almost impossible not to let something accidentally slip out. She knew she needed to take evasive action before this conversation started drifting somewhere she couldn't let it go. "Not really," she said, though she could feel her neck turning a vibrant shade of red. "That's just what Mrs. Williams was calling him." Then she yawned widely. "Thanks for the ride."

"You're always welcome, Quinn."

This time she leaned over to initiate the kiss.

Inside the house, Quinn turned off the few lights her mother had left on, leaving just the tiny one in the entryway burning, and made her way upstairs to her room. Sitting down on her bed, she reached for the framed picture on her nightstand. It was of her father, young and smiling, hoisting Quinn into the air. In the picture she looked beyond delighted, and her father's expression matched her own, his gray eyes twinkling, crinkled in laughter.

She wished she could remember it…remember him.

A tear slipped down her cheek as she traced the outline of his face with her finger. She was so deep in thought that she almost didn't hear the soft knock on her bedroom door. A second later, the knob turned, and her seven-year-old brother, Owen, stepped inside.

Wiping her cheek with her sleeve, she smiled at him. "Hey, buddy. What are you still doing up?"

"I was waiting for you to get home."

"I'm glad you did. Want to come sit up here with me?"

Owen nodded and climbed up on the bed next to her, tucking his legs up under himself. She had to smile at how sweet he looked, decked out in footie pajamas covered with train engines…one of his obsessions.

He studied her face as he sat beside her, though his eyes never quite met hers. "Are you okay?" he asked.

"Yeah, I'm okay," she said, wondering which of the two of them she was trying to convince. "How are you? Was school good today?"

He nodded. "Yeah, but Mommy still seems mad. Why is she so mad at you, Quinn?"

She sighed. There was only one second grade class in Bristlecone, and her mom was the teacher. Owen would have spent all day with her. "I really don't know."

"Is it because of where you went?"

A cold shiver ran through her. "What do you mean, Owen?"

Owen frowned. "You left this weekend. You went to…that other place. Is that why Mom is mad at you?"

Her hands started trembling, so she hid them in her lap. She swallowed, trying to figure out how to ask what she wanted to know without scaring him. "Yeah, I think that's why she's mad at me."

He looked at her thoughtfully. "You came back, though. She doesn't need to be mad now."

"Owen," she tried to keep her voice steady, "how do you know about where I went?"

His expression turned confused, for a long moment he studied her in a way that suggested she was missing something obvious. Then his expression changed again; he looked like he'd figured something out.

"I was dreaming," he said, so softly that if she hadn't been sitting right next to him, leaned close and straining to hear, she wouldn't have understood him.

A heavy, ominous feeling weighed in her gut. *Dreams.* She'd always had strange dreams herself, ever since she was little. She'd never paid close attention. Not until she'd been in Eirentheos, and the dreams had taken on a much more serious quality, driving her desperation to get to Thomas. Now she wondered just how important dreams might be.

"What did you dream, Owen?" This time she couldn't keep the shaking out of her voice, but Owen, fortunately, didn't seem to notice. Most of the time, the social challenges that Owen faced because of his mild autism made communicating with him more difficult. But, sometimes, it was easier when he didn't pick up on subtle things, like how frightened she was right now.

He scrunched up his face, deep in thought, staring at the green flowers on her bedspread, rather than making eye contact. "I don't know exactly where you were, Quinn, but you were smiling. It made you happy to be there, except one time you were scared." He glanced up at her now.

She nodded. "And then what?"

His eyes fell to the blanket again. "I don't know. Then I wasn't there with you anymore. I was here, and Mommy was sad, because you were going to stay there and not come home."

Quinn scooted closer to him, close enough that he was almost in her lap. "I came home," she said.

"I know." He nodded. "So I don't know why Mommy is mad now."

"I don't know either, buddy."

He laid his head back against her chest, and she pulled him into her lap, holding him there, breathing in the sweet scent of his freshly washed hair. "I'm just glad you're not mad at me, Owen. I don't know what I'd do right now if I didn't have you."

"You'll always have me, Quinn."

VISITING THOMAS

THE HOUSE WAS EMPTY again when Quinn woke up on Tuesday morning, even though she was out of bed earlier than she had been the day before. Her hopes that she'd be able to sleep through the night again now that she was home and Thomas was safe had been dashed sometime around one in the morning when she'd awoken from a bizarre, vivid dream.

The only thing she could remember about it was being in a field of enormous dandelions that towered over her head, much larger than the weeds could ever actually be. It scared her, after what Owen had told her last night, and she strained, trying to recall more of it, but she couldn't.

She poured herself a bowl of cereal in the still-dark kitchen, wondering how long her mother planned to keep this up.

As she carried her breakfast over to the tall island in the middle of the room, something shiny on the end of the counter caught her eye. Her keys were lying there, on top of a handwritten note.

I've decided there's really no reason you can't have your keys.

We're eating dinner over at Maggie's tonight, so you won't need to pick up Annie.

And so it was going to continue. Quinn wouldn't be able to eat at the Cunninghams' with her mom and siblings because she had to work. And, in any case, there was certainly no way she could have the confrontation she needed to have with her mother in front of Zander's entire family.

For a few minutes she entertained a mini-temper tantrum, almost deciding to *not* drive the car just to prove a point, but she managed to pull herself together enough to realize she'd get the worst end of that choice.

Besides, now she could get to school early…and alone. She texted Zander with the news, letting him know that he didn't need to pick her up this morning. Wolfing down her cereal, she made quickly for the garage, hoping William, too, would be at school early like he usually was.

Fortunately, she wasn't disappointed. Although her footsteps echoed along the empty corridors, William was standing in front of his locker, wearing his familiar purple sweater. Even though she'd known she was looking for him, she was still surprised at the relief she felt when he turned and smiled at her. It was like taking the first breath after being underwater for a long time.

"Hey," he said. "I was hoping I'd get to talk to you this morning."

"Me too. How's Thomas?"

"He's doing pretty well. Nathaniel was able to get surgery scheduled for him yesterday afternoon in Grand Junction. He had to call in some favors to manage it, but he made it happen. I was hoping to tell you before I left yesterday, but we never really got the chance to talk, and I left early so I could go with them."

"And he's…"

"He's fine. The repair Nathaniel and Lily were able to do kept his leg in pretty good shape. After the surgery yesterday, he should be up and around on crutches in a couple of weeks and have full use back in a few months."

It was good news. Although he'd always put a positive spin on things in front of Thomas, William had talked to her a few times about how much he wished they'd had the resources to do a really proper repair on Thomas's shattered femur in his world. She was glad that, in the end, they'd had the option to bring him here.

"Are you going back up there tonight?" she asked.

"I don't know. I want to, of course, but there are a number of things I've fallen behind on, and Nathaniel may be working. Thomas told me yesterday not to worry about it. We're pretty sure he'll be released to Nathaniel on Thursday morning."

"So soon? Just two days?"

"It might not be so soon if Nathaniel wasn't a doctor. There's no school on Friday, so we're probably going to try to take Thomas back home on Thursday evening."

The floor dropped out from under her. "Already? You're going to leave and go back?"

"I'm sure my parents are quite anxious to have Thomas home."

She nodded. Queen Charlotte and King Stephen would indeed be worried about their son and wanting him back. It was selfish of her not to think of that. Besides, she was sure Thomas and William both wanted to be with their family. It was just… she hadn't seen him yet since he'd been here, and she wasn't so sure she was ready for everything to be over…to go back to living her life here without them. She was afraid it was all going to feel like it had never happened.

"I'm sure they are," she said, fumbling for the right words, not knowing how to explain how she felt. "I'm just surprised… I was hoping to see Thomas while he was here."

His eyes softened in understanding. "Oh, right."

"It's okay, though." It had to be. Her life was here, not in their world.

William's expression changed to one of concern, and suddenly it was as if he could see right through her, like he understood her real feelings about it.

He shook his head. "No, I know he wants to see you, too. I could try calling Nathaniel later and ask if he could drive us up there tonight."

Nathaniel? She wasn't sure she was ready to deal with Nathaniel yet, not until she had spoken to her mother. "Well, I could drive, but I have to work tonight."

William's eyes lit up, and she realized the issue of transportation was a big one. She wondered if he'd forgotten she had a car and could drive. He had told her one time that he'd never really cared to learn to use a car while he was in her world…he didn't think he would ever really spend enough time here for it to matter, and it was a useless skill in his world, where he was an accomplished horseback rider. "How about tomorrow, right after school?"

She paused. She had a pretty good idea how her mom might feel about her driving all the way to Grand Junction with William. Of course, that assumed she would actually see her mother long enough to even have the conversation…which at this rate looked unlikely. What did she have to lose? "Sure."

As she'd expected, by Wednesday, she'd still had almost no contact with her mother. Although Megan and her siblings were still home when she woke up that morning…it would have been difficult to get out of the house before four in the morning when Quinn had again been shaken awake by crazy dreams…this time it was Quinn who stayed in her room. As much as she desperately wanted to talk to her mother, today she didn't want to jeopardize her trip to Grand Junction with William.

There was another note on the counter, though. Again, her mother had to work late and then had plans, and she wouldn't need to pick up Annie. The note irritated Quinn; her hands quivered as she read it. If she hadn't already been trying to figure out a way to get out of picking up Annie today, she might have snapped. She might have driven, right now, to her mother's work and had the whole thing out with her in the classroom before her students showed up.

But since it gave her a way to get to Grand Junction without worrying about seeing her family, she stuffed the note in her backpack and headed to school instead.

The problem she hadn't anticipated with the whole trip…and her heart sank when she realized she should have…was Zander. As soon as they'd set their lunch trays down at their usual table in the cafeteria, he turned to her, smiling. "What do you want to do today?"

She raised her eyebrows.

"We're both off work, my dad has to work late, and your mom and my mom are taking all the little kids out to some pizza and play place that just opened in Montrose. I thought you and I could go out somewhere fun together. I could take you out to dinner and then maybe ice skating?"

A hot heavy feeling settled in Quinn's chest. Honestly, she hadn't even thought about Zander when she had made certain that her schedule for the evening was free. What was she supposed to do now? After a few seconds of deliberation, she remembered her promise to herself. The truth. She would tell him as much of the truth as she could.

"That sounds like a lot of fun, Zander. But, um… I kind of already made plans for tonight."

He frowned. "What plans?"

"I told William that I would drive him up to Grand Junction to see his brother in the hospital." She stared at the table as she waited for his answer.

"Doesn't he have his own car?"

"No, actually. Does that matter?" The tone in his voice irritated her.

"Can't *Doctor Rose* drive him?"

She swallowed hard, hearing the tone of betrayal in his voice. "Doctor Rose has to work. William wants to see his brother, so that Thomas doesn't have to be there all alone for another whole night. I told him I would do it. Besides, I like his brother. I want to see him, too."

And, if she was going to be completely honest… she was looking forward to spending the time with William.

When she finally glanced up at him, the look on his face made her insides twist in knots. He was really upset…more than she would have expected. "Fine, whatever," he said, turning back to his lunch.

There was a heavy shadow over the rest of the lunch period. They both stared at their trays the whole time, but neither of them ate very much. When the bell finally rang, Zander mumbled something about needing to get to his next class a few minutes early

As soon as Zander was out of the cafeteria, Abigail cornered Quinn.

"What in the heck is going on with you? You're turning down a night out with Zander so you can run off with William Rose to see his brother in the hospital when you already spent the entire weekend there?"

She didn't know how to answer; she stood there, her face turning red, her insides going wobbly as she wondered if everyone at the table had heard her conversation with Zander.

Abigail leaned in close, her blue eyes hard and icy, and her voice low. "Are you cheating on Zander?"

Quinn's jaw dropped. Was *that* what it looked like? "No, Abbie! It's nothing like that. William and Thomas are just friends."

Abigail's expression didn't change, her voice stayed low and dark. "Well, I don't get it, Quinn. Nobody does. First, William *Rose* is talking to you, when he's never talked to another person the entire freaking time he's lived here. Then you're hugging his cousin who turns out to suddenly be his brother? Where are their parents? What is going on with that? Then you disappear for the whole weekend and it turns out you're off somewhere with them…who knows if this hospital thing is even true. And *then* I hear from Adam that the other night Zander told you he *loves* you, and you haven't even said anything back!"

By the end of Abigail's speech, Quinn couldn't even look at her. She had never really put all of that together before…what all of this must look like to Zander and the rest of her friends. The twisting feeling in her stomach grew decidedly sick, and hot tears pooled in the corners of her eyes. How had her life gotten so complicated?

"I… I don't know, Abbie. It's not all something I can explain."

"Well, you'd better figure it out, Quinn. Because you're about to lose everything." And with that, Abigail turned around and walked away, leaving her standing alone in the almost-empty cafeteria.

The room was spinning around her; her hands shook, and ripples of nausea tore through her stomach. Her first impulse was to run away, drive off, get some fresh air and some space, but the small rational part that was left knew it would only make things worse with school. Suddenly, she felt a hand on her shoulder. Startled, she whirled around.

"Hey, are you okay?" William's voice was soft, calming. She wondered how much of the exchange he'd just heard.

She blinked several times, trying to keep the traitorous tears from falling. "Yeah, I'm fine."

He raised one eyebrow.

"Okay, I don't know. Not really."

"We don't have to go up there tonight. You could stay here instead and work things out with your friends."

She swallowed hard. He'd heard everything. "No." She shook her head. "I want to go to Grand Junction this afternoon." And she did. She wanted to leave and go there *right now*, actually. Spending time with William and Thomas was about the only thing in her world that made any sense to her right now. "How about we leave now?"

He chuckled, though behind his glasses, his eyes showed nothing but understanding. "That won't solve anything, and you know it. Besides, you can't afford to miss any more classes right now. Make it through the day, and we'll leave right after school, okay?"

She nodded. His hand twitched at his side, almost as if he were resisting reaching out and touching her. A strange current filled the air between them, distracting her from the fight she'd just had with Abigail.

A shrill ringing disrupted them then, the bell warning that the next class period would begin in one minute.

"I'll meet you out front after school," he said.

She watched him walk away before she made a mad dash up the hallway to her class.

By the time her last class ended, she wasn't so sure it had been worth it to stay for the rest of the day. She hadn't been able to focus on anything. Zander and Abigail had both avoided her for the rest of the day. Even in the class they had together, Abigail refused to even look at her. Zander didn't wait for her outside any of her classes.

Just before her last class, she pulled together every bit of courage she could find, and texted her mom.

I'm going to drive William up to Grand Junction tonight to see his brother. I'll try and be home by curfew, but I might be a little late.

She knew that wasn't going to go over well. For the first part of class she had to remind herself to breathe, waiting for her mother's refusal to let her go. What she didn't know was whether that refusal would stop her from going.

It took nearly half the class period, but finally it was there, the little blinking light when she slipped her phone out of her pocket.

Don't expect us to wait up for you.

Would you have, anyway? she wondered to herself as she snapped the phone shut.

Not wanting to spend any more time in the building than she had to, she'd pulled everything she needed out of her locker before her final class and carried it all with her. As soon as the bell rang, she headed to William's locker.

"I take it you're ready to go?" he asked when he saw her.

She nodded. "Please?"

"Are you feeling any better?" William asked when they were about twenty minutes outside of town. It was the first time either of them had spoken, and she was surprised at how nice that felt, having him just sit quietly next to her, patient and unassuming.

"A little." It was a relief to be away from the oppressive, trapped feeling of the school building.

She drew in a deep breath, trying to figure out how to share her jumbled thoughts. "I hurt Zander," she said.

He was silent for a long moment. "Yeah, you did."

"What do I do now?"

His eyes were wide as he looked over at her. "I don't know, Quinn. Except stop hurting him. But I'm not good at any of this. If we were in Eirentheos, I'd tell you to ask Linnea."

The comment was almost enough to make her smile. "Why, does she have a lot of experience hiding her travels between two worlds from her boyfriends?"

He chuckled. "Everyone in my family has at least a small amount of experience in keeping secrets…*obviously*…but I was speaking more of experience in breaking guys' hearts."

She gulped. "Is that what I'm doing? *Breaking his heart?*"

"That's kind of what it looked like to me."

Now she felt even worse.

"Hey, beautiful!" Thomas said, as they entered his hospital room. "I didn't know you were coming."

"Will didn't tell you?" She frowned at William.

He shrugged. "I figured it could be a surprise."

"It's a great surprise," Thomas said, his grin reaching all the way to his twinkling eyes. "I can't believe you came all this way to visit me."

"Why wouldn't I? I've missed you," she said, leaning down to give him a careful hug. "How are you doing, anyway?"

"Great. I've never watched this much television before. Some interesting people on this thing."

She rolled her eyes. "I mean, how's your leg?" She eyed the enormous contraption that stabilized his right leg underneath the blankets. His right arm was still wrapped in a thick cast that stretched from just below his shoulder to his wrist…it looked like that had been replaced as well.

"It's going to be fine, Quinn. I'm glad there aren't metal detectors in my world to worry about, but I'll be up to my old tricks before you know it."

She smiled. "I'm sure you will."

Thomas scrutinized her face closely for a second, and then glanced up at William before looking back at her. "I think the better question here is how are *you?*"

"Do I look that bad?"

"Quinn, you look beautiful as always, but... have you been sleeping?"

She looked down at her hands, which seemed to keep twisting around of their own accord, and shook her head.

"And what's going on between you and your mom?"

Her head snapped up. "How do you know about that?" She looked over at William.

"He told me what happened at the bridge," Thomas said, not giving Will a chance to answer. "What was that about? How did she know where to find you?"

"That's the million-dollar question," she said. "She won't even talk to me this week, I've barely even seen her, and she definitely won't answer that."

"And Nathaniel refuses to say anything still," William said. "He insists that whatever he knows isn't his to tell...it's between Quinn and her mom."

"What is that supposed to mean?" Thomas asked.

"Nobody knows."

His eyes went back to Quinn. "It's between you and your mom, but your mom isn't talking to you at all."

She held her hands up in an exasperated gesture.

"So, let me get this straight. You're not sleeping, you're not talking to your mom, you're not getting any answers to a huge, terrifying question, and you're asking me if *I'm* all right?"

She sighed at his astute summary of the situation. "That just about covers it. Oh, and I just had a fight with my best friend Abigail and another one with Zander."

He let out a low whistle. "Wow."

William pulled two chairs up next to Thomas's bed, and she sighed as she sank down into one. He didn't sit in the one he'd gotten for himself though, going instead to the end of the bed and pulling out Thomas's chart. It made her smile when she realized that it was exactly what she'd expected him to do…she was beginning to understand him.

"Anything else I should know?" Thomas asked.

She looked down at her hands again, watching her fingers twist nervously. "I did find out the other night that Nathaniel was close friends with my real dad."

Both boys' heads turned toward her in surprise, and both were as speechless as she'd been when she finished telling them what Mrs. Williams had shared with her the other night.

"Do you really think something could have gone on between Nathaniel and your mom?" Thomas asked, after she'd explained the new theory she and Zander had come up with.

"I have a hard time imagining that," said William.

"Why? You think Nathaniel's never been interested in anyone?" Thomas asked.

"No, I just picture Nathaniel courting someone he actually had a chance of marrying and starting a family with. It would be awfully hard for him to consider someone from this world. Wouldn't she have questions when he disappeared back to Eirentheos? Or freak out if he told her the truth?"

Thomas raised an eyebrow. "Maybe that's exactly what happened. Maybe that's how Quinn's mom knew about the bridge."

The three of them spent the next two hours discussing every possibility they could think of, but in the end, they didn't have any more answers than when they'd started. Still, spending time with William and Thomas calmed her; she actually found herself smiling and laughing with them. She'd even almost forgotten about her rotten day by the time Thomas asked William to go down to a particular vending machine on the first floor where there was a kind of chocolate bar he liked.

William rolled his eyes, but headed for the door instantly.

As soon as he was out of the room, Thomas turned to her.

"How do you feel about Zander, Quinn?"

"What?" She'd never expected Thomas to come out and ask her about that.

"Are you in love with him?"

She shrugged, even though the question sent ice water flowing through her veins…she didn't know the answer, wasn't ready to think about this. "I've known Zander my whole life; he's been one of my best friends since I was born. I've always loved him."

"That isn't what I asked."

No, it wasn't. She knew she was stalling. "I…" she stared hard at the floor, trying to make sense of the random differently colored tiles sprinkled in with the white ones…there seemed to be no pattern to it. "I don't know."

"That's not the kind of thing you don't know, Quinn. If you were in love with him, you would know." His expression was intense as he scrutinized her face. "You're not."

She swallowed hard. "But he's an amazing guy, Thomas. He's so sweet and wonderful and fun… I don't think I could ask for a better boyfriend."

"And he loves you, I know." His gray eyes, usually so lighthearted, were serious now. "But, as much as you think you should, and you wish you did, you don't love him back."

"I care about him."

"Then be fair to him, Quinn. Do you remember in Eirentheos when I told you that you have some big choices to make?"

She nodded.

"This is one of them. You can't give Zander what he wants to give to you. It's maybe not fair, and it's probably not how things would be if you had never found the gate, but it is the way things *are*. Don't be a weed in his garden."

"Then what do I do? I don't want to hurt him."

Thomas reached for her hand, squeezing it gently. "Sweetheart, you're already hurting him. I think you already know what to do. Now you just have to do it."

As she had expected, the house was dark and quiet when Quinn got home after dropping William back off at his house. Even Owen's light was out under his door, although it was only nine-thirty. She wondered how her mother had managed to wear him out enough to keep him from waiting up for her. She decided to just be grateful for it…he didn't need to see this.

The whole drive home she had thought about what Thomas had said to her. She knew he was right. As much as she cared about Zander…and she did really love him…she wasn't in a place to give back to him what he was giving to her, what he deserved. She was already hurting him, lying to him.

Beyond just not telling him about the gate, not telling him the things that she really *couldn't* tell him, she was hiding the kisses she'd shared with both Thomas and William.

And worse, while she knew that the kiss with Thomas was never going to lead anywhere, she had no such certainties about the kiss with William. There had been something there. And although she and William had never talked about it, that same something still hung in the air between them. She'd felt it again tonight, even in the car on the way home. Earlier, when Abigail had asked her if she was cheating on Zander, it had made Quinn angry. She wasn't the kind of girl who would cheat on her boyfriend, and her best friend should have known that about her.

Except…she kind of was. If Zander had kissed another girl… well, she didn't have to dig deep to know exactly how that would have made her feel. And then if he'd chosen to spend time with that girl over going on a date?

And she knew, beyond a doubt, tonight wasn't going to be the last time she chose to spend time with William instead of someone else…instead of Zander. Even if the fact that they were from two different worlds made anything beyond a friendship impossible, he was too important to her now. She liked spending time with him, liked *him*. Maybe more than she liked Zander.

The car ride back with William tonight had confirmed that. She knew she'd been acting off after her conversation with Thomas, distracted and edgy. It was obvious that William had noticed, but he hadn't asked; he'd been content to let her be. She'd realized, though, that she *wanted* to tell him. It wasn't the right thing; she needed to talk to Zander first.

What she was doing to Zander right now wasn't fair to anybody…not to Zander, not to William, and not even to herself.

She was nauseous and her hands were shaking as she curled up near her pillows and picked up her phone. She knew he would still be awake.

He answered before the phone had even finished its first full ring, and she had an almost sickening feeling that he might have been waiting for her call. "Quinn? Hey… look, I'm sorry I got so mad at you earlier…"

She closed her eyes; a single tear dripped down her cheek and off her chin. "Zander, we need to talk."

Nathaniel's Secret

ON THURSDAY MORNING, QUINN was at school even before William. Unable to help herself, she was standing by his locker when he came up the hallway. As soon as he saw her, his expression changed to one of concern.

"Are you okay?"

She shook her head. For once, her insomnia hadn't been caused by dreams, but by a continuous replay of her phone call with Zander.

"What happened?"

"I broke up with Zander."

The shocked look on his face was almost comical. "When? Just now?" He studied her eyes; she knew they were bloodshot.

"I called him after I got home last night."

In the next instant, she understood exactly what it was that drew her to William. He didn't ask any questions, or try to tell her that it would be okay, or any other nonsense. He just took her into his arms and held her there. She rested her head on his shoulder. He let her stay there, softly rubbing her back until she finally pulled away, even though all she really wanted was to stay right there, where she felt safe.

She couldn't spend the whole day with William, though, even if she hadn't felt guilty just for wanting to talk to him. Last night on the phone when she'd told Zander that she just wasn't going to be able to have the kind of relationship that he wanted with her, the first thing he'd accused her of was cheating on him with William.

She knew that he had every right to feel that way, had felt like a liar as she'd assured him that wasn't the case. She'd had trouble looking at herself in the mirror this morning.

Today, when she had already hurt Zander so badly, the last thing she wanted was for him to see her talking to William the whole day. It felt like rubbing it in his face. So she ended their conversation before anyone else could arrive and see her with him.

The morning quickly turned excruciating. She couldn't concentrate on anything in any of her classes, even though the teachers were trying to keep things fun to hold the attention of the students whose minds were on Spring Break. There were a lot of videos.

Everyone else seemed excited and carefree about this last day of school before a glorious ten-day vacation, but Quinn was miserable. The look Zander gave her the one time she caught a glimpse of him in the hallway made her want to crawl into a hole, and Abigail wasn't talking to her either.

By lunchtime, she knew she couldn't do it anymore. There was no way she was going into that cafeteria.

She found William by his locker, putting his heavy coat on over his sweater.

"You're leaving?" she asked.

"Yes. I want to make it home before Nathaniel gets back with Thomas. There isn't anything going on in any of my afternoon classes that I need to be there for."

"Can I come with you? I can drive and you won't have to walk."

William frowned, his gray eyes concerned behind his wire-framed glasses. "Are you sure that's a good idea, Quinn?"

That's not a no. She looked up at him pleadingly. "I'm out of 'good ideas' right now, Will. I need some space just to breathe, okay? Please?"

"Let's go get your things."

William was holding her backpack for her while she turned to get her coat, when suddenly a familiar voice behind her made her heart jump into her throat.

"Nice, Quinn."

Whirling around, she found herself face-to-face with Zander. He was warily eyeing William, who was staring at the floor, zipping Quinn's backpack while red colored his cheeks.

Quinn found she couldn't meet his eyes either. "Zander... I..."

"You couldn't just be honest with me? Tell me the real reason you were breaking up with me?"

"It isn't like that, Zander!" She blinked furiously, trying to hold back the tears that were building in the corners of her eyes.

"Sure it isn't! And what is *your* problem?" he growled, turning on William. "Can't be bothered finding a girl unless someone else is interested? Or has this been going on for a long time and it's some kind of joke on me? The two of you plan this out together in the library?"

The spark that flashed in William's eyes surprised her. "That's enough, Zander." His voice was low, careful and firm and his eyes met Zander's directly.

But Zander was angrier than she had ever seen him. "Who are you to say what's enough?"

"I know what it looks like, Zander, believe me, I do. But Quinn has been as straightforward with you as she can. She and I are friends. My family has had some challenges lately, and she has been a friend to me. Now she's having a hard time, and I'm trying to return the favor. I'm sure you can understand that."

Zander didn't look like he could, at all, but he took a small step back. He stared at William, looking intimidating even to Quinn, but

William held his ground, his shoulders back, and his expression calm. For the first time on this side of the gate, Quinn was reminded that he was a prince.

"She's the one who broke up with me, been lying to me. She's not the one going through a *hard time*."

"Just because she's the one who broke it off doesn't mean it's easy for her. She cares about you. And she handled things between the two of you in private. Not in the middle of the hallway like you're doing. Don't stand there and tell me you actually care about her feelings when you're trying to have it out with her with a hundred people walking by, all of whom are going to side with you because you're more popular than she is in the first place, *and* you're the one who gets to play the broken-heart card. If you're even half the man everyone gives you credit for being, you'll walk away now, go to lunch, and let Quinn have her space."

Her eyes were glued to the floor, her cheeks on fire; she could not bring herself to look up at Zander or at William. After a long silence, Zander turned and walked away.

Quinn's hands were shaking as she and William climbed in the car. She took several deep breaths, trying to calm herself enough to be able to drive.

"I'm sorry," William said quietly.

She swallowed hard, looking up at him, although she couldn't quite meet his eyes. "You didn't do anything wrong. I should be saying 'thank you' for standing up for me. I can't believe what a mess I've just made of everything. I can't believe how badly I just hurt Zander."

He was quiet for a minute, and then he sighed. "Quinn, I know you're probably not ready to hear this right now, but *you* didn't do anything wrong, either."

She thought about arguing with him, but the only retorts she could come up with involved talking about the kiss, and she wasn't ready to go there, to explore either of their feelings about what had happened in that basement, so she just turned the key in the ignition and drove off instead.

They'd been at William's house for only a few minutes when Quinn heard the sound of Nathaniel's car in the driveway, and a sudden shiver of anxiety tightened her stomach, mixed with a new bout of anger. She hadn't seen Nathaniel since the other evening at the bridge. If she couldn't get any answers from her mother, she wanted some from him.

She followed William outside.

Thomas grinned when he saw her. "You decided to skip school this afternoon, too?" he asked when she opened the back door of the car. He was across both seats, unable to bend his leg with the splint that extended from just below his hip all the way to his toes. He was trying to remove a knitted blanket, but it was challenging to pull it up and over his leg with his one free arm, so she reached in and took it from him.

"I guess so," she said, folding the blanket and hanging it over her arm.

"She's had kind of a rough week," William told him, putting his hand on Quinn's shoulder. "We need to cheer her up."

"Easy enough," Thomas said. "As soon as you all help me get into the house."

Nathaniel appeared just behind her then, and she stiffened. "Hello, Quinn," he said.

She turned and looked up at him. His face was apologetic, almost sad. Something in his expression made much of her anger dissolve on the spot…her anger towards him, anyway. Another fierce rush directed at her mother threatened to explode her insides.

"Are you going to tell me what's going on here?" she asked.

"Quinn, I would tell you everything I could right now, really, I would, but I made a promise that I don't know how to break. I never imagined that you would find out anything like this. Can you please be patient with me until I can figure out what to do, and until I've had a chance to see how your mother is going to handle this?"

"Right now, she's not talking to me at all, Nathaniel. I haven't even *seen* her since Sunday morning. She's *avoiding* me."

"That's what Thomas was just telling me in the car."

"Speaking of Thomas, I'm cold!" Thomas said in a joking tone from his seat. "I'd go into the house while you continue your little chat, but I need some help."

Although Thomas made light of the whole situation, Quinn could tell it bothered him to be so dependent on their assistance. Nathaniel and William had to work together to lift him out of the car and carry him into the house. They were extremely efficient and gentle, but she still saw him wince a few times.

William had told her that there was no way he would have been released from the hospital already if Nathaniel hadn't been a doctor. There was still an IV port taped in Thomas's left hand, and once they'd gotten him settled on the couch, Nathaniel squeezed a small syringe full of pain medication into it. Thomas looked very pale after the exertion of being moved.

Once they were all sitting around a fire in the living room, sipping large mugs of tea brought from Eirentheos, Quinn turned again to Nathaniel.

"So you're really not going to tell me how my mother knows about the gate?"

Nathaniel sighed. "Your mother has known about the gate for long time, Quinn. How she guessed that's where you had gone, I'm not sure. I haven't had more than a passing or professional conversation with her since shortly after your father died."

"My boss at the library told me that you used to be close friends with my father."

Nathaniel sighed again and put his head in his hands, resting his elbows on his knees. He stayed that way for several minutes, clearly deep in thought. Finally, he looked up. "You really just found out that I knew your father?"

She nodded. "I mean, I guess I figured that you'd met him. You've been my doctor since I was born, and my father was alive until I was three. But I had no idea you knew him outside of that."

"And your mother is really completely avoiding you?"

"Every night this week she's made sure she and the little kids are in bed before I get home, and they leave before I wake up in the morning. She's left me a couple of notes and text messages, grounding and un-grounding me from various things."

He leaned back in his armchair, an expression on his face that she couldn't quite comprehend. He looked...*lost, maybe?* Helpless. Sad.

Beside her on the couch, William shifted, his eyes darting between Quinn and Nathaniel, concentrating intently. His posture was almost protective of her. Even groggy as he was from the medication, Thomas, too, was focused on the conversation.

"Quinn... I'm not even supposed to tell you this much. But I just... I can't keep not telling you anything. I can't keep lying to you. I've never wanted that. So... Yes, I knew your father. More than just as a casual acquaintance. More than just as a friend, even. Samuel was... my brother."

Suddenly, everything in the room grew slightly fuzzy at the edges, and she felt like she was moving. Her hand hit the couch cushion as she tried to steady herself, and William's hand landed on top of hers almost instantly. His was trembling, too.

"*What?*" Although the word was the one echoing through her mind, the voice that spoke it wasn't hers. William sounded shocked and angry. "What do you mean?"

Across from them, Thomas had sat up impossibly far, considering his casts

Nathaniel closed his eyes and took a deep breath. "It's true. Samuel was my older brother. He and I were very close...William, you and Thomas have always reminded me of the two of us."

"Wait," Quinn said, finally finding her voice, although it was small and shaky. "If you and my father were *brothers*... that makes you..."

"Yes, Quinn. It makes me your uncle."

Her uncle. Her father's *brother.* She didn't know the source of the tears that flowed down her cheeks now, didn't even notice them, actually, until one dripped onto William's hand, and he reached into his pocket to retrieve his handkerchief for her. "But...*what? How...? Why?*"

She glanced over at William. He'd moved closer to her, and his whole body was visibly shaking now, as hard as hers was. Thomas still just looked stunned.

She had learned, on her second trip to Eirentheos, that Nathaniel wasn't really related to William and Thomas...that he'd lived with their father's family since he was a teenager, and his status as "uncle" to them was an honorary one. But she'd *never* imagined that he was actually related to *her.*

"I can't even begin to answer all of your questions right now, Quinn. And I can't tell you how sorry I am that you're just finding this out now. This was never how I intended things to go."

"Does my mom *know* this?"

"Yes, she does. Not many people knew that we were actually brothers. That part we kept quiet, to protect the secret, to protect *you,* but of course Samuel shared that with Megan."

"Then... my dad was from *Eirentheos?*"

"Your father and I were both from the other world, yes."

"What about my mom?"

"She's from this world. Your father met and fell in love with her after he'd already been living here."

"Was he a… did he come here to study medicine, too? He couldn't have also been a healer."

"No. Neither your father nor I first came here to study medicine. That was an unexpected benefit I discovered after our first several trips. There were other reasons we came… things in our own world we came to get away from, and that I am not at liberty to share with the three of you, at least not yet. Really, I've shared too much already."

"Are those the same reasons you never told me you were my uncle?"

He stared down at his hands, which were pressed together so tightly his knuckles were white. "That part I never meant to keep from you, Quinn. When you were tiny, you knew…at least in a way. I used to spend so much time with you when you were little…spoiling you rotten."

"So what happened? Why have you been keeping this from her…from all of us?" William's voice still shook in anger.

"Everything changed when Samuel died. It was hard enough on Megan to know that her daughter was part of this other world that she didn't understand, and the situation was so complicated. There's still a lot she doesn't know, and she always knew we weren't telling her everything…some of it was understandably frightening for her." He glanced at Quinn. "We agreed on a compromise…that I could tell you about some things when you were eighteen, and old enough to decide for yourself. And then things changed again when you discovered the gate on your own."

She nodded, although she wasn't sure what she was agreeing to. Her brain felt overly full…like it might burst, and she was having trouble staying on the couch. "Can I…I need a few minutes to myself."

Without waiting for a response, she stood and walked out of the room.

Inside Nathaniel's bathroom, she opened the medicine cabinet and looked for something she was almost certain she'd find, as several things clicked into place at once.

There it was. A small, brown glass bottle, exactly like the one in her bathroom at home and the one in the bathroom in her bedroom in the castle. She dug in a drawer for a clean washcloth, held it under hot running water, and then opened the bottle.

The comforting scent of lavender and vanilla filled the room, and she carefully placed three drops of the oil into the center of the cloth before folding it and burying her face in the warm vapors.

When she returned to the living room, almost half an hour later, Thomas was asleep, and William and Nathaniel were both silent, staring into the fire.

"I've made a decision," she said, and they looked up, both wearing cautious expressions. William raised one eyebrow.

"I'm going back to Eirentheos with you tonight. It's Spring Break, and I'm definitely not ready to be alone in my house with my mom for ten days. I don't know when she's going to decide to talk to me about any of this, but I need some time away to figure things out, and I'm not okay staying here."

Nathaniel nodded. "I understand, Quinn, but please tell me you're not going to just take off again without telling her."

"No. I'm going to leave here for a little bit. I've barely seen Annie since I've been back, and it'll be a while, at least for me, until I'll see her again. I want a little time with her. I'm going to call Mrs. Williams and let her know I won't be at the library tonight, and then I'm going to pick up Annie from Maggie's and take her out for hot chocolate or something. Once my mom is home from work…I'm sure she'll be home early, especially if I text her that I have Annie, I will drop my little sister off, tell my mom where I'm going, and then meet you back here before dusk."

"What if your mother forbids you to leave?" William asked.

Quinn shrugged. "I'll find a way to go anyway. She can't keep me locked up for over a week. Besides, I don't think she will." She caught Nathaniel's gaze on the last part. "Will she?"

Nathaniel shook his head, closing his eyes for several seconds before meeting hers again. "She won't. That was part of our original agreement. I would stay out of the way… I would keep the secret from you, never tell you anything until after your eighteenth birthday, but she was never to actually deny my access to you…or yours to me."

"That's why she didn't stop me from going to visit Thomas last night. She was mad…she didn't want me to…but she didn't say no."

"We never, *ever* imagined that you would really discover the gate on your own, but there were stipulations in the agreement about it anyway. She agreed never to move you away from Bristlecone…away from the gate, until after you'd been told. Charlotte and Stephen wished always to be able to know how you were doing here as well."

Her eyes widened at this news. "But I'm not really even related to them."

"By blood, no. Do you *really* think that makes any difference to them? Stephen and your father and I grew up loving each other as brothers. You're as beloved a niece to him as you are to me. You always, *always* have been."

William couldn't think straight. He hadn't been able to for several hours, ever since the conversation he'd witnessed between Quinn and Nathaniel had turned his entire world upside-down. Thoughts and questions would almost form in his brain; he would almost understand some small part of what had just happened, when a new aspect of it would assault him.

Nathaniel was Quinn's *uncle?* Quinn's father was from *Eirentheos?* That meant… It meant so many different things. What boggled his mind the most was that Nathaniel had *always* known. The entire time he had lived here, William had been going to school with Nathaniel's niece, and he'd never had any idea. And his parents knew, too? What had they been thinking?

Suddenly a thousand little things made a whole different kind of sense to him…while the things that had seemed to make sense before no longer did.

And now he didn't have time to think about it anymore, because she was back, and it was time to get ready to go to the gate, to go home.

Nathaniel, who, between an extended trip to Eirentheos and arranging things with Thomas's surgery, had fallen far behind in his work, intended to help them get through the gate, but stay in Bristlecone for several more days. They wanted to make sure they got to the gate early enough that Nathaniel would have enough time to help Thomas through and then come back. His parents had planned to make sure there would be help waiting on the other side each time the gate opened until Thomas's safe return.

He met Quinn as she pulled into the driveway. It would be easier to get Thomas into the back seat of her Pilot than into Nathaniel's small sedan. And Nathaniel had already told him that he intended to drive Quinn's car back to her house for her tonight, and have a conversation with her mother. William was rather disappointed that it would be quite a long time in his world before he saw Nathaniel again to hear the outcome of *that* meeting.

He was surprised at the overwhelming relief he felt, knowing that Quinn was coming with him back to the castle. After everything she'd been through recently, and what had just happened in Nathaniel's living room, he couldn't bear the thought of leaving her here with so many people who were angry and not speaking to her. What had the girl done to deserve any of that?

He walked around the car and opened her door to help her out. Her eyes were puffy and red, so he didn't ask how things had gone with her mother. "Did you have fun with Annie?" he asked instead.

She nodded. "It's next to impossible not to. She ended up spilling half of her hot chocolate down the front of her shirt...I couldn't resist taking her into Nannie's shop to pick out something clean to wear home. Then I bought her another hot chocolate and told her she couldn't drink it until she was home."

William smiled, wishing he'd been there to see that. "Are you okay?"

"Yeah, I'm fine. Are you guys about ready to go?"

RETURN TO EIRENTHEOS

WHEN THEY REACHED THE other side of the bridge in Eirentheos, Simon and Maxwell were there, waiting for them with a wagon. William's older brothers came up onto the bridge to help him and Nathaniel carry Thomas. Simon raised an eyebrow when he saw Quinn come through the gate with them, but Max looked almost as if he'd been expecting it, greeting her with a friendly, "Glad you see you again."

Thomas smiled and joked, trying to hide his chagrin at needing assistance with *everything*, but William knew the helplessness grated on him.

"We weren't really expecting you'd be back so soon," Simon said, as they worked to arrange Thomas's leg on pillows and help him get comfortable in the wagon.

"Truthfully, he could have used a couple more days in the hospital," William said, noting the sweat on Thomas's forehead, and the fact that he'd gone a little gray. "He did just have surgery two days ago."

"We figured Nathaniel would make him stay longer, but Mother insisted we bring the wagon out here last time, too. Linnea wanted to come this time, but we convinced her that it really was too soon. She's going to be mad that she was right and we didn't let her come."

"I'm fine," Thomas said. "I'm ready to be home."

William squeezed Thomas's shoulder. "I know, buddy. Do you want some more medicine before the wagon ride? It's close enough to time you could have more."

Thomas shook his head. "I don't want to be asleep when we get there."

Quinn, climbing up near his head and finding a place to sit close to him, rolled her eyes. "Right. Because it's better to pass out from being in pain than it is to be *asleep*."

Thomas just smiled at her. "You've got your spark back," he said.

She sighed.

William walked with Nathaniel back up to the gate, and picked up the two enormous backpacks they'd dropped on the bridge. Before they'd driven down, they'd emptied Quinn's smaller backpack of her school things and filled it with as many medical supplies as they could. She was wearing the backpack now.

He felt bad that she hadn't had a chance to bring even a few small personal items with her from home…the confrontation with her mother hadn't given her an opportunity to grab anything when she stopped by her house. His parents would provide anything she needed while she was here, of course, but he was sure there must be at least a couple of things she would have liked to have.

"Do you think Quinn is really okay?" Nathaniel asked as they stood there. The look of concern on his face dissipated some of William's anger toward his un…toward Nathaniel.

"I think it's a lot for anybody to take in," William said. "Not just Quinn."

"I know. I'm sorry I've kept this hidden from you all this time. The way old secrets are coming out all the time lately, I wonder if you'll ever trust me again."

"It really depends on what else you're hiding. Because I'm getting the impression that this is not all of it."

Nathaniel met his gaze directly, and William could see the regret in his eyes. "No. This is not all of it. And I'm sorry about that; I promise that it won't always be like this. For a long time now, I've looked forward to the day when I can share everything with you. I never meant to hurt you, William. Whether I'm related to you by blood or not, you have always been my nephew, and I have always loved you."

William closed his eyes for a second, nodding. "I know. I love you, too. I just wish I understood."

"I know. It's almost dark. I'll see you soon." Nathaniel took William's hand, squeezed it, and then disappeared through the gate.

The ride back to the castle was slow and calculated. Maxwell and Simon rode up front, while William and Quinn sat in the bed with Thomas, right next to each other as they kept him company and tried to make him comfortable. Although they probably could have made the trip faster if they were walking, William kept telling his brothers to slow down. He wondered more than once what he and Nathaniel had been thinking allowing Thomas to travel so soon after his surgery.

They weren't even halfway back to the castle before Thomas relented and allowed William to give him another dose of pain medicine. The breath of relief from Quinn's direction was as loud as his own when Thomas's eyelids finally fluttered closed.

"Never again," he told her.

To his surprise, she shrugged. "I don't like to watch it, but I'd hate even more for him to be trapped there and miss another ten days here. You know how hard it is to be away from your parents. Imagine being hurt and in pain away from them."

He turned to the side and looked into her gray eyes, ringed with dark lashes that contrasted with her auburn hair. An uncomfortable feeling settled in his chest as he realized just how badly she was hurting, too.

"What happened with your mom?" he asked quietly.

She closed her eyes, and shook her head. Her hands balled into fists. "I thought about telling her what Nathaniel told me. The whole drive home, Annie was chattering at me from the backseat, and all I could hear was the imaginary conversation I was rehearsing in my head… And then I saw her. She had an expression that was half-furious, and half- something else. Worried, maybe. Devastated. And I couldn't do it. I wasn't ready, and I could tell that having that discussion now, when my head is where it's at… It wouldn't have been good."

Tentatively, he rested his hand on her knee…he knew she didn't need his words right now, but he wanted her to know he was completely there.

"So I sent Annie to put her dirty clothes in the laundry room, and I told my mom where I was going…that I would be back before school starts again, but I didn't know exactly when, that I needed some time."

William nodded silently, and as she set her elbows on her bent knees so she could bury her head in her arms, he moved his hand to her shoulders, rubbing her back softly as they rode toward the castle.

They were about halfway between the gate and the castle when, over the side of the wagon, Quinn caught a glimpse of something she didn't expect. She was straining to get a closer look, and William was turning to follow her gaze, when Simon brought the horses to a stop.

Max and Simon both climbed down from the wagon and approached the small gathering of people several feet back from the path they were on…if it could even be called a path. Though not far from the capital city, the gate was buried in a remote area. Quinn had never seen even one other person along this route on any of her trips.

The group appeared to be made up of maybe two or three families, young couples and their children, setting up makeshift tents and building a fire.

She frowned at William. "They're camping?"

He shook his head slightly, never taking his eyes off his brothers. "People don't camp recreationally in our world, Quinn. Only when they're traveling, like we did."

"So why are Simon and Maxwell so worried about it? People are allowed to travel here, right?" They did look worried, though, and Simon was deep in conversation with a man who looked to be in his late twenties; he appeared to be a leader in the group.

"It's *very* unusual for anyone to camp this close to the city. Even in the smallest villages in our kingdom, there are always inns or privately-run homes where people can find accommodations. Not to mention…we're a little, um, *protective* of this area."

After a few more minutes, Simon and Max headed back toward the wagon. The people they had been talking to started folding up their canvas cloths and extinguishing their fire.

"What was that?" William asked, as his brothers climbed back into the wagon.

"Philothean refugees. A number of people in their village were arrested ten days ago, on suspicion of helping with the resistance. They managed to sneak across the border six days ago, they said. They've been camping their way here ever since."

Quinn's jaw was on her knees. "Why would they have to sneak across the border?"

Max turned around and climbed down into the bed of the wagon as Simon began driving the horses again. "Things have changed quickly since the last time you were here, Quinn. Philotheum has become dangerous for those who don't support Tolliver…and very rewarding for those who do. He can't have been happy when his hostage slipped through his fingers," he said, nodding toward Thomas. "He knows he has to get control of the political situation in his kingdom quickly. There are rumors he plans to announce his ascension to the throne soon."

"So the border is closed between the kingdoms, then?"

"No. In theory it's still open. But for people whom Tolliver and his troops don't wish to allow to leave…"

"Like those people back there."

"Right."

"So where are they going now? Why did you make them leave?"

"We didn't make them do anything. They've been traveling hard for many days and are low on supplies and food. We gave them directions to an inn in a nearby village that will take refugees who have no family in Eirentheos."

"What do you mean…an inn that will 'take them'?" William asked.

"There have been some issues lately here, Will. Some in Eirentheos are wary of contact with strangers from Philotheum. It's hard to blame them in a way, after the poisonings, and spying, and rumors."

Quinn raised an eyebrow…she understood some of what they were talking about, but not all of it.

"There are some who even believe that we should secure the border from our side."

Simon brought the horses to a stop again, and turned around…it was obvious he'd been paying attention to the entire conversation. "That's not something we're going to discuss, Maxwell. Eirentheos is not going to cut off a connection with our brothers."

"I know how you and Father feel about it, Simon. And I've never said I disagree; only that it's a part of a bigger picture we should consider. In any case, I'm only trying to explain to William and Quinn what's going on, why, right or wrong, those people aren't able to just walk in the front door of any inn in the kingdom, so we directed them to one where they could Now, let's go. We need to get Thomas home."

When they came to a stop in the main courtyard closest to the family's living quarters, Simon hopped down. "I'll go let Mother and Father know we're here."

Thomas, who had awakened a few minutes before, tried to lift his head up far enough to see over the side of the wagon. "I want to get settled in my room before I have an audience. Please?"

The plea in his voice tugged at Quinn's heart. He was having a harder time than he was letting on. The brothers nodded and moved to assist him instead.

Of course, in a castle full of people, it would have been impossible to avoid everyone, even though they used a private entrance that led directly upstairs to the family's rooms.

They'd barely entered the vestibule when Linnea jumped up from a nearby bench, a book falling on the floor as she ran to them, relief and panic both mixed in her expression as she took in the image of Simon, Max, and William trying to carry Thomas upstairs without jostling him any more than they absolutely had to.

Linnea looked startled to see Quinn, but she didn't say anything, just reached to take one of the heavy backpacks Quinn was toting, and then the two girls walked in front of the boys, opening doors and making sure the path was clear all the way to Thomas's room and his bed.

Between the five of them, they managed to get Thomas settled and as comfortable as possible without hurting him more than necessary, though several times Quinn saw him grit his teeth.

After Simon and Max left to go downstairs, Linnea pulled two chairs to the side of the bed, and she and Quinn sat and watched as

William worked to get things set back up around Thomas's room. She would have offered to help, but she'd already learned from the weeks they'd spent here before they went back to her world that William had a system…there was a certain order of things, and while there were a few things she'd picked up on, she'd also learned that sometimes the most helpful thing she could do was to stay out of his way.

They didn't have a hospital bed, of course, but Simon and Max had helped William rig up Thomas's mattress so that the top half was elevated a little when Thomas came back here right after his first surgery. Quinn had spent many hours in this chair beside his bed, keeping Thomas company while he recovered…and William while he worked.

All of William's medical supplies were arranged in the drawers of a long dresser that Mia had emptied when he'd asked for a spot. He spent several minutes now opening and closing the drawers, re-arranging and re-stocking them with supplies they'd brought back through the gate.

Quinn looked at Thomas. He was still wide awake; the ordeal of being carried up from the wagon had been difficult, and she could tell he was hurting again. He smiled at her though, and she reached over and brushed the back of her hand down his uninjured arm. "Sorry," she said.

He narrowed his eyes at her. "*You* have nothing to be sorry about. This isn't your fault. I'm the one who ran off into Philotheum when I shouldn't have, and Harbin Rhinewald is the one who did this to me. *Not* you."

William walked around the bed toward them, setting several plastic packets down on the edge of the bed. "She means we're all sorry you have to go through this. *I'm* sorry we couldn't do the surgery the right way here in our world the first time, and now you've had to do this twice."

Quinn nodded. Thomas had already been through the worst of the recovery process once. He'd been doing a lot better before she'd gone back to her own world on Saturday night…even able to get up and move around some, and he'd stopped using any medications. And she knew he'd had another ten days of recovery after that.

This felt a lot like going back to the beginning. Although Nathaniel and Lily had done their best to repair Thomas's leg after he had first been injured, they'd worried it wouldn't be enough. They didn't have the equipment here to do the kind of reconstructive surgery that would ensure Thomas would regain full use of his leg.

"That's not your fault, either Will." Thomas said, wincing as William picked up his hand and pressed gently around the IV port.

Hot anger toward Tolliver…and toward the man who had done this to Thomas…had knocked him down a flight of stone stairs and who knew what else, because so far, Thomas wouldn't talk about it…coursed through her. She rubbed his shoulder.

"I need to take out this port and put in a new one," William was saying. "They can get infected if they're in too long."

Thomas grimaced, squeezing his eyes shut for a moment before nodding. "As long as it's you doing it."

Linnea gave up on the chair, instead climbing up near his head on the bed and settling in next to his good side. "I thought you were the one who's not afraid of needles," she teased, though Quinn could tell she was more upset than her casual words implied.

Thomas raised an eyebrow, and squeezed his sister's hand. "Well, I'm not as bad as these two," he nodded at William and Quinn, "but that doesn't mean I *enjoy* them," he said. "And at the moment, I'm just a little over the whole thing."

William gently took Thomas's arm in his hands and held it toward the girls, showing them tiny bruises in a few spots. "There was at least one nurse I wanted to shove out of the way so I could put Thomas's IV in myself. I think Nathaniel *would* have, but he wasn't in the room."

"Yeah," Thomas said, shuddering slightly at the memory. "Will, I know you were upset you couldn't get me back to Bristlecone for the surgery in the first place. But trust me when I tell you that I'm glad you tried it here at home first. I'd rather be here with less technology, and fewer resources, than to only have the option of strangers running in and out like it's an inn or something. I don't know why you think I'd rest and recover better there. Two nights was enough. I couldn't have handled all of that when I was first hurt. I was barely ready two days ago."

"I'm sure it was a little overwhelming," Quinn said, watching as Linnea brushed his hair back from his forehead. She felt awful that he'd had to spend his two nights in the hospital alone.

"Seriously," he said. "Last night, I was almost asleep after the second time someone came in to check my blood pressure and my temperature, when another guy comes in with a syringe full of something. I hold out my hand so he'll put whatever it is in my IV, but no… this is the one with the needle that he sticks in my stomach. I was awake for a while after *that*. My favorite part was that he was whispering and he only turned a low light on, so he wouldn't *wake me up*." He rolled his eyes.

"And, of course, by the time I was sleepy again, the blood pressure lady was back. When the guy came for blood at five in the morning, I think I almost cried. I *know* I just wanted to be home."

It was almost funny…except that it wasn't.

"I'm sorry, buddy," William said. "None of this is fun, I know. Someday, I am going to get my hands on Harbin Rhinewald…"

Thomas gave him a half-hearted smile, though there was a strangely dark look in his eyes. "Don't ever go near that guy, William. Really. I'm here and I'm safe now, and *none of this* is your fault. I'm sure it isn't easy on you either, having to take care of me like this. It was probably a nice break for you to have someone else do it for a couple days."

The look that flashed across William's face then made Quinn's heart give a little jolt. "It was not even a little bit easier for me, Thomas. Don't ever think that," William said, rubbing his brother's shoulder. "I love you. I hate that you're hurting, and I *want* to be here for you and helping you through it."

Somehow, a new IV port was already secured in an out-of-the way spot on Thomas's arm, and he hadn't even flinched. Another wave of admiration for William washed over her.

Only a second later, though, she cringed when William picked up a small syringe. "Unfortunately, you're not going to like me any better than that night nurse for a minute here," he said as he lifted the edge of Thomas's shirt. "This one has to go under the skin on your abdomen."

Thomas sighed. Though she could see he was trying hard not to react, his whole body tensed a little. "I know. I asked about it when they gave me another one before I left the hospital."

Although the needle was tiny, Thomas squeezed his eyes shut and held his breath during the shot. Quinn grabbed his hand and held it tightly, while Linnea combed her fingers through his hair.

"Do those hurt?" Linnea asked William when he was finished.

"I'm fine, Nay," Thomas said, probably hearing the worry in his sister's voice. "It just stings for a minute." He closed his eyes again, and then looked back up at her. "I guess that stuff keeps me from getting blood clots in my legs."

"It does," William said. "It's one of the drugs we didn't have enough of when you were first hurt. Nathaniel and I were worried the whole time."

"So, let me guess, you brought back plenty of it, right?" He meant to be funny, but nobody laughed.

"You need it a couple of times a day until you're up and walking," William's voice was tinged with a mixture of sorrow and anger...and Quinn knew exactly where the anger was directed.

"A couple of times every day? I think I'm going to need my mother," Thomas said, not entirely jokingly.

Quinn squeezed his hand again, sad as she thought about him having to go through that all alone with some stranger in the middle of the night. She felt guilty now that they hadn't gone to see him on Tuesday night, too. So what if she would have missed work?

Almost as if on cue, there was a soft knock at the door. It opened before any of them had time to respond, and Queen Charlotte peeked into the room. She hesitated for a fraction of a second, glancing at the four of them, and then nearly ran to the bed. Linnea and Quinn backed away automatically, and after placing one more piece of tape, William joined them at the foot of the bed.

By itself, Quinn's hand reached toward William's and clasped it tightly. Never taking his eyes off Thomas and his mother, William squeezed back.

"Mother," Thomas said, as Charlotte leaned down and kissed him on the cheek.

For a moment, Quinn was acutely aware of how young Thomas really was. His whole demeanor changed as Charlotte ran her hand across his forehead. As mature and skilled as he so often seemed, in reality, he was still a teenage boy. More than a year younger than she was, even. And he'd been through so much lately.

"How is he?" Charlotte asked, looking up at William. "We didn't expect you all to return so soon."

"I'm right here, Mother. I can talk." Thomas said.

"Yes, but you won't be blunt with me."

Linnea stifled a snort.

"I'm okay. The surgery went well, and I hear my leg will be okay. I've gotten over any interest I ever had in hospitals in Quinn's world. I'm still hurting, and the trip here isn't something I'd like to repeat any time soon. I'm really, really glad to be home though, and I'm happy you're here."

"He's right," William said. "And he needs some rest soon." Glancing at Quinn and Linnea, he nodded toward the door. The girls picked up on his hint, and followed him into the hallway, giving Charlotte some time alone with her son.

They were all the way out in the hall when Quinn noticed that Linnea was looking at her strangely. She followed Linnea's eyes down to her hand, and realized that it was still interlaced with William's.

Apparently he'd only just noticed that as well, because he let it drop then, although he didn't appear to be bothered. In fact, he reached up to her shoulder and gave it a gentle pat before looking back at his sister. "Do you know where Father is?" he asked.

She shook her head. "Everyone was eating dinner…we all thought Simon and Max would be coming back alone, but I just couldn't. I needed to be where I'd see him right away. I just had a feeling that you might…that Thomas would be coming." Looking over at Quinn, she frowned, "I didn't imagine *you* would be coming back so soon, though. What is going on with that?"

Quinn looked down at the floor, tracing the lines in the wood with her foot. She didn't even know where to begin.

William interrupted. "It's been a difficult few days for Quinn, Linnea. And we heard some shocking news today. I don't think she's quite been able to absorb it yet. I know I haven't. I know you've had to be patient a *lot* lately, but we could use whatever little bit you have left to spare."

Curiosity burned in Linnea's dark gray eyes, but she nodded. "We should go and open…"

Linnea's sentence was cut off as Mia ran up the hallway toward them.

"Lady Linnea! I heard that Master Thomas had returned. Is he here? Is he all right?"

William turned to face her. "Yes, Mia. He's here, and he's okay. My mother is in with him now."

Mia nodded, out of breath, worry still in her expression. Suddenly, she looked up at Quinn. "Lady Quinn! I had no idea you might be coming! Your room isn't…"

"I'm sure my room is fine, Mia. Unless someone else is sleeping in there or something."

Mia's eyes widened. "Oh, no! Lady Quinn! Your room has always been reserved just for you since you first stayed in it. I don't know that anyone ever even used it before you began visiting."

"Relax, Mia. It's fine."

"I'll have it ready in twenty minutes." The girl disappeared down the hallway.

Quinn would have called after her, to stop her, if she didn't know that Mia took pleasure in the work that she did, and that she would never calm down until everything was ready. Truthfully, tonight it wouldn't have made any difference to Quinn if she had to sleep on a couch in her clothes.

After what she'd learned today, she wondered if there was more to Mia's assertion that her room had always been "reserved for her" than Mia was even aware of.

Still not ready to handle the rest of the horde of Rose children, they decided to go to Linnea's room instead, and were walking that way, when King Stephen appeared in the hallway.

"William!" he said, taking the three remaining steps to his son and wrapping him in his arms. "I was just looking for you. How is Thomas?"

He nodded, which seemed to be enough for his father. Quinn was glad…she knew that explaining things over and over was beginning to wear on him.

"Have any of you eaten?" Stephen asked. It didn't escape Quinn's notice that Stephen didn't appear in the least surprised to see her standing in the hallway with William and Linnea. Charlotte, too, had behaved as if her presence was anticipated.

"No," William answered. "Quinn, are you hungry?"

"I… I don't know," she said. Now that she thought about it, she should be hungry…starving, really. Outside of a cup of hot chocolate with Annie, she hadn't eaten anything since William had made the two of them some peanut butter and jelly sandwiches when they had first arrived at Nathaniel's house.

"Linnea…I'm sorry to do this to you, and you can be mad at me later," William said, "but will you please go and ask someone to bring up some dinner for all of us? I'm sure it will be fine for you to go back in with Mother and Thomas soon. But Quinn and I really need to speak privately with Father."

Linnea sighed as William and Quinn followed her father down the hallway, wondering what in the world was going on *now*. She'd been waiting as patiently as she could for them to return, and now there was something *else* going on that she wasn't a part of.

She raised an eyebrow at how closely her brother walked behind Quinn, almost as if he were ready to catch her if she stumbled.She'd seen the subtle way that things had changed between the two of them when they'd first brought Thomas home from Philotheum, and she wondered how much more things had changed while they were in Quinn's world.

After Philotheum, Will had no longer kept his distance from Quinn, no longer spouted off his ridiculous assertions about "letting" her get "too involved" in their world, that by being torn between the two worlds, she'd get hurt in the end. As if any of that was up to any of them, anyway. She'd met Quinn. That girl was going to do what she was going to do.

Not that he was fooling anyone in the first place. Linnea and Thomas had spent countless evenings gossiping about it while Will was in Bristlecone, and wondering when he was going to wake up and realize how he really felt about Quinn.

It had been obvious from the first night the girl had arrived at the castle. Careful, observant, meticulous Will *not noticing* that a girl was following him closely enough to find the gate? *Right.* Really, it had been clear that something was up with this girl from the first time he'd ever mentioned her.

He'd talked about girls in Bristlecone before, come home and told everyone stories about the ones who tried to get his phone number, or who asked what he was doing over the weekend. That question was always good for a laugh around the fire in the evening, because wouldn't the unfortunate girl be surprised if he told her the answer? *"Wanna come over to dinner with my family in a different world? I'll bet you've never been inside a castle before. Don't worry…I'll take you back home after we keep you for a couple of weeks."*

But when Will had first brought up Quinn Robbins, said he'd noticed her around a lot lately, and he'd been wondering if she was watching him, it had been different. When Thomas had teased him about his "new secret girlfriend," Will hadn't laughed. He'd been defensive of the girl…insisting that she was only curious, not like the others…that she didn't have a crush on him.

And once they'd all met Quinn, and seen William around her, it had become quite clear that he truly wasn't worried she had a crush on him. Although he'd never admit it even to himself, his real worry was that she *didn't.*

She had never before seen Will the way he behaved when he'd first brought Quinn home with him. The girl had fallen on her way, and William had needed to stich up her leg. She'd arrived at the castle unconscious from a rare reaction to the valoris seed he'd given her to help her relax.

That night, William had refused to go into Quinn's room to check on her – making Nathaniel take care of her instead. He'd acted angry – at the girl for being so persistent – and at himself for "not seeing" her. He'd excused his refusal to attend to her by saying she'd be more comfortable with Nathaniel, whom she already knew.

Linnea and Thomas, though, had both seen it for what it really was. Quinn made him nervous in a way that no other girl had done before. They'd talked about it that first night, huddled together in the common room playing choice, wishing Will would get over himself and join them. They'd learned to give him his space, though. The next morning he'd still been in his huffy mood, and had run off somewhere to blow off steam.

Thomas had been taken with the girl right from the beginning, too. So much so that Linnea had been *dying* to meet her, and frustrated that she'd had to wait until after breakfast the next day. Actually, Thomas had tried to get her to give the girl privacy for longer than that, but she hadn't been able to hold off. And once she'd met Quinn, she couldn't blame her brothers. She'd loved her instantly, too.

Although Thomas would have gladly pursued the girl himself under different circumstances, it was on her second night in Eirentheos, as Linnea and Thomas danced together, that Thomas suddenly stopped, and nodded toward William and Quinn, who were dancing after being goaded into it.

"Someday," Thomas had said, "someday, that girl is going to be our sister. And I will do whatever I have to do to make the two of them realize it sooner than later."

That night, Linnea had just smiled and nodded. Tonight, she was anxious to find out just how much those two had realized.

Curious and excited as she was, though, her thoughts were on Thomas right now more than anything. She knew her mother needed some time alone with him, but there was only so much Linnea was willing to give her. She'd been separated from her twin far too much lately.

Before Thomas had left to go to Bristlecone, she had battled with her parents over going with him. Although her hopes hadn't been high that they would agree, she'd been flabbergasted at how vehemently they'd refused. She hadn't even gotten to use any of her well-planned arguments.

Her parents had been sorry; they knew how difficult it was for her to be away from Thomas. Her mother, especially, was aware of the anxiety that sometimes overtook Linnea, the feeling that she would sometimes get that something wasn't right.

But their answer had been so absolute, coordinated, unwavering, that it had made Linnea wonder what else was going on that she didn't know about. Surely she was old enough now – she was almost of age – that she could be trusted not to violate the secret of the gate. There had to be more to it than that. And now she wondered if this "private" conversation that Will and Quinn were having with her father had anything to do with it.

She would find out, and she would find out *soon*. But first, she was going to have to address the anxious twisting in her stomach that had been there since Thomas had gone back to Bristlecone…she needed to see Thomas again.

Linnea hurried to the kitchen and asked one of the servants there to have three trays sent up to Quinn's room…that was probably where they would head after they'd finished whatever they were doing. Then she asked for some soup and bread for Thomas, and after that, she practically ran back up to her brother's room.

Inside, the room, it was quiet. Her mother was sitting in a chair next to Thomas's bed, stroking his hair. He was still wide awake, but he looked a little more relaxed than he had been a few minutes ago.

"Hey, T," she said, approaching the bed and taking hold of his hand.

He smiled. "My Nay-Nay. I'm glad you came back in. I missed you."

"You have no idea," she said. "I know it was only a couple of days for you, but I wasn't ready to have you away from me like that again."

Her mother caught her free hand and squeezed it.

Thomas opened his mouth. For a second, she thought he was going to argue, give her some stupid, teasing, Thomas-style platitude, but then he looked into her eyes and he just nodded. "I know, sweetheart."

Tears dripped down her cheeks and off her nose as she leaned in to lay her head on his chest, careful not to bump or jostle him. Although she had known he was safe and being taken care of in Bristlecone, the last thirty days had been far too much of a reminder of the time he really had been missing, that they hadn't known where he was.

Linnea had worried every minute of that time that he wasn't okay. She'd tried to brush it off, the anxious feeling that had sat in the pit of her stomach and wouldn't budge. Every morning she had awakened, hoping that he'd be in his room and it would have all just been a bad dream.

Even when he finally had come home, he wasn't okay. Her beautiful, loving twin brother, who would never hurt anyone, who protected those he loved with a fierce, unwavering determination, had been so brutally beaten. It was devastating.

And during these last thirty days that he'd been gone again, that feeling had come back. She knew it was irrational, that he was okay, and that the surgery he was having would ultimately make things so much better for him. But that feeling had a life of its own, and only now, with her head against his chest, feeling him breathing in and out, could she keep that nightmare at bay.

KING STEPHEN

"DO YOU WANT WILLIAM with you while we have this conversation, or would you prefer to speak to me in private?"

Although Quinn considered the question for a moment, there was no real decision. "He knows as much as I know already," she said. "He can stay." She and William were sitting on one couch in a small sitting room, and Stephen was on another sofa, directly across from them.

For the first time since she had met him, the man in front of her didn't look like a king. Sitting there on the sofa, wearing a purple sweater and gray slacks, hollowed out cheeks, and an expression of worry mixed with apology, he didn't look like the ruler of a kingdom. He looked like a father.

He studied Quinn's face for what felt like a long time before he spoke. "So your mother told you." It wasn't a question.

She shook her head. "My mother isn't speaking to me right now. Nathaniel told me."

Stephen's eyes grew wide for a moment, and then he nodded. "How much did he tell you?"

"That my father was his brother…that he's really my uncle."

Stephen was silent again, clearly considering his next words.

"He said there was more to it that he wasn't telling me. I'm going to guess that you won't tell me, either?"

Though she didn't know how it was possible, his expression grew even more apologetic. "I'm sorry. I can't, Quinn. I've made promises…"

"Promises to my mother? What does that even matter when I find out she's been hiding something like this from me? I just found out that my father was from a different world, and my mother has been keeping that a secret from me for my entire life! How much worse could it get?"

Stephen's expression turned soft, and suddenly he was off his couch, kneeling in front of Quinn. "Precious girl, it doesn't get *worse* than that. The only thing worse than finding it out is the fact that there are those of us here who have always loved you, and we've been missing you this whole time."

She was taken aback by the sadness and apology on his face, and she allowed him to take her hands in his. He stared at her for what felt like a long time, long enough for her to see the truth of his feelings, even if he wasn't telling her the whole story. Stephen reached up and ran his hand down the side of her face. "Whatever else happens, Quinn," he said, "please know that we always loved you, and every decision we ever made came first and foremost from our need to love and protect *you*."

She had no idea how to respond to that, but she nodded, and Stephen retreated back to his spot on the other couch.

"Why didn't you ever tell me, Father?" William asked.

"What were we supposed to tell you while still keeping the secret safe? Knowing something like that would have put an enormous burden on you. Alone in a world with her? It would have been too hard."

"But why keep it a secret from me in the first place?" Quinn demanded. "Especially after I found the gate? Why does my mom get to make all of the decisions?"

Stephen shook his head. "First of all, Quinn, remember how difficult this must be for Megan. She lost her husband so suddenly, and then she was left alone with you. I know it was hard for her to think that at any time, someone from here could decide to just snatch you away or something."

Her eyes widened. "But you would never do that."

"No, of course Charlotte and I wouldn't have done anything like that, and nor would Nathaniel, but she had no reason to trust that. Secondly, the decision was not hers alone. Your father never intended for you to know everything either, not before you were of age."

"Why?"

"He wished for you to have a normal childhood, a family life in your world with him and your mother. He thought that involving you in all of this was too much for a child."

Quinn stared hard at Stephen's expression. He was telling the truth, she was sure of that, but there was also a nagging suspicion in the back of her mind that he was leaving something out…maybe a big something. "Why else?" she asked.

Stephen closed his eyes. "He also believed…and he passed this fear on to your mother…that you would be in danger here, in our world."

"In danger from *what*?" William asked, his voice taking on an edge that surprised her.

For a long moment, Stephen stared across the room at them, not answering. The expression on his face turned to one of curiosity, and Quinn realized just how close she and William were sitting to each other on the couch, and how William's posture had changed to one of protection. Her cheeks grew hot as she realized what it looked like.

Suddenly, the king glanced down at the floor and took a deep breath before he looked back up, his eyes fixed directly on hers. "Quinn, have you ever been in a situation where you have absolutely no idea what the right thing to do is? Where, no matter what you decide, you're going to end up doing something wrong, or hurting someone you don't want to hurt?"

She sank back into the couch cushions, trying to wrap her mind around the question. She thought about what she'd just done to Zander…was that only last night? Finally, she nodded.

"Well, it doesn't get any easier just because you grow up. Or just because you become a parent. And it definitely doesn't get easier when you become the ruler of a kingdom."

"So you're telling me that you don't know what to do?" she asked.

"I guess what I'm trying to say is this. The situation is complicated. If the secret of the gate were to get out… all of us would be in grave danger. And it's not all mine to share, and I'm torn between protecting you and honoring your father's wishes, and I'm afraid that whatever I do will wind up hurting you even more." He sighed. She'd never imagined that a king could look so…*vulnerable?*

"There wasn't a plan in place for what would happen if you somehow found your way here on your own, Quinn. And when you did, we were all so stunned; we had no idea how to react. How could we keep anything secret, while finding out what you already knew…finding out enough to keep you safe, the gate safe, when the only thing we *wanted* to do was to thank the Maker that you'd found us? We…Charlotte and Nathaniel and I…we all just wanted to wrap our arms around you and tell you how glad we were to see you again. How much we'd missed you."

She swallowed hard as an image of that played in her head. And then she suddenly caught a word she'd missed when he first said it. "*Again?* What do you mean, *again?*"

"Well, Nathaniel, of course, has always been able to see you as you've grown, at least from a distance. I saw you a couple of times, when you were little and I visited Nathaniel in Bristlecone for various things. Charlotte had only ever actually seen you twice. Once when your father brought you here for your Naming Ceremony, and the other time was when we went to Bristlecone for your father's funeral."

Quinn suddenly understood the expression about picking one's jaw up off the floor. "My father brought me here? I had a Naming Ceremony?"

"You wouldn't remember, of course. You were only a few weeks old…though already you looked so much like Samuel. You have his eyes, exactly."

"How could I have had a Naming Ceremony and yet nobody knows about me? Weren't there people there?"

Stephen sighed. "It was a small, private ceremony, Quinn. You saw Hannah's, and yes, it was a big deal. She's the child of the reigning king. All of my children have had ceremonies like that. But in our world, *all* children have the ceremonies. Often, they're just in a family's home, attended by close family, or during a service at a village church."

"Where was mine?" she asked. There was something in the tone of his voice that nagged at her. All of his words were truthful, but… somehow the story was incomplete.

"Yours was here at the castle. In my private chambers, actually. Your mother and father were there, and Nathaniel, and myself and Charlotte."

"My mother came here? To Eirentheos?"

"Just the once. It was overwhelming for her. I think in many ways she always had denied the truth of what Samuel had told her; it seemed like something she didn't *want* to believe. But Samuel wanted you to have an official Naming Ceremony, even though of course you already had a name in your own world. Babies born here are officially unnamed until the actual ceremony."

She nodded, remembering the baby girl that William had delivered when they were in Philotheum, remembering not knowing

Hannah's name until the ceremony she'd attended on her first visit here.

"So none of us were even included?" William asked.

Stephen smiled. "You were, actually. It was a commonplace event, you know. Simon and Maxwell were quite bored by another baby naming. Rebecca was a toddler; we had to keep stopping her from trying to pick up the baby. *You* had barely started walking. You were the youngest then, and having a baby in the castle for ten days enchanted you. *Quinn*, I think, enchanted you." He looked at both of them with an unfathomable expression.

There had been times that William had felt speechless about the situation with Quinn, but tonight he literally had no words as he led her into her bedroom after their conversation with his father. Linnea was already inside, sitting on the couch, staring at three silver trays sitting on the low table in front of her. Mia was nowhere to be seen, although the room had again been transformed from an empty guest room into Quinn's home.

He realized now that there might be a whole different story to this "guest room" right in the middle of a private, family hallway, next door to Nathaniel's room…that had never in his memory held a guest until Quinn's first visit.

"Thomas is more comfortable now," Linnea said. "I think he'll be able to sleep soon."

"Good," William replied.

"Father went in to see him."

William nodded, leading Quinn over to the couch. After his father had left the room, she'd finally broken down and cried for several minutes. Her eyes were still puffy and red, and she hadn't yet said anything to him. He couldn't blame her…he, too, was feeling shocked and drained from the events of the day.

"You need to eat, okay?" he said softly, pulling the cover off one of the trays and setting the plate in her lap.

"So what is going on?" Linnea asked, eyeing both of them. "Is everything okay? Is there something you're not telling me about Thomas?"

William stopped and knelt down in front of his little sister, looking her in the eyes. "Thomas is going to be fine, Nay. He really will. He's home, and we're taking care of him, and the worst part is done, okay?"

She nodded. "Then what is it?"

"You're going to want to eat, too, before you hear this."

WILLIAM

"HOW ARE YOU DOING with everything?" Linnea asked.

Quinn shrugged. "It's still really a lot to absorb. I'm not sure I've even really stopped to think about all of it."

Her first three days back in Eirentheos had passed in a blur. She was pretty sure she'd been in shock for most of it, and there was a lot she didn't really remember. After her conversation with Stephen, her mind had sort of shut down, and she hadn't really processed most of what she had learned.

Yesterday, she'd finally had a chance to have a private conversation with Charlotte, but the kind, motherly queen had just nodded in understanding when Quinn had told her that she wasn't ready to talk about it yet.

Charlotte had hugged her, holding her for several minutes and then kissed the top of her head before she'd gone away again, leaving Quinn to absorb herself in spending time with Thomas, William, and Linnea.

By last night, Thomas had begun showing his frustration with everyone hovering over him. He said they were too cooped up in his room, and that, given a choice, he wouldn't have been in there himself. This morning, William, Linnea, and Quinn had taken their breakfast trays into his room as they usually did.

Immediately after the meal, though, Thomas had leveled a serious look at them. "You're not hanging around in here all day. I love you all, but this is getting ridiculous. You don't even have any new stories to tell me, because you haven't *done* anything. It looks like it's beautiful and sunny outside. Go. I don't want to see any of you again until you have some color."

The girls were out in the back gardens now, sitting in the sun near the gazebo, listening to some of the younger children playing on the nearby swings and slides while they waited for William to finish the few things he had to do for Thomas before joining them.

It was a lot of work for William, being Thomas's primary physician. He had some help, between two of his cousins, Lily and Jacob, who were also healers. They helped when they could – as much as William would allow them to.

Even with help, though, William had still spent nearly every waking moment with his brother…and Quinn wasn't sure he'd been sleeping more than a few hours at night.

Linnea, too, had been Thomas's constant shadow…Quinn knew she'd been slipping into his room in the middle of the night to check on him since he'd been home.

"Well, I, for one, am not disappointed to find out that you really belong here in our world." Linnea said, interrupting her thoughts.

Quinn smiled. It wasn't the first time Linnea had told her that. "I'm not disappointed about it either. It's just kind of shocking to find out something like that, you know? And I am upset that I never knew that before."

"Me too. I would have liked to have known you the whole time we were growing up."

"Yeah…" She paused, watching as a bee flitted diligently from flower to flower in the small garden at her feet. "I would have liked to have you as a cousin always."

"Of course, I bet William's glad that you're not actually related to us by blood."

Quinn looked up at Linnea in surprise. From the grin hiding in her friend's eyes, she figured she'd been holding on to *that* remark for the last couple of days. "What's that supposed to mean?"

Linnea rolled her eyes. "You know exactly what I mean. What is going on between you and my brother, anyway? Sometimes I watch the two of you together and I wonder when you're going to be announcing your betrothal. And then the rest of the time, you make me wonder if you even know each other."

Quinn raised an eyebrow.

"You know me. I say it the way I see it."

There was a reason, she supposed, that Linnea was known for her ability to read people…perhaps it was part of her birth gift of influence.

"I don't know the answer to that, Nay. We've never really talked about it…not that we ever get a chance to."

"So there is something! When did he kiss you?"

Quinn's mouth fell open. "Who said he kissed me?" Of course, the flash burn across her face was going to give her away completely.

"Was it when you were in Bristlecone, or before that? Because there seemed to be something already going on when you came back from Philotheum."

"You're dangerous, Linnea. You know that, right?"

"When? I want details!"

"You want details about someone kissing your *brother?*"

"I don't want to kiss him. I want details about *you* kissing him."

Quinn gave an exasperated sigh, but it was hard not to admit that Linnea's excitement had her heart thumping excitedly. "Fine. It was when we were in Philotheum."

"And…?"

"I don't know… we were locked in this weird basement, and we'd just found out that Ellen was Tolliver's sister, and we were both completely freaked out, and then suddenly we were laughing about something… I don't even remember… and then we kissed."

Linnea's eyes widened along with her grin. "And then what happened?"

"I don't know. I think something happened that scared us again, and by then it was done; it had happened. We never really talked about it after that, but ever since then, things have just been… different. He's been different. I think I've been different."

"He's a guy, Quinn. He doesn't know how to do these things."

"And you think *I* do? Seriously, Linnea. I was still technically dating Zander when I kissed him. And I screwed that whole relationship up big time."

"Oh, whatever. You and Zander were never meant to be, anyway. How long do you think that could have ever lasted once you found out you were actually from Eirentheos?"

"Yeah, well, that little tidbit of information changed *everything*, but it's not like I knew that at the time."

"So you two never kissed or anything again after that?"

"No. We haven't kissed. We haven't talked about it. It's like nothing is different and everything is different."

"What do you want things to be between the two of you?"

Quinn closed her eyes for a long moment, trying to think. "I don't even know, Linnea. There's been an awful lot going on since then. Thinking about kissing William seems awfully trivial compared to everything else, you know?"

To her surprise, Linnea frowned. "Is love something trivial in your world, Quinn?"

"Um," she paused, "I don't know." It was a question she'd never even considered. "I guess sometimes it is. Or, at least, relationships when you're sixteen often are."

Linnea nodded; her face more serious than Quinn was used to. "In our world, sixteen is old enough for a girl to get married."

Quinn's mouth fell open. "Who brought up *marriage* Linnea? I told you we kissed. Once. Quite a while ago now."

"I'm not saying I expect you to marry him. I was just pointing out that here, in our world, at your age, relationships aren't *trivial*. Rebecca was seventeen when she married Howard. Now she's barely nineteen, and they're expecting their first baby."

Quinn was still struggling to concentrate after Linnea had brought *that* word into the conversation. "You said *girls* are old enough at sixteen. What about guys?"

"Men in our world are of age at eighteen. Which William will be before long, by the way."

She took a deep breath. "I don't think I'm ready to think that far ahead, Linnea. It's hard enough trying to figure out if that kiss meant something in the first place."

"Fair enough," Linnea said. "And there's no time like the present to sort *that* one out. I'll see you at lunch." She smiled and stood to walk back toward the castle, leaving Quinn staring after her, dumbfounded.

She was still staring at the path when, a second later, a different figure appeared around the hedge, making her heart thump erratically. It was William. Maybe it was because her mind was already there from the conversation she'd just been having with Linnea, but her breath caught a little at the sight of him in his neatly-pressed gray slacks and white short-sleeved polo shirt. His wire-framed glasses were tucked in his shirt pocket; he didn't need them unless he had to read something, but he always kept them close.

"Where'd Linnea go?" he asked, coming to sit down on the bench beside her.

"I… I don't know. She took off to do something," Quinn answered, trying to collect her thoughts, and willing the pink that she knew covered her cheeks to go away before he noticed.

It didn't work. "Is everything okay?" he asked.

"Yeah, everything is fine. Why?"

He frowned, studying her expression. "What's going on, Quinn? What happened?"

"Nothing happened. Linnea and I were just talking."

He raised an eyebrow, and then suddenly his entire posture changed. "Oh. Let me guess. You weren't talking about Thomas."

She shook her head.

"Or about your father."

"No." Suddenly, the bee on the flower became very interesting again.

He was quiet for a moment, and then he surprised her by putting his finger under her chin and gently turning her face until she was looking at him before he put his hands back in his lap. His expression was soft, his eyes open and friendly. "I'm going to guess that Linnea just had the same conversation with you that Thomas had with me."

Her eyes widened. The way he'd turned his body toward her on the bench, and the shy half-smile he directed at her gave her more courage.

"Do you think they planned that?"

He shrugged, smiling in earnest now. "It wouldn't be a safe bet either way. I actually kind of think they didn't. Those two are scary."

She couldn't stop the nervous giggle that slipped out. "That they are."

They grew quiet again, neither of them knowing how to continue. Quinn took a deep breath…better to keep it going now that they'd gotten this far.

"What did Thomas ask you?"

"He asked when I'd finally kissed you."

When she saw how closely his flaming cheeks matched hers, she almost started giggling again. "How do they know?" she asked.

"I think it's been pretty obvious to anyone who's been paying attention that things have changed between you and me." His gray eyes met hers, and the joking was gone.

She swallowed hard. "Yeah, I guess things kind of have."

He reached over and took her hand. His hand trembled, and she understood completely.

"I… I should be better at this," he said, and his hand shook even more. She covered it with her other hand and looked up at him. "Quinn, I don't know how to do this. I'm not smooth like Zander probably was, and I don't have the gift of charm like Thomas…all of this just comes naturally to him, but it doesn't to me. And I'm so worried that I might hurt you or upset you. So many things have happened to you lately…finding out about your father like this, fighting with your mom, breaking up with Zander. And I don't know how you feel about any of this. And I want to ask, without making it harder on you, but I don't want you to feel like you have to make some kind of a choice or a decision right now…"

By the time he stopped talking, her hands were shaking as hard as his were, but she squeezed his hands in hers anyway. She was surprised at how much it calmed her when he squeezed back. It took her several minutes to form the words she wanted to say.

When she could finally speak, she made sure she was looking in his eyes. "I'm not any better at this than you are, William. I don't have the answers to all of those questions, and it's true that I'm not ready to make any big decisions right now. But the one thing I do know is that I don't need you to be somebody else. I don't need you to be Zander or Thomas. I'm glad you're not either of them. I like *you*, Will." There, she'd said it. And now that it was out, she knew it was true.

He didn't answer out loud; the look in his eyes was answer enough. He leaned in close, and she moved toward him, too. When their lips finally touched, she was overwhelmed at the emotion that flowed inside her. Her hands found the back of his head, and she pulled him closer as his arms wound around her waist.

The kiss ended when he finally pulled away, though he brought his hand up to her face, cradling her cheek in his palm, and rubbing his thumb along the line where the blush had bloomed a few moments ago. She wasn't blushing now; the silliness and embarrassment had vanished, and she lifted her hand to place it over his.

"I can see you this time," he said, smiling.

She smiled back. Their first kiss had been in the pitch-black basement. This was completely different.

Suddenly, William looked over her shoulder, and his hand dropped from her cheek, although it stayed with hers as it fell into her lap. "Good timing, Nay," he said. "How long have you been standing there?"

Quinn turned to see Linnea watching them, looking somehow embarrassed and happy at the same time. She also looked…*worried?*"

"Sorry, Will," she said, coming closer. "I never meant… Quinn, I'm so sorry. I wouldn't have… It's just, Will…Lily needs your help in the clinic."

William was on his feet in the next instant, and Quinn and Linnea followed him through the gardens and down a path to the small clinic in one of the outer yards of the castle.

"I'm really sorry Quinn," Linnea said again as they walked.

Quinn's cheeks were red-hot again, but she looked over at her friend with a teasing half-smile. "There'd just better be a real emergency," she said.

THE HARDRIDGE FAMILY

BEFORE THEY EVEN GOT inside the clinic, it was obvious that something was going on. Simon stood on the small, covered porch speaking with a dark-haired woman who looked upset. Several children milled about in the grass and on the porch. They all looked exhausted and filthy. The youngest, only a toddler, was trying to climb the steps to reach his mother. His dirty diaper hung to his knees.

"Lily needs you inside, Will," Simon called as they approached. "Linnea? We could use you out here," he said, motioning over the children.

"Help me, Quinn?" Linnea asked.

She nodded. "What's going on?"

At that moment, Max came down the path from the direction of the castle, Charlotte and Rebecca close behind him. "Did you find William?" Max asked Linnea.

She nodded.

"Good. I'm going to ride into the clinic in the city and see if I can find another healer to help. Lily and Will aren't going to be able to do everything and help with Thomas, too."

"Wait," Quinn said. "What is going on here?"

"Simon and I were out on a ride just past the city today, and we came across another encampment of refugees from Philotheum. Several families this time; this camp has apparently been growing for a couple of days. I guess this family here found them late last night. Their father was injured in a fire when their house burned just before they left Philotheum. One of the girls is ill as well. They've been traveling like this for six days without any help. *On foot.*"

Bile rose in Quinn's throat. "Why? How could something like this happen?"

"How do you think it happened?" Max asked. "Tolliver's army destroyed an entire village last week when they found out their mayor was in the resistance."

Quinn's jaw dropped. "What?"

"Look, I'll be back later," Max said. "These people need help."

Rebecca and Linnea were already trying to round up the children, who all looked frightened. Charlotte had gone up to the porch to talk to Simon and the mother of the children.

"We need to get everyone clean and fed, at least," Quinn said, walking over to join them. "Where can we do that?"

"There's a shower in the clinic," Linnea said, "but Lily took one look at their father and told me to keep everyone outside and away."

"So we need to get them inside the castle, then."

Rebecca nodded. "We could use one of the guest apartments and have some food brought up."

"The children are frightened of us," Linnea said.

"Why?" Quinn asked, surprised.

"Oh, apparently there are some interesting rumors floating around in the villages in Philotheum about things we've done to refugees from there." Simon had come down from the porch and joined them.

Charlotte was still up there, her arms wrapped around the young woman. The baby had made it up on to the porch now and was clinging to his mother's skirts.

"If they're so afraid of us, why are they here?" Linnea asked.

"Well, we brought them to the castle, remember? They were too afraid to even try the clinic in the city alone. And the parents…their names are Connie and Eldon Hardridge…never really believed the rumors, although after the way they were treated in a couple of the villages, I think they started to. Anyway, they didn't have the choice to stay in Philotheum; they knew their children weren't safe there. Their house "mysteriously" burned down after the wrong person found out they're Friends of Philip."

Quinn's eyes widened. "They're Friends of Philip?"

Simon nodded. "Nearly all of the refugees who have come into Eirentheos are."

"But not all," Rebecca added.

Simon shot her an odd look. "I would hardly call the other ones *refugees*, Rebecca."

At that moment, one of the children, a little girl probably five cycles old, tripped over something in the grass, and fell to the ground, crying loudly. Her mother rushed down the stairs toward her. Charlotte picked up the filthy toddler and followed her.

"Well," said Quinn, "we're going to have to work on the trust thing, and get them inside."

Quinn didn't see William again for several hours. By the time they'd helped the young mother, Connie, get all of her children calmed, cleaned, and fed, it was past dinnertime. Rebecca, fortunately, had managed to make a good connection with Connie. She offered to walk with her down to the clinic to see her husband and daughter while Charlotte left to feed Hannah, and Quinn and Linnea went back to see Thomas.

When they entered Thomas's bedroom, Quinn was surprised…and relieved…to see William already in there, sitting next to the bed. She realized now that they'd all been away from him all day, and she felt bad.

"Hey," Thomas said as they entered the room. "How are the kids?"

"Better," Linnea said. "It took a while to get them to come into the castle with us. The oldest ones were convinced we were going to capture them, and send their parents to Tolliver."

"That doesn't make any sense," William said. "Why would they think we would do something like that?"

Quinn shrugged, but Linnea had talked to Connie at length while Quinn had played with the younger children, trying to get them to eat. "They're from a town not far from the capital city in Philotheum," Linnea said. "Their town is enjoying some pretty interesting prosperity and power under Tolliver's rule. Most people in their town actually *support Tolliver*, if you can imagine. A lot of the families are related to the royal line, but who've never been directly in line for the crown, and Tolliver has been making some sweeping promises about 'restoring' Philotheum to the way it 'should' be."

"And what way do they think it *should* be?" William asked, his voice incredulous.

"Well, Tolliver is rather fond of the idea that it's 'unfair' that only a first-born from the line of first-borns can assume the throne under any circumstances…I can't imagine why he wouldn't love that concept."

"No, I can't think of a single reason why the son of a usurper would want to change that," Quinn said, rolling her eyes.

"Still, that doesn't explain why they think *we're* in support of Tolliver, or that we would send people who come here to him." William sounded just as confused as Quinn was.

"I don't understand all of it, Will. I do know that Tolliver has somehow managed to convince his supporters that his marriage into our family is imminent. Or he had, anyway. Maybe they really believe Eirentheos is in agreement with what he is doing."

"There are really people who still believe he's going to *marry* you?"

"Let's just say that Tolliver's buddy 'Captain' Rhinewald wasn't so thrilled when I said something to him that was intended to disabuse him of that notion." Thomas said.

Quinn's eyes popped open wide. *"That's what happened?"*

"Among other things. Harbin Rhinewald didn't find me as, uh... charming as most people tend to. But then again, I don't feel so charming when I hear people talking about using my twin sister as a pawn to get what they want."

Linnea was aghast. "Did you really have to talk until he was mad enough to beat you half to death?"

Quinn wondered the same thing.

"In retrospect, it may not have been the best idea," Thomas answered, eyeing the needle on the syringe that William was preparing. He sighed, and Quinn took his hand, squeezing it hard, although she looked away…she still couldn't watch.

After Thomas had caught his breath again, he looked back up at them. "It did put Tolliver rather in a dither when he found out I was injured. Kind of hard to beat a guy's son to a pulp and then say, 'so, Steve, how about you let me *marry your daughter?"*

Nobody laughed.

"Now that he doesn't have me hostage anymore, and that possibility is slipping away from him, I think we're going to see him change a lot of his tactics."

"Probably." Linnea said. "When you've hung your supporters' hopes on the idea that you're going to marry an Eirenthean princess," she shuddered, "and you've apparently gotten them to buy into some prophecy that that will make you the 'true heir', then you leave yourself with a lot to live up to."

"Which is all just nonsense anyway," Thomas said. "Even his father's own oracle or whatever he was never said that anyone could somehow magically become 'heir to the throne' by marrying one of us."

They all looked at Thomas in surprise. The first time any of them had heard anything about Tolliver's "fortune-teller" had been while Quinn and William were in Philotheum, trying to rescue Thomas. Although they'd discussed it at length, and come up with their own theories, none of them knew any details.

"How do you know what the oracle said?" William asked.

"The topic came up when Tolliver was visiting with Rhinewald after I'd been injured. Bright enough, those two are, to think that a few broken bones would somehow interfere with my *hearing*."

Nobody smiled, but Thomas's expression was still darker than Quinn had ever imagined it could be. "Either that, or they really didn't anticipate my ever having the opportunity to share what they were saying."

Quinn's stomach churned, and she gripped Thomas's hand again. "So what did they say?"

"It wasn't a lot. Tolliver was extremely angry when he found out how badly I was hurt. Not that he wouldn't have liked to do it to me himself…I think the fact that he didn't get the satisfaction was part of his problem.

"He was in a rage, demanding to know what Rhinewald suggested he do now, and the idiot was trying to convince him that it didn't matter. He said the prophecy never said that the two kingdoms had to be united in order for anyone to *take* the throne, only that the "true heir" would become known by his ability to bring the two lines together and restore things to how they should be. He thought Tolliver could fulfill the prophecy by having children and having one of *them* marry into our line."

"Yeah, because that's more likely," William said, rolling his eyes.

"It's all just some purposefully vague, fake 'prophecy' anyway," Thomas said, looking around at them. "Something the oracle made up to keep Tolliver's father happy and believing his son could somehow take over the Philothean throne and have it be the right thing. I could probably make up crazy stuff like that, too, if my life depended on it."

"Well, he seems to have an awful lot of people believing it. And he's going to have bigger problems than he already does when more people find out that he was responsible for hurting Thomas like this." Linnea said.

"How do people not already *know*?" Quinn asked, stunned.

"News doesn't travel as quickly in our world as it does in yours, remember? The whole thing wasn't on the evening news," William said. "On the Philothean side, most people never even knew that Tolliver had Thomas. And he's certainly not spreading around what happened. And the majority of the people who know about it are probably keeping it quiet for their own safety."

"So they don't even know what kind of a monster Tolliver is," Quinn said.

"Plenty of them do, I think," Linnea said. "But fear of what he will do is pretty motivating to some of them as well. I think Connie Hardridge has a good idea of who was involved in burning down their house, but she almost sounded as if she expected something like that to happen She said something about knowing what chances she was taking when she joined the Friends of Philip. Tolliver's soldiers aren't kind to those who know people in the resistance."

"Some of them, anyway," William said. "We can't forget that there are members of the Friends of Philip who are *in* Tolliver's army, doing what they can to fight for the right thing every day. We owe Thomas's life to James and Dorian Blackwelder. And they're still soldiers in Philotheum."

Thomas nodded. "I thank the Maker for the two of them every day."

"I need to get back out to the clinic," William said, covering Thomas's leg with a blanket after he'd finished checking the dressing.

Quinn raised an eyebrow. "Have you eaten yet?" she asked.

"I'll have something later."

"Later when, Will? We all know you're going to go back down to that clinic and the next thing you know six hours will have passed."

He looked at her in surprise. "I'll eat, Quinn, I promise. You should all eat now, though. You can have some trays sent up."

"I've eaten," said Thomas. "Mia brought me a tray a little while ago. I wouldn't be surprised if she brings me a snack in another half hour, although I'll probably be asleep by then. I'm already feeling the stuff you just gave me."

Quinn didn't budge. "We'll have some trays brought up now. You can eat with Linnea and me, and then I'll go down to the clinic with you. I'm sure you can use more help."

"That's not necessary Quinn; it's been a long day for you, too."

"You're going to eat first, Will, regardless. You can't help them if you don't take care of yourself."

Out of the corner of her eye, she could see the incredulous look that Linnea and Thomas exchanged when William nodded. Thomas grinned, but his expression straightened when Quinn looked right at him.

They had the trays brought up to Quinn's room, which seemed to be the place they'd taken all of their meals since they'd been back.

As soon as Mia had left after setting the trays on the table, though, Linnea turned to them. "I really should go and keep Rebecca company," she said. "I'm sure she doesn't want to sit with the Hardridge children by herself all night, and I'm sure Connie won't be back up from the clinic for a while." Without waiting for them to respond, she scooped up her tray and disappeared into the hallway.

Quinn felt color creeping into her cheeks again. "Well, *that* was subtle," she said.

William chuckled. "It is Linnea," he said. "Subtlety's not her forte."

"True. And, um… I suppose we didn't exactly pick a private location earlier."

He looked up at her, surprise in his eyes and a hint of pink on his cheeks, too. "Well, consider yourself warned. If we're going to see where this thing between us goes… I have a *lot* of nosy siblings."

The heat dissipated from her cheeks, and became, instead, a slow, warm burning in her chest. "Is that what we're going to do, then? See where this goes?"

He nodded, inhaling deeply before he spoke. "I told you earlier that I have no idea how to do this, Quinn, and I don't. But I am a prince, and I have been raised to be honest and respectful. Kissing you twice now without being genuine with you and telling you what my intentions are would be disgraceful."

She sucked in a breath as his eyes met hers. The feelings she saw reflected in them were deeper than she'd imagined, and she was shocked when she suddenly felt *less* shy and awkward. "And what are those intentions?" she asked.

He looked down at her hands, and took them in his before turning his eyes back to hers. "I like you, Quinn Robbins, and I want to get to know you better. I know that right now we have a hundred strikes against us, and neither one of us knows what tomorrow is going to hold, let alone any further into the future. I don't ever want to force you into anything, and I *know* that things could change for you, and we could both get hurt."

She looked down at their hands, twisted together in her lap. "That could happen, William. I'm probably not such a safe person to get close to like this right now."

He reached up and brushed her hair back from her shoulder, clearing a spot to rest his hand. "I know what I'm getting into. And a few months ago, I would have thought this was crazy. But do you remember the conversation we had that one morning, right before I went to Cloud Valley?"

"Yes."

"I know this isn't what you were talking about, but basically you asked me if a relationship wasn't worth it, just because I didn't know what was going to happen…if I should throw away the time I have with someone now, just because I might lose them in the end. And I keep hearing that over and over in my head, every time I think of you. And I've finally decided that you're right. It is worth it. Taking this chance, for me, is worth it, even if in the end I don't get to keep you."

A single tear dripped down her cheek, and he reached up to wipe it away with his thumb, making her shiver.

She took a deep breath. "Really?"

"Of course, that's assuming you feel the same way…"

She put her finger against his lips. "I do, Will. I still can't make any promises to you, but if you're willing to put up with that for now…" the rest of her words disappeared in the kiss.

When William finally pulled away from her, they were both out of breath. He grinned at her sheepishly. "Speaking of being a prince and being respectful," he said, standing and walking across the room, "it's probably best we're not alone in a closed room if *that's* what's likely to happen." He opened the bedroom door partway before coming back to sit beside her on the couch again, although this time he put a few more inches of distance between them.

She nodded, still trying to collect her thoughts. "You're probably right," she agreed. Kissing Zander had never been like *that*.

"We really should both eat," he said, after a few minutes, when the room had finally stopped spinning. "And I really do need to go down to the clinic."

She combed through her hair with her fingers, trying to straighten it back out. Finally, she gave up and pulled it up into a ponytail. "How are things going down there anyway?"

"Not great. The father, Eldon, suffered some pretty severe burns on his arms trying to pull his daughter, Payla, out from under a bed where she'd hidden during the fire. They both inhaled smoke, and they've been traveling like that for far too long."

"Are they going to be okay?"

"I hope so. The skin on one of Eldon's arms is pretty badly infected. If Lily and I can't get the infection under control, he could lose his arm, or worse, the infection could spread throughout his body."

"He has all of those little kids." There were six of them altogether, the oldest a little girl who was only nine cycles.

"I know. This whole situation is mind-boggling to me. How they could be so afraid, and be turned down for help so many times before they made it all the way here… it's not what things are supposed to be like in Eirentheos. It's not what things are *supposed* to be like in Philotheum, either. Something has got to change, this has to stop."

"Can I go down to the clinic with you?" she asked, as he pulled the lid off his tray and picked up a biscuit.

He frowned. "You've done so much already today, Quinn. You really don't have to."

"And you've done what, Will? Sat around watching television?"

He chuckled, but then his expression turned more serious. "This is me, Quinn, it's what I do. It isn't your responsibility, though. You could relax tonight and get some sleep."

"Yeah, staying up here alone in my room is not any guarantee that I'd be able to sleep."

He sank back into the couch, tentatively setting his hand on her knee. "Dreams again?"

She nodded, shuddering slightly at how it felt, having him touch her like that. "Every night since I've been back."

His eyes softened. "What are they about now?"

"They're mostly the kind I can't remember once I wake up," she said, shrugging. "Sometimes I can hold on to tiny pieces, but mostly I just wake up way before I should, and I can still *feel* the dream. Then I can't go back to sleep."

William took hold of her hand and squeezed it gently. "What does it feel like? Are they still scaring you?"

"It's…" Quinn closed her eyes, trying to think of the right way to describe it. "They're different than the dreams when Thomas was missing. Then I would wake up just feeling terrified… and cold."

He reached for her hand now and moved closer, waiting silently for her to continue.

"These ones… I wake up kind of confused, I think. And feeling like there was something I was supposed to do and I haven't. It feels like forgetting to turn in a homework assignment or not remembering something at the store. I don't know if I can explain it any better than that."

He nodded again and then sighed. "Yeah, let's eat and then you can come on down to the clinic with me. Maybe it'll wear you out enough to let you sleep tonight."

When they reached the clinic, Lily was still inside, standing by one of the cabinets organizing supplies. The other healer that Max had brought back from the city today had only been able to stay for a few hours. The two patients, Eldon Hardridge, and his daughter, Payla, were both asleep. Although they'd kept the two of them separated in the clinic earlier while Lily and William worked on the severe burns on Eldon's arms, now they were on cots right next to each other, and Connie Hardridge sat on a chair between her husband and her daughter.

"How are things going?" William asked quietly as he and Quinn approached Lily.

"A little better, now that they're both able to sleep. Eldon should never have been traveling through the middle of nowhere like that with those injuries. The whole family is pretty sleep-deprived, and Connie looks dehydrated to me, too." She glanced again at the sleeping figures on the cots. He could see how exhausted she was.

"You should let us take care of things. Go spend some time with Graeme. Put your own kids to bed. I'll see what I can do to keep Connie drinking fluids, and we'll keep her company and see that she gets some rest."

For a moment, he thought Lily was going to object, but then she nodded. "I think I'm going to do that, William, although I don't like the idea of the two of you wearing yourselves out, either." He followed her gaze across the room to Quinn, who was carrying a full pitcher of water over to Connie. The feelings that stirred inside him as he watched her…this was something entirely new.

"I think we'll be okay, Lily. If we can keep him stable enough overnight, we'll be able to bring in some more help tomorrow."

Once Lily was gone, William went over to check on his patients. He heard Quinn talking quietly to Connie.

"Would you like us to get a cot set up for you?" she was saying softly. "We can move another one over here so you can be close to both of them all night. The rest of the children will be fine inside the castle tonight."

"I don't know," Connie said. "Are you sure it's all right?"

William walked over between them, and leaned down so that his eyes were level with the woman's. "You're safe here. I know this last week has been a nightmare for your family, but you're safe here. The children will be looked after inside, and we'll take you up to them first thing in the morning. You need to get some rest, and regain your strength for them."

Tears dripped down Connie's cheeks. "We'd heard… At first, we were so sure it wasn't true, but after so many days, and so much anger…"

William sighed. He glanced over at Eldon, whose chest was bared enough to reveal the tattoo that identified him as a Friend of Philip. He reached over and traced the edge of his finger along the circular outline. It struck him then, how odd it was that two sections in the design were raised in relief against the rest of his skin. He'd never seen a tattoo like that before; he wondered now if they were all the same.

"A lot of people here just don't know," he said. "Many of them were scarred so deeply by the poisonings that they're frightened. And they don't know about the work the Friends of Philip are doing to restore unity to our kingdoms. But we owe Thomas's life to the ones who were willing to risk everything to save him. And our goals are the same as yours and Eldon's. I think it's very brave of you to be willing to wear the tattoo and identify where you stand. You are welcome here."

Though her eyes still shone with tears, Connie nodded. "Eldon met King Jonathan once," she said. "He was only a toddler, and he doesn't remember it, but his parents have always talked about it."

Quinn looked up, interested in the story. "Really?" William said.

Connie stared down at her hands, rubbing her fingers along the edges of a handkerchief. When she spoke, her voice was quiet, still holding back tears. "His family was out one day, on a picnic near a river. Eldon and his sister, Adeline, were both tiny. They were playing by the edge of the river when Eldon wandered out too far, and got swept into a current and was pulled downstream. Their parents were terrified, of course, trying to fish him out of the river, and keep Adeline from going in after him too, screaming for help the entire time."

William looked over at Quinn and saw that her eyes were as wide as his own; he reached over and touched her shoulder. "So what happened then?" he asked.

"Suddenly, two men came riding up on their horses. Both of them jumped into the river without even pausing to think about it, and only a few minutes later, they brought Eldon back to his parents. It was only once everything had calmed down that they realized who the men were. King Jonathan pulled the blanket off his own horse to wrap Eldon in, and his friend, King Daniel, who was visiting from Eirentheos, immediately took Eldon's sister, and calmed her and played with her so everyone could focus on Eldon."

William smiled. "Daniel was my grandfather."

"Yes. This happened not long before Jonathan died so suddenly, and things in the castle started to change drastically. Eldon was one of the very first members of the Friends of Philip, back when it first became apparent…at least to some, what Hector's intentions were in marrying the Queen." Connie yawned, and William could see that she was about to fall over from the exhaustion.

"As much as I'd love to hear more, you really need to get some sleep," he said. "Quinn and I will keep watch, and we'll bring you as much water as you can hold. You really need to drink as much as you can."

It wasn't long before Connie really was asleep, and William suddenly realized that he and Quinn were alone in a room together again. It was strange; he'd been alone with her many times before, but it had never felt quite like this…as if the room were charged with some kind of electric current.

When she stood to carry the water pitcher back to the sink to refill it, he followed her.

"Thank you," he said quietly.

She turned to face him, raising an eyebrow. "I haven't really done anything special."

"That's not true. You've stepped in and helped and done so much work, without even being asked. It's really not something you have to do."

"First of all, Will, doing the right thing is the right thing. Second of all... it turns out that this is my world too, as least partially. I think I should do what I can."

His breath caught in his throat. It was going to take him a lot more than three days to get used to that idea, it seemed. "I hadn't thought of it that way," he said.

She shrugged. "Anyway, responsibility or not...it's a chance to spend some time with you."

HARD CHOICES

"ARE YOU SURE YOU'RE ready to try this, Thomas?" William asked, pulling the blankets off his brother. "It has only been ten days since your surgery."

"Do you have any idea how long those ten days have felt to me? It might as well have been a lifetime," Thomas answered, already sitting all the way up, and swinging his unbroken leg over the side of the bed.

"You need to wait a minute, buddy. Max said he would come up and help."

Thomas sighed. "I know, I know. I'm just so ready to walk around further than the bathroom. And I want to surprise the girls when they come back later, since you'll all be gone for the next couple of days."

William nodded. "I know you do. But they'll probably be gone for a while. Linnea will have a lot of fun taking Quinn to the market, so you've got time to practice. There's no rush. It might not happen today. You can't push yourself too hard." It would be a bright end, though, to what he hoped would be a good day for everyone.

Today was the big market day in the city, an event that happened only once every moon. There would be stalls filled with food and treats from all over Eirentheos. Linnea had been so excited to take Quinn. William would have enjoyed seeing Quinn's first time there, too, but, despite his warning to Thomas not to get too excited, he wanted even more to be with his brother when he stood for the first time on his crutches. Seeing the looks on the girls' faces when they returned would be enough.

"Do you think that guy, Eldon, is really going to be all right?" Thomas asked, and William knew he was changing the subject.

"He's doing better. We finally got the infection under control. He'll have some pretty bad scarring, but he'll be in good hands with Essie and Jacob once we get him up to their clinic tomorrow. It will be good for the whole family to have a place to stay…I know being in the castle all of this time has made them a little uncomfortable. I just can't believe we couldn't find something closer than Mistle Village. Things are getting really crazy around here."

"It's hard for people to trust anyone from Philotheum when it was someone from there who poisoned their children," Maxwell said, as he came into the room.

William looked up at his older brother. "One person from Philotheum was poisoning children, Max. Not the whole population. You can't blame the people of an entire kingdom for something just a few are doing."

"How are people supposed to know who to trust when the Philothean border is wide open? Anybody could just walk right in and do whatever they want. Including the kind of people who set the Hardridges' house on fire."

William had heard all of this before. Maxwell was in disagreement with their father and Simon on keeping the border between the two kingdoms open. "I don't know how I feel about it Max. On one hand, I understand what you're saying…that we have to protect our people. But we aren't supposed to be against

Philotheum, and closing the border…or treating people who make it across the way the Hardridges were treated…isn't that worse?"

"Yes. It is worse." Thomas said behind them. "Max, I don't think you understand. Yes, there are some really bad things going on in Philotheum. And, yeah, there are people who are on Tolliver's side, and they're trying to sabotage us. But most of them aren't like that. It was two of Tolliver's own soldiers who rescued me from Harbin Rhinewald's estate. If Tolliver ever figured out who they were… I don't even want to think about what would happen if the border were closed and *our* soldiers wouldn't allow them to get here to safety. They risked their lives for me."

Maxwell's expression softened, if only slightly. "I know."

"It's scary, Max, I know. But Philotheans are still our brothers. And there are more good people there than bad. We cannot let the bad ones push *us* into doing the wrong thing."

Ever since Thomas had returned from his time in Philotheum, there had been moments where William could see he'd changed, where just a little bit of the carefree spirit of his little brother had been replaced by a man who'd seen more than William had…more than even his older brothers had. This was one of those moments.

"All right, little brother," Maxwell said, "I get your point. Now let's see if we can't get you up on that leg a little bit so I can get back to at least beating you on the crumple pitch."

Later, when Thomas was worn out and Maxwell had left, William sat down in a chair next to the bed. "That was pretty awesome, Thomas." He'd made it all the way down the hall to the common room, and even been talked into presiding over a tea party for the littlest girls before he walked on the crutches back to his room. "Your recovery's been pretty remarkable. Nathaniel is going to be impressed when he gets back."

Thomas shrugged. "I've had someone pretty awesome taking care of me, Will. You've sacrificed a lot."

William felt his neck turning red…he didn't know if anyone in his family was ever going to realize that this was what he *wanted* to do. Of course there had been times lately it had been harder than it usually was to give up his free time…now that there was something else he wouldn't have minded doing with it, but even so, this was Thomas. There was nothing more important to him than making sure his brother got the best care.

He decided it was his turn to change the subject. "That was a pretty interesting speech you gave Max earlier."

Thomas shrugged. "It's how I feel about it. It worries me, actually, that Dorian and James are still there, still near Tolliver where what they did could be found out at any moment."

That thought put a heavy feeling in William's chest. "Are you doing okay with everything, T? You almost never talk about anything that happened to you while you were in Philotheum, and I worry sometimes about how hard that must have been on you."

Thomas locked eyes with him and shrugged again. "Some days it bothers me more than others, Will. I really don't like to think about it more than I have to."

William nodded, and they sat in silence for several moments.

"Speaking of things we haven't talked about," Thomas finally said, "what's going on between you and Quinn? Linnea said she caught the two of you kissing in the garden that first day the Hardridges were here."

"I've been waiting for you to ask me about that. I was starting to worry that Linnea had actually learned how to keep a secret."

"Hey, at least she's not keeping the good stuff from her poor, bed-ridden brother. You're kind of heartless, really, Will."

"Uh-huh. I'm the only one holding out *anything* here, right?" William asked, eyeing the tray of extra desserts Mia had brought up for Thomas after lunch.

"What? Mia just likes taking care of people."

William raised an eyebrow.

"Well, she's awfully cute and sweet, Will. Who could resist? Besides, she'll sit in here for hours and actually tell me things about what's going on around the castle and in her life…unlike *some* people."

"I tell you things."

"Yeah, you just leave out the best parts…like kissing Quinn. So, come on…what's going on with you and her? Honestly, you've had such gooey eyes over her lately that I was surprised when you stayed here and let her run off to the city with Linnea and Rebecca today."

"She's been cooped up in the castle the whole time she's been here, and she's been working so hard helping take care of those kids, I thought it would be nice for her to have a chance to get out and ride Dusk, and get to check out the market. Besides, it did turn into kind of a girls' trip. Even Howard didn't go."

"Keep spluttering nonsense, Will. I'll just sit here until you finally spill."

William chuckled, standing up to pace and release some of his sudden nervous energy.

"So, things are going well between you and Quinn, then?"

He couldn't stop the grin that spread across his face. "Yeah, actually they are."

Thomas's eyes widened. "*How* well?"

"I'm really starting to like her, Thomas. She's always so… there, you know? Ready to just jump in and be a part of things. And I feel like we *get* each other. We can just sit and talk about everything for hours. I think I could tell her anything and she wouldn't think less of me."

"Well, you look happier than I've seen you in a long time…at least when you're around her."

"I am. I never imagined I would actually feel this way about someone, Thomas. Really, I never figured I'd find someone who would put up with how busy I am and how focused I get sometimes on being a healer. Even these last eight days, when we've both been so busy with so many things throughout the day…when we finally do get to see each other, she just gets it. She's always spent the whole day doing her own thing, or else she's willing to spend time with me helping me do things."

"Are you actually courting her, Will?"

He felt heat at the base of his neck again. "Yeah, I kind of am. I told her my intentions, anyway, and she's still spending time with me."

Thomas chuckled. "Yeah, that might not be entirely official, but it sounds like courting. Have you told Mother and Father?"

He shook his head. "I think they both know something is up between us, but we're just not ready to make it public yet. She has so many things she has to figure out; what with her life in Bristlecone, her mom, Nathaniel… We don't know enough about where we can really go with this to involve everyone just yet."

"She does have an awful lot going on, doesn't she? How do you think she's doing with the whole Nathaniel thing?"

"I think it still freaks her out…the same way it freaks all of us out. We haven't talked about it a whole lot. She usually changes the subject pretty quickly when I bring it up, so I think it does bother her, and she's still trying to get her own head around it before she deals with *my* thoughts, you know?"

"Do you think she doesn't talk to you about it because of the way it changes things between the two of you?"

"I'm sure that's part of it, but I think it's a lot more, too. I mean, what she just found out changes pretty much everything about who she ever thought she was. And she's always been so close to her mom…"

"Yeah… can you imagine finding out that Mother and Father had been keeping something like that from you?"

William looked down at his brother, an unexpected flash of irritation filling his chest. "They have been keeping this from us, Thomas. They knew this whole time. They sent me to school in

Bristlecone with her for all these years and I never had any idea. Why would they do that?"

"What did they say when you asked them?"

"That they were trying to protect the secret, keep her safe. And that it would have been 'too hard' for me to know."

"But you don't believe them."

He paused for a moment, trying to organize his thoughts before he answered. He'd thought about this before, of course. Actually, since finding out, there had been many times that he'd thought about little else. "It's not… I don't think they're lying. It's more that their explanation doesn't cover everything about it. I mean, I get that they made some kind of promise or whatever to Quinn's mom about not telling her, I just don't understand why they would keep it secret from *everyone*, especially after she found the gate the first time."

"Would you have been able to *not* tell her? Or at least, not tell me? And if you'd told me, I would have told her, for sure."

"But it's that, right there. The fact that none of us would have been able to make it past the first two days that she was here without just telling her. I don't understand how *they* could keep it from her. Father flat out told her how happy they were that she'd come, and how much they'd *missed* her. And you've seen Mother, how she's doted on Quinn hand and foot ever since she found out."

"Yeah, that part I don't understand, either."

"Did you know that they and Nathaniel paid for her horseback riding lessons when she was little, and they've sent presents for every birthday and Christmas Quinn has ever had, even though she never knew?"

Thomas nodded, deep in thought. "You're right, Will. Not telling her once she was here is odd. Doesn't it make you think that there's something else to it?"

"I don't wonder *if* there's something else to it. It's obvious that there is. I think Quinn is going to have to talk to her mom sooner or later, and I really wish Nathaniel were here. I know there are secrets he's still keeping."

"Yeah…" Thomas stared down at his blanket for a long time before he looked back up.

"What, Thomas?"

"There is one possibility I've been thinking about. It's a little crazy, and it's probably wrong, but it would fit."

"A little crazy? As opposed to how sane the rest of this is?"

Thomas chuckled. "Yeah… something like that."

"So, your theory is?"

"It's not even a theory, as much as several questions."

"Okay, then, what are you questions?"

"All right. We know that Nathaniel is not our uncle. He came to live here, with Grandfather and Grandmother when he was a young teenager."

"Right."

"And now, we find out that it couldn't have possibly just been him. It would have had to be him and his brother…Quinn's dad."

William's eyes widened. "I hadn't even really thought about that. But, obviously, that's true."

"So, who are they, Will? They weren't related, or at least not closely related to Father, but Nathaniel's a Rose."

"So, they have to at least be pretty close to the direct royal line somewhere, but it would be pretty hard to be that close to the direct line, and not related to us."

Thomas nodded. "Exactly. And I've thought about it, Will. One time I even got bored enough to pull out a copy of the family tree. There isn't *anywhere* on our side that they would fit."

"Which leaves…" William suddenly had trouble breathing.

"Exactly."

The family's common room in their private wing was easily Quinn's favorite room in the castle. Filled with comfortable couches, arm chairs, massive bookshelves, and a little kitchen area with a small wood-burning stove, it was where the king and queen and their children spent a lot of time as a family, playing games, talking, and relaxing.

When Quinn woke up from a disturbing dream sometime in the middle of the night, she found herself drifting automatically there; it was a place she would feel comforted and safe, even when the rest of the castle was dark.

A cup of tea would make her feel better, help her relax, and maybe fall back asleep in a while, she thought. Tea was an important ritual in Eirentheos. Practically everyone she'd met here who was over the age of about thirteen drank tea all the time. Every morning began with huge pots of a rich, spicy tea at the breakfast table, and in the evening, there would always be a full kettle on the common room stove, ready for mugs to be filled again and again, mostly with a soft, sweet tea that carried a flavor Quinn could only describe as minty, though she couldn't think of anything in her own world that it was exactly like.

As soon as she opened the door, she flipped the light switch. The bright glow from the sconces on the walls blinded her for a moment, and she stood there blinking. Once her eyes had adjusted, she made her way over to the kitchen area.

After she had finally managed to open the complicated latch on the baby gate someone had built between the wall and the tall counter…Emma had apparently been quite adventurous and inventive as a toddler, requiring several different tries at a lock that would actually keep her out…Quinn encountered an obstacle that she hadn't considered.

She'd never gotten a fire going in the stove by herself before.

Usually, there was someone, a servant, around who took care of the small details like this for her...for everyone. When she stayed in the castle, it was easy to forget that she was in a different world that didn't offer all...or even most...of the conveniences and technologies she was used to. Like a stove that you could just turn on. Actually, if she wanted to heat water at home, she'd probably have just used the microwave.

While there was electricity in the castle, William had explained to her that it was still a limited resource in their world, mostly used for lights and a few other essentials...things in the medical clinic, for instance. And even though they could probably get enough in the castle to power a stove, there wasn't exactly an appliance store in town where they could buy one. The small refrigerator in the clinic was something that William and Nathaniel had somehow managed to carry through the gate.

Fortunately, she was an experienced camper and had built many fires. In the end, she didn't have much trouble getting a fire going in the little stove; it just turned out to be a lot more effort than she had expected to go through to make herself a mug of tea in the middle of the night. She probably wouldn't have bothered, except she didn't have anything else to do anyway.

Finally, though, the teapot was whistling, and she had a chance to use the purchase she'd made at the market in the city today. A little tea ball, embossed with delicate floral patterns around the sides, paid for with the strange little Eirenthean coins Charlotte had filled her purse with this morning, despite Quinn's objections.

"I've never gotten to spoil you as much as I'd have liked to," Charlotte had said. Arguing was useless, as Quinn had already learned from prior experiences...and anyway, seemed a bit cruel when it made Charlotte so happy to give things to her. It was still strange to her to know that she'd had presents in her piles from

Stephen and Charlotte at every Christmas and birthday since she was born, and she'd never known it.

Sort of in her piles, anyway. Nathaniel had told her that they mostly provided money, adding as much as they were allowed to help Megan afford more expensive things, like the horseback riding lessons she had taken for years, and vacations that her family had gone on together.

Charlotte had a wistful look in her eyes when she talked about that, and Quinn knew it hurt the queen's feelings whenever she turned down gifts from her. So instead, she'd opted for grateful, and had even had fun, carelessly bouncing from stall to stall, sampling treats and trying on jewelry with Linnea and Rebecca.

They'd spent a long time at a particularly elaborate tea stand, which was where Quinn had bought the little silver ball, as well as a few neat little mesh bags filled with interesting-looking teas. She'd picked up her own supplies of the teas she was growing so accustomed to drinking here at the castle; after spending so much time here, she knew it was something she'd miss once she went back home.

She was just settling into one of the big, cushy armchairs when there was a strange noise in the hallway. Startled, she craned her neck toward the sound, trying to figure out what it was. It didn't quite sound like someone walking up the hallway…there was another, clunking quality to it. At the exact moment she started to get freaked out, the common room door swung open, and Thomas stepped inside on his crutches.

"Oh my gosh," she said. "You scared me."

"I do sound a little frightening on these," he said, smiling as he hopped the rest of the way into the room. "I got about halfway down the hall before I started to worry that I might wake someone up. Of course, by then I was halfway down the hall."

Quinn smiled, and stood to assist him, first closing the door behind him, and then taking the crutches so he could lower himself carefully onto a couch. "What are you doing up?" she asked.

"I couldn't sleep. I've spent entirely too much time in that bed. Now that I know I don't *have* to be there, I doubt I'll sleep more than a few hours at a time. I was too anxious to get some more practice on these things to just lay there in bed." He nodded toward the crutches.

"William said you can't push yourself so hard, Thomas. You need to take it easy and keep healing."

He rolled his eyes. "Walking down the hallway in my home is hardly pushing myself, Quinn."

The tone in his voice told her it would probably be wise to let this one go. "It is good to see you up and around again," she said. "I'm sure it's been hard being stuck in one spot most of the time."

"There are worse places to be stuck than in a nice bedroom in a castle, but yes, I'm anxious to get back to my life. Did you make tea?" he asked, looking at her steaming mug, and then glancing back toward the stove.

She noticed the way he deftly changed the subject, but decided to ignore it. "Yes, would you like some?"

"I would love some. Thank you."

A few minutes later they were sitting across from each other, hot mugs in hand, the warm, soothing smell filling the air between them. They sipped in silence for a while before Thomas looked up at her, studying her closely before he spoke.

"So, you and my big brother, huh?"

She nodded, wondering if her cheeks looked as hot as they felt. "I guess so."

"You guess?" He raised an eyebrow, and her face glowed even warmer.

"I mean, yes. Me and William."

"Good." He smiled. "I'm not sure I can begin to tell you how happy it makes me to see him the way he's been around you, Quinn."

She glanced down at the floor, the red still spreading, down to her neck and out to the tips of her ears now, as panic over what he might be implying constricted her chest. "You know it's not anything serious yet, right Thomas?"

And she wasn't ready for it to be…at least when William wasn't in the room, and she could think clearly. When he was right next to her, looking at her with those compassionate eyes that sometimes felt like he could see into her very soul, everything tended to get a little fuzzy, and she would start thinking strange things, start feeling like maybe it *wasn't* crazy to be…*courting* someone from another world. Like there was actually some way this could end well.

"Does it have to be *serious* for me to be happy about it?"

"I don't know. I just don't want you to have unrealistic expectations about it, that's all."

"And what are your expectations, Quinn?"

"I don't know, Thomas. It's not exactly a normal situation. I have no idea what's going to happen between the two of us when I go home."

"Are you going to go home?"

Her heartbeat stuttered, almost stopping before she was able to look back up at him. "Of course I'm going to go home, Thomas. What kind of question is that?" She stared up at him, surprised when she realized he was smiling. "Seriously, Thomas. What?"

He shrugged. "I'm just trying to figure out where your mind's at, Quinn. Play along with me for a minute?"

"Play along with you *how?*" she asked, raising an eyebrow.

He shifted back into the cushions, rearranging himself so that both legs were stretched out on the couch in front of him, and he took a long sip of his tea before holding the mug with both hands in his lap. "Let's say…just for argument's sake…that you didn't go back home. That you decided to stay here."

"I can't just do that, Thomas. Bristlecone is my home…that's my *world.*"

"It's *half* your world Quinn. You're half from here, too. You have just as much stake here as you do there."

"Not quite…and *yes*, I have thought about it. I was born there. My father was *living there*. My mom is there. My little brother and sister are there. I haven't even graduated high school. It's not like I can just walk out right now and never look back."

"Maybe not *right now*, Quinn. But you'll graduate high school…or you won't, you wouldn't have to…you're already of age here, and our education system is quite different. It would be hard, but it isn't like you could *never* see your family again. You could go back and visit."

"And my mom would tell people what when I just disappear and reappear?"

"That you're magic."

"If you weren't sitting over there with a broken leg, Thomas…"

"You'd what?" He raised an eyebrow, a mischievous twinkle in his eyes.

She sighed loudly.

"Okay, you're right, Quinn. It's complicated for you. I get it. Just…when it comes time to make a decision…don't assume it's so complicated that there's no possible way it could work out, okay?"

"Fine, Thomas. I'll try. But believe me when I say I am *not* ready to make that decision yet, okay?"

"Sure."

"Besides," she said, staring into her teacup. "I'm not sure I'm ready to live in a world where I have to start a fire in the middle of the night just to have a cup of tea."

"Will has an electric kettle in his room."

"Now you tell me. He didn't think to bring one back for the common room?"

Thomas chuckled, but he shrugged. "This *is* a castle. Most of the time when someone wants tea, there is someone else to start a fire."

"It's not that way for everyone in your world, though."

"No, you're right. I do get it, Quinn. This world is very different from yours, and I can imagine how hard it would be to get used to living without a lot of the things you have. Most people in my world *do* have to build their own fires before they can have something as simple as a cup of tea. *Most* people in my world have to go around lighting candles if they wake up in the middle of the night in the first place. You're from a place with computers and cell phones and cars. It's not an easy decision."

HOMESICK

BY THE TIME QUINN had actually gotten tired again and been able to fall back asleep, the first hints of pale, gray light were peeking over the horizon. She wasn't ready to wake up again when Linnea knocked twice on her bedroom door and then came bounding inside.

"Wow, you're not usually asleep this late," she said, as Quinn struggled to sit up and open her eyes. "We're planning on leaving for Mistle Village in about an hour."

"Really?" She glanced over at the window. The light coming through the slit between the heavy curtains still looked faint.

"Yeah, so you'd probably better get dressed and ready." Linnea walked over and pulled back the curtains. The light still seemed off, but now Quinn could see why. The sky was overcast; billowy gray clouds covered up any trace of blue. She noticed for the first time that Linnea was dressed in dark jeans and a long-sleeved shirt.

"Is it cold outside?" she asked.

"Not cold, but cooler than usual. You'll want long sleeves and we'll take jackets and things in case it rains this afternoon. You should get ready, though. Will and Jacob want to leave on time so we can get there before the storm hits if there is going to be one."

Even though Quinn was dressed and ready to go in less than half an hour, by the time they got outside to the front of the clinic, several people were already busily getting the Hardridge family loaded into two wagons. Lily and Graeme were running in and out of the clinic, loading as many supplies as they could into the beds.

The horses were already hitched to the wagons; the two that Jacob had brought whuffled patiently in front of his wagon. Skittles, William's brown and white mare, looked a little less than pleased to be harnessed next to one of her stable mates that Quinn didn't recognize.

Walking over to Skittles, Quinn reached up and rubbed her nose sympathetically. "Good girl," she murmured.

Suddenly, there was a forceful nudge at her shoulder. Startled, she spun around to see her own mare, Dusk, starting at her in what she would have sworn was jealousy. "Oh, Dusk," she said, putting her arms around the animal's neck. "You know I love you best."

Dusk bobbed her head up and down once, snorting. From behind her, Quinn heard a hearty laugh.

"Sometimes I think that horse has more personality than the rest of us put together," William said, coming up to stand next to Quinn.

When she turned to look at him, her breath caught in her throat. Standing there as he was, in a tight, light blue sweater that set off his sparkling gray eyes and almost-black hair perfectly, it was hard to imagine exactly how he could have ever escaped her notice at school. Underneath the soft wool she could see the outlines of the muscles he'd developed through all of the manual labor he did here in his world.

When he caught her gaze she blushed, watching the color spread across her cheeks in the reflection off the clear glass in his wire-framed glasses. "Hey," he said. "Good morning."

"'Morning."

Their position, standing in the circle created by the three horses, gave them a tiny bit of privacy from the people who worked around them, and he leaned in and kissed her on the cheek. "You okay?" he asked her.

"I'm fine. Why?" she asked, frowning.

"I talked to Thomas a little bit ago. He said you were awake half the night."

Oh, right. "Yeah... it was just dreams again."

He put his hand on her shoulder, running it down to her elbow comfortingly. "Do you remember what they were about this time?"

Closing her eyes, she tried to catch the hint of an image that danced in her mind, but shook her head when she opened them again. "I remember something about dandelions," she said. "I think I was trapped in a field of them or something, but I can't really remember."

William caught her hand and squeezed it gently. "I'm sorry," he said. "I know it's disconcerting for you when you have dreams like that."

"I just wish I could remember them. It seems like they're important somehow, like I need to know what's happening in them, but I just can't hold onto it."

He pulled her into his arms, hugging her tightly. It felt good to be there, snuggled against his chest, the uneasy feeling left over from her dream was slowly slipping away. His head tipped down towards hers, their lips brushing...

"Will! Where are you?" Jacob's voice called from the porch.

He sighed and then chuckled. "I'll be right there," he called. "We need to get on the road," he said, looking back down at Quinn. "I think we've got a few hours before it rains, but I'd like to have Eldon and Payla settled at the clinic regardless."

The ride to Mistle Village was pleasant in the cool, overcast weather.

It was nice to not be feeling sweaty and sticky underneath the searing heat of the summer sun. Dusk seemed to be enjoying herself, too; her casual walk was more energetic than usual. Linnea's mare, Snow, kept up a happy pace right beside them.

They followed along a little way behind the wagon William was driving, which carried all of the Hardridge children except the youngest one…a barely toddling cherub-cheeked baby named George. They'd kept him in the first wagon with his parents so that Connie could hold on to him.

Payla, the seven-cycle little girl who had been so ill just a few days ago was doing a lot better, though William and Jacob still wanted to keep her at the clinic until her coughing had subsided more. Right now she was smiling along with her siblings as they huddled under blankets and watched the countryside roll by.

"Are you going to stare at Will the whole trip?" Linnea asked beside her.

Heat flowed into her cheeks again as she turned to face her friend. "I'm not staring at him."

Linnea raised an eyebrow.

Maybe she *had* been staring a little. Although she had seen William on horseback many times, she'd never watched him drive a wagon before, and it was surprisingly fascinating…the way he deftly controlled the horses with subtle movements of the lines he held.

"People don't drive wagons much in my world," she said. "It's kind of interesting."

"Yeah…*that's* the reason you're staring."

The blush crept further down her neck as she scrambled for a response. "And if it was a certain, cute stable hand up there…"

"If Jared was driving the wagon in front of us, I'd be staring too," Linnea said, completely unabashed. "Maybe he'd notice and actually ask me on a walk or something."

How did all of this come so naturally to some people, Quinn wondered, when it all felt awkward and strange to her? Even with

Zander, it had been hard to admit they were really dating, though Abigail had never seemed to have a problem flaunting her relationship with Adam.

With William, it was hard enough when they admitted what was going on to each other…now she had to know what to say to his sister, too? Of course, she could always keep changing the subject. "He notices you, Nay. I've seen him. I think he's just intimidated because he's a stable hand and you're a princess."

Linnea rolled her eyes. "There's always some excuse for not just coming out and taking a chance, isn't there? I'd go on a walk with him. Or a horseback ride."

"So why don't you ask him?"

Linnea raised her eyebrows. "Do girls do that in your world? Ask boys?"

She shrugged. "Some girls." She hadn't. Abigail had. "Maybe more should."

"I don't know. Here it would be weird, definitely. I'd scare him off for sure. And I think enough boys are already scared after they heard that Tolliver asked to court me. Things have dried up quite a bit since then."

"Well, you don't need a hundred boys, Nay. Just the right one."

"Is William the right one for you?"

Crap. She should have been more careful about letting *that* conversation circle back. "I don't know, Nay. I like him. We're courting."

"Can you imagine a future with him? More than just courting?"

Quinn swallowed hard. What was it with Linnea…and Thomas…pushing her thoughts to the future instead of staying grounded in now?

Being inside her own head was challenging enough. Although she'd tried her hardest *not* to let her mind go beyond the present, if she was honest, it had. The other night, they'd been in the common room after dinner, all of them just hanging out, and William had been holding baby Hannah, lifting her over his head, blowing raspberries on her tummy as she giggled hysterically, and Quinn's imagination had slipped just a little too far into an unlikely future. It hadn't helped when he'd looked up at Quinn, his eyes meeting hers, smiling the lopsided smile that made her heart turn into a puddle in her chest.

"Yeah, Linnea, sometimes I can."

When the first houses outside of Mistle Village came into view, Quinn sucked in a breath at the familiarity. She hadn't been to the little village since her first trip to Eirentheos, but at the sight of the first little stone house with smoke curling from its chimney, she knew she could have led Dusk all the way to the other side of the village, to the paddock outside the clinic without any further directions.

A thrill of recognition and excitement rippled through her middle when the low, white clinic building appeared in front of them, and Dusk and Snow followed the wagons through the opening in the wooden fence. Jacob and William brought both wagons right up in front of the big, covered porch while Quinn and Linnea walked their horses around the side of the clinic, continuing through the large, grassy paddock until they were just outside the small stable in the back.

Essie came out almost as soon as they had dismounted, and Quinn smiled as soon as she saw the familiar brown braid that had fallen over the shoulder of Essie's simple, cotton dress. On her first trip here, Quinn had spent a lot of time helping Essie in her kitchen and around the clinic, and she'd come to like Jacob's young, energetic wife who was also a healer.

"How was your trip?" Essie asked, stepping right in to help unbuckle Dusk's saddle. "I was starting to get worried it might rain while you were still traveling."

"It was really nice, actually," Linnea said, though now she was rubbing her arms against a breeze that had picked up. "Although, I think we really are going to get a storm here, soon. We should probably get the horses settled in their stalls."

Essie nodded, moving toward the wagon with the children. "I made some stew and fresh bread for lunch. Come on inside when you're finished."

When the storm did hit, less than half an hour after they made it inside Jacob and Essie's warm, homey kitchen, it was unlike anything Quinn had ever seen.

Growing up in the mountains of Colorado, she had experienced more than her share of blizzards, and sometimes in the summer they would get sudden, heavy rains that led to flash flood warnings in the small canyon area where Bristlecone was located, but the storm that raged outside the little clinic was a new experience.

While William and Jacob worked to get Eldon Hardridge settled in one of the small sleeping areas in the clinic, Linnea, Quinn, and Essie had taken the children into the half of the building that made up Jacob and Essie's home. They brought Payla into the cozy living room for now, though she was made to rest on the couch, and Essie brought over a steaming mug of clear broth for her to drink.

When the first ominous, pitch-black clouds appeared on the horizon, Quinn and Linnea followed Essie outside, and ran the entire circumference of the wraparound porch, closing heavy, wooden shutters over all of the windows.

They'd just gotten inside, and Essie was getting a fire going in the living room hearth when the first roar of thunder shook the house, causing the dishes in the cupboards to rattle. Quinn shivered at the noise.

The older children, and the tiny toddler, George, didn't seem too bothered by the crashing and banging overhead, but little Arianna, who was three, cowered in the corner of the couch, tears brimming over the edges of her eyelids.

When a new sound started, the heavy pattering of millions of raindrops against the wooden roof, Arianna began to cry in earnest.

Quinn was a little freaked out herself, especially when the wind started whipping across the outside walls, and the heavy shutters knocked against the window frames. Climbing up on the couch next to the little girl, she pulled her into her lap.

"Hey, sweetheart," she said. "Everything's okay. We're all okay." After a few minutes, Arianna relaxed into her lap, her head against Quinn's shoulder, and they sat there, staring at the flickering flames of the fire while the storm raged outside. Nearby, Linnea had pulled out a deck of cards and was playing a game with the three older children, and George toddled into the kitchen with Essie. Quinn could hear her in there asking him to hand her plates and spoons as she washed the dishes.

These kinds of storms must be commonplace in Eirentheos.

Another roar of thunder boomed overhead. It was enough to make the couch underneath her shift an inch or so across the floor. Arianna clutched tightly to Quinn's shirt, and as she did, an unexpected emotion slammed into Quinn with a thud that resounded more deeply that even the thunder outside.

She was homesick.

Suddenly, more than anything else in the world, she wanted to be in the cozy living room of her own house, with soft snow falling on the lawn outside, visible through windows that weren't shuttered closed. She wanted her own little sister to be curled on her lap, reaching her hand up into her hair the way she always did, stroking the back of Quinn's neck.

She missed the comforting sound of the television, even if it was only on so that Annie could watch Fireman Sam while she snuggled with Quinn. She wanted to be able to look over across the room and see her sweet little brother, Owen, buried in one of his non-fiction books, oblivious to the world around him, but there. She wanted to make some popcorn in the microwave and text Abigail on her cell phone, to hear the latest news about Adam.

She wanted her mom…to be able to tell her mom about the day she'd had, about the way Dusk had snuffed impertinently when she'd put her in the stable, refusing to acknowledge Quinn until she'd held out an apple.

What she didn't want was to be here, an hour ride and who knew how many days away from everything that was familiar.

She didn't realize that tears had started dripping down her cheeks until the door between the living room and the clinic opened, and William walked in. As soon as he saw her, his face changed, taking on a look of concern. He looked around the room at everyone engaged in their various activities, and then at the little girl in her lap, still staring into the fire, oblivious to Quinn's tears.

"Hey guys," he called to the kids. "Your dad is all settled in now. Why don't you all run in and see him?"

As soon as Arianna jumped off her lap and run into the other room, William took Quinn's hand and whisked her off to the guest bedroom down the hall where she and Linnea had stowed their belongings. By the time they got there, the stream of tears had turned into a torrent, and she was crying in earnest, great heaving sobs keeping time with the rumble of thunder outside.

William didn't say a word. Instead, he wrapped his arms around her and held her tight against his chest, rocking slowly back and forth and stroking her hair. She cried and cried, until she didn't think she could cry anymore, but as soon as she pulled back from him just a little, another sob broke loose from the depths of her gut, and a fresh wave of tears burst out, completely uncontrolled.

Finally, finally, when her eyes were red and raw, and there was a dull ache in the back of her throat, she was able to draw in a ragged breath, pull herself back and look at him.

"I'm... I'm sorry," she said, tracing her finger against the enormous damp circle in the middle of his shirt. "I don't even know what that was."

He put his finger under her chin, gently tipping her face upwards until she was looking into his eyes, which reflected a sense of understanding that sent an entirely new emotion rippling down through her, all the way to her toes. "Missing home?" he asked.

Her eyes widened. "How did you..."

His smile was so gentle, so relaxed that she felt completely safe with him as he reached into his pocket and pulled out a handkerchief, using it to dab the last few tears from her cheeks. "Let's just say I'm a little familiar with *that* kind of storm," he said. "Are you feeling any better now?"

"I don't know," she said. "I'm not crying anymore, anyway. I think I just feel drained."

He took her in his arms again, running his fingers down her back. "That sounds about right," he murmured against her hair.

It was better, standing there wrapped in his arms, her ear against his chest so she could hear his heartbeat, even if it was a little damp.

"How do you do it all the time?" she asked, the sound of her voice muffled by his shirt.

"What?"

"Leave home, stay in another world and miss everything that's going on with your family?"

He combed his fingers through the thick waves of her hair. "It's not easy, Quinn. It's never been easy. And, even though, in reality I do miss a lot of time with my family, I've never actually been in your world for as long a time as you've been here. I've never been away from my own world for more than five nights. I've honestly wondered before how you were doing so well with it."

She looked up at him, frowning.

"It's kind of the opposite problem, isn't it?" he asked. "While your family isn't off living life without you, you're still stuck here for a really long time, without all of the things you're used to. With me... yeah, I miss what's going on here, but I don't have to feel it so much. I pretty much only ever spend the night in your world on school nights, and I'm home for at least twenty days in between. You, on the other hand, have spent *so much* time away, and you've barely been home more than a few nights running, ever since you came back here for Simon's wedding. I wondered when it was going to get to you."

"I hadn't thought of it that way," she said.

Another enormous clap of thunder rattled the roof; the reverberations resonated deep inside her chest.

"There's not going to be a tornado or something is there?"

"No." He smiled. "We don't usually get anything like that in this part of the kingdom. We do get some pretty amazing thunderstorms around this time of the cycle, though."

"Usually?"

He leaned in and kissed the top of her head. "We won't, Quinn. Relax. I kind of like heavy thunder, myself."

She raised an eyebrow. "We don't really get storms like this in Bristlecone."

"Even in the summer?"

Her eyes widened at his question. "You're never there in our summer, are you?"

"No, Quinn. I'm not even in your world for three-day weekends. In a lot of ways, you're honestly already less of an outsider in my world than I am in yours."

"Do you ever get used to it?"

He shook his head. "I haven't. I don't know if you will."

"I don't know, either."

"Do you want to go home?"

"Um..." she bit her lip, thinking about it, suddenly remembering just how complicated everything was, that her mother wasn't speaking to her, and that her situation was different than William's. While he knew which world he truly belonged in, she was, literally, torn between the two. And she wasn't ready to deal with *that* all alone the way she'd be forced to if she went home and was surrounded by people who weren't even talking to her. "Not yet."

"Okay," he said, wrapping her in his arms again, her head settling back against his chest.

"How is Eldon?" she asked, changing the subject.

Pulling back from her just enough to make eye contact, he nodded. "He's okay. The trip wasn't quite as bad for him as I worried it would be…or at least he says it wasn't. Some of those burns on his arms are still really painful, though, and there's still a big risk of him getting another infection. I know he's happy to be back in one spot where he can relax."

Another crash of thunder shook the house, and Quinn tightened her grip on the back of his shirt.

"I guess we're all going to be stuck here in the clinic together tonight," William said. "You okay to go back out there? We can play choice or something with Linnea…she's going to come looking for us soon if we stay in here."

"Yeah, I think I'm okay now," she said. "You might want to change your shirt though, sorry."

He met her gaze straight on, a serious kind of look in his eyes. "Hey," he said, "don't be sorry for having feelings around me. You're allowed, and I'm here, okay, sweetheart?" He ran the back of his fingers down her cheek, stopping when he reached her chin, lifting it up again, this time to bring her lips to his.

FINDING VALORIS SEED

"SO, NAY, YOU STILL think you're missing out by not being along for all of the 'Adventures of Will?'"

Linnea rolled her eyes as she helped William lift the saddle up and over Skittles' back. There had been so much rain over the past day and a half that even inside the stable the ground was damp, and the air was cool and wet.

"It isn't as though I thought you were doing something exciting every minute, you know," she replied. And it was true; the evening and full day they'd spent inside the Mistle Village clinic with the Jacob and Essie and the Hardridge family hadn't been exciting at all. It had mostly been two days of being overly polite while being cooped up in a small space with too many people who were practically strangers.

He chuckled. "The exciting moments are usually…thankfully…pretty few and far between."

"I *know* that," she said. "You act like it's the first time I've ever left the castle with you. I'm allowed to go on *small* trips like when you need my help with something." As was almost always the case, she knew the main reason she'd been brought along on this trip was to help tend to the children. Not that she minded; she actually liked to feel as if she was useful and part of things.

"We're all working here, Nay. These trips aren't vacations."

How did Quinn put up with him? She admired her brother, and all of the work he did, but did he have to take everything anybody said so seriously? "I know that too, Will. You'll note that I didn't pack my bathing suit. I know you're off working and not just having fun somewhere when you're away. I just... actually like spending time with you. Sometimes it feels like you're gone so much of the time that I barely get to know you, you know?"

His expression softened; he finished tightening the straps on his side and came to stand next to her. "I miss you all the time, too, Linnea. I've never liked having to leave you behind. Of course," his tone turned teasing, "if you were always traveling with me, you wouldn't have time to flirt with stable boys."

She scowled at him. "Funny, Will. And not fair. I don't just play all day at home, either."

That managed to get through to him. "Sorry, Nay. I know that. You do work hard…and you're a lot of help on trips when you do come, too. I just meant that it's awfully hard to have a normal life and meet people when you're never home for it."

"You seem to have managed it."

The look in his eyes changed so quickly then that she suddenly wished she hadn't said anything. "Yeah, Linnea, maybe you can run off and find some guy who's from another world and whose situation is as complicated as Quinn's…everyone should try it at least once."

Her breath caught in her throat at the pain that hid behind her brother's sarcastic comment. "Sorry, Will. I didn't mean…"

"I know you didn't." He closed his eyes and pressed the tips of his fingers to his forehead.

"Hey," she said, reaching up for his hand and pulling it back down so she could see his face. "I thought things were going well for you and Quinn." A little thrill of fear clenched her stomach…she'd seen Quinn's eyes looking puffy and red the other night. Had something happened and she'd missed it? After her conversation with Quinn the other day, she'd thought things were going really well…

William looked down at her, and she could see the swirling emotions in his eyes. "Things are fine between us, better than fine really, it's just…there's always this thing between us, in the back of my mind, probably even more so in hers…how long can this possibly last? What is the future in this? I can't ask her to stay here with me. The other night she was so upset, missing her home. That little Arianna reminds her of her sister, Annie…"

If it had been Thomas telling her these things, Linnea would have told him he was thinking too far ahead, to give it some time, but it wasn't her laid-back twin, it was William. And it was clear that this was really weighing on him. His feelings for Quinn must be even deeper than she'd imagined, and this *was* a difficult situation. So, instead, she threw her arms around his neck and hugged him as hard as she could. "Things will work out, Will," she said softly in his ear.

"Do you really think so?" he asked when she finally pulled back. "Because sometimes I really worry that all I'm doing is dragging her into something that's going to make everything more difficult for her later."

"And harder for you."

He was quiet for long enough after that to make her start to worry. Finally, though, his eyes met hers. "I'm already past that point, Nay."

The deep emotion in her brother's voice almost made her take a step back. Yes, his feelings were deeper than she'd guessed. She took a deep breath, stalling as she worked to come up with the right answer. "If that's how you feel, Will, then the only thing you can do is what you already are. Be there for her. Let her figure this whole thing out and decide what she wants to do."

"What if I'm pushing her into something that isn't really what she wants?"

At this, she rolled her eyes. "William, it's Quinn. Do you really think, even for a minute, that she would be here with you if it *wasn't* what she really wanted? You can't control everything, and you don't have to. She's with you because she wants to be…that much I know for sure. I know the whole thing is crazy and complicated, but I really do believe it will all work out. It'll be awfully interesting to see how it does, though."

She hadn't realized just how much tension there had been in William's posture until his shoulders drooped visibly at the release.

He nodded. "You're right, Nay. I tell myself over and over again that I just need to let it go, and care about her while I have her here, and worry about the rest later. It's just hard sometimes."

"Well, I'm always here if you need reminding. I'll smack you upside the head if you need me to."

That actually got a grin out of him, and she didn't manage to duck away before he'd completely ruined her braid ruffling his fingers through it, so she punched him lightly on the arm. "Love you, Will."

"Love you too, Nay."

Quinn had always thought that the landscape of Eirentheos was green, but today, after a solid day and a half of heavy rains, she was astounded by the lush, rich colors of the trees and vegetation.

The sun was back in full force today as they rode toward Mistle Village. They'd enjoyed the sunshine as they'd escorted Connie Hardridge and all of the children except Payla to a small farm about twenty minutes outside of the village. There was still a slightly cool, damp feeling to the air that made the temperature feel close to perfect.

It had been an enjoyable morning, meeting the older couple who were so willing to take in the Hardridge family, and the children had loved running in a small meadow with two adorable black-and-white goats only a few weeks old.

Now, as they were riding back, William wanted to search for some valoris plants; the Mistle Village clinic was running quite low on the powder they made from the crushed seeds that worked as a mild pain reliever and relaxant. Mild for most people, anyway. Quinn had learned on her first trip here that just a tiny amount of the powder would knock her unconscious. William assured her that it would only affect her if she swallowed it, though…it was safe to pick and carry.

Quinn and Linnea followed as William led Skittles down through a heavily wooded patch that led to the river. "The plants grow best right along the river bank in shady areas," he said, bringing Skittles to a stop and dismounting. "Look for pale orange flowers."

A few minutes later, they were all down on the ground, combing through the thick plant growth along the river, searching for the valoris flowers. The rain seemed to have caused thousands of new plants to spring up overnight. Quinn had never been anywhere with so many different kinds of living things growing together in such a small space.

Almost none of the plants were familiar to her, which might have made her worry if she wasn't intimately familiar with what William promised was the only actually poisonous plant in the kingdom. She did find herself being watchful for the bright purple blooms that would signal an encounter with shadeweed; even though she'd been told that none had been reported growing in the area.

She was investigating a hint of purple, actually, leaning far over the riverbank, when she spotted the ones they were looking for…pale orange flowers with a large black center…the source of the valoris seeds.

"Will!" she called, pointing.

The flowers were a few inches out of her reach as she knelt along the riverbank. The section of the bank they were hunting along was elevated several feet from the river; the flowers were growing on a little shelf just past where her fingers would have been able to touch them.

William, who was quite a bit taller than either of the girls, lay down on his stomach near the edge, and stretched his hand down to the shelf, grinning triumphantly when he brought up a handful of the flowers. Linnea took them from him, and was tucking them into a small, leather pouch when he cried out, uttering a word that took Quinn by surprise.

"Will! What's wrong?" In an instant, she was kneeling on the ground next to him.

"I think something just bit me!" he said, pulling his hand back up, wincing as he pushed himself back up into a sitting position.

Sure enough, there at the base of his right thumb were four small wounds, all of them starting to bleed.

"Crap! What did that?" Quinn peered over the edge, but she couldn't see anything.

"There's an opening in the wall of the riverbank right at the spot where the flowers are. There's grass growing over most of it, but it's there," William said. "I think I disturbed some kind of nest…probably a river bole."

"Those things *bite?*" she asked, remembering the cute otter-like creatures she'd once seen swimming in a river here.

"Any animal will bite if it thinks you're going to mess with its babies," William said, pressing the edge of his shirt to the wounds, which were starting to bleed more heavily now. "Linnea, can you get my bag?"

Inside the clinic, Jacob was organizing some supplies on a shelf, while

Eldon Hardridge slept nearby. "What happened?" he asked, as soon as he turned around and saw them.

Linnea told him the story while he took William's hand in his and examined the bite wounds.

"That's an occupational hazard I forget about sometimes," he said when she was finished. "It doesn't look *too* bad Will. I do want to clean it out really well and get some antibiotics in you, though since it *is* a bite. You might need one stitch on this top one, but I'm not sure. It'll be fine by tomorrow, though, I'm sure."

William nodded. "That's about what I thought."

"Yeah. Why don't you go over to the house side and sit down at the kitchen table? I'll get some stuff together and come in and get it numbed up for you."

Quinn almost laughed at the face William made as they walked into the kitchen and sat down at the round, wooden table. She didn't, of course, because she knew exactly how he felt. Her own stomach twisted as she sat down next to him.

Linnea followed them in a minute later, carrying a thick, white towel Jacob had given her, and she and Quinn spread it out across the table so Will could lay his hand on it.

"I'll go grab you another shirt, Will," Linnea said, "so you don't have to sit here in that bloody one."

When Linnea had disappeared down the hall, he turned to Quinn, his face a unique shade of gray. "You don't have to stay and watch this. I know you don't like this kind of stuff."

Her chest tightened a little at the anxiety in his voice, and she took his uninjured hand in hers. "You can't get rid of me that easily, Will. Besides," she said, working to put a joking tone into her voice, "I've heard so often that you're just as bad with needles as me...you're going to deny me the chance to see the show for myself?"

"You've seen it before...when we donated blood in Philotheum."

She shrugged. "That didn't count…it was for Thomas, and it didn't even hurt."

He gave her a dark look. "I always knew you had an evil streak."

"I definitely do," she said, waggling her eyebrows up and down until he smiled. "I will leave if you really don't want me here," she added. "Otherwise, I'll stay right here and hold your hand…I just won't watch. So you tell me. Do you want me to leave you alone?"

A look of indecision crossed his face just long enough for her to have her answer. "Never mind," she said. "I'm staying."

"I should not be so bad about this stuff," he said. "I'm a healer. I *do* this to people."

"In my experience, healers are the worst patients," Jacob said, coming into the room. "Almost all of us struggle with anxieties and a low tolerance for pain. I suspect it's the Maker's way of increasing our empathy." Quinn was grateful that the supplies he carried were tucked in a small basket with a lid.

"Well, you've definitely got the empathy thing down," she said to William, squeezing his hand.

"I don't think that time when you were little helped anything either, Will," Jacob said as he sat down at the table next to them, taking William's hand and starting to poke gently around the bite marks. William stiffened, and Quinn rubbed the back of his other hand with her thumb.

Linnea came into the room then, carrying a folded shirt, which she handed to William. "I sort of remember hearing stories about that," she said. "You had stitches in your foot?"

"Yeah, that's not a memory I like to dwell on," William said, shrugging out of the ruined shirt and putting on the clean one, carefully avoiding the injury on his hand.

"What happened?" Quinn's eyes were wide as she reached for his hand again.

"Well, you have to remember, Quinn, our world is not exactly like yours," William started.

She looked up at him in surprise; until this moment she hadn't been sure if Jacob knew she was from another world, but when she glanced over at Jacob, he didn't look surprised at all.

"No," Jacob said. "This happened when Will was little, maybe about five?"

William nodded.

"It was a little while after our grandfather had died, and Stephen had just barely taken the throne."

Quinn had forgotten that Jacob and William were cousins.

"Our grandmother had decided to move back to Dreyden, the town where she was from. It's right by the seashore, and a whole crew of us went down there with her."

"It was sort of a family vacation," William said. "My mother and father took all of us kids…Thomas and Linnea were so little. *I* was little. And many of my father's siblings brought their families too."

"How old were you, Jacob?" Quinn asked, really wondering how old he was *now*…she'd never asked.

"Oh, I guess about ten cycles. Will's five cycles younger than I am."

It would never cease to amaze her how young people in this world were, when they were already married, starting families, running a clinic. It was, as William had said, a much different world than her own.

"Anyway, we were all at the beach, running around and playing, when all of the sudden Will just starts *screaming*. He'd stepped just the wrong way on a broken seashell; such a simple little accident, but it tore into his foot really badly."

She found herself squeezing William's hand even tighter.

"It was mid-summer and so many people at the time were on holiday. Dreyden is just a small town. There were only two healers there who treated injuries, and the one who was open wasn't even a fourth born."

"What?" Quinn asked. "Is that possible?"

"Yes," Linnea answered. "A birth gift isn't some kind of sentence to a particular profession when you grow up. Not all fourth-borns…not even most, really, actually go into practice as healers. They'll do other jobs helping people, or they'll work with animals, or they'll do something else entirely. Look at Lily and Graeme…they're both fourth-borns, and Graeme is even trained as a healer, but he spends more time raising the children than healing, and back in their village he was more active as a leader on the council."

"If every fourth born became a healer, we'd have more of them than we know what to do with," William said. "And there are other talents that make for good healers as well…it's not really relevant to the story whether this particular healer was a fourth-born, Jacob."

"Okay, you're right. He might have been quite talented at lots of things in his practice. Dealing with scared little kids wasn't one of them. That much I remember. Even at ten, I knew that I did want to be a healer when I was grown. Whenever Nathaniel was around, I followed him like a shadow, trying to learn all of his new tricks. At the time, I had no idea where he was coming up with some of this stuff. But anyway, Nathaniel *wasn't* on this trip, and so I went with your parents to this healer in the village, dying to see what he would do."

"And what did he *do?*" Quinn asked, scared now to hear the rest.

William turned to her, and he actually chuckled at the look in her eyes. "You make it sound like a horror story, Jacob. The guy didn't seem compassionate, but he probably wasn't a monster, either. It's not like he had a lot of choices about what to do. He didn't know the things we've learned from another *world*. And he didn't have the medications or the ideas for them that we've borrowed from there, either. They still *don't* have a clinic like ours in Dreyden, as far as I know. My foot was torn up pretty badly. It needed to be sewn up, and that's what he did. He put six stitches in the bottom of my foot."

"With no anesthetic."

"No. And no tiny little suturing needle, either." William said, shuddering now at the memory. "All I really remember is screaming the entire time while my parents held me down. It felt like it took a hundred cycles for him to finish, and even when he was done, it didn't feel better. It hurt for weeks."

For a moment, Quinn was glad that she *hadn't* grown up in Eirentheos.

"Not to mention there were no antibiotics," Jacob said, looking at her. "The next day when his whole cut started to get puffy and infected, Stephen and Charlotte cut their part of the trip short and rushed Will back to the castle. Although the older kids stayed with the rest of our families…they just took Will and the other little ones with them. So, I guess I don't even know what ended up happening with it after that."

"Nathaniel was back at the castle by then, and he took care of it," William said. "He had anesthetic and antibiotics, but I still screamed every time he got within two feet of me."

"And needles have freaked you out ever since," Linnea said lightly.

"Yeah, my excuse is not as good as yours, Will," Quinn joked.

He shrugged. "Nobody needs an excuse. Needles suck."

Quinn giggled. Linnea and Jacob smiled, but gave him odd looks, and she realized that probably wasn't a common phrase in Eirentheos. It surprised her a little that for all of the mannerisms William *hadn't* picked up in Bristlecone, that one would make the cut.

"Honestly, though, I'm sure that experience is one reason that anesthetics and antibiotics were some of the first things I really got interested in studying here. Between Nathaniel and me, we can manufacture both here in Eirentheos."

"Well, given that you've stitched me up here twice, I'm grateful for that one," Quinn said.

William smiled. "I'm sure. We still have a long way to go, though. That cut on your leg…if you'd have done that in your own world, you probably wouldn't have even had to have shots…did you know that?"

"No!" She frowned. "You tell me that now?"

"Yeah… for a small cut like that, they'd have been able to use a numbing cream and then stitch it up…no pain at all."

"And you don't bring the cream here?"

"Sometimes we do, but there's usually limited space and there are other things we're trying to bring back. I keep a little on hand at the castle clinic, just in case I ever do need it for little kids, but most of the time it's not a priority item. It doesn't keep forever, you can't always use it…your arm was way too beat up for anything but the shots…and it takes about an hour before it works, so it wouldn't have actually been practical when you injured yourself while we were walking. I meant more that if something like that had happened in your world, you'd have taken a car to the emergency room, and they'd have been able to use it there."

She sighed. "It is different here. And I know you do run out of stuff before you can bring more back."

He nodded. "Yeah… it's not like we can keep our entire kingdom stocked on medical supplies by buying them in your world. Mostly, we bring stuff back to study it and try to figure out how to make it, or something similar, with what we have here…" He stopped talking, sucking a breath between his teeth, and his other hand, still in Quinn's, clamped down hard.

"Speaking of which," Jacob said. "Sorry, Will. I figured I'd get as far as I could with that while you were distracted."

"I guess that's one way to do it," Linnea said, putting her hand on William's shoulder until they both felt him relax again. "You okay, Will?"

He nodded as Quinn heard the clink of the syringe being set down on the table. "Yeah," he said, as Jacob turned his hand over so he could get to the wound on the other side, "I think I'm just going to go with hating needles because they suck."

ALVIN

"QUINN! OVER HERE, I'M open!" Linnea called. Quinn spun around and in the same motion threw the crumple ball neatly into Linnea's waiting hands before Simon could get in front of her.

Linnea, in turn, passed the ball to Joshua, and he managed to toss it into the two-point goal just before Thomas blew the whistle from the bleachers. From the other end of the field, where he was guarding the opposite goal, William cheered.

"You're tied up!" Thomas yelled. "Half-time!"

Max's team, which included Quinn, William, Linnea, and Joshua, all headed up into the bleachers surrounding Thomas, who was keeping score and trying his best to referee from where he sat. Now thirty days past his surgery, he was doing much better. He got around really well now, but William wasn't anywhere near clearing him to play a contact sport like crumple.

Before allowing their opponents to break, though, Simon gathered them at the edge of the field. Today's game was a re-match from one yesterday, where Max's team had beaten Simon's thoroughly. As she filled a glass of water from a pitcher, Quinn could see Rebecca and Evelyn down in the huddle, rolling their eyes at each other. She giggled.

"What's so funny?" William asked, right in her ear, startling her.

She whirled around to face him. "Nothing. You boys just take your crumple a little more seriously than we girls do," she said, nodding to Simon's group.

"Says the girl who nearly knocked over my little brother a few minutes ago trying to intercept the ball."

She shrugged. "I got it, didn't I? And Daniel's fine. He knows there's tackling…he likes that part of it." At twelve cycles, Daniel was always chomping at the bit whenever he got the chance to participate in something with his older brothers. He had actually snagged a pass that had been headed for Quinn in the early part of the game. His grin had been too much fun to watch for Quinn to be bothered…but she hadn't passed up the opportunity later to steal one from him.

William grinned, then took the glass from her hand, and drained it. "Thanks."

She rolled her eyes, and he leaned in and kissed her on the cheek.

She pulled back, stunned, looking around at the small group in the bleachers. Nobody seemed to be paying any attention to them. "Are we doing this in public now?" she asked quietly.

Over the last couple of weeks, their relationship had definitely grown. They were nearly inseparable…when William wasn't off checking on a clinic, or working in his lab, although he'd even invited her in there a few times lately. But they'd kept their relationship quiet and low-key, mostly stolen kisses here and there, and one afternoon they'd managed to slip off for a long horseback ride and picnic with just the two of them.

"Officially? I don't know. But these are my siblings, and Linnea and Thomas have known for quite a while now. It's a pretend secret here, if it's a secret at all." He grinned again and picked up the pitcher to refill her glass.

"You're in an awfully good mood," she said, smiling.

He closed his eyes and took a deep, relaxed breath before opening them again. "It's a beautiful day out. It's not so miserably hot now that we're getting closer to autumn, and we're all out here together having fun. In a little while, everyone will come out for picnic dinner. What's not to be happy about?" He handed her the glass, and picked up another one to fill.

"Quite true. It's important to bask in the good days when the Maker grants them."

William and Quinn both jumped, startled at the new voice behind them, they both whirled around quickly to investigate its source.

"Alvin!" William said, his eyes wide at the sudden appearance of the older man.

"Still good with names I see, Prince William. And you, Lady Quinn, are you enjoying this lovely day as much as your companion here?"

"I... uh... Yes, I am. Thank you, Alvin."

"We weren't expecting to see you here today, Alvin. It's a pleasant surprise," William said.

Alvin smiled, his blue eyes sparkling underneath his white eyebrows. "I usually surprise myself. Never do know where the day will find me. Today I was drawn to find the pleasure of your company, maybe take in some crumple."

Quinn frowned; she was learning to associate the appearance of Alvin with significant events here in Eirentheos. The last time she had seen him was when they'd first realized that Thomas was missing. She had a feeling that his visit today wasn't coincidental.

"Well you're always welcome here, Alvin. Would you like a glass of water?" William asked, his hand reaching for the handle of the pitcher.

"Maybe in a little while, thank you. Actually, I thought I'd come to check in on Thomas and see how his recovery was coming along...

and I thought also that I might could have a short conversation with the Lady Quinn."

William looked as shocked as she felt, but he nodded. "I'll take this glass up to Thomas," he said. "He is doing much better, he'll be happy to see you, Alvin." Then he walked away.

Quinn turned back to face Alvin, wondering what he wanted. It wasn't the first time she had ever talked to him alone. In fact, she realized now that he'd somehow managed to get in a few private words with her every time she'd ever been to Eirentheos. And perhaps even more often than that; lately she'd begun to wonder...

"Yes, milady, it is me you encounter sometimes as you dream."

"What? How..."

Alvin's expression was warm and gentle as always, belying the nervous feeling his words were causing in her stomach. "Some questions are asked before we're really ready to know the answers," he said. "And you, beloved, have choices to make before you're ready for the answers to some of your questions."

Her mouth dropped open. "That doesn't make any sense. How am I supposed to make any choices before I have the answers to my questions?"

"Ah... you have it backwards my dear. You must make your choices first, and the answers will follow. I'm surprised, after discovering a world such as this one connected to your own, that you would still be under the impression that you were promised things would make sense."

She blinked. "No, you're right about that one, Alvin. Things will never again make sense to me the way they once did."

He smiled kindly at her, and she was struck, once again at how young he could look, when he so clearly *wasn't*. "The first choice you must make, Beloved, is when you are going to stop pretending that you're not going to have to have a very important discussion with your mother."

Her heart caught in her throat. That one wasn't her fault…was it? "I tried talking to her. She was the one who wouldn't talk to *me!*"

"Even so, you're hiding from her now." His expression didn't change; they might as well have been talking about the weather.

"I'm not hiding from her, she knows where I am."

For the first time, she pulled a small reaction from him. Alvin raised an eyebrow, and Quinn felt the weight of the situation on her shoulders. It was true that she wasn't actually hiding, but she had certainly run away from any possibility of talking to her mom about this. Still… "She lied to me!"

"As you lied to her."

A wild rush of indignation tore through her, and she had to take a deep breath to compose herself again. "I wasn't trying to *lie* to her. It was a secret I didn't think I could share!"

"It was a secret you chose not to share."

"What was I supposed to do, Alvin, just blurt out that I accidentally walked off a broken bridge and wound up in an *alternate world?*"

"I said nothing about what you were, or were not supposed to do, milady. I merely commented on what you already chose to do. I would also hardly call climbing up a broken bridge, closing your eyes, and stepping forward an *accident.*"

She swallowed hard. "I wasn't trying to hurt her."

"Do you think her intentions have been to hurt you?"

Were they? Quinn and her mother had always been close. Until recently, she couldn't even imagine her mother doing something to hurt her. No, she really *couldn't* believe that her mother had intended to hurt her with by keeping the secret.

"I… I never really thought about it that way."

"No, I'm sure you haven't. It's an interesting question to consider, though."

"But why? Why would she lie to me all of these years about my dad, and then still not tell me?"

"Ah... the choice to answer those questions is not mine to make, Lady Quinn. Should you desire to find out, you must ask the one whose choice it was."

"So what am I supposed to do, Alvin?"

"I can't answer that for you. It's still your choice."

"But..." frustration welled inside her chest, but the expression on Alvin's face had changed. No longer at all serious, he looked out across the field in delight.

"It appears as though half-time is over, milady. Surely you're not going to allow Simon's team to tarnish your winning record."

For a while, Quinn was able to keep Alvin's words at bay. Playing the second half of the crumple game helped. Knowing that Alvin was up in the bleachers next to Thomas gave her a push and she single-handedly scored two ten-point goals in the first five minutes back in the game. Sweat dripped from her forehead as she ran up and down the length of the field, fiercely determined to keep control of the ball.

When they took another water break a little while later, William came up to her, looking pleased but also concerned. He soaked a towel in the cool water and put it around her neck, asking if she wanted to trade places with him, and tend goal for a few minutes.

She didn't. Right now she didn't want to slow down for long enough to think, and tending goal would mean more standing and watching than she was ready to do.

Linnea caught the panicked look in her eyes before Quinn had to explain that to William though, and she quickly complained that nobody had offered to let her tend the goal for several games now.

William's eyes swept discerningly between the two girls as they made their way back onto the field, and Quinn saw the moment he caught on. His expression changed instantly to one of understanding, and she knew then that he wouldn't press the issue until she was ready to talk about it. Her heart swelled in gratitude for this boy…this man…who had come to know her so quickly and so well.

For the rest of the game, she and William were an unstoppable force as he shadowed her, anticipating her every move, clearing the path of opponents as she moved toward the goal, or leading the ball back to her hands.

Thomas called the game five minutes early because there was no chance of Simon's team catching up. Quinn could hear him grumbling as they walked back toward the bleachers.

"I get Quinn next time," Simon called to Max.

"Not a chance."

Quinn ignored their squabbling as she glanced up at Alvin. He caught her gaze for only a second, and his eyes twinkled in amusement.

"I'm going to go take a shower before dinner," she mumbled to William.

Despite her earlier rescue, it was Linnea who didn't let her escape so easily. She followed Quinn upstairs, all the way into her bedroom.

"I really was going to take a shower, Linnea."

"What did Alvin say to you? I've never seen you like this."

Quinn sighed, slumping down into one of her armchairs, allowing herself to think about and process his words for the first time. "You're not going to let this go, are you?"

Linnea beamed. "I told you that you wouldn't always feel new around here."

"Funny, Nay."

"So? What did he say?"

She pulled her legs up into her chest, resting her chin on her knees. Linnea sat down on a chair across from her, her gray eyes bright with curiosity, but also liquid with the empathy that made it so difficult to resist sharing things with her.

"He said I'm lying to my mom, and hiding from her."

Linnea looked like she was waiting for Quinn to say something else. When she still hadn't after nearly half a minute, Linnea finally spoke. "Aren't you?"

Quinn buried her face in her knees. "I wasn't thinking about it like that…like a lie," she finally mumbled.

"What would you call it, then?"

"It isn't like I had a choice, Linnea!"

"Of course you had a choice. There's always a choice."

"What was I supposed to do, Linnea? Tell her about the bridge, tell her where I was going?"

Linnea shrugged. "I don't know, Quinn. I'm not saying that. I'm not saying I would have made a different choice if I were in the same position. All I'm saying is that it was a choice you made, and you did lie, and that usually has consequences."

"That's pretty much what Alvin said. That's what he *always* says…it'salways *my choice*."

"Sounds like him, but he's right. Are you upset now because he pointed that out?"

Quinn buried her head in her knees again. "I don't know. I just wasn't ready to think about it at all."

"This isn't like you, Quinn."

She looked up at her friend. "What do you mean?"

"I mean… I've never seen you run away from a situation and hide like this before. When you wanted to know what Will was up to, you followed him. You didn't give up until you had your answer. When Thomas was missing, you ran back here without even a second thought, demanding to go on the rescue mission, not letting up until you got what you wanted.

"Now… I know you're mad at your mom. You have every right to be. She's been hiding this crazy huge secret from you, and she hasn't been playing fair. But why are you letting that stand in your way? That isn't the Quinn I know."

Her heart sank. She knew Linnea was right. "So are you saying you think I should go back?"

Linnea's eyes were intense. "I'm not going to tell you what to do, Quinn. Personally, I'd be happy if you stayed here forever. But you're never going to get the answers you want...you *need*...by hanging around here and pretending that you can ignore it forever. She isn't going to tell you what you want to know when she can't even see you."

"I'm really sorry I can't go with you," William said. "I hate the idea of you doing this all alone."

"I know. You've told me. I don't like it either, but it will be easier for me. I'll only feel like I'm gone for a day." She ran her hand from his shoulder down his arm until she reached his hand. They stood in the clearing a few feet away from the base of the bridge, talking while Linnea waited down by the river with the horses.

"Are you sure you want to do this?"

"Why do you keep asking me that, Will? No, I don't want to. It's the last thing I want. It would be so much easier to stay here for the next ten days, to help your mother and your sisters with planning your birthday celebration. But I need to."

"I know, sweetheart." He leaned in and kissed her cheek, then rubbed his thumb under her chin. "I don't mean to make it harder. This is just... new to me. I've never had to let you go since..."

She smiled and took his hand in hers again. "It's different, isn't it?"

It was different. She had a hard time believing how much things had changed between her and William during the last thirty days. Somehow he'd gone from being a sort-of friend she barely knew to someone she wasn't sure she was ever going to be able to walk away from.

The two of them had talked about this decision yesterday. A rare quiet day for William in the castle, he'd invited her out for another horseback ride after breakfast. They'd spent almost the whole day out riding, enjoying the horses, enjoying each other…definitely enjoying each other.

But after a relaxing picnic lunch near the river…and maybe a little too much kissing…their conversation had turned back to more serious things.

Ever since Alvin's visit two days ago and her subsequent conversation with Linnea, she had been trying to make this decision, to go home and confront her mother. She'd already missed the gate opening twice while she'd been here; three days would have passed for her mother since she had left.

She knew that Alvin and Linnea were right. She had to have this conversation with her mother sometime. Until she did, there would be no moving forward. She wasn't certain if choosing to go back now was brave or cowardly.

On the one hand, by going now she was taking charge of the situation, and trying to get things settled. However, another part of her acknowledged that the biggest reason that she wanted to do it now was so that if things went badly, she would still have another sixty days in Eirentheos to recover and pretend it had never happened.

Her plan was to slip back to Bristlecone tonight. It would be Sunday. She could go home, confront her mom, and be back in Eirentheos on Monday night, still in plenty of time to prepare for the big coming-of-age celebration that was planned for William's birthday.

Going back right now was a reminder of reality that she wasn't so sure she was prepared for, but she kept telling herself that she wasn't really going back to deal with her real life yet. She just wanted some answers. If she got some, she'd deal with those later, too – with Will.

"Is it safe to come back over here? Are you two through being mushy?" Linnea asked, coming to stand beside them.

William rolled his eyes, but he smiled. "I suppose so. Though you might want to leave again in a few minutes when I actually walk her to the gate."

Quinn blushed. Leaving was strange when things were so good with William here, both of them adhering to an unspoken agreement that they would just enjoy the time they had now and not worry about how things would change between them when Spring Break ended…which seemed a very long time from now, in Eirenthean days.

"Do you have everything you need?" Linnea asked, eyeing the backpack slung over Quinn's shoulder.

She shrugged. "I didn't actually bring anything with me. I have no idea what Mia packed in here."

"Your jacket, I hope," William said, walking behind her and unzipping the pack. "Yes, here it is. You should put it on. It's still a lot colder there than here."

"Aw, look. Will's a mother hen," Linnea teased, and then dodged William's hand as he reached to tousle her hair.

Quinn giggled, but took the jacket and removed her backpack so that she could shrug into it. William snatched the bag from her hand before she could set it down on the ground.

"Be safe, Quinn," Linnea said, suddenly serious again.

"I will," she said.

"We'll be waiting here at the bridge for you when you get back."

"I know." Quinn wrapped herself in Linnea's waiting arms, hugging her tightly. "I'll see you soon, okay?"

"Yeah." After one last hand-squeeze, Linnea turned and walked back down to the river. Quinn's horse, Dusk, made a whuffling noise, sounding like she, too, was upset about the impending departure.

"Are you ready?" William asked, sliding the shoulder straps back over her arms for her.

She closed her eyes and took a deep breath. "No," she said, opening them again. "I'm never going to be ready, but I'm going to do it anyway."

He paused then, and looked right into her eyes, with the kind of intensity he only occasionally unleashed on her. She almost changed her mind about going, until he started speaking. "I'm sorry it's so hard for you, and the last thing I want to do is spend the next ten days worrying about you, but I am proud of you, Quinn. And I'll be right here waiting for you when you get back."

She buried her face in his chest, hiding her tears and breathing in his scent, knowing that his reassurance extended far past him just planning on being standing here physically upon her return.

He wasn't fooled; by the time she finally pulled back, his handkerchief was in his hand. He gently wiped her face with it, and then tucked it in the pocket of her jeans. "You might need this when I'm not around," he said, leaning in to kiss her.

SECRETS

IT WAS SEVERAL MINUTES before Quinn could open her eyes on the other side of the gate. The difference in temperature assaulted her immediately…it was colder here than she had been expecting. Or maybe it just felt that way as she absorbed the difference between being in William's warm, safe arms on a late-summer evening, and standing here alone and scared on a chilly winter night.

Climbing down from the bridge was disorienting, and she felt out of place. There was no car waiting for her in the pull-off, no keys or cell phone hiding under a rock, nothing to do put pull her hood over her head, yank the zipper the last few inches, and start walking.

As she walked, she rehearsed the lines in her head that had been playing for two days, ever since that conversation with Alvin on the side of the crumple field. She knew he was right, that she had lied to her mother, too, and was guilty of hiding information. Part of this mess was her own fault.

Alvin had stayed at the castle for another full day, often locked up in meetings with Stephen. He hadn't said another word about her needing to talk to her mother, though the other night at dinner she'd caught him studying her. He had left shortly after that…she'd never told him she was going to take his advice and go home.

She'd thought about it enough, though, to realize that even if she wasn't completely innocent, she could still be angry. Wrong or right, the secret that she had hidden from her mother was *nothing* like the secret her mom had kept from her. Samuel had been her father, and she deserved to have known some of these things about him. It was beyond her why everyone would keep this from her, especially after she'd already discovered the gate and traveled to Eirentheos.

The further she walked, the angrier she became; a block before she reached her street, she had to stop herself to make sure that she wasn't actually yelling out loud. But when she finally turned the corner, and she could see her house, the fear turned to dread. How was she ever going to do this?

She paused for several minutes at the base of the driveway, seriously considering not going in. In the end, it was only the cold that propelled her forward. With the possible exception of Nathaniel's house, she didn't have anywhere else to go, and she wasn't sure if he was working tonight…that would be an awfully long walk in this bitter cold just to be left standing outside an empty house.

Her teeth were chattering by the time she reached the front door, where she stopped again. Should she ring the doorbell? No. It was her house, too. She moved the loose panel under the eave and took out the key.

As soon as she opened the door and stepped inside, she saw her. Her mother was sitting silently in the oversized chair in the living room, watching the door.

She stood there in the entryway for several minutes, trying to remember how to breathe, while her mother, too, waited wordlessly. When she finally trusted her voice, she turned to her mom. "Hi."

Another long pause, while they both looked at each other, Quinn wondered if her mother was having as much trouble breathing as she was. "Do you want to come in here and have a seat?" Megan finally asked.

Quinn had no idea what she wanted right then, but she nodded, dropped her coat and backpack on the floor, and made her way to the couch.

"Nathaniel told me he wouldn't be surprised if you came back last night or tonight to talk, but I was sure I'd made you mad enough to keep you away for longer than three days," she said. "I guess he already knows you better than I do. I should have gone down to meet you at the gate."

Quinn raised an eyebrow. "You talked to Nathaniel."

Her mother nodded, looking up, but not making eye contact. "After you left Thursday night... I didn't know what to think, what to do. Nathaniel came here and knocked on the door, but I wasn't ready to talk to him yet. He left the car in the driveway. I got up early on Friday morning and drove Annie and Owen back down to Denver. The whole ride there and back I was thinking about how I'd acted toward you, and what I'd said, and hadn't said... About how much I'd probably hurt you."

When her mom finally looked at her, tears in the corners of her eyes, the roughest edges of Quinn's anger smoothed a little.

"When I got back to Bristlecone, I went straight to Nathaniel's house. At the time, I had no idea how much Nathaniel had or hadn't told you. I didn't *know*, Quinn. When I realized where you must have been last weekend, all I could think was that he had gone behind my back and told you, when he'd *promised*. He'd promised me, he'd promised his own brother, and then he had my own child lying to me? Leaving me and running off to a completely different world where who knows what could happen?"

Quinn swallowed hard. In all the time since Nathaniel had told her about her father, she'd *never* guessed that possibility. It made sense, really, because...

"How could I have even imagined that you'd found the gate on your own? That thought never even crossed my mind. And then, last night, when Nathaniel told me what had really happened, about how confused and upset you were and then I thought about how I'd behaved toward you this week..."

Tears began to flow down Quinn's cheeks. Without even paying attention to what she was doing, she pulled William's handkerchief out of her pocket. As she brought the cloth to her face, she caught sight of his initials, embroidered in silver thread on the corner, and a second wave of emotion overtook her, mixing hot anger with the sadness.

"How dare you keep it from me in the first place, Mom? There should have never been a chance that I was 'sneaking off' with Nathaniel. I should have had a relationship with him this whole time. I should have known about the gate. I should have known *my family*."

She dabbed furiously at her tears with the handkerchief while Megan stared at the floor.

It might have only been minutes, but it felt like an eternity before her mother's gaze met hers again.

"Even if I could have told you, Quinn, I had no idea how. It's not a good answer, I know, but I don't *have* a good answer. It's not something there are lessons for, you know, telling your child that she has a secret family who lives in a hidden world and she's not allowed to know anything about them until she's eighteen?"

"That's the part I don't get, Mom. Why keep it from me until I'm eighteen? What is going to change so magically when I have a birthday that I'll suddenly be old enough to know my family?"

"I don't know! Do you think that this is how I wanted things to be? I was only a couple of years older than you are now when I met your father. Imagine, just for a moment, what it was like to meet and fall in love with this absolutely wonderful, loving man who was everything I ever wanted, perfect in every way, except he had this *little* secret."

Her mom stopped, looking down at her hands and taking a deep breath before she continued. "And I *dealt* with that, Quinn. After he finally convinced me that it was actually true, I even tried to accept it. I didn't understand it, but it was who he was, and I loved him."

More tears ran down Quinn's cheeks now, but she was too wrapped up in what her mother was saying to stop them. They dripped into her lap, making dark circles on the legs of her jeans.

"And then you came, and things became even more complicated. It was the only time he ever took me to his world, you know. He was always so adamant that it wasn't safe for us to go there, but your having a "proper Naming Ceremony" was important enough for him to risk it."

"What was so dangerous about it?" Quinn demanded. "I've been there four times now. I'm safe."

"I don't know. There were so many things he never told me about. He always just said that it was his own issue, and that he would take care of it, he would take care of everything. The only thing I had to do was help him guard the secret from you while you were a child. And then he died, and he left me here, alone with you and this huge secret, and I wasn't prepared for that. All I could do was keep my promise, keep you safe."

"But I'm telling you, I've been there. I've spent *a lot* of time there. I'm not in any danger."

"I asked Nathaniel about that last night. He said you've been safe, because the secret has been kept. Nobody knows who you really are."

"What is *that* supposed to mean? How would I be in more danger just from people finding out I'm Nathaniel's niece…Samuel's daughter?"

Megan took another deep breath, and then reached over to something that was laying on an end table beside her chair. As she pulled it onto her lap, Quinn could see that it was a large envelope, made from the thick cloth-like paper that was manufactured in

Eirentheos. "I went to the bank yesterday morning and took this out of the safety deposit box."

Quinn frowned as her mother handed her the envelope. "What is it?" It felt heavy, weighted down in a bottom corner by something that made a muffled jingling sound with each small movement.

Megan didn't answer, just pulled a tissue out of the box on the same table and dabbed her eyes with it as she watched.

She felt a strange sense of foreboding as she reached into the envelope. The first thing she pulled out was a large piece of paper. Covered with words written in elegant calligraphy, her first impression was that it was some sort of certificate. There was an entire paragraph at the top written in a language she didn't understand. She frowned at her mom.

"It's some sort of equivalent to a birth certificate in Samuel's world. You received it at your Naming Ceremony."

Sure enough, in large letters in the middle of the paper, she saw her name, or at least her first name. "Quinn Katriel *Rose?*" she asked.

"Samuel changed his last name to Barten when he came to live here. It was a secret even to people in this world that Nathaniel was his brother. That's why on your original birth certificate here, when you were born, he made Rose your middle name. The Barten was changed to Robbins, of course, when Jeff adopted you. But in his world, you were given that name at your ceremony."

Trembling, Quinn set the certificate to the side, wanting to examine it more closely later. She had a suspicion about what was making the jingling sounds at the bottom of the envelope, and she was both anxious and scared to confirm her thoughts. She tilted the envelope up, and two metal objects on chains dropped into her hands.

Although she'd been almost anticipating the appearance of a pendant, her heart almost stopped at the sight of the objects in her hand.

They were gift pendants, just as she'd expected. Both circles of the same size, one on a large, slightly tarnished chain, and one on a tiny chain that glimmered in the low light of the lamp. But it wasn't the fact that they were pendants, nor even that there were two…of course her father's would have been left for her as well. What made the room start spinning around her was the fact that the pendants were not the familiar silver worn by the royal family of Eirentheos. These pendants were gold. Philothean gold.

Holding the two necklaces in her hand, she couldn't breathe. She stared at them without really seeing them…nothing except the color was visible at all. In fact, her vision had gone blurry at the edges, and it only got worse when her hands started shaking.

"Quinn, what's wrong?" Megan finally asked, enough concern in her voice that somewhere in the back of her mind Quinn wondered how long she'd been sitting there so silently.

She didn't answer; she couldn't even remember how to make her mouth work.

Alarmed now, Megan crossed the small space and sat down next to her on the couch. "What is it, sweetheart?"

She closed her eyes, trying to unfreeze her thoughts, trying to remember how to breathe, trying to tilt the world back onto its proper axis.

"Do you… do you know what these are?" she finally managed to choke out.

"Samuel said they were some kind of necklace that they give to babies at their Naming Ceremonies in his world."

Quinn nodded. "Yes, they are. You don't know anything else about them?"

"No. I never thought anything more of them than that. I'd planned to give all of this to you at your eighteenth birthday. Although, yesterday, Nathaniel did say something that made me think there was more to it."

"What did he say?"

"He said that you might be upset when you saw them, and he wrote down his cell phone number for me, so that you could call him whenever you needed to. He said even if he was at work, he would make sure to pick up the phone for you."

Quinn took a deep breath, trying to calm the shaking. She still hadn't even really looked at the pendants, though a heavy feeling was settling in her stomach about what she might see when she did.

"Do you want to call him?" Megan's voice was wary.

She shook her head, still just trying to breathe.

"What's wrong, sweetheart? What is going on? They're just necklaces. Doesn't William have one, too? Doesn't everyone?"

She closed her eyes, steadying herself. "Yes, he does...they do." *If they were of royal lineage, they did, anyway.*

"Then what is going on? I thought you already knew all of this...Nathaniel said he told you."

"Well, clearly, he didn't tell me everything."

Megan's eyes widened. "You knew you were related to them already, didn't you? To the king and queen?"

"Sort of," Quinn managed to squeak. Except that wasn't what the pendants were telling her *at all.*

Finally her vision cleared, the shaking subsided enough for her to pull the little discs into the light so she could examine them. She started with her father's...the one on the larger, well-worn chain.

At the bottom, underneath a symbol she didn't recognize...maybe a cross between a star and some kind of flower?...were the tiny, etched letters of her father's name. Samuel Derek Rose. Hesitantly, not wanting to confirm her thoughts, but already nearly certain of what she would find, she flipped the pendant over.

It was there. Rather than the blank side that she would see on most pendants from Eir...from her father's world, from *her* world...was the circular symbol that represented the kingdom of Philotheum. A symbol that appeared only on pendants belonging to the king's own children...or those of his firstborn.

And she knew. Before she could bring herself to actually look at her own pendant, she knew. She'd heard the name, Samuel, only a few short weeks ago. The name, as it always did, had sent a little jolt of familiarity through her. Samuel was a common name; there were two of them at Bristlecone High School. So when she'd heard the name as she hid in Ellen's basement in Philotheum, she'd written it off as a coincidence.

Ellen. The second-born child of King Jonathan. Tolliver's older sister. *Samuel's* younger sister. Her *aunt*.

The shock was gone by the time she read her name at the bottom of her own pendant. Quinn Katriel Rose, the same as the name on her certificate. The royal crest of Philotheum was on the back, the symbol of the first-born child on the front. She was the daughter of Samuel Rose. Not Samuel Barten, a store manager from Bristlecone, Colorado. No. Samuel Derek Rose, the first-born son of King Jonathan. The rightful heir to the Philothean throne. And he was dead. And she was his firstborn.

NATHANIEL EXPLAINS

WHEN SHE FIRST WOKE up on Monday morning, Quinn wasn't sure where she was. She was startled at how unfamiliar her own bed in her own room felt. She was surprised, too, when she looked at the alarm clock beside the bed and saw that it was almost nine. She hadn't slept that late in a long time, and she couldn't remember dreaming about anything.

Aside from the fact that her whole body felt heavy, weighted down, almost as if she were underwater, she was actually almost rested. For just a moment, she couldn't remember why she was here, or why she felt so strange, and then a glint of sunlight reflected off the golden disks on her nightstand, and *everything* came slamming back.

Sitting there on her bed, she reached over and pulled the framed picture of her father and her toddler self into her lap.

"What were you *thinking*, Dad?" she whispered to the smiling image. "How could you keep this huge secret, and then *die* and leave me to deal with this? I'm only sixteen, and I only just found out about your world. What am I supposed to do now?"

She stared at the picture for a long time, the questions filling her brain, but no answers in sight. In the end, the only thing she knew was that she was *not* prepared to deal with being the heir to the Philothean crown. That was absurd.

After a while, there was a soft knock at her bedroom door. "Are you awake, sweetheart?" Megan asked, poking her head through the door.

"Yeah."

"Are you doing okay? You seemed pretty upset last night." She came all the way into the room now, and sat down on the edge of the bed.

"I think so."

"You want to get dressed and we could go out for breakfast?"

An hour later, Quinn and her mother were sitting in one of the familiar upholstered booths in *The Egg's The Thing*, a tiny breakfast cafe on Bristlecone's only main street. Although it was still chilly outside, the Colorado sun was shining brightly, and the little business district was bustling.

Quinn's thoughts, which had been so wrapped up in what she'd learned the night before that she'd barely spoken to her mother, were suddenly spun in an entirely different direction when she glanced out the paneled window of the cafe.

Abigail was out on the sidewalk, holding hands with her boyfriend, Adam, smiling and giggling about something with him, and their two other companions. Right next to Adam was Zander. And on Zander's other side was Melanie Fisher, a cheerleader whom Quinn barely knew.

She swallowed hard.

It wasn't fair, of course…even a little bit…for her to be upset. She was the one who had broken up with him, who had…as Thomas had said…broken his heart. And she was dating William. It wouldn't be right to be mad at Zander for moving on. It wasn't like she wanted him to be miserable. But it still stung to see it, to realize that she actually had really broken up with him, and that it wasn't going to be something she could just go back and undo.

She wondered how mad Abigail still was. When she'd found her cell phone in her room last night, there hadn't been any missed calls or messages at all.

When she looked back up, she saw that her mother had been looking in the same place she had. Her expression was sad.

"Zander was really upset when you broke up with him," Megan said. "He's having a pretty hard time with it, I think."

Quinn wasn't sure if that was supposed to make her feel better, but she felt worse.

"We were all pretty shocked, actually, Quinn. He told Maggie that he thinks you broke up with him because William's your boyfriend now. Is that true?"

Her hands twisted in the paper napkin under the table, shredding it into tiny pieces, and she blinked a few times, trying to keep her eyes dry. "It wasn't true when I broke up with him."

A deep crease appeared in the middle of Megan's forehead.

"I just…I knew I was lying to him, and I knew there were so many things I couldn't tell him, and that wasn't fair. There's been so much going on, Mom. I knew I couldn't give back to Zander what he was trying to give to me."

A few stray tears made their way down her cheeks. She reached up to dab at them with the napkin, but the whole thing fell apart, so she reached into her pocket for William's handkerchief that she'd made sure to stuff inside while she was getting dressed.

"And what about with William?" her mom asked. "You've just barely met him. Four days after you break up with your first boyfriend and you think you're ready to be dating *him*?"

"It's been a little longer than that for me, you know."

Megan closed her eyes and sighed. "Right. I always forget about that. It's so weird."

"It's very weird," Quinn agreed.

"Still, though, it's not like you have any less going on with William. How is it that you think you're ready for a relationship with him when you're telling Zander something different?"

She took a deep breath, trying to soothe the irritation from her mother's words, trying to stay calm and not begin a battle. Starting a new fight with her mom was the last thing she wanted right now.

She could see in Megan's expression that she really was confused, and she knew she was sad, too. Zander was her best friend's son. Megan and Maggie had no doubt been indulging in dreams of a future with Quinn and Zander together. It wasn't their decision, though.

"At least I'm not lying to William, mom. It's not like I could just tell Zander 'oh by the way, my dad was from a different world and I've been visiting there.' William knows."

"Just how are you planning on having a boyfriend who lives most of the time in another world?" Megan asked, nearly whispering in the small restaurant. "From what I understand, he's not planning on spending a lot of time here once he's finished with school. You still have another year of high school, and he'll be gone. What will you do then?"

She sighed. She could see that her mom had no interest in discussing the biggest, most obvious possibility. Not that Quinn was quite ready to think about that herself, especially with what she had learned last night.

"I don't know, Mom. I still have a lot of things I need to think about. I don't *know* what's going to happen. I do know that I really like William, okay? He gets me. Zander is a fantastic guy, and I hope that someday we can be friends again, because he was always such a wonderful friend, and I do care about him. But it's different with William."

The server brought their food then, and she and her mom busied themselves for a few minutes with salt and pepper and trying a few bites. Quinn had ordered a big bowl of cantaloupe, a favorite of hers, and something they didn't have in Eirentheos.

After a while, her mom looked up at her. "You're going to go back there, aren't you?"

Quinn nodded. "Tonight. William is having a big celebration for his birthday next week, and if I don't go back this evening, I'll miss it.'"

"It's not just because you're still mad at me for not telling you?" Megan's voice broke at the end, and the sound tightened something in Quinn's chest.

"No. I am still upset about that, but I kind of understand it more now that you gave me the pendants." Inside her other pocket, the pendants were smooth and cold, an unexpectedly heavy sensation against her leg.

"Are you going to tell me what upset you so much about those necklaces last night? I really thought you knew you were related to the…to Stephen and Charlotte."

"Actually, I'm not. Not really."

Megan frowned. "I always thought…"

"I didn't think anything mom. I didn't have any idea about any of this until Thursday when I left. And now… those pendants… I'm not ready to talk about it yet, Mom. I need to understand more before I am."

"You're kind of scaring me, Quinn."

"I'm sorry. I need to… I need to talk to Nathaniel."

Quinn's stomach churned as she turned onto Bray Street, heading for Nathaniel's house. Her heart had started pounding in an abnormal rhythm about an hour ago, when she'd first picked up the phone to call him, and now that she was almost here, her stomach had joined the fray.

She wasn't certain why she was so anxious about having this meeting. She should have been chomping at the bit to ask her questions and finally get…demand…some real answers, but she wasn't. After what she'd learned last night, she was afraid of what else she might learn, and what it would mean.

Nathaniel was waiting for her in the driveway…*of course he would be; why would she have expected some time to pull herself together before she went inside?* Her irritation faded only a little when she saw the expression on his face. He was much more nervous about this than she was.

Inside, Nathaniel's house looked as warm and welcoming as it ever had. A low fire crackled in the hearth near the couches where they sat down, facing each other.

They hadn't spoken at all since Nathaniel had opened her car door and given a tentative, "Hello," to which she had nodded. Now in his living room, they were silent for several more minutes, until Nathaniel finally swallowed hard, and then said, "So your mother gave you the pendants?"

She reached into the pocket of her jeans and withdrew the small cloth pouch she had found to keep them in. Pulling open the strings, she shook the little bag, and the pendants fell heavily into her hand. The image of the royal crest in the center of her father's pendant sent a little thrill of fear rumbling down her spine, as it had done every time she'd looked at it. Nervous, she rubbed it with her thumb. "Does this mean what I think it does?" she asked, although she didn't really have any doubt.

"Yes." Nathaniel's voice was soft and low but definitive.

"Why does everyone think he died in a river in Philotheum?" This was the question she'd fallen asleep to last night.

Nathaniel sighed. "I should have guessed you'd go for the hardest questions first."

She raised her eyebrows. "You think that's the hardest question?" It wasn't. Not by far.

He chuckled, and the tension between them eased, if only slightly. "No, you're right. I suppose it isn't. And I guess it's one that you really need the answer to, anyway."

Quinn waited as Nathaniel fidgeted with his hands before he started telling the story.

"I think you know some of this, Quinn, but I will start at the beginning. My father was King Jonathan of Philotheum, as I'm sure you have figured out. I was the fourth born child of Jonathan and my mother, Sophia. Samuel was my oldest brother. He was eight cycles older than me, but we were always close. I've heard stories that he doted over me, even in the cradle. We both loved our other two siblings, Ellen and Charles, but the two of them were only a cycle apart in age, and were usually in their own little world together."

"And then your father died?"

Nathaniel nodded, sadness in his eyes. "Yes, I was four and Samuel was twelve when our father…even from the beginning, we believed that our father had been killed. Later, we knew it to be true."

"Killed by who?" Quinn asked.

"As surprising as it might sound, Eirentheos and Philotheum are not the only two kingdoms in our world…"

"Right. Tolliver's father was from somewhere else, right?"

"It would be a mistake to underestimate you, Quinn. Yes, the Kingdom of Dovelnia touches the far northwestern border of Philotheum, and the relationship between the two kingdoms has historically been tense."

"Why?"

"We would get off-track if I tried to answer that question right now, Quinn, but the biggest reasons were religious ones."

She raised an eyebrow, but was silent as he continued.

"When my father became king, one of the things he most wanted was to have peaceful relations with Dovelnia. Hector was the first ambassador from Dovelnia to come to the Philothean castle in several generations."

Quinn frowned.

"At first, it seemed like things were going well. Relations between Philotheum and Dovelnia were better than they had been in many generations, and they kept improving. The strange things happened slowly, starting with Hector inviting an oracle from his own kingdom. Fortune-telling wasn't something that was practiced in Philotheum, but nobody said anything until the day he predicted the death of my father."

"What happened then?"

"At that point, my father told Hector in no uncertain terms that the oracle had to leave, or he'd send Hector back to his own kingdom as well. The oracle left, but the damage was done. Half a cycle later, my father died in the horseback riding incident. Hector convinced my mother that if he had only listened to the oracle and followed his advice, then my father would have lived. Between that and Hector promising continued peace between the kingdoms, rather than war, he and my mother were married before she gave birth to my youngest brother, Jonathan."

"Named after your father?"

"Yes." Nathaniel stared into the fire for a moment, before he turned back to Quinn. "I was so young. I couldn't understand why Samuel was so angry so much of the time at our mother and our new stepfather. Hector was always nice to me, giving me sweets and presents whenever he was around, which actually wasn't very often. I remember wanting to like him, but I couldn't all the way, because Samuel didn't."

He paused again, and Quinn sat silently, trying to absorb everything he was saying, trying to visualize it all in her head…her father and Nathaniel as young children, losing their own father.

"By the time I was eight, of course Hector had an oracle again. Not the same one…there were always rumors floating around that the old oracle had had something to do with my father's death. Many people in Philotheum believe…rightly…that there's only one real way an oracle could have foreknowledge of someone's death. But Hector, who is a quite charismatic man, was able to develop a large circle of influence as Prince Regent of Philotheum, and nobody stopped him from bringing in a new oracle, a man named Dalphius."

"Why didn't your mother stop him?"

"She was in love with him, Quinn. By that point, I think she would have allowed him to do anything. And by then, too, she was expecting his child."

"*Tolliver*," Quinn said, her voice dark.

"Yes, Tolliver. He wasn't always evil, you know. At one time, he was just a baby. Anyway, shortly after Tolliver was born was when things changed significantly in the castle. Samuel was growing closer and closer to eighteen, old enough to take over the throne himself, and now Hector had a son of his own. It wasn't long before Dalphius 'predicted' Samuel's death."

"And people actually believed him?"

"My mother did. She hadn't listened to the first oracle about my father, and she didn't want to make the same mistake twice. And there were others who wanted to believe the oracle as well, others who thought the new beliefs Hector was bringing into the kingdom were a solution to a problem that had been plaguing Philotheum."

"What problem?"

"Surely you must have wondered why there is nobody else truly fighting for the throne, Quinn? You, who notices everything."

Quinn swallowed. The thought had crossed her mind once or twice, but there were always so many other things she'd been worried about. "Ellen can't fight for the throne because she's a second-born, right?"

"Yes, traditionally only first-borns have that right. It's not Ellen's place, or Charles' or mine."

"But Charles' daughter would be eligible."

"Yes, Gianna is the next living first-born in the royal line. There are no others."

Quinn blinked. "What do you mean?"

"I mean, if something were to happen to Stephen, there would be Simon. But if Simon died without an heir, the crown would go to the first-born son of Stephen's younger brother Vincent."

"Jonathan didn't have any younger siblings?"

Nathaniel shook his head slowly. "He had one much-younger sister, Vanessa, but she died as an infant. The queen suffered a number of miscarriages, and many cycles of being unable to conceive. My grandfather, too, was an only child. For three generations, my family was able to produce only a single possible heir to the throne. There were some who believed it was some kind of curse. My mother was so afraid, as she carried Ellen… And then, by coincidence, it was during her pregnancy with Ellen that Hector and the first oracle came to stay in the castle."

"And, what? She thought the oracle had something to do with her having more children?"

"I've never had the opportunity to ask, Quinn. But these are the things I've heard through the years. These are some of the reasons that people in Philotheum have been willing to accept Hector, to challenge the beliefs they've always held and listen to his new ones. There was a lot of uncertainty in the kingdom for a long time…a lot of fighting among those who were related to the royal line, but not closely enough that it would be easy to decide where they stood…who the crown might fall to. All I know is that my mother was afraid enough for Samuel's life, and that she believed enough in Dalphius' warnings that she agreed to have Samuel sent away."

"Sent away where?"

"The plan was to send Samuel to Dovelnia, where he could learn more about the beliefs and the ways that would be responsible for 'saving' Philotheum. Hector and Dalphius had convinced my mother that it was important for Samuel to marry someone from a 'strange land', and that the kingdom would only be restored when his own foreign-born heir took the throne. And who knows? Maybe

Dalphius did have a real vision about *that*," he looked meaningfully at Quinn. "The man did really have powerful dreams sometimes. I think he allowed his own ambitions and my stepfather's desires to get in the way of gaining wisdom from them, though."

"But obviously my father never went to Dovelnia," Quinn said, pulling out her two pendants and looking at them again.

"No. Samuel never believed that Hector had any intention of allowing him to live, even if he did go to Dovelnia, and it wasn't somewhere he wanted to go. One night, Samuel had a dream that convinced him that what Hector and Dalphius were doing was completely against the Maker's wishes for the kingdom. He went to our mother, and shared it with her, in a last attempt to get her to listen to reason. He wanted Dalphius sent away, and he wanted to assume the crown early. Our mother refused, and told Hector everything. That night, Samuel disappeared. Several days later, his 'accidental' death was reported throughout the kingdom."

"But he wasn't dead."

"No. Obviously not. Although, for a long time, I was the only person in Philotheum who knew that. You see, I was there that night. Always my older brother's adoring shadow, I was in his room that night when Hector knocked on the door. Samuel shoved me under the bed, afraid of what might be coming. And he was right to be afraid. Hector did threaten him. Told him in no uncertain terms that he was leaving for Dovelnia within the week, but there was a different threat behind his words. Later that night, Samuel filled a small pack with some food and a change of clothes, and left to go to our distant family in Eirentheos."

"And then Hector just thought somehow that he was dead?"

"I don't know if Hector ever really believed that he was dead. In the morning when he discovered Samuel was missing, he did send out two guards who were not to return to the castle without proof that they'd 'taken care of' the problem. Although they did bring back a body, well, pieces of one that were enough to be convincing at a funeral, both of those guards were executed a few months later."

"And instead he just ran off to Eirentheos and they just took him in?" Quinn was surprised.

"Yes, King Daniel and Queen Helena just 'took him in.' They were already very wary of the things that were going on between Philotheum and Dovelnia, and they'd heard the rumors. They also believed that Hector had something to do with the death of my father. It was a very difficult time for your father. He was only sixteen…your age, and he had to live a completely hidden life. It was during those cycles that Stephen and Samuel discovered some old journals detailing the gate to this world, and they took it upon themselves to find it. Once they did, and they were able to roughly predict when it would open, it became a perfect hiding place for Samuel, who was constantly afraid of being discovered. It was a huge relief to have somewhere that nobody could discover who he was."

She frowned. "So where do you come into all this?"

"By the time I was thirteen, I had a good understanding of what Hector's plans were, and I'd been living in fear for a long time that somebody would figure out that I might know something about where my older brother really was. And then, I started becoming close friends with the son of one of the castle guards…Marcus Westbrook."

"The same Marcus we traveled in Philotheum with?"

"The very same. And that was my first brush with the idea that my siblings and I weren't alone in our thoughts that things weren't right in Philotheum. That Hector didn't have everyone under his spell. Marcus and the rest of his family were Friends of Philip. I started sneaking off with Marcus, sitting in on secret meetings in his home on days his father wasn't working at the castle. Sometimes Ellen and Charles would come with me, but not always. They weren't with me the night that Marcus and I, along with several other secret members of the Friends of Philip hid in the root cellar while Marcus' father was arrested by his own friends…other castle guards."

Quinn's eyes opened wide.

Nathaniel nodded. "It was a dark day. I never went back to the castle. By the time the guards came back in the middle of the night to set fire to the house, Marcus and I, along with the rest of the family, were in a safe house three villages away. Some neighbors who were also Friends of Philip made sure that the house looked like it was occupied when they came, and they made sure to spread the rumor that I had been there. My pendant was recovered from the ashes of the fire.

"Hector made it plain that anyone who would act against the crown was a traitor, even if it was King Jonathon's own son. I wasn't even worthy of a funeral, and it was forbidden for my name to be mentioned in the kingdom ever again. We eventually made it safely to Eirentheos."

"But Ellen doesn't think you're dead."

"Now, no. In the last several cycles I've become active in the Friends of Philip again, and there are a few who know who I really am. I was only thirteen when I left, and I was never much of a public figure in the first place. Outside of the highest circles of the Friends of Philip, everyone truly believes I died. Hector and Tolliver have no idea. My mother doesn't know. Even Jonathan, my youngest brother…I'm not sure if he knows I ever existed."

Nathaniel stood and walked over to the window, looking outside, where a few fresh snowflakes had begun to fall.

Even though Nathaniel's living room was cozy and warm, Quinn shivered.

Nathaniel turned to look at her again. "And outside of myself, Ellen, and Charles…and of course, Stephen and Charlotte, your existence is a heavily guarded secret."

She narrowed her eyes for a second, noting that he hadn't said that nobody else knew…only that the secret was guarded. "And what am I supposed to do about all of this?" That was the hard question. Now that she knew, what exactly did they have in mind for her? She was sixteen, and she'd grown up in an entirely different world. She certainly wasn't prepared to be the *heir to the throne* of Philotheum.

He sighed, leaning up against the small window seat. "I don't know the answer to that, Quinn. Ultimately, what you do with that knowledge is up to you. Nobody can make that choice for you."

A sudden burst of anger ripped through her chest, startling her with its intensity. "I keep hearing that, Nathaniel. 'The choice is mine,' but I don't know what that means or how that's even possible, because none of this has *ever* been my choice." She heard her voice growing louder, but she couldn't stop herself. She was almost yelling.

"I didn't ask for any of this. I didn't *choose* to have a father who was from a different world than me. I didn't *choose* to have this huge secret kept from me my entire life. And I definitely didn't *choose* to be the heir to the throne of Philotheum!"

Nathaniel was silent throughout her tirade, waiting until she'd yelled herself out and curled back into her ball on the sofa.

"Of course you didn't choose all of that. But then again, who does get to choose the circumstances of their birth? Do you think Samuel *chose* to be the first-born and the heir to the throne? For that matter, do you think Stephen did? Where you're born, and who you're born to…the choices your parents make as you're growing up…those are things nobody in any world has control over. What you *do* with what you're given…that's up to you.'"

"It's not really very fair, is it?" she asked, subdued now.

"No. I've never found much in the circumstances of life that I could call fair."

"So what do I do?"

"You don't have to decide that today. What you just learned is pretty big. I don't think it's time to jump into anything."

She nodded, staring into the fire.

"Are you going to stay here with your mom or go back to Eirentheos tonight?" Nathaniel asked after a while.

"I'm going back. I want to be there for William's birthday celebration."

He was quiet for several more minutes, before he walked back over to the sofa and sat down across from her again. "Is William courting you?"

She blushed; she and William still hadn't really discussed the details of their relationship with any of the adults in Eirentheos. While it wasn't completely a secret, it wasn't exactly out in the open like this, either. "Yeah, I guess he kind of is."

Nathaniel raised an eyebrow. "I guess I can't say I'm surprised. What are you going to tell him about all of this?"

She looked up, meeting him in the eyes for the first time during the long conversation. "I have no idea."

He nodded. "Just so we're on the same page, Quinn, I don't have any intention of telling anybody anything before you do. Except for Stephen and Charlotte, of course…they'll be expecting you to have learned this anyway, but I trust them to keep things silent."

She took a deep breath. "Thanks."

MISTLE VILLAGE

SAYING GOOD-BYE TO HER mother was a very different experience when they both actually knew where Quinn was going. After her talk with Nathaniel, she had driven back to her house and spent a little time with her mom. It was still awkward; she didn't have any idea how to explain what she'd learned from the pendants, wasn't really ready to think about what this new discovery meant for herself.

Just before dusk, her mom drove her down to the pull-off by the river. Through the window of the car, Quinn could see Nathaniel already waiting down by the bridge.

"Are you sure you don't need anything?" Megan asked, for the umpteenth time. Quinn knew she was only asking so she'd have something to say. Her mom had already insisted on taking her to the market a little while ago. She'd puttered around, not really able to look at anything, though she had come across something small she could give William for his birthday.

"I grabbed a few things, Mom," she said, patting her backpack. "But no, I already have almost everything I could need there." After her second visit, she'd realized that even taking clothes was really a waste. While the style wasn't so different there that she'd stick out badly, it was different enough that she preferred to wear the things Mia stocked in her armoire while she was in Eirentheos.

"You're sure it's safe for you to be there?"

After her conversation with Nathaniel today, she actually wasn't sure how safe she would be there, but she nodded anyway. "Yes, mom."

Megan turned to face her, deep emotion in her eyes. "I am sorry, Quinn. I never meant to hurt you by keeping all of that from you."

Quinn swallowed. It was amazing, really, how much knowing the truth had changed the way she felt about the secret. She'd tried imagining a different way to handle it…wondered how what she would have done in her mom's place, and understood just how hard it must have been. "I know you didn't. It's all just kind of a shock. I was really mad at you the last time I went to Eirentheos, but I'm not now."

"I love you, sweetheart," Megan said, her eyes shining.

"I love you, too, Mom." Quinn reached over and hugged her mother tightly for several minutes. Finally, she took a deep breath. "I'll be back in a few days. I'm not sure when."

Megan nodded. "Just as long as you come back to me."

Quinn got out of the car, closed the door, and walked down to the riverbank.

"Are you ready?" Nathaniel asked, as they stood at the foot of the bridge.

"It's weird. I've never felt hesitant about going back to Eirentheos before…apart from that first time when I thought I was going to wind up in the river."

He chuckled. "Everything is going to be okay, Quinn. Besides, I'm sure William's eager to see you."

At the mention of William, her thoughts calmed. Yesterday seemed like a long time ago right now, and she was surprised at how much she was missing him. Right now, all she wanted was to be in his arms…even if she had no idea how she was going to tell him about all of this.

Taking a deep breath, she squeezed her eyes closed and stepped forward. The chilly winter evening dissolved immediately into warm, slightly moist air. Opening her eyes, she stepped down toward the trail and looked around for William, expecting him to be standing near the end of the bridge, waiting for her as he'd promised he would be. But nobody was there. A heavy feeling filled her stomach.

Where was he? Surely he wouldn't have forgotten. No, he wouldn't have. Her breath quickened as a dreadful feeling that something was wrong quickly overpowered her. It was eerily quiet; there weren't even any sounds of animals rustling about, preparing for the approaching night. She had never been so completely alone out in the wilderness of Eirentheos before, with nobody nearby to hear her if she called.

By the time Nathaniel appeared on the bridge – the delay was always more pronounced on this side – she was on the verge of a full-blown panic attack.

Nathaniel took in her expression as he walked down to meet her on the path. He didn't say anything, just laid a comforting hand on her shoulder and looked around in concern. He shifted his heavy bag from one shoulder to another – it would be an awfully long walk back to the castle trying to lug that thing.

"Maybe he's just late?" Quinn said, though she heard her voice shake at the end.

"Perhaps the evening became a busy one," Nathaniel said, though his tone wasn't very convincing. He looked both ways down the path one more time before letting out a long, low whistle. A moment later, Aidel, his seeker bird swooped down from the trees. She chittered at him for a moment, and he pulled a strip of some kind of dried meat out of his pocket and held it out to her. "I'll send a message with Aidel, just in case, but we should start walking anyway. I'm sure he'll meet us somewhere along the path."

She nodded, although the feeling in her stomach was growing heavier. Nathaniel walked close beside her. They'd only been walking for five minutes or so when they heard the welcome approach of horses. But as the two riders drew near, her stomach sank again. William wasn't with them.

"Simon! Max! What's going on? What's wrong?" Nathaniel asked as the two of them dismounted. Dusk and Nathaniel's horse walked up beside Simon's and Max's horses, both saddled and ready to be ridden.

When she saw the look on Simon's face, panic nearly overtook Quinn. "What's wrong? Where's William?" she demanded.

Simon's eyes flicked toward her, and her heart nearly stopped before he started speaking. "William is okay, Quinn. It's not him."

"Who, then?" her whole body felt shaky; the foreboding grew darker, even as the relief about William filled her.

"Everyone is all right…mostly," Maxwell said. "But the clinic in Mistle Village has burned to the ground."

"How? What?"

"It appears to have been another attack on the Hardridge family…either someone followed them, or there are spies here," Maxwell said, his voice black.

Nathaniel looked at Quinn, confused, and she realized that he didn't know anything about what had happened to the Hardridge family.

"It's a long story," she said, before turning back to Max. "You said everyone is mostly all right? What do you mean, *mostly*?"

"Eldon Hardridge was the only one in the clinic part of the building when it happened. By the time Jacob and Essie realized what was going on and got him…he was in bad shape when we left Mistle Village a few hours ago. William and Jacob were tending him…but it didn't look good."

"Eldon *Hardridge?*" Nathaniel's voice was aghast.

"Do you know him?" Simon asked.

"Yes. What is he doing in Mistle Village? What happened?"

Nathaniel's face was white as Simon explained the earlier attack on the Hardridge family, and the condition they'd found them in. "When did this happen?"

"Last night. We received the news early this morning. The three of us rode out immediately. Father has been there today as well. He rode back to the castle with us just a little while ago. We were in a hurry to meet you back at the gate, but we wanted your horses," Simon said. "I'm supposed to take you back out there with me tonight, and Max will escort Quinn back to the castle."

"No," Quinn shook her head. "I'm going with Nathaniel."

"It's not safe, Quinn. There isn't even a place there for you to stay." Simon said.

Her eyes were hard and determined as she met his gaze straight on. "Where are you staying? Where is William?"

"In tents."

"I think I can handle that. I'm not going back to the castle to sit and worry about everyone when I could be helping." As she spoke, she walked over to Dusk. She petted her for a moment, checked the fastenings on her reins and saddle, tucked her backpack in one of the saddlebags, and then mounted her, while the three men watched in stunned silence.

"Let's go," she said, once she was settled in the saddle.

Simon and Maxwell exchanged wary glances, but Nathaniel just climbed up into the saddle beside hers, and then looked around at everyone expectantly. His shoulders were back and he looked calm, but Quinn could see how tightly he gripped the reins.

Simon nodded, and then turned to Max. "Why don't you go back to the castle and let Father and Mother know what we're doing, tell them what happened here."

"Are you sure you don't want me to take them instead?" Maxwell asked. "You could go back and be with Evelyn. I know you've only seen each other for a few minutes today."

Simon shook his head. Although his expression was bleak, his voice was strong. "It's my responsibility, Max. She's the wife of the heir to the throne; we need to learn how to do this. She's already said she will come out to Mistle Village in the morning." His gaze shifted to Quinn. "Which is what you could do, as well," he said pointedly.

Her body tensed in the saddle; she understood his subtle message. If she was going to court a prince, she was going to have to expect to wait sometimes while he took care of his duties. A faint flush of heat rose in her cheeks, but then she suddenly felt the invisible weight of the pendants in her pocket, the impossible heaviness of the decision they implied.

She wasn't merely the girlfriend of a prince…she was a princess.

"I'm going," she said.

Complete darkness hit after they'd only been riding for about fifteen minutes, and they had to slow down their manic pace just to be safe. Even when they finally reached the wide, main thoroughfare, riding was a challenge in the black night. The moon hadn't yet risen, and once they made it beyond the boundaries of the city, it was dark, and the dirt road was treacherous in many spots when they couldn't see.

Quinn and Nathaniel stayed close behind Simon; none of them wanted to be separated in the dark. Their pace was much too slow for Quinn, whose stomach churned with more anxiety every minute they traveled. She wanted to ask Nathaniel what his connection was to Eldon Hardridge, but it didn't feel like a good idea to discuss it in front of Simon right now.

Riding into Mistle Village was a strange experience. Before the shadowy outlines of the first houses came into view, Quinn could smell the smoke that still hung in the air. It wasn't anything like the tangy fragrance of a campfire, which was one of her favorite smells. This smoke was ominous; the scent of destruction and fear.

A heavy feeling settled in her chest as they rode into the town, taking a different path than the one to the clinic that was familiar to her. Before long, the faint glow from many lanterns led them into a campsite. Several small tents surrounded a much-larger one, which Quinn guessed was the makeshift clinic that Simon had described.

At the sound of their approach, a familiar figure emerged from the tent.

"Essie!" Nathaniel called, dismounting even before his horse had come all the way to a stop.

From Essie's posture alone, it was obvious that the news wasn't good. Quinn cast a heavy glance toward Simon as the two of them left their horses next to Nathaniel's, and reached the opening of the clinic just in time to hear the last part of the conversation.

"...about two hours ago, not long after you and Max left," Essie was saying, and Quinn felt like someone had emptied a bucket of ice cubes inside her chest. "I've been sitting with Connie. The children are with the Welshes."

Nathaniel's hands shook as he stepped inside the tent, and Quinn had to fight back an unexpected urge to follow him in.

Her muscles tightened in anger. This wasn't right, any of it. The Hardridges hadn't ever done anything to anybody, besides support the cause of uniting Eirentheos and Philotheum. All they'd wanted was peace, for things to be the way they were meant to be.

"Where's William?" she asked.

"He was very upset," Essie said. "He did everything he could think of to try and save that man. He promised not to go too far...if I had to guess, you'd find him somewhere near the clinic site."

The *clinic site*. The idea that Essie had to make a distinction, that there wasn't still just "the clinic" caused a sick feeling in Quinn's stomach.

"I'll walk you," Nathaniel said quietly, reappearing through the flap door holding two lanterns.

She thought about objecting, but then decided it wasn't worth it to cause anyone any additional worry tonight, so she silently accepted a lantern, and they set off in the direction of the strongest smell of smoke.

Nathaniel led her toward the clinic in silence, and she could sense how upset he was. Now wasn't the time to ask him anything.

Before they even reached the site where the clinic had once stood, thick wafts of smoke obscured their vision, billowing gray clouds dancing in the lamplight. They weren't going to be able to see anything in the darkness. They curved to the west before they hit the biggest wall of smoke, heading for the trail that connected the clinic to the main road.

Quinn saw it first, the feeble flickering of another lantern several yards off the path. She turned to Nathaniel, and he nodded, setting his own lantern down and letting her go alone.

He was curled into a ball near the lantern, with his knees against his chest and his head buried in his arms. She couldn't swallow back the hard lump that came into her throat at the sight of him.

"Will?" she said softly, when she was still about ten feet away.

His head snapped up; she'd startled him. Even in the dim light, she could see where his tears had cleared streaky paths down his soot-covered face. At first, she didn't say anything, just set her lantern down, and sat down on the ground right in front of him, crossing her legs and reaching for his hand.

He allowed her to take it, and they sat there for several minutes, not speaking in words, but understanding each other anyway.

"I wasn't expecting you," he finally said. "Max said he was going to take you back to the castle."

She snorted.

He closed his eyes for a moment, shaking his head slightly, and the corners of his mouth turned up in a half-smile. "Yeah, you're right. I should have known better. I just... I guess I didn't want to get my hopes up. This is a little too much to ask of you."

Her heart gave an unexpected little leap at his words. "So you're not upset that I'm here?"

"No, of course not," he said, his eyes widening. "I mean, I'm a mess..." he looked down at his clothes, and wiped at his cheek with his sleeve. "This isn't exactly how I wanted you to see me when you got back, but you can't imagine how much I've missed you."

"Here," she said, pulling his handkerchief out of her pocket and holding it out to him, her hands shaking at the overpowering emotion she felt at being here with him.

"I've got one," he said, smiling and reaching into his own pocket. "I just haven't been using it. It's been a long day."

"Are you doing okay?" she asked.

"No, I'm not. But I'm functioning now. I'm glad you didn't find me an hour ago, but I'm even more glad that you're here now." He uncurled from his ball, and leaned forward to kiss her on top of her head.

Her hand found the side of his face, and she traced his cheek with her finger, then cupped it in her hand. "Me too," she said.

He kissed her gently on the lips, but the current running between them right then was stronger than anything Quinn had ever imagined feeling. They didn't need the kiss, or words; in that moment she knew that he needed her as badly as she needed him. As his arms wrapped around her, she felt an overwhelming relief, as if she'd been holding her breath for a long time and was finally coming up for air. They curled tightly together there on the grass, both looking up at the sky, trying to make out the fuzzy shapes of constellations through the haze, each one holding the other for dear life.

"Nathaniel's just over there," she told him, after quite a while.

"That's probably a good thing," he said, taking her hand and sitting back up. "Although we might have to tell him about us after this."

"He knows," she said quietly. "He asked if we were...courting, and I told him that we sort of were."

He put his finger under her chin, turning her eyes to meet his in the dim light. "We are, Quinn. You don't have to be unsure about that part."

"I still don't..."

"I know, sweetheart. You still can't make any promises. How did things go with your mom, anyway? What happened?"

"Quinn? William?" Nathaniel's voice called from the blackness. "We should head back in a minute. Everyone will be worried, and I want to know more about what's going on."

At the sudden reminder of the reality of the situation, William deflated like a popped balloon, and she watched him actually grow smaller. She was right to have come here tonight.

"We can talk about that later," she said, taking her lantern in one hand, and his hand in the other. "We should go."

ELDON HARDRIDGE

IN THE LIGHT OF THE MORNING, Mistle Village was an even sadder sight than it had been during the night. The smoke was slowly beginning to clear, but there was still a light haze everywhere. The mood in the encampment was somber as they began making plans for a funeral for Eldon Hardridge, and started the long process of cleaning up the clinic site.

With little to do as a healer, William decided to keep himself occupied by helping Quinn look after the youngest Hardridge children, all of whom were too little to really understand what was going on.

He played catch with the twin boys, who were five, while the tiniest ones, George and Arianna, played in the grass near Quinn's feet.

Knowing that there would be enough sad days ahead for the children, they had all decided to wait as long as possible before telling the youngest ones. The older children were with their mother now.

Though he tried to keep a smile in front of the children, his heart was heavy. He'd done everything he could yesterday for their father, and in the end it hadn't mattered. Discouragement and anger mingled in his chest, regularly threatening to overflow.

Nathaniel was more upset than William had expected. He'd barely been talking to anyone. Quinn had told him that Nathaniel had known Eldon Hardridge, which surprised William. He'd always imagined that since he'd traveled so much with Nathaniel that he had met most of the people Nathaniel knew. Of course, their time in Philotheum had disabused him of that notion; he should have known that there were a lot more things he didn't know about the man he'd always called "uncle".

It surprised him how much better he felt, though, having Quinn back. The last ten days without her had been different in ways that he had not expected. They'd never been separated like that since they'd started courting. When she'd first decided to go back, he'd been a little sad at the idea, but had figured that it wouldn't really matter much; he'd been here without her for most of his life.

He had a hard time understanding how things could have changed so much for him in such a short time, how he could have gone from being completely okay with being on his own, here, in his own world with his own family, to spending ten days feeling lost without this girl.

It was dangerous territory, he knew. Quinn couldn't make any promises to him, and he couldn't make any to her. Even if her father was from this world, it didn't mean that she would stay here. Her family, her life, was all in a different *world*. He couldn't ask her to give that up…could he?

Four days ago, he had been sitting and chatting with Thomas when his brother had asked him if he would ever consider giving up his life here in Eirentheos to be with Quinn. At that moment, he'd realized just how far out of his depth he was with this girl…because he'd actually considered the idea.

Now that she was back, sitting only a few yards away from him, the question pressed even harder against his heart. Could he give up his whole world for her? As he watched little Arianna pick wildflowers and carry them back to a smiling Quinn, he thought that maybe he could.

When the two boys, Kevin and Blake, lost interest in the game of catch, William suggested they take turns practicing keeping a crumple goal, and he wandered back toward Quinn.

"What are you doing?" he asked, sitting down next to her.

She shrugged, holding up a string of small pink flowers with the stems tied together. "Arianna's looking for these ones so I can make a necklace for her."

He took the chain of flowers and laid them gently across his palm. "These are ameliorosa blossoms," he said.

"Okay." She shrugged again. "They're pretty."

Arianna ran up to them then, carrying three more. George toddled behind her, his hands full of several different kinds of flowers, and two kinds of weeds as well. "Pwity!" he declared.

"Yes, they are, George, thank you," Quinn said, taking them and then watching the two children run off again.

William watched her stare absently at the little girl, a lump coming to his throat as he realized that Arianna was about the same age as Quinn had been when she lost her own father. He reached to take her hand.

She turned to look at him. "So, what kind of flower is it?"

He glanced down at the blossoms she was adding to the small chain. "Ameliorosa. Also known as the healing flower," he said, pulling his pendant out from under his shirt, and showing her the flower engraved there.

A strange look crossed Quinn's face for just a moment as she looked at his necklace. He saw her take a deep breath and compose herself before she answered.

"Why are they called that?"

He wanted to ask her what that was all about, but he had a feeling now wasn't the right time. Last night, as they'd walked back to the campsite, he'd asked her again how the confrontation with her mom had gone, but she'd changed the subject in a way that let him know she wasn't ready to talk about it yet. Something about her reaction now felt the same way.

"Um," he cleared his throat, "the flowers have many healing qualities. The petals can be crushed into a salve that's good for rashes and injuries, and the stems and leaves can be brewed into a tea that helps with cold symptoms."

She still seemed distracted as she nodded and looked down at the flowers. "Is it okay to be letting her pick them?"

He smiled. "Sure. They're everywhere. If they weren't such useful flowers, we'd probably call them weeds. My little sisters love to pick them, too. They'll make huge bouquets and then leave them in piles on all of the counters and tables to wilt and crumble and make a mess."

That got her to smile. "Good. I just didn't want to be making the same kind of mistake I did last time I tried picking flowers in Eirentheos."

His stomach made a tiny flip at that memory. "Nope. Only shadeweed is poisonous, and you know that one now. The rest of the plants and flowers are fair game." He leaned in and kissed her on the forehead. He was relieved when he felt her relax against him. "Are you doing okay?" he asked softly, his face still close to hers.

"Yeah, just sad for them," she said, looking back toward the children. "And mad that someone would do something like this. What did they do to deserve that?"

There wasn't an answer to her question, the same one that had been plaguing him all night. Not knowing any other way to respond, he picked up her hand and pulled it into his lap, and they sat in silence, watching the children play in the sun.

It was late in the afternoon before Quinn ever got a chance to speak with Nathaniel privately. The king and queen had arrived shortly after breakfast, along with Max, Evelyn, Howard, Rebecca, and Linnea, and everyone had been busy most of the day.

Although there had been several offers of help, Nathaniel insisted that he wanted to prepare Eldon's body himself. Stephen and Charlotte were going to take care of the funeral arrangements, and have Eldon buried in the large cemetery just outside the boundaries of the capitol city. Eldon's body would need to be moved there.

When Nathaniel finally emerged from the tent, Quinn was the only one who saw him. She hadn't been aware of how determinedly she'd been waiting, her senses on alert, wanting to seize the first opportunity she had to speak with him, but as soon as he walked around the back of the tent, heading toward the edge of the campsite and the nearby woods, she let the plate she was washing slide back in to the wooden bucket, and followed him.

William, who was a few feet away from her, digging through a large crate of medical supplies that had been recovered from the clinic, glanced up when she stood. She shook her head at him, holding up a finger in a "wait" gesture. He raised an eyebrow, but didn't follow.

Nathaniel didn't turn around until they were far away from everyone, nearly to the tree line, although from the way he'd slowed, she could tell he knew she was behind him. When he finally did turn to face her, she was startled at his expression, at how devastated he was, at the unreleased tears that pooled in the corners of his eyes.

"You knew him well," she said quietly.

"I did once," he answered. "When we were very young."

She didn't press him for more information, sensing that he would tell her more, once the words came. He started walking again, down into the trees, and she followed along, just behind him, down through the trees and to the edge of a stream.

Kneeling down at the edge of the stream, Nathaniel dipped his hands in the clear water and pulled them up to wash his face. Quinn sat down on the bank a couple of feet away, watching quietly, studying her uncle's reflection in the water.

When he was finished washing, Nathaniel collapsed onto the ground, clearly distraught and exhausted. "I'm sorry, Quinn," he said.

"What would you be sorry for? You didn't do anything."

"Maybe that's the problem. I didn't do anything."

"What do you mean?" she asked, frowning.

"I mean that sometimes it's really hard for me to know if I made the right decision…leaving my home the way I did, hiding out in your world for all of these years, supporting Samuel in his choice to hide out, too, not pushing him to come back and take what was rightfully his."

"You could have been killed if you'd stayed."

"That's what we told ourselves, but who knows if that's really what would have happened. It's a lot harder to get away with murdering two princes than the innocents who are trying to protect them."

"Hector and Tolliver seem to have managed."

"And so successfully, too."

Quinn blinked; she'd never heard Nathaniel use a sarcastic tone before. "You know what I mean," she said.

"I know what you mean. But the fact is that neither Samuel or I *did* die at Hector's hands. I'm alive and well, and he likely would be too, if he'd stayed here, in this world."

She swallowed hard…she'd never thought about that.

"And in the meantime, Quinn… other people have died, protecting *our* secrets, fighting *our* battles."

"Who was Eldon Hardridge?"

Nathaniel sighed. "Eldon's parents were two of the earliest members of the Friends of Philip. They knew that Samuel hadn't really died. Eldon and I were close to the same age. We were the youngest ones at those meetings…"

A tingling sensation ran up her spine, and her eyes widened. "So was Eldon…"

"Yes, Quinn. Eldon was there the night that I "died" in that house fire in Philotheum. His home was the safe house we all fled to."

Nausea tore through her stomach; she had to put her head in her hands to steady herself as questions and ideas collided in her mind. When she finally looked back up at Nathaniel, his eyes were wide, concerned.

"I don't suppose there's a high chance that it's all just coincidence, then, that the Hardridges' home was burned down in Philotheum, or that someone was desperate enough to follow him all the way here to finish the job." She had to choke out the words, could barely hear her own voice over the pounding of blood in her ears.

Nathaniel inhaled sharply. "I've said before that it would be a mistake to underestimate you, Quinn. You are Samuel's daughter every inch."

"So what do you think it means, Nathaniel?"

"I would have to know more to be sure, but my biggest worry is that it means there are people who know about me who shouldn't, and that anyone in the Friends of Philip who might be able to confirm my existence is in serious danger."

"Why? Why would it matter?"

"Because if people have knowledge about me…or worse, knowledge that Samuel didn't die in Philotheum, then there is a direct threat to Tolliver taking the throne. If enough people knew there was a rightful heir, then everything Tolliver is working toward would fall apart."

"But there is a rightful heir." Quinn's voice shook on each word.

"Is there?"

BABY SEEKER

"YOU'RE UP EARLY." The sound of William's voice startled Quinn as she walked into the common room. It *was* early, she supposed. A faint glow had just begun to peek over the edge of the horizon when she'd looked out her window a few minutes before.

"So are you," she countered, raising an eyebrow.

"A little late, actually. I usually make myself a mug of tea and take it outside in time for the sunrise. Not that there's been anything *usual* about anything lately."

"That's for sure." Quinn had been back in Eirentheos for five days now, and life at the castle had been anything but normal. "So what's the hold up today that you're running so late?"

He walked over to her and reached out to her, leaning in to kiss her cheek as he took her hands in his. "Nothing. I was just waiting for you, actually."

She raised her eyebrow. "Then why did you sound so surprised when I came in here?"

"I just figured you would want to sleep in," he said, shrugging. "You've been so busy lately, and this is the first day since you've been back that there's not something going on..."

There had been something to do all day every day since she'd been back. Yesterday had been Eldon Hardridge's funeral, and last night they'd taken Connie and the children back to the Welshes' farm. Marcus, using connections within the Friends of Philip, had managed to locate Connie's younger brother and his wife in Philotheum and had brought them safely over the border two days ago…they were all together now.

Quinn had been tense ever since her conversation with Nathaniel; the weight of the decision that she faced was like a pile of bricks in her stomach. She still wasn't ready to tell William, or anyone, about what she had learned.

Forcing the thought out of her mind yet again, she looked over at him. "I don't normally sleep in very late, either…when I actually sleep at all."

The almost-lighthearted look on his face changed to one of concern at her words. "Did you sleep last night? Have you been dreaming again?"

She shook her head. "I did sleep last night," she said, rubbing his hand in hers. "Surprisingly, I haven't been dreaming at all since I got back."

His eyes widened; he looked as surprised as she'd felt when she first realized that. It had been a long time since she'd had more than one consecutive night without being plagued by the odd dreams.

The kettle on the wood stove whistled just then, and William walked over and poured the boiling water into two travel mugs that were sitting on the counter. She smiled. It was always so odd to see the little objects here and there that William or Nathaniel had so obviously brought back with them from her world. It was an odd contrast to watch him pull an old-fashioned-looking tin kettle from the wood-burning stove, and pour the water from it into two stainless steel travel mugs with vacuum lids. She wasn't sure she'd ever get used to it.

Pale sunlight was beginning to stream through the large window at the other end of the room. "So you didn't tell me why you were up at the crack of dawn, ready to wait for me to sleep in for hours."

He chuckled, carrying a steaming mug over to her while he screwed on the lid. "I have a surprise for you. Walk with me?"

"Sure."

Outside, the morning was beautiful. The air was just cool enough that she was comfortable in the light sweater she'd grabbed, and birds were chattering at each other in the nearby trees. The grassy lawns surrounding the castle glistened with dew, and the gravel of the path they were on crunched under their feet.

"I can see why you'd want to come out here in the mornings," she said.

William took a deep breath, and was silent for a moment before he answered. "It's a good way to start the day. I needed it today after the last week."

She nodded as she followed him down a back path that would eventually lead them through a small gatehouse and into the wooded area at the back corner of the castle wall.

That past several days had been stressful for everyone. The burning of the clinic had been hard on William and Nathaniel in particular; they were both very close to Jacob and Essie, and had always been deeply involved in the now-destroyed Mistle Village clinic.

Nathaniel had still been distraught and there had been long meetings between him and Stephen, and even with Connie Hardridge. One time, Nathaniel had asked if Quinn would like to join them, but she had refused.

On her second day back, some of Stephen's soldiers, following rumors they'd heard, had found the two assailants, hiding in the woods halfway back to the Philothean border. They'd been arrested, but the last she'd heard, they were refusing to talk. Nathaniel had told her he wasn't surprised by this, Tolliver's soldiers had likely threatened to harm the men's families if they were captured and talked.

Quinn had spent most of the week helping Charlotte, Rebecca, and Linnea with Connie and her children and the funeral preparations. William had been working with Nathaniel, Jacob, and Essie trying to salvage what they could from the burned-out clinic. She hadn't been able to spend much time with him.. They walked in silence now, enjoying the peaceful moment, the company, and the hot, tangy tea.

Neither one of them spoke until they'd passed the guard at the gatehouse.

"Are you going to go back out to the village today?" she asked.

"Yeah, I am. With the party the day after tomorrow, I'm sure I won't be able to go again until after. Do you want to come?"

"I promised Linnea and Thomas I'd help with some things for the party. Everybody's rushing around since there were so many other things going on."

He shrugged. "Taking care of the Hardridges was more important than a silly party."

She wasn't sure why his words rubbed her the wrong way, but whatever it was, she stopped and looked up at him. "Nobody is saying it isn't, Will, but you are a prince, and your eighteenth birthday is important to people, too."

He closed his eyes for a minute before he looked back at her. "I know. It's just that a party seems so... inappropriate with everything else going on around us."

"Except that it's a tradition, and if you decide something else is more important than one tradition, where do you stop? It's only by tradition that Simon is heir to the throne...and that Tolliver shouldn't be."

William's eyes widened, and she realized that her voice had taken on an edge that she hadn't meant to put there. It was just a topic that had been on her mind lately as she'd questioned her own place in the grand scheme of these "traditions."

"Sorry," she said. "I just... it'll be nice for me to celebrate with you too, you know."

His expression softened. "I am looking forward to that part." He leaned into her then, kissing her softly on the lips. She felt herself relax against him.

"Are you doing okay with all of this?" he asked. "We haven't really had much of a chance to talk."

She shrugged, torn between wanting to tell him everything, right now, and being afraid to tell him anything. How would he react if she did? And what would happen later, when everyone knew? Was it even safe for anyone to know? "So what's this surprise you have for me?" she finally asked, deciding on evasion, again.

His eyes lit up. "We're almost there," he said.

When the path reached a thick part of the woods, William suddenly led her several yards off of it, into a hidden stand of trees. She had no idea how he knew where he was.

"Where are you taking me?" she asked.

He didn't answer; he just kept walking. About a hundred yards later, he put his finger to his lips and pointed.

At first, Quinn couldn't tell what he was pointing at, but as her eyes adjusted to the dimmer light in the thick trees, the shapes became sharper, and a few feet ahead of them, nestled in a tree branch just above William's head, she could see an enormous nest. She looked at him in surprise, and he smiled.

He made a low chirruping sound, and a second later, a familiar gray-feathered head popped out of the nest, shiny black eyes blinking at the two of them in interest. It was Aelwyn, William's seeker bird. He made a different low noise, and she rose from her spot, hopped neatly over the edge of the nest, and glided down toward him, landing only about a foot away.

Now it was Aelwyn's turn to talk, and she made a strange noise, halfway between a squawk and a whistle. William laughed, and reached into his pocket, retrieving a package of beef jerky, which he opened and tore off a piece, holding it out to the bird.

Quinn had to smile at the intricate dance between William and the bird, as Aelwyn first turned her head away from the offering, and then reached to snatch it once he knelt down low to her. As soon as she'd swallowed it, she walked right up to him, butting her head against his pocket where the rest of the treat was hidden.

At that moment, there was a loud call from overhead, and then Thomas's bird, Sirian swooped down and landed gracefully near his mate. William withdrew the meat from his pocket, and tore it unevenly. Aelwyn eyed him warily until he tossed the larger piece in her direction. Sirian waited until she had hers, and then accepted the smaller piece.

After a few minutes, the birds had warmed up, and were strutting comfortably around the tiny clearing, and both of them even allowed Quinn to stroke their smooth heads. Up close, she was always startled by how gentle they were around people, though they were quite large hunting birds.

Once he was certain that they'd both let their guards down, William stood again and motioned for Quinn to follow as he walked toward the tree that held the nest. They'd almost reached it when Aelwyn and Sirian suddenly simultaneously flew up into the nest. Quinn shrank back, startled, but William shook his head.

"It's okay," he said.

Inside the nest, the two birds chattered in voices that seemed somehow amiable, and then a moment later, four smaller heads peeked over the edge, their black eyes shining curiously as they turned to examine the newcomers.

Quinn sucked in a breath. "They're beautiful," she said softly.

William nodded. "They've all just learned to fly."

Sure enough, after a moment, Aelwyn and Sirian took turns nudging gently at each of the babies until they'd climbed onto the edge of the nest. Then, one-by-one, almost as if they'd been trained, each baby took off, circling through the trees a couple of times before landing neatly in the center of the clearing.

"Amazing!" Quinn was delighted.

"You can pick one," he said.

"What?" she turned to him, completely stunned. "Me? Why?"

"You don't have one, and these fledglings are just the right age now. Aelwyn and Sirian will help you train one of them as a Seeker."

"But I... Doesn't it have to be someone who lives here? What will the bird do when I'm at home?"

He shrugged. "It's not a normal situation, true. But Aidel and Aelwyn cope okay when Nathaniel and I are gone. They're wild birds at heart."

"But what if I...?" she didn't finish her sentence, but they both heard the words that hung in the air, the question that neither of them was ready to think about or deal with. The biggest what-if of all.

William looked down at the ground. "You don't have to," he said softly.

Her heart sank. Now she'd ruined it.

She swallowed hard. "That's not what I meant, Will. I'm sorry, I... of course I would love to have one. It's so far beyond anything I would ever have expected or even thought... that would be an incredible privilege."

He was silent for a long moment before he looked back up at her. "Don't be sorry, Quinn. I should have realized how you might take it."

"Will... Really, I was just surprised, that's all. Is it really okay for someone like me to have one?"

"Yeah, Quinn. It's really okay." His eyes were still filled with disappointment, and a lump settled in her throat.

BYSTANDERS

AS SOON AS HE hit the open trail, William nudged Skittles, encouraging her to run as hard as she could. He needed the motion, the pounding hooves under him, the wind rushing past his face, to help him clear his head and collect his thoughts.

What had he been thinking, pushing Quinn like that? He'd promised her that he wouldn't…that she could have the time and the space she needed to get her own life sorted out first. He couldn't even imagine how difficult this must all be for her, and so many things had already changed for her lately.

She had apologized several times for her first reaction to his offer of a bird, and he'd done what he could to convince her that he wasn't mad at her. He was the one who had taken things too far too fast.

He'd just gotten excited…yesterday on his ride back from Mistle Village he'd been startled by the familiar sound of Aelwyn's call overhead. He'd followed her all the way back into the nest, excited at how proud she'd been to show off her tiny flock to him. It had been clear that it was her way of telling him that it was time to choose one of the babies to be trained as a companion seeker. The rest of the fledglings would soon go off on their own into the wild.

Last night, he'd told Thomas about it, and the two of them had gone to their parents with the idea of allowing Quinn to choose. He'd barely slept all night, as his mind raced further ahead than he should have allowed it to.

By the time he'd gotten up this morning, he had convinced himself that not only was he going to take her to the clearing, but to take it a step further. He'd been going to ask her if he could formally announce their courtship at his birthday celebration.

He was going to have some serious words with Thomas when he got back tonight for suggesting *that*.

If he kept pushing Quinn this hard, he was going to end up forcing her right out of his life, and the idea of losing her made his insides twist in ways he'd never known they could. He wasn't sure how it had happened, but somehow that girl had taken over the top spot on his list of priorities.

He didn't know what he would do if he lost her now…and if he wasn't careful, that was exactly what was going to happen. And it would be his fault.

He was surprised when the low outlines of the houses in Mistle Village appeared suddenly on the horizon. He'd been riding harder than he'd realized. The trip had taken him half as long as it usually did.

As he eased up on the reins, Skittles slowed to a trot, and he was glad he hadn't loaded her up with the saddle bags as he'd originally intended to. She had broken a sweat, but seemed to have enjoyed the workout as much as he had. They stopped at the river so she could have a rest and a long drink before going the rest of the way to the tent clinic on the outskirts of the village.

William paused before he entered the tent, looking off in the distance toward the burned-out site of the clinic building. From where he stood he could see several people digging through the rubble, trying to salvage what items they could, and hauling the ruined wood and debris away. They hoped to get a new building erected before the end of carperos...autumn, and at least finish the half that served as Jacob and Essie's home before days began to grow chilly.

Inside the tent, he was surprised to find Nathaniel alone with several patients. "What's going on?" he asked, looking around at what appeared to be a mother and her three young children, two boys and a girl, all of whom looked close to the same age, somewhere between six and eight cycles, though one of the boys was definitely the oldest of the three. The boys sat together on one of the two portable cots they'd set up; the younger one had a fresh bandage wrapped around his lower leg.

"Oh, hey Will," Nathaniel said, looking up from where he stood over the little girl's cot, listening to her chest with his stethoscope. "Glad you're here. This is Mara Halpern," he nodded toward the mother who stood by her daughter, "and her little girl, Clara. The boys are Wesley and Darren."

"Hello, Mrs. Halpern," William said, looking at the woman. When she turned her face to him, he was surprised at how frightened she looked, and at how dirty she was. The three children were filthy as well. "I'm William."

"Yes, hello Prince William. Please, call me Mara."

He nodded. "What's going on?" he asked again.

Mara's lower lip trembled as she glanced around at her three children.

"They just got here about ten minutes ago," Nathaniel said. "She brought them here because Darren over there fell near the fire pit and got a pretty good gash on his leg. But Clara has had a bad stomachache since yesterday, and she's been getting worse."

William looked down at the little girl for the first time. Her face was pale and sweaty; she looked like she was nauseous and hurting. He watched Nathaniel gently prod at her abdomen, and when he touched the lower right quadrant, Clara cried out. He looked up at his uncle in alarm.

Nathaniel looked at Mara, his gray eyes shining with the kindness and empathy that William strove to emulate. "We are going to take care of you and your children, Mara. Everything is okay; you're safe here. But William and I are going to step outside and talk for a minute, okay?"

The woman didn't look convinced…if anything she looked more frightened, but she nodded.

"Appendicitis?" William asked, once they were outside.

"That's what it looks like. I want to get some blood and look more closely to be sure. We just don't have half of what we need here without the clinic."

William closed his eyes, turning his head toward the sky, trying to breathe, and silently berating himself for not loading Skittles down with more supplies for the trip here. "The castle is the closest real clinic. Do you think we have time to get her there?"

Nathaniel shrugged. "I have no idea, and I don't even know what the bigger risk would be…that it'll rupture and she'll become septic on the way, or the risk of doing it out here over a dirt floor without half the supplies we need…"

"Who knows what kind of infection she could get from that," William said. "And out here we wouldn't be able to treat her as well if she did."

"So we try moving her," Nathaniel sighed. "We're going to worry that poor woman half to death. She's from Philotheum."

William's eyes popped wide. "Another one? How did she get here?"

"I guess there's another small group camping out somewhere not far from here. There are two more children, one older and one younger back at the camp with her husband. They thought we'd be less likely to harm a woman, so she brought the kids here by herself. That little boy in there has a cut that needs at least five stitches, but thank the Maker that he got hurt this morning, or she would have never brought Clara before it was too late."

William thought he might be sick. "She thinks we would hurt her husband. She's not going to trust us taking her and her kids back to the *castle*."

"I had just gotten her to trust me a little," Nathaniel said, putting his hand over the left side of his chest, where William now knew there was a tattoo that marked him as a member of the Friends of Philip. "But she looked pretty afraid again when you walked in."

"Where are Jacob and Essie?" William asked.

"Jacob is over helping at the clinic site…there was no need of him here when he left. But Essie went out to a farm about half an hour from here to help the midwife with a twin birth."

"All right, well, I'll go get Jacob while you talk to Mara. See if you can convince her to let us treat Clara at the castle."

Half an hour later, William found himself alone at the clinic with Jacob and the three Halpern children. His muscles were tight with anxiety as he looked at the little girl's gray-tinged face. He understood their mother's concern. She didn't want them to take her and her children anywhere without getting her husband first.

Although she'd decided to trust Nathaniel, she'd been wary of Jacob and William. He had seen the difficulty of the decision ravage her features just leaving the three children here while Nathaniel took her to find her husband. She'd almost taken Wesley with her, but the boys had put up a huge fuss about being separated. William, worried enough about helping Darren with his cut, had just barely convinced her to leave the brothers together.

After she left, they went to work over the little girl. Jacob tried to keep her calm while William got an IV started. Among the many other things the clinic was short on, they were out of valoris seed powder…a mild remedy that William usually used to alleviate minor pain and help keep patients calm.

Fortunately, they did have enough pain medication on hand that once the IV was in, Clara was able to fall asleep. Once she had, William helped Jacob carry some supplies outside so that he could get one of the wagons ready to serve as a temporary ambulance.

They were certain now that it was appendicitis, and though they very much wanted to get Clara to the castle clinic to perform the surgery, they talked and made plans for an emergency appendectomy here if it became necessary.

As he loaded some blankets and pillows up onto the bed of the wagon, William looked up at Jacob. "Do you think they're going to trust us long enough to get Clara back to the castle?"

Dark, heavy circles hung under Jacob's eyes. He suddenly looked so much older that it was hard for William to believe that his cousin was only five cycles his elder. "I think it's hard for anybody to trust anyone they don't know right now, Will."

William frowned. "Do you trust them?"

"I do," his cousin sighed, "but only because I saw the woman's tattoo. Half a cycle ago, the Friends of Philip was something I'd just barely heard a few stories about, and now, I'm starting to distrust anyone who doesn't wear the symbol."

William's eyes widened. "Have you joined, Jacob?"

"No. I've thought about it. I do support their mission…I want the kingdoms reunited more than anything."

"So what's stopped you?" William felt strange himself about the issue…he wasn't sure what he thought.

"I know it's bad, but when I first heard about all of it, I thought of it as a Philothean issue…they're the ones with the wrong people in the castle…why should it be our problem?"

He heard the 'but' in Jacob's voice. "What changed?"

"This!" said Jacob, throwing up his hands in the direction of the tent that now served as his clinic. "The people I've met who are Friends of Philip, who want what I want…who believe in the right thing enough that they're risking their lives for it. The first time I thought of joining, Essie and I both thought it was too dangerous. Why risk it? Why become a target if people found out?"

"You're already a target," William pointed out, glancing toward the horizon at the old clinic.

"Yeah, I am. And even if we weren't already being attacked, just for helping people, just for doing *the right thing*, Essie and I are both starting to realize that we can't just stay out of it and go about our own business, and still be the people we want to be."

William frowned. "What do you mean?"

"I mean…look at what's going on, Will. There are hundreds of these Philothean refugees now…they're huddled in these camps, they don't have the things they need, and they can't find shelter, and *why?* Most of it isn't because of a few dozen evil people from Philotheum who actually mean harm to them. It's because of all the people who 'don't want to get involved,' who just want to stay in their safe little villages and pretend that everything is okay. Or worse, they want Stephen to close the border and for the whole kingdom to look the other way from the things that are going on over there."

William swallowed hard, a strange feeling forming in the pit of his stomach. "I never thought of it that way."

"Until recently, neither did I. Now I can't stop thinking about it. This isn't the world I want my child to grow up in."

William raised an eyebrow.

"Yes, Will, Essie and I are expecting a child. We just found out, right before all of this happened."

Back inside the clinic, while Jacob finished getting the wagon ready,

William approached the two little boys, the supplies he'd readied hidden in a small, covered box.

"Hey guys," he said quietly. "Do you want to see something fun?"

Wesley, who was the oldest, eyed him warily, but nodded along with his younger brother who, even with a leg that was hurting him, was enthusiastically curious.

Even though he hadn't loaded the saddle bags this morning, William was never completely empty-handed when he arrived at a clinic. He reached into the smallleather pouch he always carried and withdrew a toy. It was a small puzzle game he'd bought in Bristlecone, a brightly-colored cube covered in small squares. He took a few minutes now to show the boys how to twist and turn it, trying to match up the colors on each side.

They were fascinated. He let them play with it for several minutes, showing them a few tricks and getting them comfortable before he patted Darren softly on the knee, just above the bandage that Nathaniel had wrapped around his leg.

"Hey buddy, can I take a look at your cut while you play?" he asked, purposefully keeping his tone light.

Darren nodded, still absorbed in the game, but Wesley's attention immediately honed in on what William was doing. He gave the protective older brother a friendly smile, but the boy relaxed only a little.

Darren whimpered when William tugged gently on a part of the bandage that had gotten stuck, and Wesley's glare turned angry. "Don't hurt my brother," he said.

"I'm just looking at it right now," William said, as he examined the cut. Nathaniel was right. It was going to need several stitches. He looked over at Wesley. "Hey, can you help me with something over here for a minute?"

"What?" the little boy asked, when William had gotten him out of his younger brother's earshot. "What are you going to do to my brother? You're not going to make him cry and then go to sleep like my sister, are you?"

William's heart did a little flip at the boy's concern. "We only gave your sister a little medicine to make her sleepy because her tummy was hurting so much," he said. "We're going to fix it soon, but right now the best thing she can do is rest. She's going to be okay."

"Will she wake up again?" Wesley asked, tears pooling at the corners of his eyes, and William's heart ached even more.

"Of course she will. Everything is going to be fine, buddy."

"Are you going to do that to my brother?" Some of the tears were starting to drip now.

"No, I'm not. He's going to stay awake, and you can stay sitting next to him the whole time to make sure, okay?"

Wesley nodded, wiping his cheek on the shoulder of his shirt. William reached into his pocket and took out a handkerchief; the motion of handing it to the little boy made him think about Quinn. He hoped she was doing all right back at the castle.

"Are Clara and Darren twins, Wesley?"

"Yes." He dabbed at his eyes with the crumpled-up cloth, sniffling.

"I thought so. Did you know that I have a brother and sister who are twins and they're just a couple of cycles younger than me?"

"You do?"

"Yup. And I love them very much, and I always try to protect them, too. You're doing a really great job as a big brother."

The look in Wesley's eyes was very slowly becoming more trusting.

"I do need your help, though Wesley. Do you think you can help me?"

"What do I have to do?"

"I need to clean out your brother's cut, and I need to fix it so it can heal the right way and it won't get infected or give him a bad scar. But I don't want to hurt him when I do that, so I need to give him some medicine to make just that little part of his leg go to sleep for a while."

Wesley raised his eyebrow skeptically. "He doesn't like medicine."

"Nobody does, Wes," William said, meeting his gaze. "And he's really not going to like this kind, because I have to use a little needle to put it just in his leg."

Wesley's eyes popped open wide.

"Yeah, I know. It will sting, and he's probably going to cry for a few minutes, but then that part of his leg will fall asleep and he will feel better. Do you think you can sit by him and hold his hand and help him keep his leg still?"

"Maybe." Wesley still looked dubious, and William had to smile.

"We're not going to talk about the needle, though, okay? Not even if you see it, although you probably won't, because I have a special way I like to hide it while I'm using it. I won't lie to him…I'll tell him when it's going to sting a little, but talking about the needle is a little scary. Can you just talk to him about other stuff, like maybe his favorite game to play or his favorite thing to eat? Can you do that for me?"

"I'll try."

William couldn't help smiling again. It was an honest answer. "Awesome. Thanks, little man."

"Prince William?"

"Yeah?"

"You're not going to stick needles in *me*, are you?"

William looked him right in the eye and smiled. "No, I'm not."

MYA'S REVELATION

QUINN WALKED BACK INTO the castle slowly after saying good-bye to William at the stable, still upset with herself for ruining his surprise. She barely gotten inside the hallway to the family's quarters when Linnea pounced on her.

"So?" Linnea said, smiling widely.

"So what?" She frowned. Had she missed something else?

"Which one did you pick?"

She felt her face and neck flush hot. "You knew?"

Linnea rolled her eyes. "Were you really under the impression that people keep secrets from me around here?"

She raised an eyebrow at her friend, "I suppose not many." Of course, Quinn knew of several secrets people were keeping from Linnea, her own included, but it wasn't like she could say anything.

"So? Which one?" Linnea's eyes shone with curiosity and excitement.

"The one that's a solid light gray color except for the patches of white on the chest and wings."

"Oooh, good choice!"

By that point they'd reached the door to Quinn's bedroom, and she was surprised to find that the door stood open. As soon as they entered, she could see why. "Do the two of you ever hang out in your own bedrooms?" she asked Thomas, who was sitting on her couch. His injured leg was propped up on her coffee table.

He shrugged. "Yours is a nice change of scenery. Besides, we were waiting for you, wanting to hear how the bird-picking went."

"You were right, T. She picked the one you thought she would."

Thomas's eyes lit up as he smiled widely. "I've been calling that one Raeyan. It's perfect for you."

"You can name it something else if you'd like, though," Linnea said hurriedly.

"I don't know; it's kind of a nice name. I don't know anything about naming seeker birds…and at least that one's a name I'm not going to have to learn how to pronounce."

Thomas chuckled. "See, Nay. I knew what I was talking about."

"Does the name mean something?" Quinn asked.

"Um… it's something like 'trusted guardian'."

"Well, that's appropriate then." She sat down in one of the armchairs and put her own feet up on the table. Her thoughts were still in a tangle; she couldn't decide whether Thomas and Linnea being in her room right now was a welcome distraction or an annoyance. After she'd sat there silently for a moment, she realized that the two of them were still looking at her expectantly.

"What?"

"Anything *else* happen on your walk?" Linnea asked.

She frowned. "Like what? We saw some rabbits, too."

"That is so not what she's asking," Thomas said. "What else happened between you and Will?"

Now she was confused. Nothing else *had* happened, at least nothing noteworthy besides her overreaction, and they didn't know about that. "I really don't know what you're talking about."

Thomas and Linnea never looked more like twins than when they both reacted the same way to something. Watching them both roll their eyes at the same time was almost comical.

"Do you think she just doesn't know that him asking her to formally announce their courtship at the party is a big deal?" Linnea asked her brother.

Suddenly the room felt like it was spinning. "What?" she managed to splutter.

Linnea's eyes widened, and pink lines spread across her cheeks. "He did ask you, didn't he?"

"He didn't ask me anything, except about the birds. *What* was he supposed to ask me?" And why did his siblings have to know everything before she did? Her heart pounded heavily in her chest as she wondered just how badly she'd upset him over the bird thing. She'd already felt terrible enough.

Both Thomas's and Linnea's faces were beet red. "Sorry, Quinn," Thomas said. "I had no idea we'd be ruining anything by saying something."

Quinn blinked furiously, as she tried to regain her composure. The pain in her chest threw her off balance. He'd been going to ask her about that and now he hadn't? What did that mean? What had she done?

"Quinn…" Linnea walked toward her, a sympathetic look in her eyes.

Suddenly, there was a soft knock at the open door, and Quinn looked up to see King Stephen standing there, looking a little concerned. She'd never before thought how nice it might be if she were a chameleon, capable of blending into the background on a moment's notice.

"Oh, hi Father," Linnea said, the red coloring in her face reaching all the way past her hairline and to the tips of her ears now. "How long have you been standing there?"

The look Stephen directed to his children right then might have made Quinn laugh if she hadn't been so mortified. "Long enough to hear the two of you crossing the boundaries of decent privacy, as usual."

They both looked down at the floor.

"I do believe there's a good deal of silver that needs polishing downstairs," Stephen said, in a tone that caused both Thomas and Linnea to slink out of the room immediately.

Once they were gone, Stephen's eyes fell back on Quinn.

"How are you?"

"I'm all right, thank you." It was a lie; she was barely holding herself together, and she'd never felt quite this awkward talking to him before.

"We haven't really had a chance to talk since you've been back."

"No, we haven't."

"Do you have a minute now?"

She nodded slowly, taking a couple of deep breaths. Her thoughts were spinning so wildly that she wasn't sure she was capable of maintaining a conversation, but she'd try.

Stephen closed the door to her room and came over to sit down on the couch that Thomas had just vacated. They both sat there for a moment, just looking at each other…she had the feeling that he wasn't quite sure what to say to her, either.

Finally, he spoke. "How are you doing with everything?"

She closed her eyes and took another deep breath before she answered. "Apparently not as well as I thought I was."

He chuckled under his breath, though his gray eyes shone with sympathy. "That sounds about right. It's a lot to take in. Nathaniel told me that Megan gave you the pendants."

"Yeah." Quinn reached deep into the pocket of the woven pants she wore for the little pouch she'd stored there. Carefully, she unclasped the safety pin that held it in place, and pulled the pouch into her hand. The pendants inside jingled together softly.

"She gave me the pendants, and Nathaniel told me the whole story. Or at least what sounds like the whole story. I'm learning that there's always some part of things I don't know about."

"It sounded like he told you most of things that are relevant. He told you who he really is and who your father was."

"Who I am," she added raising an eyebrow at the word 'relevant', but choosing to let it go for now.

"Yes. Who you are."

"Well, that's the part I'm having the most trouble with," she said. "I'm not entirely sure what I'm supposed to do with that information."

"I imagine it changes a lot of things for you, Quinn."

She looked up at him, meeting his gaze, a little wave of irritation crashing into the sides of her stomach. "Is that what it's supposed to do? Change everything for me?"

He sighed, his expression shifting to one that looked almost...*guilty?* "I don't know the answer to that. There's nothing about this situation that's the way it's 'supposed' to be. Or at least, the way I wish it was. I said something to Alvin once, about not knowing what I was supposed to do about any of this, and he told me that there's no such thing as *supposed* to...that there is only whatever situation is in front of us today, and the choices we make in dealing with it."

"So what do I do now then? What choice do I make?"

"Ultimately, that decision is up to you. No one else can choose for you."

The anger rushed in so fast it took her by surprise; she didn't even know where it came from. "I keep hearing that. Everyone says 'the choice is mine,' but it doesn't feel that way. It feels like everyone else has been deciding everything for me my whole life, and now they're waiting on me to make some kind of 'choice' that's really going to be what they wanted the whole time. What is it I'm supposed to be deciding, exactly, Stephen? I don't even know! What are my choices?"

His face was red now, and there was a definite look of guilt in his eyes. He was silent for several minutes, watching her closely as she tried to calm herself, by taking deep breaths.

She raised her eyebrow, and he finally spoke. "I don't know if I can even answer that question and be fair to you, Quinn. I'm trying to be as honest as I can here, but I'm not a neutral party in this. The Maker knows I've tried, I've done my best to sit back, to stay out of your way so that in the end the decision you make is really yours. But I have a stake in this. And I've already interfered more than it was my right to."

"Interfered *how?* You're not the one who told me any of this, you're kept it from me as much as anyone."

Stephen looked down at the floor, avoiding eye contact with her, and cold trickles of fear seeped into her chest.

"I interfered with your mother, even against your father's wishes, prohibiting her from taking you out of Bristlecone."

She nodded…she'd known about that, but she had a niggling feeling that that wasn't all he was talking about.

"But at least that helped Nathaniel to be able to know you, and left the door open to your making your own choices eventually. And, honestly, I never fully agreed with Samuel's decision to keep everything from you. The much bigger interference of course, the one that crossed the line, really…that I sacrificed my own son's choices for…was when I sent William to Bristlecone to be near you."

Quinn's blood turned to ice in her veins. "You did that because of *me?* Not for him to study medicine?"

"That *was* a big reason, and it's certainly the only reason *he* ever knew about. But no. We could have found other ways for him to gain that knowledge here, maybe not as in-depth, but I'm not sure we could have brought ourselves to let him go there at such a young age for that reason alone."

"But why? Why would you send William to be near me? I never really even *knew* him in Bristlecone."

Stephen sighed. "It's complicated, Quinn."

A sudden flash of intuition nearly knocked her out of her chair. "This was your plan all along, wasn't it? I'd meet William, find the gate, and learn about my real world... and then what, Stephen? I fulfill this prophecy you claim not to care about? I marry your son and take over the Philothean throne, re-unite the kingdoms?"

Stephen wouldn't make eye contact with her; his face grew even redder, and she felt her muscles constrict in rage. "Are you serious?" she asked in a low, cold voice.

"I told you I'm not a neutral party. And I'm human. I don't always make the choices that are the right ones. I know I shouldn't have. That my only responsibility was to wait on the Maker. I justified it by telling myself I wasn't actually forcing anyone to make a certain choice. But I did stack the deck, yes."

"You 'stacked the deck.' Like a *card game?* So it's some kind of a game to you? My *life?* William's life?"

His Adam's apple bobbed up and down twice before he managed to choke out an answer. "No, it isn't a game. But it is what I did." He stared out the window now, still avoiding looking directly at her.

"Are you apologizing?" she asked.

He finally looked at her, with an expression she couldn't begin to understand. "I don't know if I'm sorry."

Quinn stormed out of the castle, her heart racing, and tears streaming down her cheeks. She couldn't remember ever having been so angry before in her life. Everything...her whole life, the time she'd spend in Eirentheos, her relationship with William...had all been a set-up. Something planned by someone else.

She thought about going and getting Dusk, or about heading back into the woods where William had taken her this morning, but she knew she would have to deal with servants in the stable or the guard at the gatehouse to get to either of those places, and she couldn't do that in her current state. So instead, she retreated to the farthest corner of the castle gardens, well past the gazebo and the flower beds, and she found a small stone bench near a wall.

Though she'd been crying already, as soon as she collapsed onto the bench, the sobbing began in earnest. Past rational already, her thoughts became a soundless, incoherent blur, as she cried and cried until she ran out of tears. Or at least she thought she had, because when she'd finally stopped, she pulled the handkerchief out of her pocket, and when she saw William's initials embroidered in the corner, a fresh stream started.

Eventually, though, she really did cry herself out, and she sat there on the bench, feeling too drained to think anymore, too numb to move, and she just stared at the neatly-trimmed bushes a few feet away from her.

She almost jumped out of her skin when one of them moved.

Quinn stared at the bush, trying to figure out what she had seen. It had only barely quivered, and she'd almost decided that it had just been a small animal stirring inside, when she suddenly saw a small pair of brown-leather Mary Jane shoes poking out at the bottom.

She sighed, wondering how long Alice had been sitting over there. Wiping her eyes one more time, and blowing her nose before stuffing the handkerchief back into her pocket, Quinn stood and walked around the large bush.

The little girl was sitting there on a tree stump ringed with flowers, a large notebook in her lap, and a pouch of colored pencils open beside her. She didn't look up until Quinn was standing directly in front of her.

"Hi Quinn," she said, before looking down again to exchange a blue colored pencil for a green one.

Quinn raised an eyebrow. "How long have you been out here, Alice?"

"I don't know," Alice answered, beginning to fill in some of the leaves she'd traced. Quinn recognized the bush in her drawing. "I can't tell time yet."

Her answer made Quinn chuckle. Alice's eyes met Quinn's. "Are you all right?"

"Yes, sweetheart. I'm fine."

"Why were you crying?"

Quinn swallowed. "You saw that?"

Alice nodded. "I saw you were crying when you were going outside."

"You've been out here the whole time?" She was startled.

"Yes." Now the green pencil went carefully back into the pouch and a pink one came out. Apparently undisturbed, Alice began sketching out the pink flowers that dotted the base of the bush.

"Isn't somebody going to be wondering where you are?"

Alice looked up at her again. "I told Emma I was going outside with you. I'm sure she told someone."

Quinn closed her eyes. If she'd told Emma, then surely everyone in the castle knew the little girl was with her by now. "How old are you now, Alice? Four?"

"Five," the little girl said, without looking up from her drawing. "I had my birthday when you were gone."

"I'm sorry I missed it."

Alice looked up at her, all wide gray eyes behind her glasses. "Maybe you can come to the next one."

Quinn smiled, lowering herself down onto her knees in front of the tree stump. "Maybe I will, Alice. I would like that very much."

"You're going to William's birthday party, aren't you?"

"Sure I am."

Alice's eyes penetrated hers now, with a depth that surprised her. "William really missed you when you were gone, you know."

"I know. I missed him, too."

"He was scared you might not come back."

"Did he tell you that?"

"No, he just looked worried when he talked about it. But I told him you would come back and go to his birthday. And you did." A tiny smile appeared on her serious little face.

"You were right." Quinn had to swallow down the hot sensation that rose in her throat at the image of William looking worried as he talked to his little sister.

"Emma says he loves you."

Heat flooded her cheeks.

"But I told Emma it's none of her business."

"Emma thinks everything is her business," Quinn chuckled thinking of spunky little Emma, who reminded her of a boisterous combination of Thomas and Linnea.

There was a little twinkle in Alice's eye. "So does Linnea."

Quinn couldn't help giggling. "You're right, she does."

The pink pencil went back to work, meticulously shading the petals of the flowers. "I think you love William, too, Quinn."

Quinn swallowed hard, her eyes sweeping over the little girl, so intense, sitting with her legs curled up beside her, the skirt to her blue dress smoothed neatly over them. "I definitely love you, Alice," she said, kissing her on the top of her head.

"I love you, too, Quinn."

After her conversation with Alice, Quinn took the little girl back upstairs in the castle. She was calmer now, but needed time to process what had just happened. She sincerely hoped that her bedroom was empty…as much as she loved both Thomas and Linnea, she wasn't prepared to deal with them again right now. What she wanted was a hot bath with lavender and vanilla oil.

But, although there was no sign of Thomas or Linnea in the upstairs wing, when she reached her room, it wasn't empty.

"Is everything all right, Lady Quinn?" Mia looked up from where she was putting neatly folded clothes into the armoire.

"I'm okay, Mia," she answered, knowing that her blotchy face gave her away. "How are you?" she asked, trying to shift the conversation.

"I'm well. I'm just trying to catch up on some tasks I've gotten behind on."

"You've been a little busy lately, haven't you?" she asked wryly. Mia had been spending *a lot* of time with Thomas.

A splash of pink colored the girl's cheeks, but she met Quinn's gaze. "As have you, Lady Quinn. How are things with William?"

Touché. The fact that the sweet maid seemed to have caught Thomas's eye should have alerted Quinn to the likelihood that there was more spunk hidden under Mia's quiet demeanor than she had guessed.

It had always been almost too easy to talk to Mia, though. "I don't know," she found herself saying. "Things have been really wonderful…until I think I messed them up today."

Mia raised an eyebrow. "This is about William asking if the two of you could make your courtship official?"

Quinn swallowed hard, but nodded. "Except he didn't ask."

"Do you really think he didn't ask because he'd changed his mind about it?"

She blinked. That possibility sounded a lot more absurd coming out of Mia's mouth than it had swirling around inside her mind, all muddled up with her insecurities. "No. He probably didn't ask because he was afraid I'd be upset or that I'd think he was pushing me."

Mia's bright green eyes were gentle and sympathetic. "I don't think you've 'messed things up,' Lady Quinn. I think that you and Master William are both doing the best you can in a complicated situation."

Something in Mia's voice caught Quinn off-guard. She frowned, scrutinizing Mia's expression, suddenly realizing that Mia knew more than she should have. Possibly far more, but Quinn decided to start with the simplest issue first. "How do you know what happened with William and I this afternoon already? Thomas and Linnea haven't come back up yet."

When Mia's eyes fell to the floor almost instantly, Quinn's intuition flashed. "What do you know, Mia?"

Trembling, Mia moved the basket of clothes and sank down onto the ottoman. "I've known some things for a while, Lady Quinn…had suspicions about others. But today…" She looked up for a brief second, apprehension in her eyes before she looked down again, pulling her thick, black braid over her shoulder and fidgeting nervously with the end. "I was trying to get some chores finished earlier, and visiting with Thomas and Linnea at the same time. I'd just gone back into your bathroom to put away towels and tidy up when you came upstairs."

She frowned, trying to understand, and then dread froze her muscles as she realized what Mia meant. "Earlier? You were in there earlier? The whole time?"

Mia's nod was almost imperceptible. "I wasn't trying to eavesdrop. I just… I didn't want to barge in on you…"

Nausea twisted her gut. *Mia had heard everything.* Not just about William and the birds. There hadn't been time for her to escape once Stephen was in the room.

"Before…" Mia's voice shook. "Before you get overly worried, may I show you something?"

Quinn was too deeply in shock to do anything but nod.

Mia straightened, and then reached for the collar of her navy-blue work dress. Quinn stared, stunned, knowing what she was about to see before Mia had managed to pull her dress far enough to the side to reveal her tattoo.

"What?" she breathed. "Why? How long have you…"

"As soon as I turned sixteen, I joined. My family has worked in the castle for three generations."

"Really?" she realized that she'd never asked about Mia's past or her family.

"Oh, yes. My mother attends personally to Charlotte and Stephen. Before that, she attended the children, as I do now. My father is a guard, but his mother had this job before my mother or I did. Both my grandmother and my mother attended your father when he lived here, in the castle."

Quinn's eyes were wide. "It's supposed to be a secret, Mia! I haven't even told William yet. Or Thomas or Linnea. Are there more people who know?"

"I know it's a secret, my Lady. Until today...I knew about Samuel, that he hadn't died in Philotheum as most believe. I didn't know that his heir really existed, and of course I had no idea it was you. Although I'll tell you now that Thomas has at least some idea that there's more going on than you've shared. He's not certain if you even know what, but he has begun to believe that Samuel and Nathaniel were from Philotheum. He knows that I'm a Friend of Philip, and that I know a lot about the resistance, or else he wouldn't have shared with me as much as he knows... but he has no idea about many of the things *I* know. I've known about Samuel...and Nathaniel, too, of course...for a long time, but until today I never really believed..."

"Do you know anything about Eldon Hardridge?"

Mia closed her eyes, her features taking on a grayish hue. "Yes. Most of us in the Friends of Philip here in the castle believe he was persecuted and followed because he knows about Samuel and Nathaniel. It is what he believed, as well. He had no idea anyone had followed him into Eirentheos this far, though. He would never have put Jacob and Essie in danger like that."

It was hard to breathe. Quinn sank down onto the couch and put her head in her hands.

Mia came over and sat beside her. "I won't say a word, Lady Quinn. Not to anyone, I promise."

Quinn looked up into Mia's eyes, which seemed to be filled with sympathy even more than knowledge, and she knew, somehow that she could trust the girl. "So you heard what Stephen did? The position he put both William and me in?"

Mia nodded. "I did. And I don't agree with it, but it seems to have worked out all right in the end."

"Really?" Her anger flashed again. "You think this is all right?"

Mia shrugged, seemingly unconcerned with the sarcasm in Quinn's voice. "Do you regret meeting William?"

That stopped her cold. The answer came without thinking; even the idea of not knowing William now was like a knife in her chest. "No. But that doesn't make what Stephen did okay."

"It doesn't. But he can't change it now, Lady Quinn. And it's your own reaction to the situation that will determine the outcome now. In the end, he didn't force either of you to do anything. I'll be honest. I love seeing you and Prince William together. The two of you… What's there is not there because of what Stephen did. You can't let someone else's bad decision change what's growing between you."

Quinn nodded, although she still had no idea what to think or how to respond. Now she *really* needed some time to herself.

"It has been a challenging day so far, Lady Quinn. Can I draw you a bath?"

Even in the hot water, with the comforting scents filling the air around her, it took a long time for her muscles to loosen, and her thoughts to begin to unsnarl. She thought about the things that Stephen had told her. It still angered her that he had so deliberately put William in the position he had, but slowly she realized that Mia was right. That didn't have to get in the way of how things were now between her and William.

And, in a way, so what if Stephen and Charlotte had always hoped that she and William would end up together? It wasn't as if they'd forced it to happen. The relationship had bloomed all on its own. It wasn't really any different than her mom and Maggie hoping she'd choose Zander.

Even as she calmed, and some of her anger dissipated, she ached inside for William. The sacrifices he had made to spend all those years in Bristlecone had been enormous and difficult. It had hurt him to spend so much time away from his family and to feel so isolated.

And he'd made the sacrifices without even knowing all of the reasons. And it might have never paid off in the end for him at all. It still might not.

This morning she had hurt him again, and she resolved now that she wasn't going to do that anymore. So there were a lot of questions that she didn't have the answers to right now. How she felt about him wasn't one of them. And neither was the way he felt about her. As soon as he got back from Mistle Village, she was going to tell him that she was ready to make their courtship official.

And now that she was truly aware of just how fragile the secret about her father was, she knew it was time…she had to tell William.

TRUST

RELIEF FLOWED THROUGH WILLIAM as the castle gate appeared before their small caravan. He and Nathaniel huddled around little Clara Halpern in the back of the wagon, and she wasn't doing well. They needed to get her into the clinic and get the surgery started *now*.

As they drove on to the main bridge leading to the castle, Nathaniel stood and climbed up onto the wagon seat next to Clara's father, Josiah, who had been driving. Taking the reins from the man, Nathaniel slowed only slightly when they reached the guard stand. "We're going to the clinic," he called to the guards inside. "Please help everyone else with the horses, and then bring them down to meet us."

William looked up in time to see Ben, a guard whom he'd recently gotten to know rather well when they'd traveled together, nod and step outside to assist the rest of the family and some friends of theirs from Mistle Village who'd agreed to ride the horses back and accompany them on the journey.

"Let my mother know there are additional guests for dinner," he yelled, hoping Ben could still hear him.

"I'm sure someone will take care of that," Nathaniel said, driving the wagon down to the clinic at the far corner of the castle.

As soon as they'd reached the small building, Nathaniel and Josiah hopped down, and rushed to lower the gate at the back of the wagon.

"William, please go on inside and start getting things set up. We'll get her inside, and I will talk to her parents." Nathaniel said.

He nodded and hopped over the side of the wagon, running up the stairs into the clinic, and making his way to the small operatory in the back. They didn't need to use it very often, but kept it ready just in case. William flipped on the lights and began scrubbing the small table in the middle of the room.

"Is there anything I can help with?" He jumped, startled. He hadn't heard anyone come into the clinic yet.

"Quinn!" he said, turning around. "What are you doing out here already? We just got back."

She nodded. "I was waiting for you to come back. I saw you rushing around and I came to help if you needed it. So what can I do?"

"Grab one of those sheets over there and help me get this table covered."

"What's going on?" she asked, as she helped him shake out the sheet.

"We've got a little girl with appendicitis. We should have operated in Mistle Village, but without the clinic it's so dangerous..."

At that moment, they heard Nathaniel's voice in the clinic. William glanced through the door and saw him carrying Clara as gently as he could. Her parents followed him, both looking white and shaken. Tears streamed down Mara's face. A second later, Jacob appeared in the doorway.

"Will," Nathaniel's expression was pleading as he carried the little girl into the operatory. "Let Jacob and I take care of Clara, and you handle Mr. and Mrs. Halpern and the children, please?"

He felt Quinn's eyes on him.

"They don't trust me, Nathaniel."

"They do now…after you took care of Darren. And the boys know you and trust you. They'll let you get them into the castle and cleaned up and fed."

William sighed, but he nodded. The idea of performing surgery on a child still made him anxious anyway. He had only assisted in a few similar procedures so far.

Quinn followed him out into the main room of the clinic while Jacob walked around them and into the operating room.

Mara and Josiah Halpern were standing in the middle of the room, looking lost and helpless. Through the window, he could see their other children wandering around near the wagon. Although Wesley still hovered over him protectively, Darren looked almost completely recovered from his earlier trauma, although his dirt-caked face was streaked from the tears he'd shed earlier, and sticky, too, from the copious amounts of candy William had rewarded him with once the stitches were in.

"Is Clara going to be okay?" Mara asked anxiously.

"It's scary, I know, Mara. But I'm sure she's going to be fine. Nathaniel and Jacob will take good care of her. We have the right medicines here. She'll be asleep the whole time, and she won't feel anything. You'll need to stay here with her for a few days while she recovers, though."

He was surprised by how wide both of their eyes grew at this news. Mara and Josiah looked at each other, terror plain in their expressions. He frowned. "You're safe here, you know. No harm will come to your family here at the castle."

The look on Josiah's face was not trusting at all. "What are you worried about?" William asked.

He saw the man's hand reach protectively over the left side of his chest, where he assumed a tattoo hid under his shirt.

"He's worried we'll be arrested," Mara answered, though her husband was shooting her a look that clearly indicated he wished she wouldn't speak. "We've heard stories, about others."

A weight settled in William's chest. "Those stories aren't true Josiah. The only arrests that have been made in Eirentheos are to those who have done our people harm. We have arrested some for poisoning our children, for burning homes and clinics. But not for escaping to safety with their children."

"In Philotheum, the Friends of Philip are being blamed for everything. When we first decided to leave, we believed it was different in Eirentheos. But we kept hearing rumors..." Josiah slumped into one of the chairs along the front wall of the room.

William sighed. Simon had told him about some of the rumors. "We believe those rumors are being spread by those against your cause...others coming across the border from Philotheum and targeting the border towns and the refugee camps. They want to weaken the Friends of Philip. My father and my oldest brother believe that in a way it's a positive sign, an indication that the resistance is gaining in strength and power, and those who are against the cause are starting to see it as a real threat."

Quinn looked at him in interest...he hadn't yet shared this with her.

"So it is true that King Stephen supports the resistance - the Friends of Philip?"

"Yes, Josiah, he does...as do I. Our goals are the same as yours...to see a proper heir on the throne of Philotheum, and to restore the brotherhood that our kingdoms rightfully share. And our goal here, tonight, is the same as yours as well. To see your family cared for, clean and fed, and for your beautiful little girl to be healthy again. You are not in danger here. Can you trust me, please?"

"I don't see that we have any other choice right now." Josiah answered.

William closed his eyes and took a deep breath. "Fair enough," he said. "I'm sure that the two of you would like to stay here, and be with Clara as soon as they are finished. If you will allow it, we will take the other children up to the castle and help them get bathed and fed. Later we can bring them back, or take you up to them. As long as the surgery is uncomplicated, we'll be able to take Clara up to an apartment in the castle tonight where she can stay with you and we can care for her there."

Quinn and William had almost made it to the door to go outside to the children when Josiah came up behind them. "Prince William?" he said in a low voice.

"Yes?" he turned, surprised. Something in the man's tone made him feel the need to step slightly in front of Quinn.

"I do trust you now, thank you. But I'm going to warn you…it wasn't so wise for you to just trust me. You should have asked to see my tattoo, and my wife's as well."

"What?" William's eyes widened and his heart rate accelerated.

Josiah pulled back the collar of his shirt, revealing the design, an intricate coupling of the seals of Eirentheos and Philotheum. He noticed again that some of the details in the pattern were oddly raised. "You can trust us, too…but I'm telling you to be more careful, please. Always be certain of who you are talking to, even if you think you know."

Still feeling strange, and his heart still beating faster than normal, William nodded, then turned and led Quinn out of the clinic.

Although they spent much of the evening together, caring for the Halpern children, it wasn't until much later in the evening that Quinn finally had the chance to speak to William alone. She was in the common room with Linnea and Thomas. They'd eaten dinner in there with the children while Nathaniel and William were getting Clara settled in a guest apartment with her parents.

Now they were playing a game of Choice while sort of keeping an ear on the shrieks and giggles coming from the playroom across the hall. Every few minutes one of the younger children ran in, needing something. Quinn had just finished tying the back of a dress-up costume for Emma and was watching her skip back to play when William walked past the door.

She turned to look at Thomas and Linnea. "I'm going to go talk to Will," she said, setting her cards face-down on the table.

"Sure, leave when I'm winning," Thomas teased, grinning.

Quinn rolled her eyes. "Hey, Josh!" she called across the room, to where Joshua sat in a chair, absorbed in a book. He'd come upstairs only a few minutes ago. "Why don't you come play my hand and take Thomas down a peg?"

At thirteen cycles, Joshua was next in line after Thomas and Linnea. They often treated him as if he were still younger than he was, but Quinn knew that he loved to be included when they did things. She was right; he grinned and came right over.

She found William just outside the doorway to his bedroom. He looked exhausted, and there were still tiny spatters of blood on the leg of his pants. She almost turned around before he saw her; she wasn't sure this was the right time to bother him…maybe tomorrow when he'd rested, but he must have heard her approaching, because he looked up when she was still a few feet away.

She was startled by the violent little stutter in her heartbeat when his eyes lit up.

"Hey," he said walking her direction and meeting her halfway.

"Hi," she suddenly found it difficult to speak over the sound of her heart pounding in her ears.

He smiled. "Want to come in for a minute?" he asked, walking back toward his bedroom door.

She nodded, following him inside and over to one of the large, overstuffed sofas in front of the fireplace. They never spent much time in William's bedroom…he worried about impropriety when they were alone, and it just somehow wasn't a room where they spent much time when they were hanging out with his siblings.

His room was easily the most eclectic out of everyone's bedrooms. On her first trip to the castle, Quinn hadn't even known he had his own room. He rarely slept here, preferring to be with Thomas when he was home. This room was more just a private space where he studied and worked, or retreated to when he wanted time alone. Huge, built-in bookcases lined an entire wall, filled with a crazy variety of books from both her world and his. Several shelves held devices and toys that he'd clearly brought back with him. There were more than a couple of empty candy wrappers, too – the packets of Skittles always made her smile. The two big bags of them she'd purchased as the only birthday present she could think of were stowed carefully in the bottom drawer of her armoire.

A long table under the window served as a mini-laboratory. There were three microscopes, and an assortment of test tubes, bottles, jars, and many things Quinn couldn't even identify.

"How are you?" William asked, as she curled up at the end of the couch.

"I'm good," she said, though her heart still fluttered nervously. "How is Clara?"

"The surgery went very well, and she's going to be fine. I think they'll all be much better after a couple good nights of sleep." He sat down on the other end of the sofa from her, sighing and leaning his head back into the cushion. "What have you been up to this evening?"

"Helping out with the kids, but..." her heart pounded a little more furiously now, "mostly I've been waiting to talk to you."

His face fell, and her stomach gave a sickening lurch. What was wrong? What had she said now?

"Quinn... I'm always going to be busy like this. I thought you realized that. I can't always be around every time you want to talk."

Oh. Tears threatened at the corners of her eyes, and the sick feeling spread outward from her stomach, as she fought back the urge to flee. She had almost decided to make her exit when, suddenly, she understood. She didn't know *how* she knew, but she did. She understood William's reaction perfectly. *You can do this.* Of course he was defensive. She'd pushed at him once already this morning, and now he was exhausted. As her heartbeat thundered in her ears again, she looked up at him, meeting his eyes.

"Will," she said softly, "I know that." She moved, sliding herself across the couch until she was sitting on the cushion next to him. Curling her legs up under herself, she faced him. Her hands were shaking, so she hid them in her lap. "I know you were busy. I'm not upset that you were, okay? I wasn't upset. I wasn't impatient. I was just waiting."

His expression softened a little, and she took another deep breath.

"I might have been busy all night, Quinn. I'll probably be going back to check on Clara again in a little while."

She nodded, still looking him in the eye. "I know." Steadying herself as much as she could, she reached for his hand. She hadn't realized just how nervous she was about the gesture until the relief when he reached back toward her nearly knocked her over.

She looked down at his hand, nestling her fingers in with his, before she looked back up at his face. "It's what I wanted to talk you about, Will. I'm here, okay? If it would have taken you all night, or until tomorrow, or *whatever...whenever* you come back, I want you to come back to me."

Although his expression was even softer now, she could see surprise in his eyes. He reached to take her other hand in his. "What are you saying, Quinn?"

She closed her eyes for a moment, trying to get the right words in her head. Another deep breath…it would be best to start at the beginning.

"Look, Will, I know I hurt you this morning, that I ruined your surprise."

"Quinn, you didn't…"

She shook her head and reached up, touching her finger to his lips. "I did. You have been unendingly patient with me, and I don't know if you even realize how much that means to me."

His mouth twitched again, and she raised her eyebrow. "Just listen. I know what the reality of this situation is. Actually, after today, there's a lot more we're going to need to talk about. But I want to tell you this part first. Whatever else happens, I know that what I really want is you. I want to know you. At the end of the day, you're the one I want to tell everything to…even if it's the next day."

William moved closer now, and she could feel his hands trembling in hers. "We don't know…" he started.

"I know we don't. But I've been thinking about this. And the thing is, I don't want to miss this time with you just because of what *might* happen. I want to be with you and we can just see what happens together."

He blinked, a hint of moisture in the corners of his eyes. "That's what I want too, Quinn. I feel like I've spent my whole life holding back, not really getting involved in anything. And you were right, in the end all that's really done is it's made me miss out on time I could have been enjoying with people I care about."

He paused, and she saw him swallow a couple of times. Although seeing him like this put a strange heat in her own throat, she squeezed his hand reassuringly.

"I was going to ask you today if it would be all right with you if we made our courtship official. I want to tell my family about us, and I would like to formally escort you at my birthday celebration."

She nodded, her thudding heartbeat taking on an entirely new pattern "I would like that very much, Will." And she leaned in this time to kiss him, her bottom lip grazing his top one as his hands found their way around her back.

Neither one of them wanted to pull away; even after the kiss ended, they sat there for several minutes, her forehead against his cheek as their fingers wound and unwound. Finally, though, he leaned back far enough to be able to look into her eyes.

"What did you mean when you said 'after today there's a lot more we're going to need to talk about'?"

She sighed, pulling her knees up to her chest. "Of course you heard that."

He raised an eyebrow, reaching for her hand again.

"Give me a minute," she said, taking a deep breath. She stood and walked around the room, needing to expel some of the sudden nervous energy that had overtaken her.

"Quinn! What's wrong?" William asked, concerned now, standing and walking over to her.

She couldn't make her mouth form the words, she had no idea where to start or how much to say. Trying to collect herself, she stared at the pattern in the parquet floor so intently that the lines and shapes began to blur together.

"Okay, Quinn, you're worrying me here. What is going on? If we need to talk about something, then just tell me. I'm sorry I overreacted a minute ago, but I'm not going anywhere. I need you to trust me, please."

Just before the lines in the floor disappeared entirely, she realized that she was making this harder than she had to. She took a deep breath. There was no way she could keep this from him forever anyway. And he was right…she needed to trust him. For the second time that day, she reached into her pocket and withdrew the little drawstring pouch.

He frowned when he saw the little bag in her hand. "What…?" he started to ask, but she lifted her finger, shaking her head.

After carefully easing the ties open, she turned the pouch over, and the pendants fell into her hand.

William gasped before he'd even picked one up to look at it more closely. "One is yours, isn't it?" he asked.

She nodded, picking up the shinier one and laying it in his outstretched hand. "The other one is my father's." That one she held between her thumb and forefinger, rubbing it nervously.

William didn't speak as he held the pendant up into the light, examining it carefully on both sides. All of the color had drained from his face, and his hands began to shake visibly, the tiny chain of the pendant vibrating against the back of his hand.

"Quinn Katriel *Rose*," he finally breathed, in a voice that was almost inaudible.

She nodded.

He looked at her now, shock the most dominant emotion in his eyes. "You're the rightful heir to the throne."

She nodded again.

They stood there for several minutes, William turning the pendant over and over in his hand until Quinn started to feel dizzy. "I think… I need to sit back down," she whispered.

Without a word, he followed her back to the couch, where they sat in silence again, for what felt like a very long time.

Finally, he took a deep breath. "How long have you known?"

"My mom just gave me the pendants when I went home a few days ago."

He was quiet again, and her throat started to feel very tight; she had trouble pulling in a deep breath. Her knees came back up to her chest, and the longer he was silent, the tighter she curled into her ball. "Are you mad at me?" she managed to squeak.

Instantly, his expression unfroze, and he turned his entire body toward her. His eyes swept over her, taking in her posture, and in the next second he was sitting next to her, gently reaching deep into the ball to put his hand over her heart.

"Hey," he said, in a voice so gentle it made the tears that had been hiding behind her eyes begin to pour, without warning, down her cheeks. "Quinn, of course I'm not mad at you. Why would I be mad at *you* about this?"

She shrugged, still huddled tight behind her knees. "Because I didn't tell you right away? Because it doesn't make any sense? Because…because what in the *hell* am I supposed to do about this, Will?"

After he'd walked Quinn back to her room, William did not go to check on Clara as he'd told her he was going to. If Nathaniel wanted to keep secrets like *this* from him, he could take care of a patient for a while on his own, too.

How could Nathaniel…his parents…anyone else who knew about this keep it from him for this long?

He'd glanced into the sitting room and the play room when he'd walked by and seen that they were both empty…everyone had migrated to their bedrooms for the night. *Good.* He walked all the way to the end of the hallway and stopped just outside the door to his parents' private apartment. He knocked…three sharp raps on the door…and then waited. He knew they would still be awake.

His mother answered the door, already in her dressing gown, his baby sister curled in her arms.

"Will!" Charlotte said, surprised. "What's going on?"

Before he could answer, his father appeared behind her. "I'm guessing he needs to talk, Charlotte. Come on in, Son."

THE BIRTHDAY PARTY

"THAT SHOULD NOT BE allowed."

Quinn turned from her spot in front of the mirror in her bedroom to see Thomas standing in the open doorway. She raised an eyebrow. "What?"

"You, looking like that. It should be expressly against the law. Nobody will be able to pay attention to anything else tonight."

She blushed. "I'm sure that's not true."

He walked across the room to stand next to her. All day yesterday and today he'd been practicing walking without using his crutches at all. She was impressed how well he was already doing.

Thomas raised an eyebrow at her reflection in the mirror. "Not true? Have you looked at yourself?"

She looked. It *was* a pretty dress, the full skirt overlaid with a crisscross of purple velvet strips with complex flowers cut out of them. The top was form-fitting and simple, held up by lacy spaghetti straps. Mia had spent over an hour braiding her auburn hair in an intricate pattern until it hung just right at the nape of her neck.

She turned to Thomas. "You clean up pretty nicely yourself."

He grinned. "That's never been a secret," he said, shaking his shoulders so that the purple velvet cape he wore rippled down his back.

Quinn rolled her eyes. "I thought you were escorting Mia? You won't be paying attention to her?"

"That's a given. I haven't seen her yet; I'm picking her up in her room on the way there. I know she did that to your hair, so really it's a compliment to her."

"I hope so," Quinn said, punching him lightly on the arm. "She was quite excited when she left here to get herself ready."

"Found it!" Linnea called, as she came back into the room, holding up a tube of lipstick Quinn had once brought her from Bristlecone. "It's the final touch."

"I can do it myself, you know," Quinn said as Linnea stood in front of her, brandishing the make-up.

"You won't use enough if I let you do it," Linnea answered.

"There's a fine line between your version of enough, and looking like a clown in the circus," Quinn said.

"What's a circus?" Linnea asked.

She sighed and stood still, allowing Linnea to have her fun. Although she liked to tease her friend, she had discovered that Linnea actually knew what she was doing when it came to make-up, unlike Quinn, who felt hopeless most of the time when it came to stuff like that.

"Thomas and Linnea, it's about time to be getting downstairs," Rebecca called from the doorway.

"We'll be there in a minute," Linnea said.

Thomas looked at Quinn. "Really, sweetheart, you look beautiful. We'll see you in a few minutes?"

She nodded, suddenly feeling like she had no idea what she was doing. "Provided I don't fall on my face on the stairs."

"Not going to happen; I'll be holding your arm," William said, coming into the room.

"Will." Her lips broke into a grin, her heart skipping a beat at the sight of him in his formalwear…perfectly pressed black pants, a crisp, white button-down shirt, and the purple velvet cape fastened at the neck with a silver pin bearing the symbol of Eirentheos. The silver of his wire-framed glasses looked as if it was made to match.

Relief, too, overtook her as he entered the room. It was the first time she'd seen him today; he'd left early this morning to do something, and knowing how William often disappeared like that when he was upset about something, she'd spent a good part of the day nervous, wondering if it had anything to do with her. Yesterday, too, there had been so much for everyone to do with party preparations and he'd been so busy with Clara Halpern and her family, that she hadn't really had the chance to talk to him, to see how he was really feeling about what she'd told him the other night.

"Wow," he said, coming to stand in front of her and taking her hand in his. The look in his eyes melted her anxiety away almost instantly. "You're so beautiful, Quinn."

Heat flowed from the top of her head all the way to her toes, bringing with it a new kind of feeling, a certainty about him that she hadn't fully felt before. She stared into his warm, gray eyes, seeing so clearly who he was, and understanding how she felt about him. As strange as this whole situation was…this part, with him, was right.

Thomas and Linnea grinned at each other. "We'll see you downstairs," Thomas said, leaning over to plant a kiss on the top of Quinn's head before he hobbled out of the room after his sister.

William watched as they disappeared through the door, and then turned back to her. "I have something for you," he said, reaching inside his pants pocket.

Her breath quickened as he pulled out a little purple pouch. "What is it?"

"Open it," he said, setting it in her outstretched hand. The crushed velvet was impossibly soft and light sitting on her palm while William untied the satin drawstrings.

Reaching inside, she pulled out a delicate silver chain. It was too small to be a necklace…

"It's a bracelet," he said, "a traditional courtship gift. I had it made so you could wear it tonight."

Hands shaking, heart hammering, she held it up in the light so she could see it more closely. Suspended in the center of the chain was a small silver band. On one side of the band were his initials, and the symbol on his pendant, the ameliorosa flower. The reverse held Quinn's initials, QRR, and an engraving of a rose.

She looked up at him, her eyebrows knitting together.

"I figured it was best for now, to keep the name you're used to. We can always have it changed if you make a different decision."

"And the rose?"

He shrugged, slipping the chain around her wrist and fastening the clasp. "It seemed… appropriate."

She rubbed her thumb over the design. "I guess it kind of is. I feel bad now. This is much nicer than what I have for you, and it's your birthday." Feeling awkward now, she stared down at her wrist, watching the little silver bar dangle there, catching the rays of evening light through the window.

"Hey, Quinn… you've already given me what I really want tonight." Gently, he put his finger under her chin, lifting her face until her eyes met his. When she finally smiled, he kissed her on the forehead.

"What do you have for me, though?" he asked, grinning.

She walked across the room and pulled the little gift bag out of her armoire.

William's eyes lit up when he felt the heft of the bag. He pulled out the tissue paper and grinned at her.

"It's really not much," she said.

His eyes were moist as they met hers. "It's perfect, Quinn. The kind of gift that could only come from you."

"I don't have something to give to you for our courtship."

Kissing her forehead again, he took her hands in his. "I know you don't. You didn't have any idea what to expect. Believe me, I know what it's like to be in a world where you don't understand the traditions and formalities, and every day it seems like there's something else you were supposed to do, but you had no idea."

She squeezed his hand, thinking of all of the years he must have felt like that at school. "What was I supposed to get you?"

His hand went into his pocket yet again, and she gasped as he withdrew another silver bracelet. The chain on this one was much heavier and thicker, but the silver bar was the same. "Put it on me?"

Her hands trembled as she tried to figure out the little clasp on the chain. "You're not supposed to have to buy your own present," she said.

"Hey, sweetheart, none of that." His hands tightened on hers, and he leaned down to meet her gaze again. "Do you honestly think that matters to me? You're willing to walk down there on my arm tonight. *That* is my courtship present. I always thought I'd be making that walk alone, Quinn. That my crazy, divided life would make it impossible to meet someone that I would be ready to take this step with. And by some miracle, you're here. I didn't buy the bracelet because I needed a present; I bought it because I wanted us both to have them, that's all."

She stared at him, stunned, blinking back tears.

"Is it too much?" A hint of nervousness had crept into his voice. "Tell me what you're thinking."

She closed her eyes for a minute, trying to force her scattered thoughts into coherent sentences. Finally, she took a deep breath. "I was just thinking how amazing you are, Will. And how sad I am that all of these years you've been right there, and I never knew anything about you. All this time…I only saw what everyone else saw…the studying, the seriousness… how could I have missed *you*?"

Closing his eyes, he shook his head. "You saw more of me than anyone else ever did…you still do. And I will never be able to fully express how much that means to me, how grateful I am to you." With that, he pulled her into his arms and held her tightly for a long moment.

"You ready?" he asked, dabbing softly at her eyes with his handkerchief, removing the evidence of her emotion a moment ago. "It's almost time to be downstairs."

"No. I have no idea what it is I'm actually supposed to do," she said, as a different sort of nervousness started swirling inside her stomach.

He smiled. "You don't have to do anything. It's really just a birthday party. You have to hold my arm, walk into the dining room, and sit down at the table with me. It's almost the same as any other night."

She breathed in and out a couple of times. "Except for all the extra people, right?"

"Right." He leaned in to kiss her cheek. "Thank you," he whispered against her hair.

She pulled back just far enough to look into his eyes, reaching up to run her finger down the side of his face, smiling.

He kissed her softly on the lips - just a quick brush, though it was enough to send another flash of heat rippling through her chest, and then linked her arm inside his, the little silver chain jingling softly. "Shall we?"

William had been right…she didn't actually have to do anything. Once they reached the entrance to the grand dining hall, there was an announcement about William; his formal introduction as an adult prince, and then he led her to the seat next to his at the high table. There were a few interested second glances and whispers as he led her between the tables on his arm.

There was one glance in the crowd that seemed a little *too* interested in the new development between Quinn and William…that of his cousin Gavin. She didn't know him very well, only enough to know that she neither liked nor trusted him. The look he gave her as she and William passed his table made her shiver.

It was different to be sitting at a table with just the king and queen, and their oldest children and those they escorted. Because it was a celebration for him, William sat right next to his father with Quinn at his side. Simon sat next to Charlotte, his wife Evelyn beside him. Tonight, he wore the heir's crown.

The head table sat at the front of the room, slightly elevated so that the guests could see William. It reminded Quinn of a wedding dinner in her own world. From where she sat, she could see Thomas and Linnea at a round table just in front of them, the two oldest at a table filled with Stephen and Charlotte's younger children. Linnea had baby Hannah in her lap. Jared, her date, was keeping toddler Sarah entertained with a rousing game of peek-a-boo.

When Thomas caught sight of Quinn watching them, he waggled his eyebrows at her, making her giggle before he turned his attention back to his own date.

Next to Thomas, Mia's cheeks turned a soft shade of pink when Quinn caught her eyes. She looked very lovely, with her dark hair flowing down past her shoulders, and wearing a soft, yellow dress for the occasion. Thomas seemed happy with her there; his eyes were on Mia most of the time, and more than once, Quinn caught a glimpse of the two of them flirting. She enjoyed seeing them like this.

The crowd gathered in the dining room wasn't as large as she had been expecting. There were maybe only a hundred people seated at the tables scattered throughout the hall. She looked at William curiously. "There aren't that many people here," she said.

"No, it's not actually that big an event. It's mostly family here, and people of importance in Eirentheos…mostly family," he smiled.

"It's just a birthday party," she said, echoing what he'd told her upstairs.

He nodded. "Just a birthday party."

On Quinn's other side was Maxwell and the girl he had brought, a pretty young woman named Catherine. Although she seemed very nice, Quinn didn't know much about her. William had told her that she and Maxwell had only been courting for a few weeks; they hadn't made anything official.

The dining room looked beautiful tonight; the tables were draped with purple and silver tablecloths, and enormous bouquets of purple and white flowers occupied the center of each one. Servants darted in an out near every guest, filling glasses with a thick, yellow juice that Quinn didn't recognize. Soft music drifted through the room from a small group of musicians set up in the corner.

Everyone chatted amiably, nibbling on a mixture of roasted nuts and dried berries from silver bowls that sat between every two people. She noticed that nobody touched the glasses of juice, though, so she left hers alone.

Quinn had eaten the nut-and-berry mix before; it was a sort of appetizer that appeared before fancy dinners here in the castle. Although most foods here at least resembled things she was familiar with at home, there was one very unusual kind of berry in the mix, an odd green with an irregular shape. At the first couple of dinners she had attended in Eirentheos, she'd been afraid to try them. At Simon's wedding though, Thomas had convinced her to taste one, and after that, she'd been hooked. Nothing in her world compared to them.

Now, between polite conversations, she found herself surreptitiously digging through the bowl, looking for those green ones. She was just reaching for the bowl a third time, when William nudged her softly with his elbow. She looked up at him, abashed at being caught, but he only winked and dropped a small handful of them on her plate.

The heat flowed through her chest again.

After a few minutes, Stephen smiled at William, and then he and Charlotte stood. A hush fell over the room immediately.

William put his hand on Quinn's knee then, and, heart beginning to flutter again, she looked up at him and smiled, placing her hand over his.

"Charlotte and I would like to thank you all for coming here tonight," Stephen began. "It is a very rare privilege for a man to be blessed not only with the love of a kind, upstanding, and beautiful woman," he looked over at Charlotte, who was stunning tonight, in a long, flowing purple gown, her delicate silver tiara perched atop her dark curls, and she returned her husband's enormous smile, "but also with these children who, even in their youths have shown themselves to be courageous, loving, and sacrificial in service to others and to the Maker."

He paused then, as the guests clapped, and he looked down at William, smiling and extending his hand toward his son, who took it and stood up next to him.

"Tonight we're here to celebrate William as he comes of age, an extraordinary son even among this group of extraordinary children. I don't know if I could ever find the words to express how proud Charlotte and I am of him. His compassion and care toward others will no doubt be held up as an example to other healers for generations to come. We raise a toast tonight, and drink the juice of the sunfruit…may the rest of your life bring the same sweetness and life to our kingdom that your childhood has. We love you, Son."

Stephen paused to smile as everyone applauded again, and then he cleared his throat. The dining room quieted immediately. "We have yet one more reason to celebrate this evening, as William makes official his courtship to the Lady Quinn, who has already found her way into the hearts of our family. Tonight, we ask the Maker for his blessing over their courtship and for his guidance as their relationship continues to grow."

As the crowd stood and cheered, Stephen and Charlotte pulled William into their arms. Tears ran unchecked down Queen

Charlotte's face as she reached for Quinn's hand, and then pulled her up and into a hug. Before Charlotte let her go, Stephen leaned in close to them.

"Whatever happens, Quinn," he said softly, "I want you to know how happy it makes both of us to have you here, and to see you and William together. I've never seen either of you as happy as you are with each other."

Tears stung the corners of her own eyes as she nodded, unable to come up with the right words. After a moment, William's hand found hers again, his fingers rubbing the thin chain of her bracelet as they all sat back down, and the servants began bringing out the dinner dishes.

AFTER DINNER

AFTER THEIR PLATES HAD been cleared away, William led Quinn outside onto the main patio. It was just beginning to grow dark and the hundreds of candles that had been placed in sconces running down the castle walls and all along the low wall surrounding the raised terrace gave the whole place a warm, flickering glow.

He had seen it this way before, but the celebration had never been for him. He was a little surprised by how emotional he found himself over the whole thing, over actually becoming an adult, and having his own party. It had really struck him for the first time as he had taken Quinn with him up to the head table at dinner…escorting a girl to a place that, for his whole life, had been reserved for adults.

He supposed it meant he could make his own decisions now. It was a thought that had been running through his head all day…since two nights ago after he'd talked to his parents, really.

He couldn't believe what they had told him, and he wasn't sure whether to be angry, or furious…or grateful. At different points during the last two days, he'd been all three. What shocked him the most were the moments he wasn't completely, staggeringly livid…which was the emotion that would have made the most sense. He had no doubt about how he would have felt if he'd found all this out three months ago.

All these years he'd thought he was in Bristlecone for reasons that were actually his choice, but he hadn't been. He'd been there to help keep an eye on Quinn, like some kind of crazy spy, even if he'd known nothing about it. His parents and Nathaniel had spent the last nine years hoping the two of them would find each other and hit it off.

They'd been set up.

And she knew.

And she was still here, still holding his hand, next to him at his celebration, announcing their courtship together, wearing his bracelet. All night, he'd been moving his wrist a little more often than was strictly necessary, just to hear the soft little jingle of his own jewelry, to feel its comforting weight against his wrist.

He didn't know how Quinn was doing it, standing here with him, not freaking out over what had been done to them. He wanted to ask her, but he didn't think that discussing it at the party was the best idea. He felt badly now that he'd taken off earlier, blown off some steam by riding Skittles all the way to Mistle Village and back. Although seeing the ruins of the clinic again had helped him put things into perspective about why his parents would be willing to take such a huge risk, or at least why they'd want one more set of eyes on the true heir to the throne.

As he looked at the girl standing next to him, he was in awe of how in control of herself she seemed…more so than he felt. Most likely, she was just as confused as he was; he couldn't imagine what it would be like to suddenly find out you were the heir to the throne in a kingdom in a world you'd never known existed.

Confused as he was, though, his only real instinct was to stay next to her, to the girl who had somehow come to be the most important thing in his world. And he knew, now, that he would support her in whatever she wished to do.

More than anything, he wished the choice wasn't *so* desperate and confusing. If only she'd grown up in this world, knowing her destiny always... He knew that there was no use in "if only," but he truly wished that at the very least their kingdoms were at peace in the way they should be.

He'd made a decision late last night that he hadn't yet shared with anyone. Although he had always wished for Philotheum and Eirentheos to be at peace and joined together the way the Maker had intended, lately, the need for it to be so had intensified inside him.

The idea had been simmering in the back of his mind ever since his encounter with the Halpern family, since he had seen how much trouble they had trusting him, when he so desperately needed them to. And especially after the conversations he had had with Jacob, first at the clinic, and then three nights ago when Jacob had told him that he'd made the decision.

Now that William knew about Quinn, knew what was really at stake, it had become more than an idea; it was something he felt he had to do.

He was going to join the Friends of Philip.

Quinn followed him to a distant corner as more musicians down on the lawn below began to play. Looking into her eyes now, he wondered if there was ever really a time he'd been angry she'd discovered the gate. He couldn't even hold on to the anger he'd been feeling toward his parents for using him...both of them...the way they had. Because if they hadn't done it...hadn't sent him there, or hadn't hidden the truth from him...there was no way this girl would be standing in front of him right now.

"Thank you," he said to her again, putting his arms around her waist, swaying softly, not caring if his tempo matched the music.

She smiled, playing absently with the pin at his neck as her eyes met his, and he was amazed at how well he could read what was there. He saw her almost blow it off, almost make a remark that would undermine her part in this, and then he watched as she decided not to, and she nodded softly at him instead.

If he lived another hundred cycles, he would still never find the words to describe what that look did inside his heart.

He leaned down, brushing his lips softly against hers, and her arms reached up around his neck.

"All right, Will, even if it is your birthday, and even if you are officially courting her now, you still can't monopolize Quinn all evening."

William rolled his eyes and turned around to see Thomas grinning at them, mischief in his eyes, Linnea and both of their dates just behind.

"Are you sure about that, Thomas?" William teased. "Perhaps it's just an adult matter you're not ready for yet."

Thomas only laughed. "Stick to healing, Will. I don't know what you see in him Quinn; he can't even pull off a joke with his baby brother."

Quinn and Linnea both giggled as William punched Thomas lightly on the arm.

"Come on sweetheart," Thomas said, "I need to get in at least one dance before it's time to cut the cake."

"There's birthday cake in your world, too?" she asked.

"Well, in our castle, anyway. Since about eight cycles ago. We'll probably dance the Hokey Pokey again later, too."

William's blushed slightly, although right now it would have been very difficult to dampen his mood. "Dance with me, Mia?" he asked, extending his hand while Thomas whisked Quinn away.

It should have been a perfect evening. Quinn helped him cut into the elaborate chocolate cake decorated with purple and silver roses, and William thoroughly embarrassed himself when Thomas dragged him into the center of the circle during the Hokey Pokey.

He had just handed Emma off to Joshua and finally gotten Quinn back for a slow dance when he noticed that something wasn't right.

The crowd seemed a little smaller than it should be, and when he looked, he couldn't see his parents anywhere. Across from the dance floor, over by the drink table, Evelyn was chatting with Howard and Rebecca, but her face didn't look quite right…none of their faces did, actually, and Simon wasn't anywhere, either.

Thomas and Linnea were still dancing…he'd just stolen Quinn back from Thomas, actually…but a feeling of unease settled over him.

"What is it?" Quinn asked, looking up at him. With her head on his shoulder, as it had been, she'd probably felt him tense.

"I don't know," he said, shaking his head. "Just… something."

She looked around at the other guests now, too. "Where are your parents?" she asked.

"That's what I was just wondering. I don't see Simon, either…or Max."

Quinn's whole body stiffened in his arms. "Something's wrong. Let's go."

The door to his father's office was closed, but William could see soft, yellow light pouring out from underneath. When he his hand hesitated in the air, Quinn reached forward and knocked, hard, three times. A moment later, Simon's face appeared through a small crack. He didn't look right; there was a strange shadow over his features, and a deep crease between his eyebrows.

"William," he said, "you really should be outside. Your guests..."

"Let us in, Simon." Quinn's voice was firm, almost forceful, and a strange emotion rippled through William's stomach at the sound of it.

Simon, too, looked taken aback, and he held the door wide for them to enter, and then closed it behind him.

Both of his parents were inside, and when he saw them he knew that Quinn had been right; something was *very* wrong. His mother and father sat next to each other on one of the couches, holding hands, distress plain on their pale faces. Across from them, on another couch, were Marcus Westbrook and his son, Ben.

The four of them stood as soon as they saw Quinn and William, which made him feel strange. Although he had known Marcus all his life as one of his father's personal guards, and he'd grown up knowing Ben, he'd recently gotten to know them both much better when they'd come along on the journey to rescue Thomas.

Marcus and Ben both looked extremely upset now, and a sense of panic started flickering inside William's chest.

"What's wrong?" Quinn asked.

Marcus looked down at the floor before he began to answer, which made William's panic grow, the flickers steadily becoming sharper against his ribcage.

"We've just received word that Dorian and James Blackwelder have been arrested."

Quinn gasped beside him, and his own knees suddenly felt softer than they should. "What? When?"

Marcus sighed, a shadow crossing his features. "Come sit down Lady Quinn, Prince William. We'll tell you what we know."

William led Quinn over to a pair of upholstered chairs that made another side of the square where everyone had been sitting and talking. His two older brothers sat down across from them, and they all turned their attention back to Marcus.

He cleared his throat. "About an hour ago, we received a message, carried by Ellen's bird." He nodded toward the low table sitting in the middle of them, where William could see a heavy, folded paper. The wax seal embossed with the Philothean seal was broken open. "You can read it if you'd like," Marcus said, as his gaze followed William's, "it says that she found out this morning that Dorian and James were arrested on charges of treason, and they're being held at the castle, awaiting trial."

"Which they will most surely be convicted of," Ben added.

Next to him, Quinn had gone completely white. "And what will happen to them?" she asked.

William reached over and took her hand in his, holding it tightly as Marcus answered. "They'll be executed."

Her hand tensed inside his, growing cold and clammy. "For rescuing Thomas."

"Ellen's letter says that the official charges list espionage and disobeying direct orders as examples," Marcus said, his eyes on the floor again. "But yes. Most certainly it's a result of their involvement in returning Thomas to us."

"So what can we do?" Quinn asked. "How do we help them?"

Across the room, Simon's posture changed as confusion flittered across his face. William could see Maxwell change, too, but his confusion was mixed with annoyance.

"I understand that you are concerned and upset, Quinn," Simon said, "but it really isn't your issue."

Her hand broke away from William's as it balled into a fist. He watched as she took a deep breath, though she didn't speak right away. He wondered what was going through her head; knowing she would be torn by Simon's statement. Torn by a decision she wasn't ready to make yet…a decision that would ultimately distinguish whether an issue such as this one had either nothing to do with her at all, or if, as the rightful ruler of Philotheum, it would belong to her more than anyone.

His father spoke before she could, turning to look at both Simon and Maxwell. "We'd like to speak to Quinn alone for a moment. There are guests outside we're neglecting, Simon… Max."

The annoyance on Max's face shifted to outright anger, but he stood and walked toward the door. Simon turned to his father, more confused than ever. "And Will? It's his party."

Stephen's eyes fell on Quinn. "That's up to you."

William felt, more than saw, Maxwell's jaw drop.

"He can stay if he wishes," she said, reaching for his hand again. She looked up at him, and he could see in her eyes that she wanted him there, but she was leaving it up to him. He squeezed her hand, knowing she would understand his reply.

The look on Maxwell's face told him that he was going to have to answer to his brothers later, but he wasn't leaving Quinn unless she told him to.

"We'll go out with you," Marcus said, as he and Ben stood. The look Marcus directed at his father, though, told William the answer to something he'd wondered about.

"Marcus and Ben know," he said, after the door had closed behind them. "About Quinn."

"Yes," his father agreed. "Marcus has always known. Ben was told much more recently."

"But before we went to Philotheum with them," Quinn said.

Stephen looked at her, a hint of wonder in his gray eyes. "Yes, before then."

William wondered how she knew that…wondered if there was anything else she hadn't told him yet, and realized he wasn't sure he was ready for the answer.

"What can we do to help the Blackwelders?" she asked.

Stephen sighed heavily, and Charlotte reached to take her hand in his. He looked…older, William thought. "I don't know if there's anything we can do. Relations between our two thrones are at a standstill. Hector sent a message a few days ago letting me know that if I'm not going to 'promote peace' between our kingdoms by allowing our families to join together, then the least I can do is actively support Tolliver's ascension to the throne…at the end of the season."

William saw his own horror reflected on Quinn's face. "How long is that? Summer is almost over, right?" she asked.

"Summer *is* over," William corrected gently. "Or Eternolis, as we actually call it. We celebrated the beginning of our harvest season…Carperos…while you were in Bristlecone."

She raised an eyebrow. "I guess I missed that one. So which end of season is he talking about?"

"The end of Carperos…thirty moons from now," Stephen said.

Her eyes widened. "That seems like a long time."

"I doubt we actually have that much time before he really starts pushing against us. I don't think he has any intention of there being peaceful relations between our kingdoms, although he did send another offer of marriage along for Linnea."

White-hot anger bubbled up in William's stomach, and his hands clenched tightly at his sides.

Stephen saw the expressions on their faces and nodded. "Of course, I doubt that Hector has any idea what happened recently with Thomas. I believe that was Tolliver acting on his own. However, I don't think that particular offer merits even a response."

"Oh, it deserves a response, Father," William spat, unable to restrain himself.

"Exchanging hostilities is not going to further our cause. Even if he doesn't know the extent of what his son has done, I don't think Hector really believes we would allow our daughter to marry him," Charlotte said quietly.

"We think he's mostly using the offer to stall us, anyway," Stephen said. "He needs more time to get his people and troops in support of him, and against us. In the meantime, he would prefer to continue to undermine our own peoples' confidence in us, and attempt to force *us* to close the border, so he can claim that we've initiated the hostilities, despite the fact that his kingdom has been poisoning our children and tracking down and killing innocent people."

Everyone was silent for a moment as those words hung in the air.

Finally, Quinn cleared her throat. "So you need to act."

"Yes."

"And the hold-up is me." She was sitting up straight, and her chin was taut, but William could feel her fingers trembling. His own surprise was heavy and thick…he hadn't processed this whole thing that far yet, but he realized now that she'd pegged it correctly.

"Yes, Quinn. We never wanted to force you into a decision, but ultimately, what you decide will be the determining factor in how we proceed."

She swallowed hard. "What would you have done if I'd never found the gate…if you hadn't been able to tell me anything until I was eighteen?"

"We'd always prayed that another solution would present itself before we had to make that choice. We've walked a fine line in our dealings with Tolliver for a long time now…first with Rebecca, and then with Linnea. If Thomas hadn't decided to go searching for Lily, it's likely that we could have continued to stretch that out for a while longer."

"And what is your other option, Stephen?"

"If you choose not to fight this battle with us, Quinn, we will attempt to install Charles' daughter, Gianna as the heir apparent, and Charles as Prince Regent, until she is of age."

"Why have you not done that already?"

Stephen sighed deeply, and William was surprised when his mother began speaking, instead.

"I know you were raised outside of our world, Quinn, outside of our beliefs. I don't actually know if you were raised to believe in the Maker at all."

Quinn's eyes widened again, "I think that's a little different in my world," she said.

"We don't actually believe it is, Quinn," Charlotte said. "But either way, we have always believed that the Maker has his own plan for our kingdoms, and that it is only by following his lead that we will have the peace and prosperity he means for us to have."

"And you think the Maker wants me to be the heir of Philotheum."

"We believe that's who he made you to be."

Quinn dropped William's hand then, and she stood, walking around to the back of the chair she'd been sitting in, and leaning her hands against it. He turned around to watch her. "If that's true, then exactly how is *any* of this my choice?" Her voice trembled.

Stephen's eyes were soft when he looked up at her, though there were dark, heavy shadows beneath them. "It's always your choice, Quinn. Nobody can force you to be anything…not even what you were born to be. You could return to your own world and never look back."

She paused for what felt like a very long time before she nodded. "And where would that leave you?"

He stood now, walking over closer to her, meeting her eyes. "It would leave us in the hands of the Maker, and we would do what he leads us to do. He hasn't yet directed us to do something other than wait on you, and so we haven't."

"And we won't, Quinn," Charlotte said. "We may not understand the Maker's plan, and it's difficult, sometimes, when things look like they're crumbling around us, not to take matters into our own hands and try to fix it."

"Maxwell is struggling with it very much," Stephen said. "He thinks we are making a mistake now, but Charlotte and I, though I'm sure we will continue to make many mistakes, we truly believe that it's never a mistake to wait on the Maker."

"Does Max know about me?"

"No, he doesn't. But it doesn't matter. He knows enough to make his own choices about what he's going to believe, and who he is going to trust."

"So what do I do now?"

Stephen sighed. "Right now, tonight, Quinn, you get your first taste of what it might be like if you do choose to be the ruler of a kingdom. We've gotten some terrible and distressing news, but there is a celebration going on outside, and not one of us can afford to be away from it any longer."

ALTHOUGH WILLIAM AND QUINN both did their best to switch back into "celebration" mode, the rest of the party had a strained feeling to it.

As soon as they got back outside, Linnea pounced on William, dragging him off to the dance floor, while Thomas took Quinn's arm.

"What's going on, Will?" his sister asked. "And don't blow me off this time; I'm tired of not being included in anything. I'm almost of age, too, you know."

William closed his eyes for a moment and then nodded. "I know you are Nay." He did feel bad at how often things happened that Linnea didn't get to be part of. And he felt even worse, because there was something else he'd taken away from her recently, too, something that he now realized might not have been the right decision.

"Look, Nay, we just heard some really bad news, and I can't talk about it right now and stay at the party and do what I need to do…and I think Quinn feels the same way. I promise I'll fill you in on it tomorrow, though."

And he would…at least the parts that were his to share. But the hurt didn't disappear from her eyes.

A little way across the floor from them, he could see from the expression on Thomas's face that he and Quinn were having a similar conversation. As hard as he tried to enjoy the rest of his party and entertain his guests, dancing with everyone, he was preoccupied the whole time, always watching Quinn, wondering how she was doing.

All of this was an awful lot for a sixteen-year-old girl from another world to absorb…too much, he thought. Finding out that she was the heir to the throne in a kingdom in another world was bad enough without walking into the middle of a war, too.

She was holding it together impressively, though. As he watched, she danced with Thomas, with his older brothers, even some of his cousins, though he chuckled quietly when he saw her excuse herself for a few minutes when his cousin Gavin was approaching. She smiled and laughed, looking every bit like it was all natural to her, as if she belonged here. He was surprised to find himself following her lead, trying to navigate his interactions with his guests with the same grace she was showing.

It was only when she danced with him again that she seemed to let her mind wander back to reality, and then the deep crease showed itself between her eyebrows, and her hands trembled slightly in his.

When the night was over, William upset his siblings again by asking for a few minutes alone with Quinn as he walked her up to her room.

As soon as he'd closed her door behind them, she looked up at him. "Well, *that* wasn't how I envisioned your birthday party."

He smiled softly. "No. I guess things really don't go according to plan sometimes."

"I don't have any idea what to do, Will." She sank down onto her couch.

"I know you don't." He perched on the edge of her small table, putting his hands on her knees, tracing the lines of velvet flowers on her skirt with his fingers, trying to sort out his own thoughts.

"Part of me wants to run off to Philotheum tonight and tell Tolliver to get off my throne and send Dorian and James back home, right now."

His eyes widened for a second…it surprised him that she'd actually thought that far. Trying to keep the pressure off her, he chuckled. "I know, love. I don't think it's that simple though."

"No, it's not. Especially because the other part of me *really* wishes that the biggest thing I had to worry about right now was how I'm ever going to get my grade back up in World History."

At the moment, part of him felt that way, too. "Maybe you've been studying the wrong world," he said with a wry grin.

Quinn snickered, and the suddenness of the noise caused him to burst out laughing, too. The pair of them sat there, laughing hysterically for several minutes. "In either case," she finally agreed, out of breath, as she was overcome with another bout of the giggles.

When she was finally calm, though, her expression took on a serious tone that erased all of the laughter from the last several minutes.

"What are you thinking, sweetheart?"

Her chin shook as she swallowed, the crease on her forehead deepening. "I was thinking that I want to join the Friends of Philip."

Somehow, her words didn't surprise him at all; that should have seemed all wrong to him, but it didn't; it felt right. Still, he had to ask the question. "Are you sure, Quinn? You're still not obligated to this world, you know? I don't think you should make any huge decisions this fast."

She stood and walked over to the window…he could see from her posture that she was deep in thought, trying to figure out how to express what was on her mind. He waited while she looked outside for a long moment before finally turning back to him.

"I don't know a lot of things, Will. But it's too late now to pretend that none of this ever happened…maybe it's even too late to pretend that I never should have followed you and walked off that bridge. I don't know what it was…but I don't believe it was just a freak accident anymore."

She turned back toward the window again, looking out as her voice dropped low, almost as if she was speaking to herself more than she was to him. "I know now that I can't ever just completely walk away from this world. No matter what I decide, this is still half of who I am. This is who I was born to be. And I don't know everything. I don't know what I believe, and what I don't. But I can see what's right. And I know whose side I'm on."

As she finished, a warm feeling settled in his chest. He stood and crossed the room to her, taking one of her hands in his, and with the other catching a long tendril of her auburn hair that had slipped from the intricate braid. Her breath caught as he twirled the strand around his finger, and he looked into her eyes, the warm feeling inside of him growing more intense, building slowly into something more, a warm glow that spread through every part of him.

"I love you, Quinn."

He hadn't planned on telling her that, hadn't known until that moment that it was true. He didn't have any idea how she would react…she'd probably feel like he was pushing her, except he wasn't. He knew what the stakes were, knew that there was a good chance that he couldn't keep her regardless, but at that moment he knew…down into the deepest part of his being, he knew that it didn't matter. None of it, not how they'd gotten here, not where it was going to go, mattered. He loved her, would always love her, and she deserved to know.

She didn't look away, which was encouraging, though he saw the surprise register somewhere in the depths of her gray eyes. As he watched, other emotions battled there, too, though she grew completely silent, until she finally did look down, studying the way their hands were entwined. When she finally looked back up, her lower lip trembled.

"We were set up, you know. The whole reason your parents sent you to Bristlecone was because they hoped you and I would somehow meet and hit it off." Tears welled in the corners of her eyes, and her hands were shaking now, too.

He lifted a finger and pressed it softly against her lips. "I know."

"You *know?*"

"Yes, the other night, after you and I talked, I went straight to my parents' room. We had a long conversation about it. Very long." He shook his head, trying to dispel the memory.

"You're not mad?"

"I was, Quinn...not at you," he added quickly, feeling her hand grow clammy in his. "It wasn't your decision or your fault. You were a pawn in this game, too."

"I didn't tell you."

The fear in her voice hurt his heart. He moved his face close to hers, looking her in the eye. "You just barely found out, yourself. I didn't have any idea how to bring that up in a conversation, and I knew you already knew."

"So... when did you decide you weren't mad about it?" She was looking down again, her voice so quiet he had to strain to make out all of the words.

He sighed, taking one of her hands in both of his now, studying the texture of the soft skin, tracing it with his finger. "I don't know that I've actually decided I'm not mad. What I *have* decided is that as far as my feelings about you are concerned, how we got to this point...whether it was by accident or someone else's ridiculous design...it doesn't matter. It's how I feel. I love you."

His breath caught as she finally returned his gaze, her eyes searing through him, somehow seeing right into the depths of his being. "I love you, too, William."

There were no words to describe the way the feeling exploded in his chest then. If he'd felt he was consumed a moment ago, it was nothing compared to this…to her returning his feelings. Their lips touched then, and the warm glow suddenly sparked into a flame, a raging fire that flowed through every part of him, burning away any doubt he'd ever had about her, replacing it with something new.

The kiss went on for a long time, building in intensity until he finally pulled away, knowing exactly what was going to happen if he didn't, desperately hanging on to the small piece of him that knew he didn't want to take that from her, not until the day when he could pledge every part of himself to her.

It took several minutes for them to recover, both of them out of breath as they stumbled back, Quinn to the couch, and him to an armchair a safe distance away.

When he finally felt he could speak again, he looked over at her. "Are you okay?"

She blinked. "Um… more than okay, I think." The edges of her lips curved up in a half-smile for a few seconds, and then suddenly the smile faded and a crease appeared between her eyebrows. "Why? Are *you* okay?"

She looked so worried that he couldn't help dashing back toward her. Sitting down next to her on the couch, he stretched his hand toward her, and gently turned her face to meet his. "I'm perfect, Quinn. Even with everything else that's going on…I've never been this happy, never imagined I could *be* this happy."

He paused, trying to swallow back the new kind of nervousness that had risen in his throat. "I just… I know your world is different from mine. I never thought about girls there, never tried to understand how this whole thing works there. And I don't know what you expect from me…when I'm pushing you too far, or… or when you might be wishing for something more. I don't know what you and Zander…"

She put her finger against his lip, silencing him. "I know you're not asking, Will, I know. But Zander and I kissed…that's all. You and I have done more than Zander and I ever did… and I'm good with this. This…you and I, where we are, where we're going… it all feels right to me. This is good."

Relief washed over him in an enormous wave, although a new worry edged in at the corner of his mind. "You know it's not that I cared what you and Zander…"

She frowned. "Really, Will? You wouldn't care? I mean, I appreciate that you're trying to be so open and understanding about everything, but if we were talking about you and another girl here…I would *care*."

The second wave of relief took him by surprise; the breath he hadn't realized he'd been holding exploded out of him in an unexpected chuckle. Quinn was smiling, her eyes soft and warm, and she took his hands in hers.

He squeezed her hands gently, rubbing his index finger against her thumb. "Our worlds are so different… the rules are much simpler here…what's expected and appropriate when you're courting, and what's not."

"It's not so different, Will," she said, shaking her head. "Not for everyone, anyway. I was raised… Well, my mom did marry someone from your world, so…"

He smiled, leaning in to kiss her on the forehead, amazed at how much better he felt having this open between them. "So we're on the same page about this…*both* of us okay with the way things are."

"Like I said… more than okay."

Pulling her into his arms, he held her against his chest for a long, comfortable time, thinking that he'd never felt so safe or so calm before. Quinn's breathing, too, was soft and slow as she played absently with the pendant she'd pulled out from under his shirt.

He kissed her hair, deep in thought now. "I was going to tell you…maybe not tonight, but tomorrow, that I've decided the same thing. I want to join the Friends of Philip, too."

There was no surprise on her face as she looked up at him. She simply nodded, as if it were the most natural thing in the world for him to say right now.

"There's something else I haven't told you." He hadn't intended to, actually, because he'd already made a decision about it...or he thought he had, but tonight at the party, and after everything that had happened in the last couple of days, it had come back into his mind, and he knew, now, that his original decision had been wrong.

She raised an eyebrow, sitting up and turning slightly to face him. "More secrets?"

"Sort of."

"Well?"

"When a prince...or a princess...comes of age in our world, it's traditional to take a journey around the kingdom, visiting villages they've never been to, and getting to know the people there, helping out with a project, that kind of thing."

"Yeah, I heard about that," she said. "But Linnea said you'd decided not to go...she was really mad, actually. Something about the next youngest child gets to go on the trip, too?"

"Yes, that's the way it's supposed to work."

"So what made you decide not to go, and to risk the wrath of Linnea?"

He sighed, his eyes tracing the trail of flowers on her skirt again. "I guess, in a way, I was feeling like it didn't really apply to me. I *already* have traveled to so many of the villages, helped with so many projects, gotten to know so many of the people. I even went along on Rebecca's trip two cycles ago, when I was the next-youngest. It seemed...I don't know...superfluous to take another trip just because."

Quinn frowned again, but she didn't say all of the words he could see hiding behind her eyes. "And now?"

"And now...after the conversation earlier tonight, *and* the one you and I had the other morning...I realize that as a prince, I can't just decide what things to be a part of, and which ones I can just blow off, even if I think my excuses are good. Well, I *can*...my parents were upset, but especially given the higher level of danger, it was my *adult* choice to go or not go. I can choose that, but what does it say to the people of our kingdom, and to my family? Even to myself, really?"

"And definitely to Linnea."

He nodded. "Right. I wasn't making the decision only for myself. And it wasn't fair."

"So you're going to go?"

"Yes."

Tiny creases appeared in the corners of her eyes. "How long is the trip?"

"Usually for an entire moon."

"Wow." Her throat quivered as she swallowed. "When would you go?"

"Before I answer that," he said, meeting her eyes again, "I should say that I would like you to come along with me."

Her eyes widened. "Is that allowed?" The concern in her expression made him smile.

"Encouraged, actually, if we're courting. If I wasn't courting anyone, one purpose of the trip would be to meet more young ladies."

"We're definitely courting," she said, narrowing her eyes.

He grinned. "I think we've established that."

"Just saying."

"I would want to leave soon, in maybe three or four days."

She nodded. "I still have plenty of time before Spring Break ends. I'll come."

"Good." The heavy feeling had been sitting in his chest without his even noticing, until suddenly it was gone, and he felt oddly light. *This* was the right thing to do. "Although," he paused now, rethinking the timing, because he really did want to take care of the other thing first. "I want to join the Friends of Philip before I go. I want to be clear about where I stand…with my people and with myself."

Quinn nodded. "So what happens with the whole "next youngest child" thing when there are twins? Who gets to go? Is Thomas even ready to travel?"

"I'm not leaving Linnea behind this time," he said. "I feel bad enough. She was really devastated when I told her I wasn't going."

"What about Thomas?" she asked.

"I don't know. Probably. His leg is doing much better now…I think he could safely travel in a wagon. But we could just ask him."

CANCELED

AS QUINN HAD EXPECTED, Linnea was ecstatic when William told her he planned to go on the trip after all. He had apparently managed to find her as soon as she woke up in the morning, because Quinn had just finished getting dressed when Linnea came bouncing in to her room, excited about the news.

She stood there with her hair still dripping as Linnea gushed about finally getting to go "on an adventure" with Quinn and her brothers.

"If Thomas is able to go," Quinn said.

Linnea raised an eyebrow. "It's Thomas. He'll find a way."

"That I will," he said from the doorway. "I'm sure I'll be just fine." He came in the room, smiling as usual, but Quinn noticed that his demeanor was off, just a little bit, as it so often had been since his time in Philotheum.

He caught her studying him, and he must have noticed that she was more somber than usual, too, judging from the look he gave her. "So what happened last night at the party, Quinn?"

A heavy feeling washed over her. As devastating as the news about the Blackwelders had been to her last night…she was dreading Thomas's reaction. "You might want to sit down," she said.

"Yeah, that's probably a good idea." William's voice, coming from the doorway, startled her. He came in and closed the door behind himself.

Although Linnea was upset after Quinn and William told them what they'd heard about Dorian and James, by the end of the story Thomas had gone completely white. He sat in one of the armchairs, perfectly still, and staring at a small vase on the table, not saying anything.

Quinn looked over at Linnea, who shook her head, her eyes growing wide as she looked at her twin brother. Although he was still the sweet, lighthearted Thomas that they loved, there were times they all had seen how his time in Philotheum had affected him more deeply than anyone wanted to admit. This was one of those times.

Linnea moved over toward him, hovering close by, but they could all sense that he wasn't ready to be touched, and they waited.

Next to Quinn on the couch, William had gone rigid; his breathing was shallow as he waited to see how his brother was going to react to this news.

She didn't know how many minutes passed before Thomas looked up again, but it felt like a long time. When he finally spoke, though, it wasn't about Dorian and James…not exactly anyway.

"Why were you included in all of this Quinn?" he asked. "It's not because the two of you are courting that you were allowed in that room," his eyes darted between William and Quinn. "If anything, he was included because of *you*. Why?"

A cold sensation rippled through her body, sliding from the top of her head, all the way to her toes, enough to make her shiver. Her still-damp hair now felt like a hundred icicles. She looked up at William, pleading in her eyes as she struggled to decide what to do.

The look he gave her in return told her that he understood what she decided either way, but that the choice was up to her.

She wasn't even quite sure why it was so hard for her to tell them…why it had been hard to tell William. It wasn't as if she liked keeping secrets. And she loved and trusted all of them. As she'd thought about it during the past several days, the only explanation she could come up with was that telling them made it real…made it something she couldn't just walk away from and pretend it never happened.

But hadn't she just decided last night that she couldn't do that, anyway? This was real, and regardless of what she decided in the end, these people she cared about…who cared about her…deserved to know.

"Quinn? Are you all right?" Thomas finally asked, and she wondered just how long she'd been sitting there, staring into space.

Nodding, she closed her eyes for a moment, and held up one finger. Then she stood and crossed the room to her night table, and pulled open the little drawer where she'd stowed the cloth pouch before she went to sleep last night. It hadn't yet made it into her pocket today.

Linnea's gasp when Quinn held up her pendant was audible. "Bole splick!" she spluttered.

"Linnea!" William said sternly.

Quinn frowned, confused.

"It's impolite. Trust me," he said, though a grin teased at the corners of his mouth.

"And entirely appropriate for the occasion," Linnea countered, taking the pendant into her hand to examine it more closely. "How long have you been keeping this from us?" she narrowed her eyes.

Quinn swallowed hard, and tried to keep her voice from shaking, hoping desperately that Linnea wasn't going to be extremely mad at her over this.

"She found out when she went back to Bristlecone this last time," William answered for her. "And Nay, I know you love Quinn, so think for a minute before you decide what you're going to say next."

Linnea nodded, her eyes on the pendant as she turned it over in her hand, examining every detail closely. "Wow," she breathed, when she finally looked back up at Quinn. "This changes everything, doesn't it?"

Quinn closed her eyes and took a deep breath. "You're the second person who's said something like that to me…and I still don't know whether it does or not."

She felt William's arms around her waist, and when she finally opened her eyes, the look on Linnea's face had changed from one of shock to one of sympathy.

"Yeah, I can see where that would be difficult," Linnea said. She was trying, and it made Quinn smile.

"It's still a secret," William said. "Quinn still doesn't know exactly what she's going to do now that she knows, and it's not exactly something that needs to be advertised to everyone."

"Not to mention the incredible danger she would be in if this became public knowledge."

They all turned to look at Thomas, who was still sitting in the armchair across the room…they'd almost forgotten he was there, too.

His face was pale, but he didn't look quite as shocked as Linnea. Something about his expression made Quinn feel cold again, like a block of ice had formed in the pit of her stomach. "Did you know something about this, Thomas?"

He sighed. "Not exactly, no. But I had some suspicions… wondered…"

Quinn frowned, remembering her conversation with Mia, wanting to know exactly what Thomas's suspicions were… "Wondered *what?*"

"Whether Nathaniel was actually King Jonathan's son…and whether you were *that* Samuel's child."

A noise somewhere between a cough and a choke exploded from William's throat? "What? You didn't tell me you suspected *that*, Thomas…only that you thought maybe Nathaniel and Quinn's father were Philothean. Why would you have even thought Samuel *had* a child? He was supposed to have died when he was a teenager. Nobody knew he was still alive!"

The shadows underneath Thomas's eyes grew darker. "There are people who know, William. And there are even more who believe that it's possible. Samuel's body was never recovered, at least not enough of it to convince everyone. Tolliver fears that the man his father hired to follow Samuel into the woods that day and murder him wasn't completely trustworthy…if you can imagine. After the funeral, that guard was executed." Thomas paused while the rest of them absorbed the impact of that statement.

"He's been afraid for many cycles now, actually, that Samuel is still alive and will show up to challenge his claim to the throne."

When all three of them stared at him in stunned silence, Thomas shrugged, answering their silent question. "No. I don't think Tolliver ever expected me to make it back here alive. Not once I was injured…he knew what sending me back in this condition would do. He wanted to get as much information out of me as he could, and then make it look like an accident…like I'd done something stupid while I was in Philotheum and gotten myself killed. I'd probably have been dead before Dorian and James got to me if he hadn't wanted to investigate rumors that people might have known I'd been captured."

"Those weren't rumors," William said. "People did know."

"Yeah…and I wonder how many of them have been arrested, besides Dorian and James?"

"Why haven't you shared any of this, Thomas? Don't you think some of this information would be helpful to have?"

"I've shared some of it Will. And… I am sorry I haven't shared it with you. It's just…you all have had so many things on your minds lately, and you were all so upset about what happened to me, anyway…"

"Have you told Father?"

Thomas closed his eyes. "I've told him some of it. But, I don't know… I can't explain why I haven't shared everything. It's just… a feeling I've had."

"Yeah, Thomas," Quinn said, irritation rising in her voice. "Keep following those feelings. Look where it got you last time."

His eyes met hers, one eyebrow pointed up in a v-shape. "Was I wrong, Quinn? Unaware of the danger, yes, I'll give you. But wrong? Was there really nothing going on with Lily to be concerned about?"

A loud knock on the door startled them all, and the door opened before Quinn could even catch her breath to say, "Come in."

King Stephen strode purposefully into the room, followed closely by Nathaniel, who closed the door behind himself. "I had a feeling I would find you all in here," Stephen said. As he walked toward them, his eyes fell on Quinn's small coffee table, where the pendants now sat. "Have you told them everything?" he asked, cocking his head toward Thomas and Linnea.

"Depends on what you mean by everything," she answered warily. "I told them everything I know."

Stephen smiled, though it didn't reach all the way to his eyes. "I'm not keeping secrets from you any more, Quinn. There isn't any reason to. Did you tell him them what we learned last night?"

"Yes."

Nodding…Quinn wasn't sure if the look on his face was relief over not having been the one to share that information…Stephen looked over at Thomas now; they could all see in the paleness of his face, his stoic expression, how much the news of James and Dorian's arrest really had impacted him. "I'm sorry, Son. The news we've just received isn't much more promising."

Quinn and William both looked up at him in alarm. There were dark circles underneath Stephen's eyes; she wondered if he'd slept at all last night. Just thinking the question felt like swallowing a rock. His position right now was the same one she contemplated putting herself in every time she looked at that pendant and considered what it really meant.

"What's going on now?" she asked.

"We've just received another message from Ellen," Nathaniel said, with darkness in his voice that made Quinn shiver. William's hand found hers again. They discovered yesterday afternoon that Tolliver planned to send soldiers to raid her house, looking for 'fugitives'. Ellen, Henry, their guard, Ryan, and two couples who were staying with them all managed…barely…to get across the border safely late last night."

"Would Tolliver have actually done something to Ellen? His own sister?"

"I'm sure he would have no problem having her killed, Quinn, if he could get away with it. Right now, I think he still has a public image to maintain, and I don't know that he would actually have had her arrested, but the rest of them…Ryan, Natalie and Andrew Gramble and their new baby…"

She clutched William's hand tightly at that image, remembering the sweet young couple whose baby girl William had delivered while they were all hiding together in Ellen's basement with Tolliver upstairs. He rubbed the back of her hand with his thumb in a way that was probably supposed to be reassuring, but since his palm was sweating as badly as hers, it had the opposite effect.

"They're safe now," Stephen said. "They're in Anwin with Charles and Thea. "It does mean, though, that we've lost our most important contact with the Friends of Philip inside Philotheum. Ellen and Henry are planning on traveling here to the castle in the next couple of days."

"And what else?" Quinn asked. She could tell from Stephen's expression that there was more.

He sighed. Nathaniel pulled one of the chairs from the table under Quinn's window over near the couch, and Stephen sat down in it, looking like he had no idea where to start. Finally, he cleared his throat. "We heard some things this morning that give us reason to believe that sensitive information has been passed to Tolliver."

"What kind of information?"

"Information about you, Quinn."

The room suddenly started spinning. "What *kind* of information about me?"

A dark shadow passed across Stephen's face. "It's my fault, really. I should have seen it, should have been more careful, I just thought my own family, my own sister's son would never cross such a dangerous line..."

"Gavin." Thomas said, acid coloring his voice to a tone that in different circumstances would have shocked Quinn. It wasn't a question.

"Yes," Stephen said, his own voice low. "If we hadn't been watching so closely for birds, trying so desperately to keep any communications from Ellen secure, he would probably have never been caught. He's been messaging Tolliver directly."

"Why?" William exploded off the couch, fury in his voice. "He's always been kind of a jerk, yes, but *this?* What's in it for him?"

"I don't know, William. I don't understand it myself. I haven't spoken to him yet...haven't even told his parents anything. I need some time to think, to figure out what I am going to do."

"What has he told Tolliver?"

"I don't know. The message he was trying to send this morning was about the two of you making your courtship public last night. I don't know what else he knows, or what kinds of things he and Tolliver have been looking for. That's what I'll be trying to find out."

"So why are you in here telling us all of this now?" Quinn wondered.

Stephen's expression was pained. "I hadn't intended on it, not until I had at least gotten a handle on the situation myself, but then a little while ago I heard some of the children chattering, saying you'd decided to go on your trip after all, William."

"I... I *had* decided that, yes."

"It's far too dangerous," Nathaniel said. "We don't know everything that Tolliver knows, but if he has any suspicions about who Quinn really is…or about the connection that's now public between the two of you…"

"I am going to be making a decision today about whether the time has come to close the border," Stephen said. "Regardless, for now…and for the foreseeable future…*all* of you will be staying close to home."

A WALK

"I THINK A WALK might be good," Thomas said.

Quinn nodded slowly. Out of the corner of her eye she saw William and Linnea do the same. They'd all been sitting in stunned silence in Quinn's room ever since Stephen had left to go discuss the situation with Simon and Nathaniel had gone to check on Clara Halpern. The pendants still sat in the middle of the low table. They all avoided looking directly at them, although their very presence was a force that hung thick in the room.

"We should go see the birds…let Quinn and Raeyan get to know each other, and start training." Linnea was already up and halfway to the door. The rest of them were slower. For the first time, Quinn thought the fact that Linnea had been kept back from being directly involved in some of the things that had happened might be to her advantage.

Although she knew that it hadn't been easy on Thomas's twin, Linnea's scars didn't run quite as deep as the rest of theirs. Ever since last night, Quinn had been unable to shake the image of the first time she'd met James and Dorian Blackwelder, when they'd shown up at

Ellen's doorstep in Philotheum, first scaring her, William, and Nathaniel half to death in their uniforms, and then taking them to Thomas, who'd been so broken...

The memory had replayed itself even in her dreams last night...not her usual strange dreams, but a nightmare that hadn't ended when she'd awakened this morning. Dark shadows underneath William's eyes told her that his night might have been similar. And Thomas... she couldn't imagine what this news must be doing to him.

Outside, the sun was shining, and there was a hint of a breeze, making the temperature perfect. In almost any other circumstances, the weather would have brightened her mood immediately. Trying to compose herself, she took several deep breaths, inhaling the sweet scents that drifted from the gardens. As they stepped onto the gravel path that would lead them around to the south side of the castle and then the woods, William ran his finger down the inside of her arm before taking her hand in his. She shivered at the sensation, and suddenly an entirely different memory from last night flashed across her mind.

Heat flooded her cheeks...not the nervous, uncertain kind she was so used to, but something more. She looked up at William, meeting his half-smile with one of her own. He glanced at Thomas and Linnea, who were both ahead of them, neither one paying attention, and then he leaned down, touching his lips to hers.

"Are you okay?" he asked quietly against her ear.

She nodded. "It was a good idea to come out here. I'm actually excited to see Raeyan again." The mixed feelings she'd had about accepting the gift of the bird had disappeared. She didn't know when it had happened, but sometime in the last couple of days she'd come to terms with the fact that this world belonged to her every bit as much as the one she'd grown up in.

She still had no idea what she was going to do, what part either world was going to play in her life going forward. There were still huge decisions to make, and plenty of outside forces that would try to make those decisions for her. But she'd accepted that it was true...what she'd told William last night...that she was never going to be able to just walk away from this world, or deny the part of herself that belonged here.

It was too deep now...her feelings about everything, the anger that resounded in her chest over Tolliver's actions, her worry over the Blackwelders; she had the first stirrings of understanding about who she really was, and what that might mean.

Whatever else she was, she was a Philothean princess. And she could have a bird. She thought about the fledgling as they walked, remembering his bright, black eyes. Raeyan...*trusted guardian*. Well, she could use one of those.

They were just rounding the corner to the southwestern gatehouse when, up ahead of them, Thomas slowed, looking around and then turning to the rest of them.

Quinn frowned; something was wrong. "What's going on?"

"There's no guard," Thomas said.

Even before they reached him, she could see that he was right. The gatehouse was empty, the door closed. Nobody was anywhere around.

"That's not supposed to happen, is it?" She frowned. This entrance to the castle wasn't used much by anyone outside of the family; it wasn't convenient to much of anything besides the woods and a trail that eventually connected to the one they took to the gate.

"No. Not ever."

"Could whoever's supposed to be here maybe just taking a break?"

"No." William shook his head. "Someone...an apprentice, usually...comes around every two hours to give each guard a short break, and a longer one every four. If there was an emergency in the meantime, they're all equipped with really loud whistles. We'd have heard something like that."

"So what do we do?"

Thomas sighed. "I guess we go back and tell someone that nobody is here."

"Not all of us," Quinn said, an ominous feeling building inside her. "We can't just leave it open."

"Nobody ever comes back here, Quinn," Linnea said. "I'm sure it's just something small, and it will be fine for a few minutes."

"Is it worth taking that chance, Linnea? On the same morning they found Gavin sending messages to Tolliver?"

Linnea swallowed hard; the seriousness of the situation suddenly registering in her expression. "Are we really at that point?" she asked. "Where someone would do that?"

William nodded toward the splint that still dominated Thomas's leg, a dark look in his eyes. "I don't think we can ignore that possibility. What if there's already someone inside the wall who doesn't belong? Or just outside?"

"Then we can't just stand here talking about it," Quinn said. "Linnea, let's go."

The two girls took the gravel path at a run, although as soon as she'd turned her back on Thomas and William, dread overtook her, and she was terrified about leaving them alone there. What if there was someone inside the walls of the castle? She couldn't imagine any reason for an empty gatehouse that was *good*.

They didn't waste any time, running straight to Stephen's office. With everything that was going on, surely someone was in there. The door was closed. Quinn knocked loudly three times, and then tried the knob without waiting for a response.

Stephen was just standing up from behind his desk. Nathaniel and Simon looked up at them in surprise.

"What's wrong?" Stephen asked.

"Simon," he said when they'd told him, "get Marcus to get out there and get Thomas and William in here *now*. I want the gates closed and the entire grounds searched. The entire family needs to be in our wing and accounted for. Quinn and Linnea, stay right here. I'll send someone to walk you upstairs."

Linnea's face had gone pale by the time the door closed behind the three men. "We can't even walk ourselves upstairs? What's going on here?"

"You're asking *me?*" Quinn was stunned by what had just happened, and Stephen's over-the-top response had turned her worry about leaving Thomas and William alone outside into full-blown panic. Her heart pounded out of control and she couldn't draw in a deep breath.

"Hey, Quinn, I'm sure he's just being cautious. My Father gets a little zealous sometimes about us." She could tell by the change in Linnea's tone that her friend had seen how close to the edge she was getting, and in a different circumstance, she might have been impressed at how quickly Linnea had pulled herself together.

"I know," she said, but it didn't sound right. Her voice came out in ragged gasps. How long would it take for someone to come and get them in here?

The two of them stood in silence. Linnea kept sending calming glances Quinn's way, but it wasn't helping. For the second time that day, Quinn thought about just how lucky Linnea was not to have lived through the details of Thomas's rescue. Right now, she was battling the memory of the last time she'd been this worried about William, the night she had traveled with Ben to Ellen's house, and William and Nathaniel had been so delayed in meeting up with them.

Although she hadn't admitted it to herself before, that was probably the night she'd first realized how her feelings toward William had changed. She would never forget the way she had felt when he had finally come through that door, taken her in his arms...

A quiet knock on the door a few minutes later nearly made Quinn jump out of her skin. The doorknob rattled after a second, and she realized the door was locked.

"Who is it?" Linnea called through the door.

The door was heavy and thick; they had to strain to hear the voice on the other side, but after asking twice, Linnea said, "I think it's Ben."

Quinn nodded, even though her heart beat even more erratically as Linnea unlocked the door. She was still too worked up to feel any relief when it was Ben who entered, dressed in his full, flowing purple uniform, the silver crest of Eirentheos huge in the center of his chest. It couldn't possibly be that easy for an on-duty guard to just disappear.

"I'm supposed to take you upstairs," he said.

"Are Thomas and William back inside yet?" Linnea asked.

"I don't know. All I was told is to come and get the two of you and take you upstairs and then see who's there and who's not."

Upstairs, Ben escorted them to the door of the family's wing, and then he disappeared. The hallway was busy as the Rose children filed in from various lessons and activities they'd been attending. Quinn's panic grew when she didn't see either William or Thomas, and all she wanted was the quiet of her room.

Linnea was just closing the bedroom door behind them when it was pushed open again from the other side, and Thomas and William both came into the room. At the sight of them, Quinn fell apart. Her knees went weak, and tears started dribbling from the corners of her eyes.

Thomas and Linnea both looked at her in alarm, but William just walked straight over and pulled her into his arms.

Nobody said anything for several minutes while he held her tightly, stroking her back, though she was aware that Thomas and Linnea were watching her closely. Finally, when she was breathing normally again, she looked up at him. "Sorry," she said.

He kissed the top of her head. "Don't be sorry. We are fine, though. So far, nobody has found anything wrong, besides the fact that Paul, the guard who is supposed to be on duty there, is missing. You were right to act so quickly, but everything is okay."

William led her over to the couch and sat down next to her. "That was a pretty minor freak-out," he said, smiling. "I've been waiting for a big one for a while now."

She frowned at him.

"What? I've almost had a few of them myself over everything we've found out recently. I'm honestly not sure how you're doing it."

"Do you *want* me to freak out?"

Across from them, Thomas chuckled. "We sort of do, Quinn. The rest of us feel like we can't until you've had a turn first."

She rolled her eyes.

"So what do we do now?" Linnea asked. "Just wait?"

"Yes, I think we just stay in here and act like everything is normal, except we stay inside," Thomas said. "I think I'll go find us some snacks and some cards, actually."

"And I should go check on the Halperns," William said, looking at Quinn apologetically and squeezing her shoulders. "Will you be okay without me for a few minutes?"

She nodded, calmer now. "Now that I know you're safe."

Linnea was quiet as William and Thomas walked out of the room. Once the door closed, Quinn looked at her friend, noticing her silence. The pendants were in Linnea's hand again, and she was examining them, a strange look on her face.

"Really crazy, isn't it?" Quinn asked.

Linnea nodded, not looking up from the pendants. "I never would have guessed something like this… Nathaniel… you."

"Are you mad at me for not telling you?" Quinn heard the small shiver in her voice; she wasn't sure she could handle a battle with Linnea on top of everything else that was going on.

Linnea's eyes flashed up, a strong emotion burning in their gray depths, but it wasn't anger. Quinn could see that instantly.

"Of course I'm not mad at you. I mean, I'm sure there was some anger in my first reaction, but mostly I was just stunned. It's a lot to take in…I'm sure it's a lot more for you."

Quinn shrugged, not really knowing how to elaborate on her feelings about it…not entirely sure what her feelings *were*.

Linnea stood, holding the newer, shinier pendant in her hand. She walked over and reached up around Quinn's neck, securing the chain with a twist of her fingers.

The cool, smooth weight of the pendant against her skin made her gasp.

"When are you going to stop pretending you haven't decided anything?" Linnea asked, in a voice that was barely above a whisper.

"What?" Quinn breathed, her heart pounding. "I *haven't* decided anything, Nay."

Linnea didn't answer for a long moment; she curled herself into one of the armchairs and eyed her contemplatively. She frowned. "Okay, so maybe *pretending* wasn't the right word. But honestly, Quinn, what are you going to do? You really think you're going to go back to your other life in your world and just be okay with that?"

Had she even thought about it? She swallowed hard, trying to imagine it now. "I don't know. I was happy before. I have a good life there, you know, Nay." Her throat constricted as she thought about home, her mom, Owen, Annie, everything she had in her own world.

"Yes, *before*. You have a childhood there, Quinn. You have a good family, I've heard. You have school, a couple of friends, you've had a boyfriend. I'm sure it's all very nice. Do people in your world still live with their parents and their little brothers and sisters once they've reached adulthood?"

Quinn sank down onto her couch, absorbing Linea's question. There were times that Linnea still seemed to be younger than her, still underage and carefree. And then there were times when it was obvious that even if she was younger, Linnea's life was different than hers; she'd been raised to think differently, and she *had* lived more days, experienced more things that Quinn had.

"I don't know, Linnea. It all changes when I graduate, but I don't *lose* it all. I'll still have my mom, my family. I was never even sold on the idea of going far away to college. There's a decent school an hour away from home. Besides, I'm *not* an adult yet, in my world."

"What's the age of adulthood there?"

"Eighteen…for men and women."

"So that's what? Two more cycles for you? Years? Whatever you call it?"

Quinn sighed. "About one more year. I'll be seventeen in… I don't know not quite two weeks in my world, I think."

"Wait a minute. It's almost your birthday, and you haven't told anyone?"

"It hasn't exactly been the biggest thing on my mind, Linnea," she said, rolling her eyes.

"But, it's your *birthday.*"

She narrowed her eyes, and Linnea held up her hands. "Okay, we'll talk about that later. But still, you wouldn't lose all of that coming here, either, you know."

"What are you suggesting? That I just disappear from my life and go back and visit on the weekends? People would ask questions. Besides, if I took the throne…" her voice shook just saying the words, "if I took the throne, I'm sure I'd be living in Philotheum, nowhere near the gate."

Linnea's eyebrow formed a sharp v. "Haven't thought about it at all, huh?"

She sighed. "Of course I've *thought* about it, Linnea." More lately than she cared to admit. "But nowhere in those thoughts have I even come close to a decision."

"Meaning…you also haven't decided to go home and stay there."

She reached for the pendant around her neck, rubbing her fingers over the etched surfaces, looking down at her name, engraved in the gold. "No," she sighed. "I haven't decided that, either."

CHANGE OF PLANS

"WE HAVE A SERIOUS problem," Stephen said, his eyes heavy and dark.

Quinn's heart sank to the bottom of her ribcage. After a long afternoon of being kept inside the castle, keeping the younger children entertained, Stephen and Nathaniel had finally come upstairs and asked to speak privately with William and Quinn in her room. She'd asked if Thomas and Linnea could join them as well, but Stephen had refused, making her wonder what else could be going on that was a secret now.

"Have you found Paul?" she asked, starting the conversation, because both Nathaniel and the king seemed to be reluctant.

"No, we haven't. We sent some guards to his house in the city a little while ago and they found it deserted. The neighbors informed them that his wife and children left a few days ago; they'd heard they were going to visit relatives but they didn't know any details. Paul was quite obviously there at some point today. He reported to the castle this morning."

"And now he's just gone?"

Stephen's eyes were on the floor as he began his answer; his hands clenched tightly together. "Marcus led the search of Paul's home. While he was there he discovered some very... disconcerting letters.

Stephen stopped talking then for long enough that Quinn and William both looked over at Nathaniel in concern.

"Apparently," Nathaniel said, "Paul's wife has family in Philotheum, a twin sister it sounds like. Recently…since around the time we brought Thomas back, they've been getting some very distressing messages from her. The details are fuzzy…the letters of course don't tell everything, but between the letters and what little information we've been able to get from Gavin, it appears that Paul may have agreed to intentionally leave that gate unguarded."

"Why?"

Stephen looked up now, as shaken as Quinn had ever seen him. "Tolliver has been attempting to orchestrate a way to kidnap Linnea."

"What? Why? What does he think that would accomplish?" Quinn was almost shouting; her hands were shaking now.

"I can't pretend to understand the motivations of that..." he paused, closing his eyes, "I don't know. I can only guess that if he actually got his hands on her, got her back to the castle, that he thinks I would agree to the marriage, to keep her from being harmed." He looked down at the floor again. "I probably would." His voice was quiet and small.

"So is there someone in the castle? On the grounds? Is Linnea in danger?" William had stood, was pacing frantically back and forth to the window, glancing down onto the wide lawn below.

Stephen cleared his throat. "The thing is... from everything we can tell, this was supposed to happen tomorrow. Paul wasn't actually supposed to leave; he was just supposed to let someone in. They know you've all been using the back gate a lot to visit the birds."

"What happened to change the plan?" Quinn's heart was still beating erratically.

"We don't know. We're rather hoping that he may have disappeared today as a way of warning us. Paul has worked as a castle guard for many years. This is a very difficult situation. It seems that Tolliver is not above threatening the families of every guard in the castle if it would get him what he wants."

"How many guards have families in Philotheum?" Quinn asked.

Stephen shrugged. "What does that matter? I'm not going to go through my guards and clear out those who do. That's probably more than half my guards, and it's unfair to them. Most are completely trustworthy, like Marcus and Ben, who are among those with family in Philotheum. I'll be more careful. I'll double them up; no more situations where anyone is working alone for now. Trade them off more frequently, maybe. But I'm not going to sink to his level, Quinn."

She nodded. "So what are you going to do?"

He sighed heavily, and when he answered her, his expression was grave. "Right now, I'm going to do what I need to do to protect my daughter. Until all of this is sorted out and I can figure out exactly where Tolliver is trying to go with this, and where all of our vulnerabilities are, I am going to send Linnea where she'll be safe, where all of you will be safe until we know what how we're going to proceed. The gate opens again tomorrow evening. Nathaniel will be taking you, William, Thomas, and Linnea back to Bristlecone."

Quinn swallowed hard as she tried to wrap her mind around all of this. She was going back home tomorrow? It startled her to realize that she hadn't even been keeping track of the days; she wasn't even sure how long she'd been here. Finally, she looked back up at Stephen as William came to sit back down next to her. "You need me to make a decision, don't you?"

"Yes."

She nodded, meeting his eyes even though her entire body was trembling. "Is it all or nothing?"

Stephen frowned. "What do you mean?"

"I mean, is it I either decide to take my place as the heir to the throne or I stay in Bristlecone?"

His eyes widened. "Of course not, Quinn. You obviously know what I hope you will choose. I'm sure you know what I wish your father would have chosen…if he had, you wouldn't be in this position right now. None of us would. I will stand behind you with either…whatever…choice you make."

His eyes met William's now, and Quinn could see the enormity of the emotions reflected there. "That goes for you as well, Son." His gaze drifted for an instant to William's and Quinn's hands, twined tightly together now. "I know what I've done, and the position I've put you in, but the final choice is yours, and I will respect whatever you decide to do."

Quinn hadn't realized how much that question had been weighing on her, how trapped she'd felt by the possibility that by not choosing what everyone wanted her to, she'd lose everything she'd come to care about, this family of hers that she'd come to know and love…William.

She really was free to choose. The fact was both infinitely freeing and crushingly heavy.

"However," Stephen added, "with the heightened danger to the four of you in particular…in the absence of a decision from you that will change our course of action, I am asking you all to remain in your world until further notice."

William's body jerked forward slightly, and he made a choking sound, but he didn't say anything. Nodding, Quinn pulled him tighter to her side.

"I can understand that," she said. "But there's one more thing."

Stephen raised his eyebrows.

"I want to join the Friends of Philip before I return to Bristlecone," she said. "If that's possible."

"So do I," William said, squeezing her hand.

Stephen and Nathaniel looked at each other, and Nathaniel nodded. "You need four members to approve," Nathaniel said, "but we have that in the castle. I could try and arrange a meeting for tonight."

"You're sure, Quinn?" Stephen asked. "I don't think you should make big decisions until you've at least been back home and had time to think away from all of this."

She knew that his suggestion made sense; it would only be logical to take some time, especially time away from this world before committing herself so deeply. But she also knew that she didn't need the time. About this much at least, she was certain. Whatever...*whoever* she was in her own world, in her other life, she was also the daughter of Samuel Rose. If things had been different, she would have been raised as a princess of Philotheum. She needed to acknowledge that...needed that connection to her father, even if she never stepped up to his throne. "I'm sure, and I'm ready to do it now, before I go ho... before I go back to Bristlecone."

Stephen stared at both her and William for several long minutes before he finally nodded. She could see in his eyes that he understood the decision for what it was...a declaration without being a promise.

"We can arrange a meeting tonight...in the council room after dinner."

"Yes," Nathaniel said. "I'm going to go and speak to Marcus." His eyes met Quinn's, and she was taken aback by the depth of the emotion in them, or rather, the emotions. There was relief, fear, maybe even a hint of...*pride?Love?*

What surprised her even more was how deeply some of those same emotions resonated in her own heart.

"Will you please send Linnea and Thomas in here on your way?" Stephen asked, as Nathaniel stood to leave.

"I cannot believe I am finally going to your world." Linnea's eyes were brighter than they should have been, given the circumstances.

The four of them had been sitting in silence for several minutes since Stephen had left the room.

"It's not a vacation, Nay," William said. His fingers, twined with Quinn's, tightened.

Linnea rolled her eyes. "Is that your new motto, Will? Every time I go somewhere with you, I get to be reminded of how hard you work all the time, and how seriously you take everything? It's also not a funeral. I know there are serious things going on here, but this trip could be fun, instead of a bad thing. I've been wanting to see where you spend the rest of your time for as long as I can remember. You don't have to ruin it for me."

Quinn looked over at Thomas, and saw that his eyes were as wide as her own. She tensed, waiting for William's reaction to Linnea's attack, but after a few seconds, he relaxed beside her.

"You're right, Nay. I shouldn't be so grim about it; we can go and have fun. At least nobody will be trying to kidnap you in Bristlecone."

Thomas's jaw dropped. "You're good for him, Quinn."

Her cheeks grew warm as she glanced nervously up at William, but his expression was warm, and he leaned down to kiss her cheek. "Very good," he agreed.

There was a knock on the door then, so tentative that at first Quinn wasn't sure she'd actually heard it, but then Thomas stood to answer it.

Mia came into the room looking uncertain, though she smiled when Thomas put his arm around her shoulders and led her over to where the rest of them were sitting.

"I heard you're leaving?" she asked, looking around. "I was told to begin making preparations for all four of you to leave tomorrow."

"Yes, that's right," William said.

"And you don't know for how long?" Mia looked up at Thomas.

"No," he said. "It will feel like a long time for you. I'm sorry."

As she watched the exchange between the two of them – the glances and unspoken words – Quinn could see that things had grown more serious between Thomas and Mia than she had known.

Mia shook her head. "It will be good to know that you're safe. Things are too uncertain here right now."

William had grown rigid beside her again, and Linnea looked concerned, too. It took Quinn a minute to understand what their problem was…they were worried that Thomas had shared more with Mia than he should have.

"Mia," she said quietly. "You need to show them."

Mia nodded, and stepped closer to them before pulling back the collar of her dress.

Linnea sucked in a breath. "How long?"

"Almost a cycle now. Since I turned sixteen."

"Did you know about this, Thomas?" Linnea demanded.

"Mia told me a couple of days ago," he said, "right after she told Quinn."

Linnea's and William's eyes both flashed to her.

"I guess I'm better at keeping secrets than I thought," Quinn said, a little guiltily.

William put his arm around her shoulder. "It might be a necessary skill for a…" he broke off his sentence, glancing back over at Mia.

"It's okay, she knows my secret, too."

"Wait a minute! You told *Mia* before you told us?"

"No, Lady Linnea. It isn't Lady Quinn's fault. I… I overheard a conversation I shouldn't have." She looked at Quinn. "I haven't told anyone, I promise, not even Thomas. I wouldn't." Her hand went over her heart, over the tattoo.

"I know you wouldn't, Mia.

"Do all the Friends of Philip know?" Linnea asked.

"If anyone does, they've never shared it with me," Mia said. "I can't say that I'm happy I know. It's an enormous secret that carries more responsibility than I'd like. To be honest, even knowing the little I know about your world has been a burden."

Again Quinn was reminded of how much depended on the decisions she had to make. She couldn't blame Mia for how she felt…the weight of her responsibility was humbling and terrifying.

"I think I want to join the Friends of Philip," Linnea said.

Everyone turned to look at her, and Quinn's stomach twisted as she realized that she and William hadn't shared those plans with her.

"Father won't allow it until you're of age," Thomas said.

"How do you know?" Linnea turned on him, frowning.

"I've already asked. He'll consider allowing me to do it at sixteen, instead of waiting until I'm eighteen, but definitely not before."

Linnea threw her head back against the couch cushion. "You already asked him? Without telling me? Anyone else have a secret to share while we're at it?"

There was a resigned half-smile in William's eyes as they met Quinn's.

"William and I are both joining the Friends of Philip before we go back to Bristlecone," Quinn said softly.

THE FRIENDS OF PHILIP

"YOU'RE BOTH CERTAIN ABOUT this?" Nathaniel asked. His words were to both of them, but his eyes were on Quinn, scrutinizing her expression.

After dinner, Nathaniel had asked Quinn and William if they would join him on a walk outside, before the meeting where they would declare their intentions to join the Friends of Philip.

Quinn was silent for a long moment, meeting his gaze as she considered his question. She was sure… but she did want to make sure that she had put thought into all of the aspects of her decision. Her stepfather, Jeff, had always called this "due diligence". She swallowed hard; it was oddly painful thinking of him here, now, when for so long she'd pushed thoughts of home out of her mind.

"What would my father…Samuel…have wanted me to do?"

A shadow crossed over Nathaniel's face. "He never intended for you to have to make this decision on your own. Honestly, Quinn, once you were born, it was something he struggled with immensely himself. He was a good man, with the potential to be a great king, but he was human, just as you are, and things aren't always so simple. For a while, when you were tiny, he considered the idea of just staying in Bristlecone forever, of keeping you safe there, of never even sharing the secret with you."

"And then?" William was curious, now.

"I think he started to realize that some of his choices had been mistakes, and that he sometimes even regretted ever running away in the first place."

"Even though if he'd stayed he'd have been killed?"

Nathaniel shrugged. "We don't know that's what would have happened, Quinn. It might have all worked out if he had stayed and fought for what was rightfully his."

William's hand closed tightly around hers as she closed her eyes, deep in thought for several seconds. Finally, she nodded. "I'm sure I want to do this. I'm not ready to decide what it means, but I'm sure about this."

William had only been in his father's council room a few times before; he couldn't even remember when the last time had been. A sharp intake of breath beside him as they approached the thick wooden doors told him that Quinn was more nervous than she was letting on, and he tightened his grip on her hand.

Stephen was there, waiting just inside the door as William, Quinn, and Nathaniel entered. He had been leaning against the back of one of the tall armchairs that made up a small sitting area near the front of the room, but he stood up and came over to meet them at the door.

He doesn't look like a king, was the first thought that entered William's mind. It was an odd thought to have…his father rarely did look like a king to him, except maybe on special occasions. But today, maybe because he'd been thinking so much about Quinn, and the decision she was facing, thinking about her father and the choices *he'd* made, it really struck him that Stephen was really only an ordinary man with an extraordinary responsibility.

As his father wrapped him in a hug, William offered up a quick, silent prayer for him and for this meeting tonight.

They weren't alone in the room. Marcus was there, already seated at the enormous table, along with Luke Willoughby, another of his father's personal guards. The two men stood as they approached. William raised his eyebrow at the sight of Luke here at this meeting…that explained Mia. She was Luke's daughter. He wondered if tonight's meeting would hold any more surprises.

"Hello Master William." Marcus said, holding out his hand in greeting. "And Lady Quinn."

William had to withdraw his hand quickly from Marcus' and reach to steady Quinn, who had stumbled backwards slightly, as both guards lowered their heads respectfully towards her.

If Marcus noticed her reaction, he didn't acknowledge it. "Lady Quinn, this is Luke Willoughby, I believe you know his daughter, Mia."

Quinn didn't falter again; she smiled widely and reached to take Luke's hand. "If you're Mia's father, then I'm sure I like you already. It's a pleasure to meet you."

"And you as well, Lady Quinn."

When he had first begun courting her, William had thought about how difficult it might be for Quinn to adjust to the idea of having a relationship with a prince. As a child of the king, William often had to contend with heavy obligations, formal events, and diplomatic relationships. He knew it wasn't always easy to deal with the constant demands of his position. Simon's wife, Evelyn, still had difficulty with it, and the one girl Maxwell had been halfway serious with about a cycle ago, had eventually broken up with him over it. Max had been hurt pretty deeply.

Tonight, though, watching the way Luke and Marcus, two guards he'd known his whole life, bowed their heads low when they spoke to Quinn, deferring to her, made him realize for the first time that he'd had it wrong. If she decided to acknowledge her birthright, *he* would be the one doing the escorting and smiling.

As they sat down at the table, William put his hand under her elbow, rubbing it gently under the pretense of assisting her. She glanced at him, giving him a slight smile before turning her attention to the four men sitting down with them…his father, Nathaniel, Luke, and Marcus.

"King Stephen tells me that both of you would like to join the Friends of Philip," Marcus began, cutting straight to the issue.

"Yes." They answered simultaneously. William wondered if Quinn's palms were as sweaty as his were becoming.

"Do you understand what you're getting yourselves into?"

Quinn frowned; under the table, William put his hand on her knee, smoothing the lacy, white fabric of her skirt. Briefly, she touched her hand to his, and her slight tremble calmed as she touched him.

"I'm sure we don't know all of it," William answered. "Everyone here knows about Quinn?"

"Yes," Stephen answered. "It's still a secret, even among members of the Friends, but Marcus has always known, and we informed Luke only recently. I'm sorry, Quinn, but we are reaching a point where, given the safety concerns, and especially with you and William courting officially, we have to expand the circle. Luke is highly trusted, and we felt confident in sharing the information with him."

Luke looked at Quinn. "I still can't believe it, Lady Quinn, but I swear I will guard your secret with my life.

William wasn't certain how she would react, and he was surprised when she just nodded. "It's not going to be possible to keep the secret for much longer, I don't think."

"Are you genuinely considering accepting your role, milady?" Marcus asked.

She closed her eyes and took a deep breath. William tightened his grip on her knee, but this time she was so deep in thought that he wasn't sure she noticed.

When she opened her eyes, she didn't answer his question, instead asking one of her own. "Tell me about the Friends of Philip."

Marcus' eyebrow went up almost imperceptibly, and out of the corner of his eye, William saw his father give a tiny nod.

"What do you know about the history of our kingdoms, Quinn?"

She shook her head. "Not much, really. I heard a story once, about the twins… but I don't think I was paying close attention at the time."

"The version of the story in the children's history books," William clarified. "I think she read that during the poisonings."

"Those were the books that were poisoned?" Luke asked.

"Yes. Interesting, don't you think?" Nathaniel answered, and the two of them exchanged a look. William had never really thought about it before…that the poisoned books were the ones which taught about the shared history of the two kingdoms.

"Anyway," Marcus looked back at Quinn, "that's a fairly simplified version of the story. It's true that Philotheum and Eirentheos were once one much larger kingdom. At one point, in fact, all of this was Philotheum."

"And then there were twins, right?" she asked. "And they didn't know which one of them was the first born?"

"Yes." Nathaniel spoke now. "The story is that it was a very difficult birth, and the queen nearly died. It's an old story, and the records aren't completely accurate, but the thought is that the babies were handed off to a young nursemaid. It wasn't until the next morning, when it looked as though the queen might actually live, that anyone realized there might be a problem. Nobody had any idea which baby was which; what boy was the heir to the throne."

"I guess you can't exactly flip a coin over something like that."

Luke looked panic-stricken over Quinn's joke, but Stephen chuckled. "No, not exactly."

"So they just decided to split the kingdom in half and share?"

"Well, it wasn't quite that simple, Quinn." Although there was a smile hiding in the edges of his expression, Marcus' voice was serious. "Actually, for many years, the king and queen made no decision at all. Hoping it would all work out on its own, I suppose."

"We call it *the dandelion choice*," Stephen said.

Quinn's entire body stiffened and William looked at her in alarm. "What's the *dandelion choice*?" she asked.

Although she'd re-composed herself nearly instantly, William patted her knee softly as he answered. "When you plant a garden, no matter how carefully, there will always be weeds…plants that work their own way in, tend to themselves, and multiply. A gardener has two choices. He can carefully cultivate the plants he has placed there, feeding them, watering them, and vigilantly guarding them against the weeds…"

"Or you can let the weeds in," Quinn said.

"Yes. Some weeds, dandelions in particular, are quite useful, and even beautiful. They provide food, medicine, decoration, entertainment. You can even make a kind of coffee from ground dandelion roots."

"So why not just have a dandelion garden? It's easier." The level of understanding in Quinn's voice was frightening William a little.

"It's easier, and there are even some advantages, right. But deciding to have a dandelion garden is, in many ways, a choice to make no decision at all. You don't have to make that choice. If you just don't decide anything, the dandelions will decide for you."

"Is that so bad?"

"It's not…until you reach the point where you have no control over the situation at all. The dandelions start to go everywhere, choking the life out of any other plants in your garden, starting to spread outside your fence. Eventually, you're at their mercy…it's no longer your garden; the dandelions have taken over."

"And you can no longer have roses."

William frowned; he couldn't remember ever having talked about this with her before. "No. Choosing 'the roses' is the opposite of choosing 'dandelions.' Roses are delicate, difficult to cultivate, and early on they're easy to kill. They need lots of sunshine, water, food, and care. They're vulnerable to bugs and weeds. And growing them can even be painful. With the roses come the thorns."

"But if you put the work in…"

"Right. If you make that choice, put in the work, there's nothing more beautiful than a perfect rose."

Quinn nodded, closing her eyes for a long moment. "So they just didn't decide; and the 'dandelions' took over."

Stephen raised an eyebrow; William could tell that his father was as surprised by Quinn's reaction as he was. "It was a very tenuous time for Philotheum in many ways. After the birth of the twins, the queen was never able to conceive again…Philip and Aaron were it. And there were other relatives circling, saying that if they couldn't make a decision, then maybe it was time for another branch of the family to take over the throne. One cousin in particular…Norman, the son of the king's second-born brother, had married a royal from Dovelnia and moved to the far eastern portion of the kingdom. It was mostly wilderness, sparsely populated and largely ignored, and he was basically ruling there, sort of setting up a kingdom of his own."

"Here, you mean?" Quinn asked. "Philotheum is the western part, Eirentheos the eastern, yes?"

"Yes, Quinn. It would have been the part of the kingdom that is now Eirentheos. I'm getting to that." Stephen exchanged a wary look with Nathaniel.

"And there was a problem with the kingdom this guy was setting up?"

"Yes. The people of Dovelnia…where this man's wife was from…have always challenged our beliefs about the Maker. They've always maintained that we…the original Philotheum, and later the two kingdoms of Philotheum and Eirentheos…don't rule our people with enough power, that we use our beliefs as an excuse not to take advantage of the resources we have, both physical and human, to 'improve' our kingdoms.

"They believe that a king should be someone with strong power over his people, that the people aren't wise enough to decide on their own how they should live their lives…they require a king to interpret messages from the Maker and enforce those messages in law. In Dovelnia, the king has absolute power, and he rules through appointed religious leaders who own land and govern the people in small townships. The people become very dependent on these leaders.

"Norman, in his short time reigning over this portion of the kingdom, acquired quite a large amount of wealth. His 'people' were practically slaves, living under those to whom he had gifted land…gifts that, of course, were not his to give. And his influence was spreading."

"Like a dandelion."

"Exactly like a dandelion. Meanwhile, the king had become elderly and ill, while two potential heirs were doing nothing, making no decisions."

"Did they fight over who would take the throne?"

"Philip and Aaron? No. From all of the stories, it was never a battle. But it was a lack of making a decision."

William couldn't be sure, but he thought that Quinn squirmed a little at his father's words.

"So what happened?"

"The stories say that a messenger from the Maker himself appeared, separately to both Aaron and Philip. I don't know if the messenger appeared physically, or in their dreams," Stephen spoke now. "The legends say that it's where the story of the dandelion and the rose came from. But whatever happened, it was Philip who eventually proposed the solution. It meant a war, to remove Norman from his rule, but they did it. Afterwards, the kingdom was divided equally along the Philotheos River. Philip allowed his brother to choose which side to take as his own. Eirentheos wasn't much at the time. The already small population had been devastated in the war, and there was a lot of rebuilding to do, but it's what Aaron chose. He wrote in his private journals that watching his brother make that decision had convinced him that Philip was the true leader…that he must have been the firstborn, and he deserved to rule the more powerful kingdom."

"And Aaron's half became Eirentheos." Quinn said. William could tell by the faraway sound of her voice that she was thinking deeply about this.

"Yes. Although until very recently, the two kingdoms operated very much as one, two parts to a complete whole." Stephen reached toward the middle of the table, and picked up two small, metal objects. William had been too preoccupied to notice them lying there before.

When he held the first one up, they could see that it was a little silver replica of the Eirenthean seal, the same symbol that appeared on William's pendant. The second object was a gold replica of the Philothean seal. For a moment, Stephen held them separately, one in each hand, and then he moved his hands together, joining them. They watched as the two separate images joined and became one complete design, the design of the tattoos worn by members of the Friends of Philip.

"Why a tattoo?" William asked. It was something he had been wondering about for a while now. "Doesn't it make you a target if you're captured?"

"Yes, it does. Especially now," Marcus answered, looking William in the eye.

"Then why do it? Why make yourselves vulnerable like that? It would be a whole lot easier to hide your membership in the Friends of Philip if you didn't have it *tattooed* across your chest." *And less painful*, he added secretly, although he doubted that was an issue for anyone else, and he'd promised himself that he wouldn't make it one for him, either.

"That's the point, isn't it?" Quinn asked, with that understanding tone her voice sometimes had, the one that raised the hair on the back of William's neck.

"No, it isn't." Nathaniel answered.

William frowned. "What's the point? What am I missing?"

Quinn turned to face him. "The Friends of Philip aren't trying to hide their identities. They believe in what they're doing."

"What about all of the refugees? Why are they coming here? What about families like the Hardridges?"

"Almost all of them *are* families, William…people who are worried about the safety of their children," Nathaniel said. "Most of them came here with the intent of setting up their children and one parent somewhere safe, while the other parent went back into Philotheum. Some of them only sent one parent in the first place. Some with family here in Eirentheos have left their children and both parents returned. Eldon Hardridge was planning on going back there before he was killed."

Nathaniel's face had taken on the expression that William had seen often lately, ever since Eldon's death. It was grief, yes, and anger, too, but... Nathaniel had been different since then, and William knew there was more on his mind than he was letting on, and he had a feeling that Quinn wasn't the only one on the cusp of a major decision.

"So the Friends of Philip are not worried about people finding out who they are."

"No," Marcus said. "We're not advertising it, of course, but when members of the Friends of Philip are caught; we aren't afraid of letting them know who we are, and how many of us there are fighting for what we believe is right."

"For a long time, I wasn't sure what my part in this was supposed to be." Stephen spoke now, a deep, sad look in his eyes. "I knew, of course, that I wanted the peace between our kingdoms to be restored; that I wanted Samuel to return and fight for his throne, and even when he died, I always held out the hope that you would return, Quinn. But it has taken these recent events…nearly losing Thomas, watching you have the courage to go after him, even though you didn't know who you really were… and then watching my own people behave the way they have. It still shocks me to know that so many in Eirentheos are so willing to look the other way, to allow these terrible things to happen to those who are really our brothers. And I realized that at least some of it was because I, as their leader, haven't taken a strong enough stand. I've waited, and negotiated, and I've never made it clear where my loyalties lie.

"And then to have both you and my own son, seeing so clearly…making a decision that I hadn't yet committed to… I was so proud of you both, and ashamed that I didn't do this earlier."

Stephen stood, and William's eyes widened as his father pulled back the collar of his white, woven shirt to reveal a tattoo, still red around the edges.

"It is time for our kingdoms to come back together, and I'm ready to do what it takes to make that happen."

COMPLICATIONS

"DOES IT HURT?" Quinn asked, eyeing the equipment that Nathaniel was setting up on the table near her couch, where she was sitting, curled up next to William. She wasn't sure why she asked; she already knew the answer. William put his hand over her shaking one. It was an attempt to calm her, but since he, too, was pale with anxiety, it wasn't very effective.

Nathaniel stopped what he was doing to look over at her. "It's several needles poking into your skin lots of times," he said, matter-of-factly. "It hurts. The first few minutes are the worst, before you get used to it. After that, it's mostly just really annoying."

"Then there's the part at the end..." she shivered, beginning to feel cold in the thin camisole she was wearing, as she glanced down to the spot where, a little while earlier, Ben Westbrook had already stenciled the interlaid symbols in black drawing ink. The design was already on William's chest, too, waiting to be made permanent.

Last night, after they'd learned about Stephen joining the Friends of Philip, they had invited several more people into the room. Marcus had performed a simple ceremony initiating both

Quinn and William into the secret group, and they'd made their promises to uphold the mission of rejoining the kingdoms and protecting the other members.

They'd also shown them the tattoos, something that Quinn had never looked very closely at before. They were inked in a special blue pigment, which could only be made by certain members of the Friends…different from those members who knew how to draw the tattoos. They were lucky, it turned out, that Josiah Halpern was staying at the castle with his family. He was the only one nearby who knew how to craft the pigment.

The tattoos were special in a different way, too, they'd learned. After the tattoo was drawn, a third artist was involved, usually a healer, who injected another substance made from the crushed leaves of certain plants underneath two particular sections of the design that caused scar tissue to form, and those sections to raise slightly in relief to the rest of the tattoo.

Nathaniel, prince of Philotheum as he was, alone among the Friends of Philip knew both how to ink the tattoo and raise it.

While several members of the Friends had other tattoos…many of Stephen's guards had the symbol of Eirentheos on their upper arms; the raised portions of the Friends tattoos made them unique.

Ben had described the raising process as quite painful…itself another way of weeding out any who might seek to join their group dishonestly. Nobody had disagreed with him, and Quinn had spent most of the morning pacing nervously.

William gently squeezed her hand. "I'll be right here the whole time," he said.

Linnea grabbed a blanket off of the end of the bed and laid it across Quinn's lap. "We're all here."

"Why am I doing this again?"

Nathaniel raised his eyebrow and looked over at her, but William just smiled. "You know why, unless you've changed your mind."

She pressed her lips together and shook her head. "I know what I want and where I stand. I'm not going to let a little bit of pain stop me."

"That's my girl," Thomas said. "You'll be fine. It's the first thing I'm going to do on our sixteenth birthday."

"Ladies first, T," Linnea said.

"Fine. Right after you, *little* sister."

Last night, Stephen had agreed that both Thomas and Linnea would be allowed to join the Friends after their sixteenth birthday, even though Thomas wouldn't yet be of age. Simon had also informed his father of his intent to join. Maxwell was still wary of the whole thing, and Stephen confessed to the rest of them that it worried him a little, but he hoped Max would at least accept their decision and support it.

Quinn looked up at William. "Are you ready for your turn right after me?"

He shrugged, kissing her cheek before he answered. "I can't let the girl I love do something I'm not willing to."

Linnea snickered. "Remind him of that one when you're about to have a baby."

Red flooded instantly from Quinn's head to her toes, heat replacing the chill she'd felt a moment ago. "Linnea!"

As always, Linnea was unfazed. "Somebody around here has to daydream about the fun possibilities between you two, instead of all of the heavy decisions and gloom all the time. Don't worry…I've only got colors picked for the nursery; I haven't started sewing anything yet."

William rolled his eyes at his sister. "Let's take care of first things first, Linnea." He squeezed Quinn's hand, and she was surprised once again at how easy and natural things between them had become. Not so long ago, he wouldn't have been so cavalier about someone throwing out teasing comments like that. Nor, she realized, would she.

"Okay, Quinn," Nathaniel said, holding up the tattooing device. It was something he'd designed himself, taking ideas from both traditional ones used here in this world, and ones he'd studied in Quinn's world as well. This one used light electric currents that could be generated by friction, rather than plugged in.

Her stomach twisted into knots and she felt lightheaded as William scooted to the end of the couch and pulled her head into his lap. Nathaniel, William, and Thomas all looked away as Linnea helped her pull the thin strap of the camisole off her shoulder and tucked a towel around her lower chest, leaving just the stencil exposed.

Linnea settled herself on the floor next to the couch and took Quinn's left hand in hers, while William firmly gripped the right.

There was a click, and then a low vibrating sound came from the small machine in Nathaniel's hand.

"You're sure?" he asked one more time.

Quinn nodded, and then squeezed her eyes shut.

"I still can't believe I'm actually going to Bristlecone with you tonight," Linnea said.

"I just wish your first trip was going to be under different circumstances," Quinn answered, as Nathaniel paused to wipe away some of the extra ink. He had been right; the first few minutes were rough, but after that, she'd been able to relax and keep up with the conversation.

It *was* annoying, and she held her breath again for a second as he started back up; he'd long since stopped trying to convince her not to do that; it happened every minute or so, and she just couldn't help herself. William ran his fingers softly through her hair as she looked down at Linnea.

"I don't see why I have to let the fact that someone's trying to kidnap me here affect my time *there*. Maybe it will be a break for all of us."

Thomas chuckled. "Always the optimist, Linnea."

"And you're not excited about going?"

"I won't be able to *do* anything there. I'm going to have to stay in hiding. If anyone recognizes me, I supposedly just had major surgery, what… a week ago or something?"

"Yes, a week," Nathaniel said. "It will be Tuesday night in Bristlecone. I was going to have to be going back to work anyway."

Quinn wasn't sure she was ready to go back, to try to fit in to her life at home with all of this new information and this huge decision hanging over her head. Part of her was worried, too, about how being back there was going to change things with William.

At home, she was just a regular junior in high school who had broken up with her boyfriend just a few days ago. Here…she and William had managed to become more deeply connected in just over a month's worth of time than she'd ever imagined possible. Certainly more connected than she'd ever been with Zander.

Nobody at home was going to understand that.

And she knew that this was it, too. Whatever she decided during this time she spent in her own world was going to change her life forever, in both places.

Nathaniel was almost finished inking William's tattoo when there was a knock on the bedroom door and Stephen entered without waiting for an answer. He closed it tightly behind him, and Quinn could tell from the look on his face that something wasn't right.

"What's wrong?" she asked.

His eyes went straight to Nathaniel. "Can I speak with you alone for a minute?"

Nathaniel nodded, silencing the tattoo machine and setting it on the table. "I'll be right back…I think."

"Yes, he'll be back soon." Stephen glanced across the room at Mia, who had come in and begun folding some of Quinn's clothes. She hadn't been planning on taking anything with her on the trip…and now her shoulder hurt too much for her to even think about carrying a backpack, but she'd let Mia work anyway, suspecting that her real motive was to have little bit more time in these last hours with Thomas.

"Mia, I'm sorry to interrupt, but Charlotte was asking for you."

"Yes, Your Majesty," Mia said, bobbing her head toward the rest of them in apology, and ducking out of the room behind Stephen and Nathaniel.

"I wonder what's going on *now?*" Thomas said, setting down one of Quinn's shirts he'd been folding for Mia, and looking at the closed door.

Quinn sighed. The pain, the lack of sleep the night before and the nervousness she'd been battling for hours now had started to get the better of her. She felt completely drained. "Probably something else cataclysmic. Maybe Tolliver's just arrived."

Thomas chuckled. "Probably. It's starting to get that bad around here, isn't it?" Though he was joking, she could see that he was anxious, too.

She looked down at William. "How are you doing?"

He raised an eyebrow at her. "You made this look easier than it is. *Ow.*"

She coughed. "Right. I'm sure people would line up around the block to do this after watching *me.*" William wasn't going to have any clean handkerchiefs to take back to Bristlecone with him after that. She'd ripped one of them completely in half when Nathaniel had first stated the injections that would raise part of her tattoo. Somewhere in the middle of it, she'd nearly thrown up.

Ben had lied. "Quite painful" didn't cover it. Excruciating might have been closer. She wasn't going to tell William right now, but it wasn't hurting any less as time went on, either.

And yet, she'd done it. Though it was hurting now, the biggest thing she was feeling was pride…pride that she had done something that she was so afraid of, pride that she'd made a decision and gone through with it.

For William's sake, though, she almost wished that he hadn't been there to watch. Most of his color had vanished after seeing that, and it hadn't come back yet. She suspected it wasn't going to until after his was done.

Understanding the true implications of the tattoos had made her think…she had spent a good part of last night really weighing whether she should do it or not, put a permanent mark on herself, put her trust in something she didn't fully understand.

But after she'd gone to bed, for the first time since she'd received the pendants, she'd dreamed. As often was the case, she couldn't remember fully what it was about when she'd awakened, but she remembered seeing herself with the tattoo. Another image had been flickering through her mind as well. One so familiar that she couldn't be certain it had actually been in last night's dream, or if it was just a memory. The image that had appeared in her dreams hundreds of times before, all the way to the earliest dreams she could remember.

It was a vision of a perfect white rose, more perfect, more beautiful than any flower she'd ever seen when she was awake. And far more dangerous, too. The whole stem of the rose was covered in thorns. So sharp that their edges glimmered in the sunlight, the thorns spiraled up the stem from the very spot it emerged from the rich, black soil to the base of the luminescent bud.

And now she understood. This trip home, for her, was supposed to be time to distance herself from all of this, to take stock and look at her life at home, and really make a decision, but after that dream…

The rose had been in her mind all morning, so vivid that when she closed her eyes, she could actually catch a faint whiff of its perfume.

When Nathaniel had grilled her again this morning, several times, about how serious the decision was, how she didn't have to make it now, it hadn't been difficult to tell him that she knew. She'd close her eyes, and the rose would flicker there, and the certainty would come.

William, for his part, hadn't wavered. He already knew what he believed, whom he trusted, which side he wanted to stand with in this battle. Although she'd checked herself several times, making sure that her choice had nothing to do with his, his absolute steadfastness had made it easier for her, steadied her.

She wasn't ready to say anything…wasn't ready to admit the truth even to herself… but part of her already knew. Her decision to join the Friends of Philip had been a decision of far more than that.

"I meant the tattoo part, Quinn. You were awesome; for a few minutes there I thought that maybe people who get them for fun weren't completely crazy. This hurts. I'm really about to change my mind on the other part."

"You can't," Thomas said. "You're too far into it now. You'd be trusted far less with an unfinished symbol than just not having one in the first place."

"I know. I keep telling myself that. This is just a bad time to take a break."

Quinn rubbed the back of his hand sympathetically. She leaned down to kiss his cheek, stopping to whisper in his ear, "It does give me a chance to enjoy the view unobstructed, though."

He rolled his eyes, but squeezed her hand. William was taller and lankier than Thomas. It was easy to forget how much physical labor he did, and overlook how muscular he actually was. His lying across her with no shirt was her one consolation for the pain she was in.

"I'm still going to do it, even after watching you two today," Linnea said. "If I ever do have to see Tolliver again, I want him to know exactly how I feel."

Thomas nodded. "Me too. You can come see *me* without a shirt then, Quinn."

She blushed…both Thomas and Linnea could be relied upon to hear *everything* she didn't want them to hear.

"And what would Mia think of that?" she struck back.

He shrugged. "She spent so much time with me when I was sick in bed that she's probably bored of the sight by now."

Quinn rolled her eyes. Thomas was an impossible, shameless flirt, but she had to love him for it anyway.

The door opened then, and Nathaniel and Stephen came back into the room, both of them looking anxious. Nathaniel sat right back down on his chair next to the couch and picked up the tattoo needles.

"What's going on?" Quinn asked.

Stephen took a seat across from them. He was silent for a moment, watching as Nathaniel started back up with the tattoo. Quinn saw his hand drift absently toward his chest, to where his purple shirt covered his own fresh mark. "We have a problem," he finally said.

"Clearly," Quinn said. "What's going on now?"

The way everyone's attention snapped toward her at her remark told her that her tone had betrayed just how badly today's events had stretched her nerves.

Almost everyone, anyway. Stephen and Nathaniel didn't seem to notice, which scared her even more.

Stephen sighed. "A little while ago, Simon and Marcus rode down to the gate, just a routine surveillance run, as we usually do. They've just returned."

William's shoulders tensed underneath her, and she suddenly felt like she'd swallowed a rock. "And?"

"There is a large group of Philothean refugees camped out in the entire area. The gate is surrounded."

Quinn frowned. "More Friends of Philip?"

"No," Nathaniel said, shaking his head. "Marcus isn't sure who this group of people is, or how…or why…they made their way here, but they seem to be ordinary citizens."

"And I don't suppose we can just go strolling through there and disappear through a gate that doesn't exist," Thomas said, standing and beginning to pace.

"Can you ask them to move?" Quinn asked.

"We could, possibly, but it would take time… and…and we're not sure how easy it would be to do so without raising some suspicions."

Ice water replaced the blood in her veins. "Why do you think they'd be suspicious?"

Stephen closed his eyes; dark gray streaks had appeared under his cheekbones and on the sides of his neck. "Because we've also just found out that Gavin may have known more than he should about William's…and your…comings and goings, Quinn. It's possible that Tolliver knows something about the gate."

"And it's terribly coincidental that people would show up in that same area right now," Nathaniel added, not looking up from his work.

Quinn's eyes widened and her heart sped to a manic pace. "So what does that mean?"

"It means we're not going to Bristlecone," Linnea said.

The quiet whirring of the tattoo machine ceased. "No, we're not. Not now and maybe not anytime soon."

OTHER BOOKS BY BREEANA PUTTROFF

The Dusk Gate Chronicles
The continued adventures of the Rose family in
Eirentheos and Philotheum

Rumpelstiltskin's Daughter
A new take on an old fairy tale

COMING SOON
The Gatekeepers
An all-new adventure featuring some familiar characters

Visit www.BreeanaPuttroff.net to find out more!

www.ingramcontent.com/pod-product-compliance
Lightning Source LLC
Chambersburg PA
CBHW051631180726
48284CB00006B/1680